The

UNBECOMING

of

MARGARET
WOLF

ALSO BY ISA ARSÉN

Shoot the Moon

The

UNBECOMING

of

MARGARET
WOLF

A Novel

ISA ARSÉN

G. P. Putnam's Sons
New York

PUTNAM
— EST. 1838 —

G. P. PUTNAM'S SONS
Publishers Since 1838
An imprint of Penguin Random House LLC
penguinrandomhouse.com

Library of Congress Cataloging-in-Publication Data

Names: Arsén, Isa, author.
Title: The unbecoming of Margaret Wolf : a novel / Isa Arsén.
Description: New York : G. P. Putnam's Sons, 2025.
Identifiers: LCCN 2024003642 (print) | LCCN 2024003643 (ebook) |
ISBN 9780593718360 (hardback) | ISBN 9780593718384 (epub)
Subjects: LCGFT: Queer fiction. | Novels.
Classification: LCC PS3601.R744 U53 2025 (print) |
LCC PS3601.R744 (ebook) | DDC 813/.6—dc23/eng/20240223
LC record available at https://lccn.loc.gov/2024003642
LC ebook record available at https://lccn.loc.gov/2024003643

Printed in the United States of America
1st Printing

Title page art: Theater mirror © Ysbrand Cosijn / Shutterstock
Book design by Alison Cnockaert

To the wolves, that you may someday eat well of your monsters;

And to Luke, for all our small joys.

H of H: I cannot rise. Too heavy with filth and sin.

Th: Give me your hand.

H of H: I'll stain you.

Th: I'll take it.

—ANNE CARSON, *H of H Playbook*

The
UNBECOMING
of
MARGARET
WOLF

Prologue

Christopher Street
1955

ONLY TWO THINGS had come with me all the way to New York City from south of the Mason-Dixon Line: a bottle of Wild Turkey from what I once called home and an orange telephone. I lived in a basement unit on Christopher Street that tended to take on a bottle-green tinge from the scummy light that pushed through the single mail-slot window high up on the street-side wall, and I liked to think the orange complemented the space quite nicely.

The line trilled as I waited for it to connect me to Edie Bishop's apartment a few blocks down the road, where the West Village took on a slightly more bourgeois cant. I turned a shallow lowball cup around between my fingers a few times, one of five mismatched glasses I'd magpied over time—it was Jim Beam, not the Wild Turkey; I only slugged straight from the old bottle when I was celebrating something. The rattan chair I'd rescued from the curb gave a crackle as I shifted my seat.

The connection clicked. "Bishop."

"Have you met the new ingénue Ezra hired?" I lipped at the glass and transferred the handset to my other ear. "Apparently he did pictures in California."

"A new one? Now?"

"I know." The telltale *chip-chip-chip* of Edie making a drink on her end scored the line. Great minds. "I already gave him flak for it—he spends all last year grousing about his budget, and he hires someone from *California*. I don't think there are any designs of getting him to bed; I think he just feels bad for him."

"Would I know his name?"

I sipped. "Shoard, Wesley Shoard. I haven't seen him in anything."

Edie made an unassuming grunt. "Maybe they weren't the most legitimate pictures."

I rattled my ice shallowly. "Not sure. He's handsome. Seems nice enough. We're getting a drink tomorrow."

An audible smirk emerged in Edie's voice—"Oh?"

"Stop."

"What, stop?" She was clearly still smirking. "Tell me about him."

I rolled my eyes. "He's a fencer. Great posture. Incredible eyes, like quicksilver. Handsome as anything. Studied at Oxford, did a Rhodes stint in Britain before enlisting. Navy."

"You sound halfway in love already," Edie said. I shook a chunk of my own ice into my mouth.

"Couldn't be," I said around it. "He's queer."

Ezra Pierce, the director of the Bard Players on Commerce Street, collected his company like teeth scattered on the curb after a brawl. We were all of us strays, blacklisted or rich enough yet stymied by arrest records, the city's shiniest if unpalatable dross, which Ezra molded with pride and a wealth of lenders that were best not examined in direct daylight.

Lisette Greene, one of the other women in the company, was a divorcée from Oshkosh who made her way to Manhattan by way of sex work and good instincts. Our comic lead, Irwin Drake, went by the mononym Chap and could be found drying out in an overnight cell at least two weekends out of every month. As for myself, I had escaped the fate of becoming the second-rate wife of some third-rate racketeer from Cherokee Park, Kentucky—and landed myself in the muck of more dangerous relations in Richmond, Virginia, but that was neither here nor there, and in the past besides.

And now there was Wesley Shoard from California, formerly of the pictures, doing Shakespeare with the rest of us. He would be a fine addition to the company if his pedigree held up under Ezra's high expectations. Our theater on Commerce Street was a far cry from Broadway, but we were good. That was all that mattered to me.

"That's hardly stopped the most audacious," Edie said.

"No? He had a commission as a lieutenant."

Edie made a considering sound. "Officers *are* usually more hard-lined with their preferences. Is he any good? Remind me what you're putting together this season."

"*Twelfth Night.*"

"So he's your Orsino?"

"At least he'll appreciate the buckskins," I said. I looked at myself in the mirror across the apartment—my hair was still in rollers.

If I stretched my arms out wide, I could almost touch both walls of the place at once. The room was a shallow shotgun shape. A sagging armoire stood beside the knocking radiator. My bed shrugged up against one wall like a figure trying to shield itself from rain. A sheepish kitchenette stood past my table and chair.

I had dressed up these droll basement digs with framed art and furniture dragged in from other people's castoffs—a sofa with corduroy upholstery that was still more mint green than gray, a side table carved from a knotholed length of unstained wood, an eclectic collection of candlesticks set up throughout the apartment to fill it with a warm, sparse glow instead of the harsh and hideous glare of the ceiling fan and its limping arms. The place looked better in lower light.

My best find was the long gilt mirror, nearly four feet across, that took up one whole wall and gave me the perfect setup to pace and practice my lines. I could watch my face and my entire body at once, tuning my performances just so.

I primped at the rollers cinched against the nape of my neck. It was a slow Monday. I was meeting Lisette for lunch in SoHo in two hours, giving myself a good dish with Edie before she headed off to do God only knew what with her day off.

Edie Bishop didn't act, not anymore, but she had deep pockets and good taste and the ear of every producer worth his salt in the city. She had scooped me under her wing after she'd watched me botch an audition for a screwball sex comedy from the other side of the cattle-call casting table within the first month of my arrival to the city. I'd read from *Macbeth*.

Those men in there, she told me point-blank in the particular balsa-wood coil of her Aussie accent, her fine red mouth pecking from one of her brisk and toasted cigarettes, *they aren't looking for talent. They're just looking for the best set of tits in the bunch.*

Is that what you were doing at the table with them? I asked, leveling a look at her. *Looking at our tits?*

The keen smile in Edie's eyes sparked with laughter. *I have a friend you should meet, Ms. Wolf.*

The friend had been Ezra. He hired me after hearing the same monologue in Edie's apartment two weeks after I met her—Lady Macbeth, my favorite of Shakespeare's women. *Yet here's a spot*, et cetera, et cetera. I'd been with the Bard Players ever since.

"True; he won't have to try very hard to make your Cesario scenes smack of mixed-up sex," Edie teased.

"Wesley seems perfectly kind," I said, "he really does. Is there any gossip going around about him yet?"

"How new is he?"

"I think he only just got settled after the holidays; he's nearby, somewhere off Morton. He walked me home after our first rehearsal."

"What a gentleman."

Edie Bishop wasn't quite patron, not quite mother, not quite friend. I got the sense she saw glimmers of herself in me, from when she was also a wandering talent on the short side of twenty-five trying to make something of herself. Edie's glamour was ageless. I could never quite tell if I wanted to be her or impress her. Usually, both.

"I'll ask around the uptown scene next time I'm there," Edie said. "Does he go to parties?"

"I should hope so, he's too pretty not to."

"They probably already know his Social Security number and blood type. Those queens in Lenox Hill are better than the Federal Bureau."

Edie let me go after more idle chatter—her obnoxious downstairs neighbor was finally readying to move out in the coming months, taking the noisy parties with him; I'd gone to an opening off-Broadway that could have used another month of rehearsing.

"Alright," Edie finally said, "ooroo, Margot; come for coffee soon, won't you?"

"Of course, call and I'll be there."

"See you, luv. Bye." She hung up first, as always.

I looked at myself in the mirror as I listened to the dial tone, the orange handset pressed to my cheek and the powder-pink of the rollers peeking through the shiny brown hair wrapped around them. As

I replaced the handset on its cradle, I peered for a moment at my forearms, bare inside the bell sleeves of the dressing gown I'd bought at a costume warehouse clearance.

I had been doing it for as long as I could remember, roving angry red scratches along the insides of my wrists and elbows without even realizing it. It started when I was girl, but I never could recall exactly when or why.

The habit was at its worst when my nerves heightened. I'd done my best to hide it from my mother when I was small—the hideous rashes left behind were an embarrassing manifestation of anxieties dreamed up for nothing but the perversely comforting weight of owning them: that something terrible would happen to my mother, because she had no husband to protect her for most of my life; that I would suddenly stop breathing in my sleep and never wake up again; that awful, dark things lurked in the corners and would sink their teeth into me if my vigilance slipped.

I ran my thumb over the roughened skin there, shallow scars from years past. The scratching was my warding ritual, the way I dispelled the fear of my own loneliness. To be alone was to be afraid. Luckily, with work and ambition and the daily chaos of the city, I hadn't felt the need to do it for a long time.

Pleased with myself, buoyed by a good chat with Edie, I got up to put my face together for lunch.

Margaret Wolf was my own creature, and nothing could take that from me. What mattered to the people who came to watch me onstage was not the sad little thing I had been once, but rather the women I became night after night. If this—the basement apartment, the two-bit theater company—was the best I was to have for the moment, I would make do until I could rise. The play was the thing.

There was no going back the way I'd come. There was always a bigger role to aspire to. There was always something better waiting just ahead.

There must be. Or else what was any of this stumbling forward for?

In front of the mirror forty minutes later, dressed in a smart tweed set in teal with my face painted, I put on a hat and smiled at my reflection in the gilt mirror. I left the apartment and stepped out onto Christopher Street.

The buildings had taken on a fiery rosiness in the noon sun. The West Village was comfortable, familiar, inspiring to me in its off-kilter way. Manhattan was a place where monumental things happened, but the Village stood on the west side like a scab proud of its pucker along the spotless skin it held together—the seedy pride of unflappable moxie. It felt like home to me.

I made for the train with my shoulders drawn back and my hat angled to catch the warmth of daylight on my face. A new production was about to begin. I would become someone else, take on another life, and give the little girl at the core of me the proof that I loved her best and dearest.

1

The Edison

EZRA PIERCE WAS of the same generation as Edie Bishop, eccentric and stubborn and in possession of very specific tastes. Edie preferred ballerinas, and Ezra was fond of fawnish little bastards.

We had been rehearsing *Twelfth Night* for the last eleven weeks, and Ezra was lining his pockets with good karma and the assurance he knew exactly what his leads were up to the night before opening by treating Wesley and me to dinner. We met at the Edison. Ezra was accompanied tonight by an insufferable student called Benjamin— *Full name, my dear. Not Ben. Never Ben. Too gauche. A-haw!*

Wesley insisted on covering the bill. "It's the least I could do, maestro," he teased as he reached into his sport coat for his wallet after we finished sipping our coffees and dessert liqueurs. Another braying laugh leapt from Benjamin-Not-Ben—*A-haw!*—who had been mooning over Wesley since the moment we sat down.

Who could blame him? Wesley was a vision. He carried his trim, elegant figure with the springy surety of an athlete as he moved through the world with an attentive kindness that made it painfully clear he didn't understand how attractive he was. He had thick, wavy hair the color of crow feathers that shone near-blue in stage lights and sunshine alike. Those bright eyes of his, so gray they must have been a devil to capture on film, always seemed to be laughing *with* you, and when he smiled a single dimple came to life on his left cheek.

Late into the afternoon of our first drink together, Wesley and I gave each other the rundown of our rambling histories. He'd grown up in Maine, taken to sailing, and stayed in California after completing his naval service on the Pacific front. I'd carefully dowsed from there for the story of what brought him to the city and discovered that the one who ruined it all for him—to land one in Ezra's employ, there was always someone who ruined it all—was called Andrew: a magnetic casting director with Hollywood in the palm of his hand. He folded Wesley so smoothly into a vertiginous lifestyle of drug-addled parties that by the time Wesley realized the art-films Andrew secured for him were only ever screened at adult theaters, it was too late to get out with his reputation intact. He'd become nothing but a pretty pet trapped in a four-year cloud of vices.

It was the cold slap of reality that woke him one morning, and Wesley's nasal mimic of the incident over his third gin sling had made me laugh despite the distant pain settled like silt at the back of his gaze—*Collect your things and get out, Shoardie. The valet will put whatever you can't carry in the driveway for you. Twenty minutes, or faster if you can swing it; there's a breakfast meeting that I'll absolutely shit to be late for.*

And from that morning forward, Wesley's name was mud in all the places Andrew could reach to sully it. No studio would let him so much as darken the doorway of their soundstages, not even the least reputable. With nowhere else to go, he sought the theater again. The part of him that lived for Shakespeare had long been dormant, but it was to Shakespeare and the boards that he returned.

There was much of my own story in his. An instinctive resonance ran between us as I shared mine in turn: Lexington, then Richmond, then here; the private hell in those early places, and the scrappy life of my own making.

We got along like a house on fire, a cracking good match both onstage and off. It really was unfortunate our proclivities weren't more in line.

"Shall we?" Wesley chirped, tucking the cash under the ashtray at the center of the table, and stood to pull my chair out for me.

In the lobby, we fetched our jackets from the coat check. Wesley gently shook mine out and offered it.

"Is that the one you found on sale last fall?" Ezra asked at the end of a fresh cigar as he lit it, nodding at my silk bolero. He was a tall, narrow man with an imperious nose, on which he wore brass pince-nez. His wisping white hair and well-groomed beard were in tame order, which was rare to see—I was used to him brooding through the empty house of the theater during rehearsals or the wings on performance nights, twisting his fingers into his goatee as he stewed on new ways to eviscerate his cast for failing to read his mind.

He was a phenomenal director, a genius eye for staging and a savant-like ear for the text, cursed with the shortest fuse I'd ever seen. Edie attributed it to the exhausting company he chose to keep, the simpering Benjamin-Not-Bens of the world. *It makes him feel young, I think, the exasperation.*

I turned in place as Wesley put on his hat. "You'd know better than I would," I said to Ezra. "It all blurs in the closet."

"Heard that at a party last week," Wesley said briskly, grinning.

He held out a hand to Ezra and ignored another laugh from Benjamin—*A-haw!* "Thanks for having us, Ez."

"Ez?" Benjamin raised his eyebrows and pursed his lips. He was a soft-edged cellist from the Juilliard School. All the boys who let Ezra stop over in their love lives liked to fancy themselves seasoned but were usually so doe-eyed I just ended up feeling sorry instead of truly disliking them. I truly disliked Benjamin. "You *hate* nicknames."

Ezra shook Wesley's hand, blew a purple-tinged cloud of smoke from his nostrils, and leaned in to air-kiss both my cheeks goodbye. "He's the only one who makes them sound dignified," Ezra said. "Somehow. Nothing to it, darling, just don't muck up the show."

The tips of Benjamin's ears turned pink. I dug my gloves out of my purse and realized with a quick tightening in my chest that I had scored my arms with roving pink threads in repetitive passes under the table as we'd eaten. *Shit.* I tugged on each one swiftly before holding out a hand to Benjamin.

"Lovely to meet you, Ben."

Wesley and I walked out together. I took his elbow when he offered it, and he shot me a small, secretive smile. "That was *cold*," he muttered.

Wesley lived a few blocks away from me in a third-floor walk-up that smelled of singed black tea. His apartment was spartan and tidy, kept with the efficient hand of an ex-officer. He had no roommates, no art on his walls, and an impressive bar cart.

"So is trying to flirt with his date's employee the whole time," I said. Wesley snorted.

"I'm a grown lad." He patted my hand on his arm. We stopped at a crosswalk and waited for the light to change. "But I *do* appreciate a knight in shining armor."

I smiled at him, his profile cut cleanly against the dark in the mottled wash of neon signs and halogen bulbs glowing. He noticed me watching and grinned. "What?"

"Nothing." I rubbed at his arm through the linen of his sleeve and tugged us across the street when the light went green. "I'm just happy. I'm looking forward to opening."

"I like happy Jack," Wesley said as he fell into step, letting me lead the way. "You're fun when you're happy."

He'd been calling me Jack since he first saw me in my Cesario costume, claiming I wore trousers better than half the men he knew, and had I ever considered doing drag? The name stuck, and every time he said it, a warm sense of belonging came in to fill the small, empty places left wanting inside of me. He was my friend. It made me feel as precious as a creature of Eden given its proper title for the very first time.

The air was calm and perfectly temperate, the deep clutch of spring settled down over the city, and the bustle of the street had begun to turn over from evening to night.

I had once believed Lexington and Richmond were the biggest cities I would ever know, the places most full of life in the entire world. A fond scrap of memory wagged through me when we passed a gentleman with a velveteen coat and matching hat—I recalled my old director at the Richmond Revue, Ansel Jensen, sitting in the empty house between shows and teaching me how to recite iambic pentameter as I swept the aisles.

We stopped in front of my building at the top of the basement stairs. Next door, the pharmacy threw its sterile fluorescent shout onto the sidewalk. Wesley removed his hat.

"I'm for a nightcap," Wesley said. "There's a party on the pier. Care to join?"

I knew exactly what a party on the pier entailed, and ordinarily I would have jumped at the chance. Those parties were riotous islands of secret, shuddered joy, filled with men in dresses and wigs, women in suits more handsome than any heartbreaker in the city, and everyone in between with their arms slung over one another's shoulders and sipping from the same glass.

A party on the pier was where I first saw Edie's social prowess at work, invited into the sacred space of the city's underbelly to meet her there. She had asserted herself as my ambassador on the upper level of a building tucked into the narrow shrug of Charles Lane, where I'd looked down and gone dizzy to see the packed milling-about of every colorful someone below.

Over the wail of the band, Edie had told me of Ezra—and from Ezra came regular work and this rare, fine friendship with Wesley. I could pinpoint every good thing that had happened to me since arriving in Manhattan on that single party. The magic of the city was fickle, but kinder to me than any other place I had called my own.

Wesley was watching me expectantly for an answer. I gave him an apologetic smile. "I can't," I said. "It's too close to opening. I'm antsy."

"Aren't we all?"

"I know. I'm wound up. It's better if I just try to get some sleep."

Wesley looked amused as he leaned in and kissed my cheek. "You sure? I'm going to run myself down."

I reached up and put a hand to his cheek in farewell. "I know, I'd just get in your way. Have fun. Thank you for dinner. Don't stay out too late, remember call is five-thirty tomorrow."

"Should I phone if I'm going to be past curfew?" he teased.

"Only if you end up in the drunk tank."

He turned his face, grinning, and kissed the tips of my fingers. As Wesley stepped back onto the sidewalk, he replaced his hat on his head with a flourish.

"Sir," he announced into the dark, the light from the streetlamp pouring over him like a spotlight, with his voice pitched in the higher register he took on when he parroted my own lines at me as Viola, "shall I to this lady?"

"Ay, that's the theme," I sallied back, digging for my key in my purse. "To her in haste."

The deadbolt always took some wrestling to get open. There were four units along the narrow hall, and a shared bathroom at the end of it, which was only ever clean when I set to it with a scouring brush and the end of my patience.

Home.

I undressed to my slip and stood at my vanity with its uneven legs to rub a pasty dittany along the insides of my arms. The cooling soothe of it was familiar, faraway, and I stared at the fine pink furrows before going to the kitchen.

I wasn't nervous. I *wasn't*. It was going to be a good show. It was a comedy—everyone loved the comedies. I trusted Wesley, and I trusted myself. We would be great together.

So why now, why the old habit rising like a portent?

I picked up the bottle of Wild Turkey and peered at the contents. After nine years, the bottle was still one-third full. If *Twelfth Night* opened well, I would toast to myself with a small sip after making my way home in the wee hours after the cast party. I put it back in the cabinet and made myself a slapdash martini. I was out of olives.

My script sat on top of the pile on my table. I flipped to the beginning, sat down in front of the mirror, and began to run my lines aloud.

I put myself back in the space Jensen once taught me to access— *Get in their heads, Margot, feel yourself step into their lives. You can become anyone with enough imagination. That's the power of the theater: transformation.*

It used to frighten me how deeply I could feel. My mother had insisted it was a blessing, a light from the good Lord to allow me the full glories of His gifts, but for the longest time I could only see it as a curse on my small, useless body. I saw no point to the miserable ability, no reason for my highs or the sweet agonies that came with them, until I found the stage.

To bend an audience to my will was my sole sense of control in this life, the only one I truly owned. I could make people laugh, cry, gasp, fear, desire; in thrall to artifice in their seats, they had to behold me, to see me for all that I was: an unstoppable force. On the boards, I was more than a woman. I was a conduit. The stage was the only place fit to tame these strange passions.

I reached the end of the fifth act. I poured another drink, ran my thumb very gently along the inside of one wrist, and started again from the top.

◆ ◆ ◆

WESLEY AND I became inseparable during *Twelfth Night*. I'd marked a tangible change in myself for the better since we had become friends, and Edie agreed—no matter how much she teased me for such a girlish attachment to a man like Wesley, she was right. I adored being around him. He carried a certain lightness, a sense of unshakable humor I longed to embody. It was a joy to bask in the warmth of his ease.

Rumors flew, of course. The rest of the company made bets and gossiped in poorly covered whispers about whether or not Wesley and I were fucking. We hadn't, nothing near it—but we spent lots of time together outside work, and where there was the smoke of actors being friendly offstage burned the fire of sharp-tongued conjecture.

Twelfth Night had been open for three weeks and was receiving perfectly average reviews, as I expected. It wasn't the kind of show that moved critics to tears or any feelings much bolder than plain enjoyment. But Ezra was content, so we were allowed to take our days off for ourselves instead of spending them refining, refining, ever refining under his watchful eye.

Chap pawned a ticket for a new off-Broadway farce on me when other plans came up for him on an odd Wednesday. I didn't have anything better to do, so I took myself out. I had a smart little dinner with Edie at the all-night diner on Canal Street before she went off to a preview she was dreading—"It's *Antigone*," she said, sneering over the edge of her coffee cup. "Nobody likes *Antigone*. Do you like *Antigone*? See there, you look positively stricken. My point exactly."

I ducked a brief, spitting rain between awnings and overhangs to get to the theater in Chelsea. It was less a theater and more of a walk-in closet with rows of seats put in. There were fewer than a hundred of us in the audience, which meant the house looked packed. It would serve the actors' egos well.

I tried to enjoy the show. Truly, I did—but it was maudlin and affected, too confident in its own misery, and it left my curiosity so lacking that I found more entertainment in surveying the characters in the audience in washed-out relief from the stage lights.

A man with thick muttonchops and his wife fought a nodding, sneaking sleep farther down my row that took them each in turn; first him, then her, then him, then her. Just ahead of me, an older woman with a feathered hat shook her head subtly to herself, which made the feather wag in the dark with quick, harried jumps.

And there, two rows from the front, sat Wesley and a companion.

Their shoulders were touching, subtly. Wesley was watching the stage with impressive effort, his eyes narrowed as though reading a sign very far away that might make clear where the hell this plot was going. His companion, a buttoned-up professor type, looked bored to tears.

The pressure of my eyes must have drawn some sensation in him, as Wesley stilled and turned to face me. Confusion limned his expression in the dark, but after a moment he smiled. He gave a small, twitching wave. I sent one back and looked away as I noticed Wesley's date turning to look at me as well.

At intermission, I ordered a dirty martini from the bar in the lobby. Too dirty; I was debating tossing the glass of brine surreptitiously into the plastic ficus tree beside me when Wesley approached with his friend.

"Are you dead of boredom yet?" he muttered, leaning in to kiss me hello on both cheeks.

"Only halfway," I said, "but the final act might seal the coffin."

"I think the butler did it."

"The butler *always* does it."

Wesley's friend cleared his throat carefully. Wesley started and ushered him forward by a step with a sheepish look on his face. "Jesus, where are my manners—Jack, this is Wallace Miner. Wallace, this is my co-actor, Margaret. Margaret Wolf."

We shook hands. His palm was warm and slightly sticky with sweat. I gave him my most winsome smile. "A pleasure. Are you also in theater?"

"Ah, no. Linguistics."

I nudged Wesley with my elbow. "Does this one talk your ear off about all his favorite soliloquies?"

"I don't—do much theater, usually, Shoardie, would you like a drink?"

"Vodka tonic," Wesley said, touching Wallace barely on the waist as he peeled away to find the end of the concessions line.

I gave Wesley a doubtful look until I was sure Wallace was out of earshot. "He's a charmer," I said lightly.

Wesley shot me a wry smile. "I know. It was either this or a lecture on semiotics, and he wants me over for a drink with *his* friends later tonight, so this was my bargain." He slid his hands into his pockets, pulling out his leather cigarette case from the left one. "I thought it would be more interesting, Chap was going on about it all last week."

"He gave me his ticket," I said, and Wesley barked a laugh around the end of a cigarette as he popped it between his lips. He held the case out to me. I offered my lighter from my purse instead of taking one. Wesley leaned forward to let me give him the flame.

I tried another sip from my martini, grimaced, and held it out to Wesley. He tasted it, recoiled, and dumped it into the ficus before handing the empty glass back to me.

"Are most of your friends professors?" I asked, peering around at the eclectic crowd. Wesley made a considering sound.

"Some." He exhaled and waved his hand vaguely in the air. "I like them a little older. Comes with the territory."

"A refined palate."

"Exactly." He ashed into the fake plant and examined the fresh cherry end. "How do you think *Twelfth Night* is going?"

I shrugged and leaned alongside Wesley's casual ease. We both looked out over the milling audience—I could see Wallace looking out of place and impatient behind a woman wearing a boa so voluminous it nearly swallowed her face.

"I think it's going fine," I said. "I don't know. I'm a poor judge from the middle of it, especially since it's a comedy."

"You don't like the comedies?"

"Oh, I *like* them. There's just less . . . subtlety to them. Barefaced. Not so many layers to the characters."

Wesley nodded on another steady inhale. He caught my eye with a whiff of mischief, as though he had a rich secret about Lisette or Richard, our stage manager. "I heard," he muttered, "that Ezra's planning the Scottish play next."

My stomach dropped. "What?"

I looked at him immediately and caught the quiet pride in his expression, gossip being the currency of the theater. "The fall opener," Wesley hummed.

My heart hammered to a sprint. Sweat prickled along my underarms and the palms of my hands, the soles of my feet.

"If you're joking," I said, fighting to keep myself poised, "I'm going to be *very* upset with you."

Still smiling, Wesley's brow creased with curious confusion. "What? It's just a rumor."

"From whom? Where did you hear it?"

"Greg, from props. Ezra put in an order for more sugar blood and a bunch of *Highland-style daggers*."

I scowled. Part of me didn't want to believe him. I didn't want to get my hopes up. I had no patience for being disappointed, but I had never craved any role more thoroughly than Lady Macbeth. "That could be any number of the tragedies."

The lights flickered—five minutes until the show started again. Wesley sucked on one more mouthful of smoke before stubbing out his cigarette in the poor fake plant. He kissed me on the cheek and searched my gaze. "I have to collect my linguist. What? You look like you've seen a ghost."

"It's nothing," I blurted, and squeezed his hand. "I'm fine. If you're wrong, you owe me a drink."

"Alright, Jack. Have a nice night, won't you?"

"Of course. Enjoy your linguist."

I slipped away into the ladies' room. I shut myself in a stall and squeezed my eyes shut, jamming the heels of my hands against the sockets until I saw colors.

Ezra was going to do *Macbeth*. The chance of a lifetime, finally within reach. The only thing I had ever truly let myself want—the life I wanted more than any other to embody, and learn, and dwell in.

I forced myself to steady my breathing. I could do it. I was good enough.

Two voices roiled in my mind, both of them from Richmond, the angel and devil clinging to my shoulders.

Think of her motivations. Jensen used to coach me as I polished the footlights of the Richmond Revue's playhouse, picking up every odd job he would give me until he finally agreed I was ready to take a part onstage. *What could push a woman like her to such lengths? What must she have faced? Build her story for yourself, and it will move through you with the text.*

And there behind him within me loomed Hollis, cold and malformed in untouched memory. *You're too green, Margaret, I've told you a thousand times!* I could still hear, smell, feel the words on the fine hairs of my face from his sour hiss as he crowded me against the vanity in the dressing room locked behind him. *You play the roles I see fit to give you. Now put on the goddamn dress and be grateful.*

"Stop it," I whispered urgently to myself. I shook my head, wagged out my wrists to keep from scratching, and left the bathroom, the emptied lobby, the strange little theater, in a rush for home through the shower pelting down outside.

◆ ◆ ◆

I DIDN'T EVEN bother taking off my shoes before I was rummaging through old folios back in my apartment, exhuming my copy of

Macbeth. I peeled it open with trembling hands and took a moment to stare at the gentle pen strokes of Jensen's direction notes.

I had loved him with all the innocent ferocity of girlhood. He was arrested on a degeneracy charge only days before our own production of *Macbeth* was due to open, in a rash of police raids on queer bars all over Richmond. The Richmond Revue fell apart swiftly in the aftermath, and I ended up at the Halcyon across town under the direction of Michael Hollis.

I poured myself a straight shot of rye from the kitchen cabinet and sat down with the script. I would get this role. I would finally bring this woman to life: ambitious, and sure of herself, and filled with power of her own making.

2

The theater on Commerce Street

INTERMISSION, HALFWAY THROUGH our penultimate show of *Twelfth Night*. I'd done well as Viola, Viola-as-Cesario, parading around in my trousers and skirts and kissing both Wesley and Lisette to bawdy hoots and cheers from the audience. At least they were having fun with it. It was fun. It was all just *fun*.

I could hardly concentrate on anything fully since Wesley told me about *Macbeth*. I couldn't quit thinking about it. I'd scratched my arms raw in the wings without even realizing it between my scenes tonight in the first half.

Halfway through smearing a fresh layer of Covermark over the insides of my wrists, mind stuck on Lady Macbeth's motivations instead of Viola's, the door to my dressing room swung open. I jammed my hands under the vanity table and looked up through the mirror to find Wesley shutting it again behind him.

"I should have knocked," he announced. He looked scattered.

I frowned. "Are you okay?"

He shook his head, twitchy with preoccupation. I indicated the sofa with a nod. As he sat, I turned slightly away from him with one shoulder and set back to my arms. I was to have them bare with my final costume.

"Is Ezra wringing you out, too?" I asked without looking up. "I think his latest, that flautist, is spending all his nerves before he gets to us. I give it another week before they're done."

I glanced up and found Wesley watching me distantly, as though only halfway conscious of the world moving around him. He didn't blink for a long time.

"Wesley."

"Does that hurt? What happened?"

He was peering at my arms, the half-covered scoring standing out red against my skin. My cheeks heated with shame. I scoured the sponge in the makeup pan and painted another heavy smear over my left wrist. "Nothing. I'm allergic to the lace."

Wesley made a sympathetic sound at the back of his throat, then crammed his thumbnail into his mouth and set to chewing. He'd been late to call today. I hadn't had a chance to see him offstage.

I let him stew in the privacy of silence until he leaned forward with his elbows on his knees and his head in his hands. He gave a great groan, and I set down the makeup sponge with a clatter.

"*What*, Wesley."

"I'm sorry," he said through his fingers. His voice was wet and miserable. My chest clenched to find the pitch of it only steps away from tearfulness.

I put the sponge aside and took to the sofa beside him. "Tell me."

"It's stupid," he moaned, and then tossed his head. "It's not *stupid*, it's terrible, but it's— God, do you ever wish you could un-fuck somebody?"

I couldn't help the laugh that scraped itself out of my mouth even as I raised a hand to hold it in. Wesley turned to look at me with his temple propped on his fist, curled up as though shielding his soft parts. "Yes," I said as evenly as possible, "I think we all do."

Wesley shook his head and raked his hair back from his forehead with both hands. Traces of his face powder were stuck to the roots, shimmering pale against the glossy black. "I really fucked up, Jack. I feel like such an idiot."

So, it was a breakup then. He had a tender spirit. I patted his knee. "Oh, stop. Someone's heartsick over you, what's new? Half the Upper East Side—"

Wesley stopped me with a hand collecting mine, pulling it into his lap. I looked down at the join of our fingers in silence as he squeezed with quiet ferocity.

"It's no one new," he said very softly. His voice was shaking. "It's . . . Andrew. He. Well, I told you he kept me comfortable, close at hand, and I—I thought that was it, I really did, I mean, God, Margaret, the *people* he knew . . ."

I let Wesley find himself in the silence of recollection. He stared into the middle distance of the threadbare rug and wrapped his other hand around mine, clinging—I followed suit and held his in return. "Is he in town? What did he do, Wes?"

Wesley gave a warble of stiff laughter. "Do?" Wesley opened a hand at the shabby hovel of the dressing room and hacked another bitter chuckle. He looked more unglued than I'd ever imagined he could be. His chin wobbled. "He backed me into a fucking corner, let me think I was safe with what little he let me keep, that's what he did, and now I'm going to lose it all!"

"Wesley." I shifted to face him and took his face in my hands. I turned him to look at me and angled for his eyes until they actually met mine. "Take a breath, slowly: What. Happened."

Wesley set his jaw and took my hands down from his face. "The Committee is investigating me."

My stomach dropped. "Fuck, HUAC?"

"Exactly," he spat, looking away to pinch at the inner corners of his eyes.

"How do you know it's them? What do they think you've done?"

"I got a call last month, felt fishy but I didn't make anything of it. Then Mrs. Beebe across the hall said two men let themselves into my apartment the other day, and—and if they find anything . . ." His mouth twisted up with miserable fury. He tossed his head. "I can't be put on a list, Margot. I *can't*."

"You won't be. They can't do that, they—"

"Can't they? They arrested Frank from the club on Ninth two weeks ago on suspicion. Not a lick of evidence." Wesley stared hard at me, begging me to refute it. When I couldn't, he groaned again and dragged a nervy hand down his mouth.

"Well, what could they have on you?" I tried.

". . . I may have gone to a Party meeting or two after Andrew and I were done."

I didn't want to chide him, but my mouth still drew into a firm line. "Wesley."

"I know! I was upset, it was a—a stupid fucking rebellion!" He threw a flat hand at the wall as though convincing it of his cause. "But even if I hadn't, they could muster up anything they want. I have an Equity card; I'm already two steps from—from Bolshevism in their eyes, and if they've been watching me, they know the sort of company I keep. I'm done for, Jack. *Done*."

I watched him rage at himself and wished I could do anything to help. "He was well-connected then," I said gently. Wesley snorted.

"Understatement."

I took his hand again and pulled up close to press our sides together from shoulder to ankle. "I'm sure it will be alright. Lay low. Don't give them any reason to sniff after you, and they'll forget about it. You'll see."

Wesley shook his head. He seemed to surrender to a very deep and bothersome truth before heaving a sigh and sliding down onto one knee in the space between mine. He brought my hands to his mouth and squeezed his eyes shut, summoning strength.

"I'm so sorry," he whispered, speaking directly into my knuckles, "but it's the only sure way. Could you . . . Jesus. Would—would you marry me?"

Oh, no.

No. I couldn't let him do that. It was unfathomable cruelty. To invite him to sew himself to me would be like tossing a kitten into the deep end of a lake.

I had to tell him. He had to know what he was signing up for.

"Wesley," I blurted—but couldn't bring myself to say anything more. What was the truth, really? That I was afraid of myself? That being alone without the noise of other people's poetry as company made my heart race and my gut clench, panicking over nothing but the silence?

My mouth hung open around a blank syllable. He watched me without blinking, expectant and fevered. What was it, really, that was so wrong with me? I couldn't put it into words. I only knew that it felt wrong to be in my own body sometimes. Was it a disease? Communicable? Would I doom him just as surely as a blacklist would?

"Please." He gave a damp, desperate chuckle. "I . . . please. I know I'm asking for too much, but . . ."

A long silence stretched between us. In the hallway, bright laughter passed the door shut tight.

"You're—you really are one of my favorite people in this city, and you wear a pair of trousers better than most of the men I've known. It would hardly be a—a chore for me," Wesley tried at teasing, but his eyes were full of misery and his voice broke. A sharp surging inside me rattled—*Unsex me here, and fill me from the crown to the toe topfull of direst cruelty.*

I could protect him.

A sense of purpose flooded through me with a shape I'd only known from the middle of a scene. I blinked at him. *Protect him.* I had never had that role before: protector. I had always been treated as a commodity, fit more for being broken than the careful work of breaking.

I leaned down and ever so gently kissed him on the mouth. "Alright," I whispered against his painted, chapped lips. "Of course I will."

He leaned up across my lap and hugged me tightly around the middle. I held him in return, pressing his head to my heart. *Protect him.*

I could do that.

I would.

When Wesley sat back on his heels, dabbing at the edges of his eyes to keep the stage makeup from slipping, I saw the pallor had retreated somewhat from his gaze. "Thank you," he rasped. His mouth wobbled into a vigorous smile. "I can't . . . You're a doll. Thank you, Jack."

The call for five rose through the whalebone halls of backstage. I patted Wesley heartily on the shoulder and nodded at the makeup on my vanity on my way out the door. "Get yourself tidied. You can use my kit."

I found Ezra scowling at the set from stage right, vulturing by the stage manager's desk. I snatched the cigar from his mouth and sucked in a punishing, stinking mouthful. He glared at me.

"I heard you're doing the Scottish play," I said. Ezra's glare compounded. He plucked the cheroot back and shook his head.

"This is *exactly* why I was waiting to say anything until after we closed," he hissed, leaning in with his voice low. "I knew you were off these last few days, who was it? Who told you?"

His gaze quickened past my shoulder, and I glanced over to see Wesley leaving my dressing room with a fresher face to set himself on the other side of the wings. Ezra grunted and meditated on a slow pull of purple smoke.

"You two are worse than a mated pair of turtledoves," he sneered, his nostrils pluming.

"Who do you have in mind?"

Peering sidelong at me, Ezra was silent.

"For the Lady," I insisted. It was hard to keep the fight in me under Ezra's singular scrutiny, but I managed not to let my voice go small.

"Not Banquo?" He fixed me with a tart look. "Malcolm? Duncan, perhaps?"

I grabbed the cigar from between his fingers and stubbed it out on the exposed brick wall beside the stage manager's desk—Richard was across the stage, unable to squawk about keeping the ashes away from his precious production book.

"I know you already have it cast," I said. "I need to know one way or another, Ezra, I—"

"Oh, come off it, Margaret, it's you. Of course it's you."

I stared at him as the air rushed out of my lungs.

Ezra gestured at the side of the stage where Wesley had gone to take his place ahead of curtain. "Turtledoves you may be, but I'd be a fool not to recognize whatever . . . *mess* there is between you as certified fucking gold onstage."

I couldn't speak. A white fuzz buzzed and bloomed between my ears.

It was me. *She* was me. I was her. I was finally going to do it.

Ezra looked at me flatly for several long moments. He raised one bushy eyebrow. "Anything else?"

"We're getting married," I blurted, and blinked. That's right. I'd just agreed to marry Wesley. "Wesley and I, we—he asked me to marry him."

Ezra made a soft, intrigued sound. He drew his hand slowly down his beard and smiled not unkindly. "One thing after another with you two, isn't it? Never a dull moment."

◆ ◆ ◆

WESLEY AND I were married with little to-do in a small chapel the following Monday, with only Edie and Ezra along for witnesses. Ezra smoked through the whole thing. Edie insisted on taking us for cocktails afterward, despite it being eleven o'clock in the morning.

That night, the party at the warehouse on Bank Street called for costumes. Wesley tarried on my doorstep with his hat in both hands after walking me home from the bar, his cheeks blushed with the effort of a brisk walk and the briefest chill that was beginning to gnaw at the edges of the air. "I thought we might go as bride and groom," he said. "But I'll wear the veil—do you have a tux?"

"Bring me a bow tie," I said. "I'll see if Edie has a men's jacket that fits."

She had four. I chose one with black silk lapels.

When we showed up at the pier after sunset, Wesley with a tulle veil pinned to his hair, I accepted the glass of champagne his friend passed to me as he opened the doors for us. We surrendered to the hilarity of the night, the first of the rest of our life together, the unseen and glittering future.

I was Margaret Shoard now, and soon to be Lady Macbeth. Everything was exactly as I could have dreamed.

I found Edie holding court by a concrete pillar wrapped with sagging yellow crepe paper left over from some other day's reason to celebrate. She was dressed as an exotic bird, fuchsia pink and draped in feathers. Starry-eyed women and eager young men surrounded her like colorful petals falling open around the matrix of a budded flower, the familiar look of desperation for success splashed across all of their faces.

"Margot!" She hailed me with a beckoning wave of her hand when I sidled through the crowd to get to her. I ignored the sharp glances.

Her gaze was bright and glittering with drink. She was the sort who held her liquor by way of deepened elegance and wit rather than sloppy dissolution. Edie smiled and excused herself neatly from the crowd with an air of being freed from a particularly uncomfortable bind. Her shoulders relaxed, and she steered me confidently toward the bar with a hand at my upper back.

"Congratulations, luv," she said at my ear over the roar of the crowd and the music—Wesley had been pulled into the eddying circles of his friends. I would find him later.

"I'm really pleased with the whole thing," I said. "I am, truly."

"I'm sure you are. If you're set on going for a man, he's the best of them."

"Did Ezra tell you about *Macbeth*?"

Edie rolled her eyes and passed me a fizzing glass. She tapped her drink against it. "Take one evening to not think about work, darling. It makes you look peaky."

She sipped with a smile in her gaze. I mimicked her.

"By the way," she said, "I've got you a wedding gift."

I made a tetchy sound. "I told you not to."

"Well, you live in a pit and Wesley has all the wrong eyes on him; I think you newlyweds rather need a place to call your own."

She dug into her clutch and held something out to me—a set of keys. I frowned.

"Edie, what—"

"Just don't throw any raucous parties like the last tenant. The fifth floor gets *beautiful* light around midday."

I gaped at her, and unable to think of anything else, said again, *"What?"*

"I've covered the first two months of rent and got a damn good rate for you on the rest of it." Edie pressed the keys into my hand and closed my fist around them. "Ezra's going to start paying you both a little more with the Scottish flap, so you'll be fine on your own from there."

I stared at the keys. This happiness was too much. I wasn't made to hold so much *good* in my body at once. An itchy sense of dread seeped in with each foggy heartbeat in my ears—but this was neither the time nor the place nor the reason for any of that. Not tonight.

I threw my arms around Edie's neck and kissed her square on the mouth. She laughed against my cheek, bright and fragrant. "Thank you," I said at her ear.

"Go enjoy your evening, poss." She lifted my arms from her shoulders and kissed my knuckles, leaving a bright print of her lipstick behind. "Don't let me keep you."

It was a perfect night. I drank too much and didn't care. My feet felt lighter than air, and I had a mild headache from so much happiness as I moved through the crush of it. Wesley's friends crammed us into a cab at midnight and told the driver to take us to the Marlton. We laughed the whole way there, leaning on each other across the middle seat, dizzy with joy.

When we arrived, Wesley carried me over the threshold into a sumptuous hotel room. The bed was an ocean, and the long statements of the windows were garlanded by crisp linen curtains.

Here was the first real step into our lives braided together. Private. Safe. The door latched after Wesley kicked it closed behind him. He spun me in place, my husband, and I clung to his neck, ardent, burying another peal of laughter there.

My husband. The title like a shield, and mirroring my own new identity sitting miter-like on my own head: *wife.* I leaned back and gazed up at Wesley, looking him full in the face.

"Are you happy?" I asked. He smiled and set me down on my feet. My heels settled into the thick, plush carpet like lawn sod.

"I'm *elated*, Jack."

"Good. Help me out of this penguin suit."

Wesley pushed the jacket from my arms as I unfastened my trousers and kicked them down to my ankles. I reached up to begin plucking pins from my hair. Across the room, a tall mirror above the dresser showed us from a distance—Wesley at work on my shirt buttons, his own suit immaculate, the pinned veil lost to the party.

Wesley turned me with a steering hand on my waist once my shirt hung open and unclipped the bow tie from the back of my neck. As I kept at my hair, already a fistful of pins in one hand and still more to free, he tugged feather-light at the open collar of the shirt and peeled it from my shoulders.

I stood before him in my underthings. He stared at my body as I watched us through our reflection for a long moment—beholding him, beholding me.

Wordlessly, Wesley thumbed at the lace strap over my shoulder. He marveled at it with a shallow frown. I put the hairpins down on the edge of the vanity beside me and helped him finish the work.

Away came the longline clutch of my brassiere. My garter belt slid off with both our hands hunting its closure around my waist. I unhitched the catches on my stockings as Wesley unhooked and shifted the girdle down my hips, and I balanced myself on Wesley's shoulder with one hand to roll away my last pair of nylons without any runs. I kicked off my shoes, shimmied down my lace briefs, and finally stood naked before him.

Wesley stared at me through a protracted silence with his hands resting on the rounds of my shoulders. He swallowed and roved his fingertips down to stroke with measured, careful curiosity across the small swell of my left breast. His forefinger traced a slow circle over the pink ridge of my nipple. Tears sprang to his eyes.

"I will never have the words," he rasped, staring at his hand on my body, "to say how grateful I am for you."

"You don't need to tell me," I insisted gently. "I know it. I do."

Wesley shook his head. "I'd say it six ways to Sunday, but—truly, whatever I've done to deserve this, I wish I knew so I could keep doing it. Over and over again, I'd do anything to make you happy, Jack. I *swear* I would."

He trailed off and clenched his jaw. I lulled him and reached up to redirect his hand into mine, carding our fingers together. "It makes me happy to keep you safe, Wesley."

"Does it?" he whispered. His chin wobbled. "God, I—I thought I was stove up, and now here you come, saving me from my own mistakes."

I wrapped him into an embrace, guided his face down to the dip in my shoulder, and felt his body wrack with the tremor of his first sob. I shut my eyes briefly and murmured tender nothings to Wesley while he came apart in my arms. He clung to the bare skin of my back and pulled me to him. I opened my eyes and found our reflection in the mirror again: The disparate halves of us joined messily, jigsaw edges matching in perfect harmony despite our misalignments—a rude, hysterical punch line.

I could learn to love the humor in it over time, if only to have him. I rested a hand on the back of Wesley's neck.

"You're entirely too dressed to be crying so hard," I muttered into the side of his head. He chuckled wetly into my hair and stepped back to let us divest him as well.

Wesley's gaze stayed fixed to the carpet as I lifted off his jacket and plucked open his bow tie. He shrugged off his suspenders and unhooked his cummerbund. When he set to his shirt buttons, I paused to tip his chin up and search his expression.

"I know what I'm getting into," I promised him.

Wesley abandoned his shirt for a moment to take me by both sides of the face and press an ardent kiss to my forehead. "I'm in debt to you, Jack," he whispered into my skin. "I mean it. You're saving my life."

I stroked a hand along the back of his arm. "No debts. It's a partnership. I'll protect you," I murmured, "and you protect me. Easy."

Wesley sniffed a soft, piteous chuckle into my hair. "You don't need protecting. You're a force of nature."

My heart lurched with a sweet thrill. I angled back to look at him full-on. "I wouldn't have said yes if I didn't need you, too."

"Here's another vow," Wesley said gently. He sniffled and drew himself up, blinking quickly. "I will do anything you ever need from me, whenever you need it, to protect you, too. Tit for tat. I swear."

I smiled.

Both of us undressed, I gathered him up onto the bed. We laid beside each other and finished picking the pins from my hair.

Heavy with drink and revelry and the weight of our new shared life, Wesley drifted off while we daydreamed aloud; the things we wanted most in life, the small specificities we would grow to discover about each other, the fresh start that awaited in the new apartment.

Together, there was so much we could carry in a shared grip.

I traced the slope of Wesley's shoulder and marked how peaceful he looked when he slept. I counted his breaths, the slow march of them automatic in his body's drive to live, and swore I would train that same instinct into my own body.

Perhaps standing beside him would teach me how.

Perhaps I would finally want to learn.

3

Sixth and West Washington Place— Shoard Downs

OUR NEW BUILDING was an Italianate wonder made of stern, green brick, which had been built smack-dab in the middle of the last century and boasted higher ceilings and more windows than I ever could have dreamed.

The apartment afforded two bedrooms with a fairly large kitchen and a handsome study. The only things I brought along with me were my own clothes and cosmetics crammed into a few suitcases, the gilt mirror, my orange telephone with a new place of honor in the kitchen, and the bottle of Wild Turkey poured out over all this good fortune lately to its halfway mark. Wesley's furniture, far more curated and less ramshackle than mine, made up the most of our space.

A fine view of Sixth Avenue scrolled out below us, and we looked directly into the building across it, but neither of us minded. We got good light, just as Edie promised, and we'd be spending most of the daylight hours catching up on sleep or out rehearsing anyway.

Wesley and I finished hauling boxes upstairs by mid-afternoon. All of the windows were open to the airy, temperate weather. *Every place worth its salt needs a nickname,* he'd said with a proud grin, working at the cork of a bottle Edie had delivered earlier. *I'm calling it Shoard Downs.*

We sat beside each other on Wesley's old steamer trunk and passed the bottle between us as a welcome gift and congratulation at once— just yesterday afternoon, Ezra had posted the cast list for our next production:

MACBETH, Thane of Glamis—Wesley Shoard.
LADY MACBETH—Margaret Wolf.

The future ahead bloomed with potential. To see my name alongside that role was nothing short of surreal.

Wesley surveyed the morning's handiwork, the slogging up and down of our belongings through the stairwell, as I picked idly at the edge of a faded pinup sticker advertising Miami—the trunk had traveled with him to and from Oxford, Maine, California, scads of other places I could only imagine.

"Well," Wesley said briskly, "I'd call this a very good day indeed."

He passed me the bottle with a wholly satisfied smile I couldn't help but return.

"You and I," I said, accepting the wine and swiping a slouching lock of hair back from my forehead, "have different definitions of 'good.'"

I took a swig. Wesley watched me fondly.

"I thought that mover was going to have a conniption when you took that box from him," he said.

I scoffed. "It was *dishware,* and he was going to hoist it upside down. You would think common sense was a little more common."

I gave him the bottle again. He examined the label. "This is the sort of vintage we should really be savoring from a glass."

With a broad gesture at the rest of the room, our lives now joined as one into a madness of boxes and scattered furniture, I turned to and fro as though soliciting direction. "If you want to look for the glasses, be my guest."

Wesley grinned. He took another pull from the neck.

The sounds of this part of town eddied in through the windows, still very much the unique mutter of the West Village, but a less-manic patter than what used to chatter through the street-level port-hole in my old apartment. It felt as though I could finally draw a full breath, where light pushed in with the express purpose of buoying my spirits into the day.

I could be happy here. *We* could be happy here.

It was Sunday. I had never taken an extra day off before. The afternoon before me seemed endless.

"You have a standing appointment this evening, don't you?" I asked Wesley, not looking directly at him. He chuckled.

"You know my schedule better than I do."

"I only figured."

Wesley made a pleased sound, sipping again. He nudged my trouser leg with the butt of the bottle. "You figured right, but—you know."

When I looked over at him, he had his elbows propped on his knees and was staring at his shoes. He'd worn an old shirt today to allow for the sweat of effort, his cuffs rolled to his elbows and his collar open. His hair had come loose from its usual order, curling gently about his ears with sweat.

"I don't have to keep on with them, if you don't want me to," Wesley said, not stilted but certainly not barreling forward with confidence. He held the bottle out to me like an afterthought. "My . . . appointments."

"Wesley, if you think—"

"I can cut back," he said quickly, as though the courage to say anything would leave him if he let me speak. He rubbed the corner of the wine label with his fingernail. "If you'd rather me stay here for a while, to—settle in, or, whatever you need, Jack. I can just . . . be yours."

He looked away from me, but he reached between us on the trunk and took my hand. When he squeezed my fingers, I returned the gesture and sat patiently until he glanced up at me. I held my free hand out for the bottle and drank a wide glug.

"If you think I expect you to table yourself," I said, "then you're even more of a martyr than your repertoire lets on."

Wesley sniffed a chuckle and searched my face. "Yeah?"

"Of course. This," I insisted, gesturing between us, "is whatever we want it to be."

He stared at my knuckles meshed against his. Tugging at me gently, Wesley lifted the back of my hand to his mouth and kissed it. "What do *you* want it to be?" he asked there.

I took another drink and swiped the side of my fist across my mouth. "All I need it to be is happy. If continuing to see your friends is what makes you happy, then I want you to keep doing that. Just promise me you'll be careful. No more Andrews."

"No more Andrews," Wesley said gently. I passed him the bottle and watched him take a swig—his mouth, his jaw, the firm line of his throat.

Curiosity took me. "How does it work?"

"How does what work?"

"Your friends. The . . ."

Wesley raised his eyebrows. "The trade? You've never asked before."

"Never quite wondered, but now I'm much closer to it. So."

Vaguely amused, Wesley looked up at the vaulted ceiling and

thought for a moment. "It's . . . different," he said, "but also similar. In some ways."

"Similar how?"

Wesley grinned, wide and unafraid. "Do you really want the details?"

I nodded.

He explained it to me, dry and perfunctory, with the demonstration of a few practiced gestures for the particulars.

I squinted. "That's all?"

Wesley laughed. "What do you mean, 'that's all'? It's sodomy, people have been arrested for it."

Despite the taboo, he seemed smug; proud of his own muster.

I made a doubtful grunt. "Just sounds like taking the alley entrance instead of the front door to me."

Wesley laughed again, and he overbalanced before tipping off the trunk. He dragged me down after him by the ankle, and I followed with a hand out to make sure the bottle wouldn't topple—although there was hardly any left to spill.

I sprawled out where I landed and smiled up at the ceiling.

"We are, perhaps, drunk," Wesley announced as he splayed on his back as well. Hot pride filled me in a rush. *I* had done that. *I* had put contentment there in his heart, lodged like an arrowhead.

I sat up beside him with my knees curled under me and gazed at him, long and prone and mine. "I'm awfully pleased with us," I said.

Wesley rolled his head to face me. Along the soft inner skin of his lips, the wine had stained a very gentle purple. "We're on our way, Jack."

I smiled to myself and rested a hand flat on his diaphragm, rising and falling gently with each breath. He was warm. We sat in silence for another protracted spell.

"Do you think I can do it?" I asked gently.

"Do what?"

"Be Lady Macbeth."

"Of course you can. You're going to be phenomenal."

Restless, I began to flex and relax my fingers against the fabric of Wesley's shirt. "I have so much . . . *expectation* built up in me around it, I don't know."

"Well," Wesley hummed, "even coming from the same person, every role becomes new before it's done."

"Is that it?" I fussed blindly with one of his shirt buttons, pushing it out of and back into its loop. "They always take such hold of me. It's like the character kicks Margaret out of the chair and lives inside me for the duration of a production." I nodded at our boxes. "And some unpack their stuff, stick around more thoroughly than others."

"What about Jack?"

"What about what?"

"Do they kick Jack out alongside Margaret?"

I smirked. "Jack *owns* the place. Especially when he's happy. He's got the best taste."

Wesley chuckled, his belly jumping softly under my hand like the very current of joy. I bit my lip and felt a flare of possession.

Nothing of his nature changed the fact I was genuinely attracted to him. Anyone would be. I wouldn't have agreed to marry him if I wasn't, which was shallow at best and downright selfish at worst.

"You're a wonderful actor," Wesley said, and it was such a private assertion that I believed him. I looked over his face and found it softened with drink, laid bare with affection.

Much of the same must have shone in my eyes. Wesley reached down and ran his thumb up and down the inside of my wrist. Neither of us spoke for some time. If he felt any of the old ridges from my anxious scratching with the soft passage of his touch, he said nothing about it.

"I suppose we should consummate this venture one of these days," Wesley said plainly. My heart lurched in my chest.

"Do you want to?" I stammered. "I mean. *Can* you?"

Wesley gave me a wry look. "You said it yourself, it's just a different tack. Of course I *can*."

"I know, but—"

"Do *you* want to?"

"Yes." The admission sliced easily into the stillness. I swallowed, not looking away from him or even hazarding to blink. "I—yes."

Wesley's eyes flashed. Sparks drew beneath my skin.

"Then come here and let me look after you, Jack," he murmured.

He pulled me down to him, or I followed—it was impossible to tell which of us moved first. We kissed, and it held the same simmering heat as every kiss we shared onstage—but this, here, was different. Newer, charged with fresh and forward purpose.

I clutched at the buckle of Wesley's belt until he steered me to settle myself up onto his hips, to lean down and cling to his collar as we delved together into the strange depths of this new secret we shared.

"Same idea," I gasped against his mouth when he went for the closure of my slacks, "but—have you—?"

"Yes, yes," Wesley panted, his eyes squeezed shut as I felt him stir beneath me. "I've got you; come here."

I shuddered when his left hand found me, gently hunting, and he hushed me as he brought his other hand against my back under the loose tails of my shirt to steady the angle of us. It had never been like this with Hollis—*he* had touched me like an ornery creature, like he was afraid that tenderness might have freed in me some idea of what I really deserved.

Here, by Wesley's hand, came every measure of that kind and quiet awe with which I had long dreamed of being touched; as though in having fled my life unwittingly, it delivered itself to me now tenfold.

Our clumsy limbs knocked, near-missing with *sorry*s, *oops*es, *here*, *let me*s, as we breathed, gasped, and laughed into each other's mouths. I shed my trousers and undershorts before working open Wesley's fly and asking again, mostly to appease my own nerves, "Can I?"

I had my hand around him, which made his brows pull together with an ecstatic, ferocious need. I was mostly just marveling—I didn't know it was possible for a man to function after half a bottle of wine. Perhaps Hollis was of even weaker stock than I had known.

"It's your show, Jack," Wesley panted, flexing his hands on my flanks and trembling sweetly the whole way.

The feeling was singular from this position, odd and marvelous and wholly unique. I had only felt the breach before from flat on my back or pressed forward into the sheets—or the carpet, if Hollis was impatient—but this wasn't about Hollis. Hollis was long gone, a charred myth of what once was.

Wesley was here, and urgent, and vital, and mine, mine, *mine*.

As I found a soft hitching pace, I followed it like a pointing hound into a thicket of river reeds. Beyond the open windows, the city sang its familiar tune.

Wesley clung to me so dearly the flesh of my thighs dimpled under his spanning grip. When I covered his hands with my own, clinging right back, dragging the novel weight of my wedding band across his tendons, Wesley shivered; stilled; broke. He gasped, his head tipped back and his shoulders bowing gently against the floor, his eyes still firmly fixed shut.

I remained suspended in cotton-headed bliss, floating leagues beyond my own body as Wesley sagged and caught his breath. I let my own eyes fall closed and imagined what that might feel like, to put forth instead of consume—to be devoured instead of to devour.

"Thank you," I said, my voice rough and awed.

Wesley gave a pale titter, his torso leaping softly beneath me. "You are *quite* welcome."

He helped me maneuver off him, foal-legged, and I staggered into the bathroom.

Shut tight in privacy and still buzzing across the outline of my body, I cleaned up and rinsed my hands under the faucet—the novel luxury of an en suite toilet, with pipes that didn't make a wheezing rattle like they had on Christopher Street.

I stared through my flushed and wide-eyed reflection. I'd been taking birth control pills from my rheumy physician for two weeks, figuring I would only ever keep up appearances by playacting the compliant wife with a husband who expected his dues. That was what a good wife did, after all: She kept up appearances.

I examined myself in the mirror, my flushed cheeks and my dilated pupils, and ran my fingertips along my lips. "Come, you spirits, that tend on mortal thoughts," I whispered. Frisson shot through me, sparkling down the length of my neck. I swallowed and drew my entire carriage up ever so slightly.

I had everything. I had the role, the apartment, the husband of my dreams. Nothing could break me.

"Unsex me here, and fill from the crown to the toe top-full of direst cruelty! Make thick my blood. Stop up th' access and passage to remorse, that no compunctious visitings of nature shake my fell purpose, nor keep peace between th' effect and it!"

I stepped closer to the mirror and stared hard at myself, into myself, drawn so close to the glass that it fogged softly with each breath and I could hardly make a difference of my features.

When I emerged again into the naked apartment, I forwent dressing and remained in only my shirt and brassiere. I unlatched my suitcase and dug for the bottle of Wild Turkey.

Wesley had collected himself, mostly—his belt remained unfastened and his buttons open to his undershirt. He lit a cigarette. "This is the most fabulous apartment," he said, still sprawled on his back. "I love it. Shoard Downs. We should take Edie out to that place by the park as thanks."

I uncorked the bottle and took a sharp swig before holding it out to Wesley, standing over his loose-limbed ease.

He grinned up at me. "Another wedding gift?"

"From home. Home-home, Kentucky. I take a few sips whenever good stuff happens."

Wesley peered at the bottle. His gaze softened. "There's a lot left."

I took another mouthful and peeled my lips briefly over my teeth for the burn. "Make me a deal."

"Another?"

"A deal, not a vow."

Wesley tipped his head back and exhaled a rarified piston into the air. "Shoot."

"For as long as we've got together, give me reasons to drink it and you can help finish it."

Wesley lifted the cigarette up to me and smiled. "Deal."

I gave him the bottle and accepted his smoke. He sipped as I drew, and I laughed more freely than I could ever recall as he winced against the taste.

◆ ◆ ◆

WE WERE LEARNING the neighborhood and finding spots we could call ours—corner stores, the dry cleaner's, various routes and paths through and around the landmarks that made up a day's errands between rehearsals. I had a favorite coffee shop around the block, a lunch counter that knew us as regulars, and several nighttime joints that knew how to pour Edie's drinks just the way she liked them the second she walked in the door. I had everything I ever could have asked for—and then, of course, the role.

Our *Macbeth* was going to be stunning. Wesley and I were made for it. Ezra's feedback for us got less and less involved, and some days he would even forget to critique us. Had Wesley not also been there to witness it, I would have sworn I was hallucinating.

Nevertheless, anxiety plagued me. I couldn't quit telling myself I was going to ruin it. My conviction was either too fierce, or not enough. I was either exactly manic enough in the Lady's ambitious destruction, or completely overdoing it. Nobody was saying these things to me besides myself—and nothing anybody said otherwise convinced me. My mood changed like the tides, and with it my sense of peace.

Wesley did his best to keep me centered, but I could tell it wore on him. I hated feeling like a burden.

When he was out, I hunkered into the chaise with a drink and went over and over my lines. I held myself back from pacing—to pace at this stage of preparing would upset the careful placidity of the poetry. So I read and recited in near silence, on my own under the light of a single lamp.

The doorknob rattled well after midnight with the telltale fumble of Wesley juggling his keys on the other side of it. I looked up from my page but didn't move to stand.

Wesley stumbled through the door, his hat off and tie undone, and shut it gently behind him. He was humming a tune to himself as he toed off his shoes, chuckling a little when he pitched forward, and I noticed when the hall lamp caught him that he had a small red mark on his neck just above his collar.

"Was it fun?" I asked.

Wesley jumped, one hand braced against the wall, and dissolved into a minor pleasure of relieved laughter when he saw me there.

"Christ, I thought you'd gone to bed."

"I can't sleep. How was the party?"

"Bona, bona, bonaroo," Wesley sang as he strolled over in sockfeet. He pointed at the folio, grinning rakishly. "You've read this one already."

"It's a favorite."

"You're *my* favorite, Jack." He was giving me a silly little smile when I looked up at him and raised an eyebrow.

I nodded at the mark on his neck. "Looks like you were someone's favorite tonight."

Wesley's cheeks flushed a soft pink as he reached up to touch at his throat, as though he could still remember the feeling of whoever's mouth had put it there. "He was . . . nice," he determined. That was the most he ever revealed to me if I asked about them, whether his companions were *nice* or *fine* or *perfectly kind, actually.*

"I'm glad you had fun." I shut the folio and stood up, and Wesley pulled me close.

"It's all fun," he said, sighing. "So bold and blue, cackling about this and that and who-she-do. But I like quiet, too. I like our home."

Awkwardly slipping my arms up to reach around his shoulders, I returned the embrace briefly. "I'm glad," I assured him, patting his back. He sniffed a laugh against my neck.

"Truly! I do! I've never really cared to call any place home, not 'til now." He pulled back and lowered himself onto the chaise, laying out long with his jacket askew in his liquor-limbed ease. He always looked more delicate after coming home from one of his uptown parties. I wondered when, if ever, life might twist itself around to let him be this way always, unbound by his defenses.

"You're a peach." He sighed again, lolling his head to the side to peer at the wash of the nighttime avenue below. "I really, madly adore you. I don't feel like I tell you that enough. Has anyone ever told you they love you?"

Standing over him, I petted a hand through Wesley's hair, the pomade already worked most of the way out. "I'm glad you had fun."

"I love you, Jack."

I gave him a brief, wincing smile. "You're punchy."

Wesley grinned and hid his face in my hand, peeling open one eye to look sideways at me. "Trade sticks, huh?"

I set down my script on the end table and curled up against him, wriggling along Wesley's side to wedge us both onto the slim cushion. Against his collar, I smelled a light cologne with a floral touch.

"He certainly smells nice," I muttered. I watched a small, inward smile fade up on Wesley's mouth.

"He was a ballet dancer."

"A *ballet dancer.* Edie would be proud. Been in anything we'd have seen?"

"No, he's new to the city. Young."

I swatted Wesley gently on the shoulder. "I thought you liked them older."

"Oh, I do. But everyone at So-And-So's was already paired off—this poor chicken looked at me from over a drink, big eyes all nervous, and asked if I had a smoke. I couldn't say no."

"A knight in shining armor," I cooed. Wesley rolled his eyes before shutting them and shifted his shoulders to pull me close.

"I think he was just knocking off the spell of it, you know how it goes; the nerves, that . . . dive into the deep water. Putting his head under for the first time." Wesley paused to free a wide, jaw-round yawn. "I was more than happy to get him over the threshold."

I regarded my husband and this careful way in which he cared. I *didn't* know how it went, and that was the crux of it. But here was his kindness again: the sharing with me. I put my head to his shoulder and sank into the way his fingertips played lazily with the hair curling at my nape.

"What happened here?" Wesley cooed with blithe concern. I opened my eyes and managed not to flinch when I felt his fingertips on my inner arms, where I had scratched them faintly raw earlier that night. My stomach swooped.

"It's fine. It's a big role, I'm just anxious. Don't worry about it."

Wesley frowned at me, his eyes so vivid and shiny I could swear they would burn right through me if he stared for long enough.

"Is there anything wrong?"

"Nothing is wrong. I'm fine, Wes." I pecked him lightly on the mouth. "I'm glad you had a nice night."

I made to get up, but Wesley caught me gently around the waist when I swung my legs over the edge of the chaise. He stared shortly into nothing for a moment, putting words together at the back of his mind. "If you aren't . . . happy," he said, then stopped, drumming up the complete thought. "I don't want you to fall on your sword for me any more than you already have."

"What do you mean?"

"Well, it—" Again, Wesley cut himself off. Whatever merrymaking he'd done had slowed down his quick wit to a sleepy crawl. He dragged his hand along my hip and let it rest on my thigh. "Distresses you. Clearly."

He was looking sidelong at my arms.

I smoothed his hair back from his forehead. "It's alright. I promise. It's nothing new."

Wesley scowled.

"It's not your fault," I said gently.

"Do you want to have sex?" Wesley asked, still hiding in my dressing gown.

"Not particularly, but I'll lie here with you a little longer."

"Alright."

He gathered me up again to cozy along his side. I hugged close to
him and counted the steady march of his breathing, borrowing his
calm. I willed myself to quit imagining dangerous solutions to un-
formed thoughts.

"Wesley," I murmured.

"Hm?" His voice was cloudy, narrow and drowsy.

"Do the roles ever steal you from yourself?"

"How's that?"

"In the thick of it, do you ever . . . put yourself too far in them, and
forget who you are?"

"What," Wesley yawned, roving his nose against the side of my
face, "like losing your place on the page?"

I stared at the ceiling in the dark, tracing the shadows with my
eyes. "Never mind."

I left him to his dreams. I hoped they were as kind to him as his
parties, his friends, the glittering endurance of their impervious
survival.

I hoped he would never know this uncanny feeling of mine well
enough to name it.

4

The theater on Commerce Street, opening night

WE OPENED *MACBETH* on a Friday. The house was packed. The applause was still roaring in my ears.

I stumbled into my dressing room after the second curtain call, still in my nightgown from the final scene, sugar blood crusted under my fingernails. The play had it right; no matter how I scrubbed, it didn't come all the way out.

"I'll be there!" I called over my shoulder into the hall as the rest of the company bustled, laughed, cheered, and capered, celebrating our victory. "I know, Harry's—I heard, we're all going to Harry's! I'll meet you there!"

I shut the door and locked it. Leaning back against it, I took a heavy breath in; held it; blew it out.

A manic titter kicked up from my chest and dissolved quickly back to a stricken silence.

I'd done it. I'd done it, and they loved me.

The craving to scratch at my arms burned white-hot.

I tried to ignore it. The Lady's final words rang hard and heavy through my head—*What's done cannot be undone. To bed, to bed, to bed!*

My entire body was trembling. I couldn't feel anything but a faint buzzing like chalk shrieking across a blackboard from head to toe. I ground my teeth and slapped myself several times against the sides of my head. "*Stop it*. Get back here. Come back, Margie."

I'd become the Lady.

They loved me.

I would never feel so powerful again.

That was it, wasn't it?

I began to pace, tugging my hair out of its pins and folds and curls. That was the stuff, never mind that she ended up dead. Everyone died, someday. Somehow.

I was a force of nature.

Conviction, that much of it, women weren't meant to hold that for ourselves. We were supposed to be apart from it, killed to restore order if we so much as tasted a lick of it. If I tried to bring *any* of her into my waking self, it would ruin me. It didn't fit. It just wasn't done.

My breath picked up, jogging hard in my chest. I began to cry.

That sense of control, of action, the taste of it onstage made it so painfully clear to me that I'd never owned a single day in my life. I'd *never* been in control. The only thing I had ever truly done for myself was run: run from home, run from Hollis, run under Edie's purview, run into a marriage with Wesley. My fate had never been mine. I was made to steer and veer and speed like a poorly handled Hudson Hornet in the dark of night, no headlights, weaving between every hurdle.

This was no way to live. This was not a life.

I needed to break something. I needed to scream. I needed to tear myself apart.

Wesley had sent a crystal vase of yellow roses ahead of me that afternoon, waiting on my vanity when I arrived for call with a handwritten card tucked amid the petals—*To my Lady, This is only the beginning. —W.*

I hurled the vase at the wall. It shattered apart in a brilliant, violent spray.

The roses looked so strange on the floor, little baby birds punted from their nest with wobbly necks bent sideways and limp. Around them, the carpet glittered with the splintered remains.

An inquisitive tapping on the door brought Ezra's voice to the jamb: "Margot? Everything alright?"

I crouched beside the best of the wreckage and marveled at the danger of it.

Another knock. "Margot?"

I squeezed my eyes shut and shook my head—I could hear three men at once saying my name, Ezra-Hollis-Jensen-Hollis-Ezra. My vision began to tunnel, fuzzy black blooming like mold around the edges of reality.

"Where's Wesley?" I called, without looking away from the glass.

My flesh itched to be addressed. Marked. Parted.

"What do you need, did something fall? I heard—"

"No," I said, my voice high and panicked at the back of my throat. "Go find Wesley, please, it's—it's important, I need him."

It *was* important. I had to tell someone. I couldn't be alone. I stared and stared and stared at the glass, my forearms screaming.

"Why?" More knocking. "Margaret, what—"

"*Get Wesley,*" I snarled, rounding on the door as though gnashing at an outreached hand.

I was not piloting my limbs. I was a passenger in my own body. The Lady was still in me, she would—she would always be in me, I had brought her to life; I had created her, birthed her, I could never let her go again. We were the same, we were so much the same, she was me and I was her, but she had *power.*

I didn't want to be free of her. I couldn't. I needed her.

I reached into the shattered pile and turned over a particularly rude cleat of crystal in one hand. My fingertip beaded with blood when I tested it.

The knocking evolved from polite tapping to several raps from the side of Ezra's fist. "Richard is fetching him, Margaret, open up. *Margaret.*"

Go get some water, and wash this filthy witness from your hand.—

Why did you bring these daggers from the place? They must lie there. Go carry them and smear the sleepy grooms with blood.

My hands are of your color—

"But I shame to wear a heart so white."

I snapped my attention to the mirror. Lady Macbeth in all her finery, crown and stole and heavy chains of office, her woolly hair piled in regal braids, stood behind me in the reflection.

"*Devour,*" she bade me, and all fell to dark.

♦ ♦ ♦

THE FIRST THING I saw upon waking was Wesley looking at me like I might dissolve any moment.

"*Oh.* Hey. Thank God; hey, Jack. How—how are you feeling?" He whispered to me so gently, as though to hear too many words might wound me further.

He was so wonderful. I was so doped that I could swear I heard one of his monologues piping in through the radio across from the hospital bed.

I'd been put up in a small room painted the color of baby shit, perhaps because I had done something awful. I pushed at my very dry lips with my lumpy tongue and only looked at the bandages on my wrists through my periphery. Wesley was wearing a suit mottled with hideous bloodstains dried to a rusty brown, bow tie undone—he had attempted to comb his hair into a begging sort of order at some point, but he'd missed a spot: An ornery curl sprang out at the back of his neck.

"Where is she?" I croaked. I sounded like a wounded goose. Wesley smoothed a hand over my hair, matted down into the brickish pillow under my head.

"Who? Edie? She's just down the hall; she had questions for the surgeon."

Not Edie. Who . . . Christ. I didn't know. I nodded at the radio. I couldn't lift my arms. "Could you turn that off?"

Wesley flipped the power switch, and I realized the broadcast had been a late-night talk show. Not *Macbeth*. It clicked off right in the middle of a gaudy bout of audience laughter.

I leaned into the broad warmth of Wesley petting across my forehead. He had large hands and his fingers were careful, so very particular. He cast the refrain of that worried look on me. I surprised us both by laughing.

"What?"

"I'm sorry." I sighed a little into my malformed, drugged hilarity. "I suppose you'd rather be at a party right now."

Wesley's expression twitched like one great seizing muscle. "Don't be ridiculous. Here with you is the only place I need to be, Jack."

His hand was still in my hair, the tendons tight even as he soothed a soft thumb along my cheek. I stared at the shape of my feet under the blanket and wondered distantly what they had done with my shoes.

"Is Ezra upset?" I asked.

Wesley made a wheeze that probably meant to be a chuckle. "Ezra is *livid*."

I laughed again, a great jag of it that made my shoulders leap. I didn't feel it turn into the sharp, untamable bolt of tears until Wesley lulled me and softly swiped at the tears under my lashes.

"Did I ruin it?" I whispered. I wanted to reach up and cling to his arm, keep him there, but I couldn't move my hands. I turned my face and buried it in Wesley's palm instead.

"You did nothing of the sort." He kissed my forehead and left his mouth there at my temple for a moment. "You were sensational."

"Are you going to commit me?"

I felt the shiver chase up Wesley's spine as though it were my own. He stepped back and regarded me, clear-eyed and serious. "I could never. Not *ever*."

Sniffling hard, I nodded. "I'll get better," I said.

"You will," Wesley murmured, "of course you will."

I tried to wet my lips again and tell him how badly I wanted to believe us both. But Wesley held a cup of water with a straw up to my mouth for me, so I drank instead.

Smart, heeled footsteps stopped in the hall, then a brisk knock on the door kept ajar. Edie entered and took careful stock of me from over Wesley's shoulder.

"The doctor wants to speak with you. Did she just wake up?" she asked.

Wesley nodded.

Edie plucked idly at an invisible thread at the edge of his jacket. "Have you eaten?"

"A bit."

His chin was beginning to stubble—I could see it beneath a measure of stage makeup he'd missed with the sponge, or maybe not had a chance to get at before . . . He was so beautiful. *Hail, Macbeth.*

"Go see the surgeon, then find something hardy," Edie said. "Take a break, poss, put your head down."

She ushered Wesley from the room. He took a long look at me before turning away down the hall, straightening his jacket and squaring his shoulders in spite of the misery clinging to every inch of him.

Edie stood and watched me for a long moment. She had a fox fur around her shoulders, a matching pillbox hat fixed to the crown of her head, and a pair of emerald-green gloves the same shade as the silk pencil dress pouring down over her body. From above her, the fluorescent light cast a gold pall over the plinth of her. She looked like an angel.

I told her as much, and she scoffed. Edie nodded down at my arms, slack atop the stiff hospital sheets. "Those bandages will match that new chiffon of yours."

Edie rummaged through her clutch as she crossed to stand beside my bed. From somewhere down the hall beyond the open door, an unhurried metallic beeping started up.

"Your name is everywhere tonight. Did you know that?" Edie slipped a cigarette from her case and offered it to me. I nodded in the vague direction of my hands.

"I don't think I can hold anything."

As if it was simply the thing to be done, Edie tugged off one glove and lit the cigarette before holding it to my lips.

I leaned forward and thought of Ezra's long-suffering poise, the same grin-and-bear-it professionalism with which he and the others of Edie's generation held themselves. The idea that his stores of patience with me might one day run dry made my nerves shiver—I took a deep drag on the smoke and refused to think about it.

With her hand at my mouth, infinitely steady, Edie began to tell me exactly how news of my dressing room episode had fluttered out through the ranks of the social strata like ripples from a thrown stone.

"Did you really get ten minutes of applause?" she asked.

"Eight," I croaked.

Edie hadn't been in the audience tonight. Edie never came to opening nights. She waited for the comfort of a few good shows to work its way into the company before coming to see any of our performances.

She looked at me with an impenetrable, incisive gaze. "How did it happen then?"

Apparently I'd bled like a stuck pig, one of the costumes was ruined after Wesley tried to stanch me with it, and a stagehand fainted at the sight.

"I don't know." I nodded at the water again, and sipped as Edie offered it with her other hand. A trickle of it slipped past my mouth, and Edie swept it away with the edge of one finger. I shook my head. "I can't . . . What were they saying, what did you hear?"

I smoked from Edie's fingers and heard about the salons and clubs and private parties across the city that were awash with my name. A strange delight overtook me at the idea.

I didn't allow myself to think properly on the fact Edie might never see me as Lady Macbeth. For just one night, I was on everyone's mind. People *knew* me.

Edie ran a hand through my hair, just as Wesley had done, and took her own brief draw on the cigarette. She watched me steadily and did not blink. Her eyes were so blue I wanted to drown in them.

"Most women would simply take to bedding someone unadvisable instead of all this," Edie said. "You really have it out for yourself, don't you?"

"Sorry."

"Oh, don't apologize. You're terrible at apologizing. You've made your bed and now you'll have to lie in it, but at least you did it with a bang."

She was quiet for another protracted moment.

"I told you when you got married," she said, and then stopped herself briefly at a thought. "He's the best of them. He is. You'll never find another man willing to love you warts and all the way Wesley does. He's a rare sort."

I frowned. "He has his own share of uglies."

Edie made a very measured sound, considering. She was still petting my hair. "You must be kinder to him, Margaret."

I looked up at her in silence. My mind was moving like congealed soup. Edie ashed the cigarette and held it close so I could reach it again, burnt down just past halfway. "He's a mess. Ezra told me he could hardly speak when they were calling the ambulance. They couldn't get him to let go of you to get you here, he rode along with the medics."

She turned away from me and looked intently at nothing. "I would never tell him this," she said, "but please understand me. You attempting some . . . last hurrah, or whatever you want to call it, this has sheared *years* from his own life. You have to recognize the violence in that. And not just to yourself."

I held very still. I stared at the ridges of my covered feet again and did not imagine the taste of dirt.

"I don't tell you this to . . . blame you, I don't know. Maybe I do. Maybe I'm angry at you." Edie adjusted her stole with one hand, rolling her shoulders smoothly and drawing up a little taller. "I only think you should know the reality of it, *especially* if you're serious about building any lasting future with him. You absolutely cannot do this again."

The room was quiet. The beeping down the hall persisted. I counted it inwardly like the sluggish, drugged-down tick of my own pulse.

Edie cleared her throat. "And so long as I'm being honest, I may as well be selfish. I've no stake in anything you do beyond my own pride, but if you'd carried off this folly, then I'm not entirely sure what I would have done with myself, either. So."

I tsked my tongue gently against the insides of my teeth, bone-wet in their straight, solid rows in the rest of my mouth, so soft and strange. "That isn't fair, Edie."

"I never said it was." Edie took the cigarette back, drew it to the filter, and stubbed it out in the ashtray on my bedside table. "But it's the truth."

She put her hand back in my hair, the one with the glove still on, and swept it down to the back of my neck. I shut my eyes and sank into the feeling of being held. Tears prickled behind my squeezed-tight lashes.

"Quit this foolishness," Edie murmured. "Quit looking for a way out, because it doesn't exist. Face life like the rest of us, in all its hideous beauty."

I sniffled hard around a sob. My throat clicked and skittered with uncontrollable sorrow. "I don't know who I am anymore, Edie," I managed to weep.

"Oh, hush. Of course you do, darling. Of course you do. You'll learn."

I didn't believe her. I was a ridiculous, impossible creature, too many people in one body—Margie, Margaret, Margot, Wolf, Shoard,

Jack, every bloodied woman I'd ever embodied and then slain on-stage. My own near miss of an ending.

I was tired. That was the crux of it. I was so very deeply tired, and I didn't know where I would ever find relief from myself to rest.

From down the hall, the beeping stopped.

Somewhere, Wesley had hopefully found a place to catch up on sleep.

Life, the spiteful bleed of it, would keep on whether or not I sought to join in.

5

Shoard Downs

I SPENT THREE days at the good hospital near Gramercy before they released me with a packet of care instructions for Wesley, as though he was bringing a wounded puppy home from the pound. I took my first hot bath since before opening night and stared at the ridged, black lines of nylon sutures on my arms held fastidiously away from the water as Wesley washed my hair.

Our apartment was dark except for the single standing lamp left on beside the bookcases. We had decamped to the chaise in the sitting room, me lying across it and Wesley on the floor with his knees drawn up.

The minor tremor in my fingers had died down after the first day, as my nerves began the slow work of righting themselves. The surgeon, a serious man with a heavy brow and very steady hands, deemed me lucky I hadn't truly wrecked anything. I could hold my own cigarettes now.

The rest of the Bard Players had brought me flowers and meals between calls—although never Ezra himself, as hospitals tended to remind him he was just as human as the rest of us.

"Be honest, Jack. Is it my fault?"

I turned to look down at Wesley at his question, in shirtsleeves and nursing a bottle of gin in one fist. He had slackened his personal rule of not drinking during a show run since his every free moment offstage was spent at my bedside; I refused to let him quit the run entirely, we needed the money more than I needed company. Ezra had apparently hired in an understudy for the Lady from a different company, and nobody would tell me straight if she was good or not. They all just made noise about how opening night had been singular, and how proud I should be.

My free hand was loose and lazy, combing steadily through Wesley's hair in ceaseless, comforting rote. "Don't be stupid," I said, "of course it isn't your fault."

"Feels like it's my fault."

"You aren't the one who put the glass in my hands."

"Wasn't I, though?"

The bottle sloshed with Wesley's next sip. I took another mouthful of smoke. Through the open window, the whine of a siren passed on the street below.

"This whole thing feels like my fault," he repeated, but this time on a whisper. A brief and subtle rage slithered between the gaps in my ribs.

"Well, it isn't. Please stop saying that."

Wesley was glowering at the middle distance when I glanced down at him. Silence persisted for a moment.

"I've heard about this," he announced. "Hysterics. It happens when women aren't getting their needs met."

"'Their *needs met.*'"

"Do *you* remember the last time I took you to bed?"

I ran the filter of the cigarette against my bottom lip. "That's neither here nor there, it—"

"Of course it is," Wesley spat. "If I don't give you the very basics of a proper fucking marriage, then this mess is *my fault.*"

"*Stop it,*" I snapped. "I said yes to you, Wes, I knew exactly what I was signing up for. This had nothing to do with you. Let it be mine."

Wesley took another slug of gin before settling the foot of the bottle against his bent knee. He shook his head to himself. "Well. Whoever's fault we want to call it, you really scared me."

Another long pause sat heavily with us. I ran my thumb along the shell of Wesley's ear and felt him shudder as he leaned into the touch, unable to hold himself back from seeking comfort.

He drew a shaky breath. "I love you," he said, stark and shattered. "You know it. You have to know it, I-I love you in our own strange way, but if it isn't enough for you, you need to *tell me* instead of . . . this. Again. *Ever* again. Making plans for—for what life would have been like, I don't want to do that. I *won't.* I don't like thinking about who I might be without you!"

His voice trembled with a fever I had never heard in it before, not even in his most tragic roles. I drew my hand flat against his brow and leaned his head back gently to rest against the edge of the couch. I tendered my fingers upward into his shallow widow's peak. "I know," I said over the sound of him struggling to hold in his tears. I tended him with a hush. "I'm sorry, Wesley. I know."

I looked down and saw his chin buckle. "I can do my part," he said. "I—I'll get myself help. There are ways, I can—I can change, if you need me to, I—"

My hand stilled in his hair. "What?"

"I can be different, J—Margot, there are—they have treatments, places where—"

I tugged at the roots of his hair sharply enough to make him gasp. "Don't you dare even *think* about that."

A pitiful spillage of tears tripped up from Wesley's chest. "I've been thinking about it," he sobbed.

I turned him with ginger care to face me, to look at me full-on with those terrified, sweet eyes of his, over-brimming with awful shimmer.

"That's just as much violence as what I did," I said, searching his face. "*Stop it.* I promise you, you promise me. Not *ever* again. Do you hear me?"

Wesley sniffled messily. Surrender shuddered past the fear deep in his gaze. "I promise," he rasped.

"Good." I eased my grip on his hair and smoothed my hand over the crown of his head. I tapped off the end of my cigarette before taking one more tidy drag. "Perish the thought you've been anything but a boon to me," I murmured. "You're wonderful. Believe that, if you can stand it."

Wesley drew in when I handed him the cigarette, obedient. His cheeks hollowed shallowly. His eyes were still pink and wet but the fear in them had deadened by the smallest bit. There had always been an aspect of the hare in him, as there was in me, a fevered animal that only ever wanted something else's jaws around it.

I could give that to him. Together, we could cradle each other in our teeth and never let them shut.

"I need you to tell me, Jack."

"Tell you what?"

Wesley took another mouthful from the cigarette. He looked away as he exhaled, the very edge of his mouth twitching as he gathered himself. "You keep me so far away from you. If you need—*when* you need something from me," he said and looked me straight in the eye. "When you need me, you tell me. This never happens again. You *tell me*. Alright?"

I nodded, blinking away my own bolt of exhausted, frustrated tearfulness. "I'm sorry."

"Would you quit *apologizing* to me, Jack; just tell me you'll try, and mean it."

His voice flashed with the brittle efficiency of an officer petitioning a wayward cadet to quit behaving like an idiot: You'll get yourself killed doing that; do you think this is all a game?

I swiped at my eyes and sniffed hard. "I'll try. I *will* tell you, I promise."

Wesley heaved a wracking sigh. He shifted up to his knees and gathered my free hand to his mouth, pressing a fervent kiss to my knuckles with care not to move my wrists. "I love you," Wesley whispered, and I thought of the day he asked me to marry him.

I had to let him in. I had to protect him.

"I love you," I said, and I knew it, and I meant it. I squeezed his fingers and chased the promise with a tight draw on the last of the smoke.

We sat in the silence of licked wounds, tending to our own quiet vices. When Wesley finally stood, he leaned down to kiss me. His lips tasted of salt.

"I'm for bed," he said. "Are you coming?"

"I'll be in later. I'm not tired yet."

He took stock of me for a moment with sluggish, half-drunk darts of his eyes before sighing and trudging to the bathroom with the bottle still in hand.

I stared through the window into the building across from ours.

The bedroom of the woman who lived inside was empty, with the television on. It shouted jagged splashes of monochrome light into the dark room. I thought of my mother in earnest for the first time in years.

She married the shiny new preacher in town when I was fourteen. The day of her wedding, Mama helped paint my face to be her maid of honor and told me all about the privilege of becoming somebody's wife.

Wives are the masters of the home, she told me, patting a pretty pink lipstick onto my cupid's bow. I had never worn makeup before. That had been the most exciting day of my life back then—my first part to play, aside from simply being my mother's daughter. *We raise the babies and cook the meals and make everyone comfortable, because without us there would be no warmth in the world. Wives are the keepers of kindness.*

Where was that power beyond the weight of homemaking? I had no designs to be anything but married. I didn't want to be a mother. What transformative potential existed for me as a wife if I wasn't going to follow the script I'd been given?

There was so little point in only *tasting* ambition, never chewing or swallowing it—power, respect, all of it mine by proxy, artifice alone. Without direction, I had to make up the rules to this as I went.

But I had to be here, and for good. For Wesley.

I dabbed at my eyes with the edge of my sleeve and curled up on my side. I wrapped my arms around myself, careful not to press on the sore straits of my scars, and wondered who I was to become.

◆ ◆ ◆

REPLACED.

What an ugly fucking word. I had never thought about it before, but it really was hideous.

Excised. Tossed aside. Put back on the shelf. *Replaced.* Like I was no better than a sheet of plastic, draped lazy and limp over something rotten.

I blinked rapidly, as though seeing better would change the meaning of the word. "You're kidding."

Ezra's office was tucked deep into the veins of the theater, overstuffed and cramped with the folios and contracts from years of past plays. No windows, only one door in or out, and bursting with paper. Above us, the feet of the stage crew yammered as they practiced a changeover.

"Probation," Ezra said, easy as anything, removing his pince-nez to fiddle them idly between his fingers. "Protracted."

"Replaced," I repeated, tasting the depth of its cruelty for the first time.

Ezra held in a sigh and canted his eyes up at me in exasperation. "You aren't in any fit state to perform, Margot. You have to see that."

My stitches had been removed the week prior. I applied a vitamin salve twice a day to the skinny red lines; the nurses told me it would work wonders—*See here*, one said as she lifted the edge of her blouse, indicating a flat and barely there smudge of silvery skin on her waist, *I had my appendix out and now you can barely tell.* I was back to routine with Wesley, lunch at our favorite café three times a week and going with him to parties again with my new rotation of evening gloves.

I was alright. I was alive. I could forget this ever happened and move on.

But none of that mattered if I couldn't work.

"Ezra," I said, but stopped when my throat caught on spiny frustration. I swallowed and forbade my voice from rising. "When did you decide this?"

He sketched a simpering shrug at me. *Twelfth Night* was still open on the far end of his cluttered desk—*O Time, thou must untangle this, not I. It is too hard a knot for me t'untie.* "We've had to make do without you in the meantime," he said, "and after the first few shows I realized we could give you the space you need to recover without compromising the integrity of the run."

I held up the undersides of my arms to him, showing him the evidence, and relished privately the way he flinched from the sight. "I appreciate it, as I'm sure my understudy has, but I'm recovered *now*. I need to work, Ezra."

"You need to rest."

"Are you my doctor?"

"I'm your director," Ezra said coolly, leaning back in his chair, "which strangely seems to hold more weight to you. Do you realize how close you came to dying in my theater?"

Good, I nearly blurted. I clenched my jaw and said nothing. Someone above pelted from stage left to right with a quick clip. From the wall behind Ezra, our poster for the company's inaugural performance of *Romeo and Juliet* stared me down with my adolescent-looking signature beneath Juliet's name.

"You have to let me work," I said, and hated how my voice wobbled.

Ezra sighed. "The only thing I have to do is look after my cast."

"By cutting me loose and letting me—what, waste away in my own apartment?"

"By protecting the rest of them from the stresses *you've* caused," Ezra said evenly, enunciating every word.

Aghast, I stared at him. "What the hell does that mean?"

"You didn't have to see the mess you made."

"I had to *feel it*!" I jabbed a finger at myself and crossed to the short side of the desk, where I could almost loom over Ezra. He sat and looked solidly up at me. "I'm not the one who pushes the company to their fucking limits to get the performances I want!"

Ezra raised his thick, silvery brows. "If my methods distress you, perhaps probation is more fitting than I'd thought."

"Jesus, Ezra!"

Sighing, Ezra unfolded into a full stand and fingered the first button of his jacket closed again. Any height advantage I had disappeared. I crossed my arms and glared at him.

"Margaret. I appreciate your devotion to giving every blaggy old bitch in our audience a reason to crow about a cursed production and garnish ticket sales like this. But if it's truly my methods that drove you to it, then I think it's best we take a long break from each other. Professionally."

He didn't try to soothe me in any way beyond that. Ezra's hands were in his pockets and my own fists were stuffed under my armpits, and the impasse between us was so vast I wanted to cry.

I settled for taking up the paperweight on his desk, a cheap cast of a Rodin with two hands barely touching, and hurling it at the far wall.

It bounced off and thumped to the floor, where it rolled to a pitiful stop on the carpet. Nothing broke.

"This is a mistake," I seethed, not looking at Ezra. I could feel him watching me curiously.

"No, I really don't think it is, darling. See this time for the gift it is, and we can talk again when you're feeling better."

My horrible, stupid eyes began to well up. I turned my face to the floor, where the statue had lolled to a stop, one of the hands begging for alms while the other pushed it away. "What's your metric for me feeling better?" I ground out.

"Well, that will be for you to decide, won't it?" Ezra settled back in his chair and placed his spectacles on his nose. He gestured at the door, the sight of him blurring quickly in a wash of sable and pink as my gaze shivered with unshed tears. "Leave the door open when you go."

In my haste to leave, ripping it open, I let the door bounce back on its hinges. As I strode into the slim aisle of the halls, I heard one of Ezra's frames judder from its nail and crash to the floor. I hoped it was the *Romeo and Juliet* poster.

Outside, the sun stung my cheeks. I pawed at my eyes and hid my face in a silk scarf that I wrapped hastily around my hair before cramming on a pair of sunglasses. Summer was shedding one final wash of itself, venting the last of the heat before autumn, and I was sweating in earnest by the time I reached the stretch of smaller theaters and clubs just north along Seventh Avenue.

If Ezra wouldn't give me work, then someone else would.

But I should have known he'd been talking.

Everyone had been talking.

Three different directors in the West Village made careful niceties before telling me in their own avoidant ways that I was a liability.

A risk.

Poison.

Fuck them. I didn't need them.

That was a lie—I didn't *want* to need them. I wanted to be a self-sustaining creature who didn't need to throw myself into fictional bodies to make sense of my own.

My anger drove me even farther uptown, to the pond in Central Park where I usually liked to take air and watch the ducks mill around. When I sat down on the bench and took a moment to push my breath back down, reality caught up to me.

I was done for.

6

Jane's Backside, Twelfth and Greenwich

"IS WESLEY HEADING out tonight?"

Edie had brought me to one of her spots to rattle me out of my funk—people stared less at two women drinking liquor at three o'clock in the afternoon.

"Maybe. He might have something arranged, some . . . schmooze, or another."

For the last nine weeks, I had been in a mood. Lowercase m.

In a mood, I wasn't the same risk I would have been in a Mood. In a Mood, I would have tried to hurt myself. In a mood, all I wanted to do was lie on the carpet in the middle of the room without stockings on and get drunk.

Though I had tried at first to throw myself wholesale into keeping house—cleaning and cooking and running all my little errands—I discovered I was fantastically terrible at everything else besides spinning records, staring through the television set during daytime programming, and wallowing. I had stopped looking forward to dinner invitations and ignored the side of my closet where my cocktail dresses hung, opting instead for the dour comfort of the few ensembles with which I didn't have to wear a girdle.

The Bard Players were doing *Much Ado.* I helped Wesley run his lines and pretended it didn't gut me as every pointed syllable reminded me of exactly what I'd lost.

"Do you ever go with him?" Edie asked.

"What, uptown? *God* no."

Edie smiled sideways at me. "Do they scare you, the shinier they get? They hunt in packs, you know."

I mocked an arch look at her. "Exactly."

"I'll bet Wesley fills the ears of any poor thing who falls for him with nothing but how wonderful you are."

I snorted. "Maybe."

"I'm serious. You're a myth to every queen in the city, I bet half of them make sacrifices in your name like Sybil on the fucking mount."

I laughed. It felt good—Edie was good at making me laugh.

"How is he, by the way?"

"He's quit handling me with kid gloves, so that's something." I rattled the ice at the bottom of my glass, peering to measure whether the dregs were worth another mouthful or not.

The day Ezra cut me from the company, Wesley and I'd had our most explosive argument yet. We were hardly ever at each other's throats, but this had been a good, hearty row. I shouted at him for not reading Ezra's mind, and he shouted right back— *Honestly, Jack! Trying to predict Ezra's choices is even more of a fool's errand than being upset by them; listen to yourself! You're smarter than this!*

Deflated in the aftermath, we sat together on the chaise and split a glass of port. Wesley had let a lunch with a photographer in Tribeca slide past on the clock to stay and hash out my misery, so I at least owed him the drink.

What do I do? I had said, the fight finally sapped from me, my head leaned on his shoulder.

What do you want to do?

I feel . . . cornered, *Wesley, I don't know who I am anymore.*

Shh. Hey. I'll talk to Ezra.

And tell him to, what, throw another fistful of dice on me with the chance I'll snap again?

I'll talk to him, Jack.

I think I broke one of his frames. I threw a paperweight.

Good arm.

"Can I ask you something?"

Edie was chasing the lime around the bottom of her glass with the end of her stirrer.

"Of course," I said.

"You'll answer me honestly."

"Why wouldn't I?"

Edie sipped off the last of her drink and thumbed neatly at the edge of her lipstick. "Why are you still so miserable?" she asked, as breezily as starting up the next thread of gossip.

I stared at her. "Are you serious?" She looked at me expectantly, and I gave a disbelieving huff. "I haven't worked in over two months, Edie."

"And before Ezra, you hadn't worked for even longer than that. Jobs will come and go, it's all the game."

"I *know* that."

"So why are you surprised?" Edie said with intentional calm. I took stock of my breath—shut my mouth and slowed down for a moment.

"It's not easy," I said evenly. I twirled my glass around on the spotty wood varnish. "I'm not . . . used to it, at this level. I thought the Players were a sure thing."

Edie reached over and patted me briskly on the back of my hand. "Nothing is a sure thing. Do yourself a favor and don't develop some white whale complex. There are plenty other femme fatales to be played when you're back on your feet, and half of them wear far more flattering outfits than those shapeless wool sacks."

I said nothing, frowning into my cup. She didn't know what this felt like. How could she? Edie was a powerhouse. I was just somebody's wife.

Edie looked down her nose at me. "Do you want my advice?"

"What I *want*," I groused, "is my job back."

"Well, it won't come back if all you're going to do about it is get blotto and hide from your husband."

I winced. "I'm not hiding."

"You know I'm right."

"Well, you don't have to rub it in," I snapped, but made no move to get up. I raised my hand and ordered another drink.

Edie watched me as the bartender made quick work of it. She leaned up onto her elbows for a moment. "Have you really grown so afraid of your own failure," she asked me gently, "that you won't stand up and try again?"

"I've told you not to measure my career against yours," I said into my fresh glass.

Edie rolled her eyes up to the ceiling. "I'm not *measuring*. I'm being perfectly objective. Everyone learns this shit as they go, nobody gets a primer."

I snorted. "You've never had a husband." I swallowed half the drink down in one go.

"Oh, as if it's any trial for you, with the arrangement you two cooked up."

Edie seemed to catch herself and glanced down as though to cram the words back in her mouth. I knew the feeling all too well. My chest tightened. I turned my cup around between my fingers.

"Wesley chose me," I said, only glancing up when I was sure she'd quit looking so sorry for me. Edie gave a resigned nod.

"That he did, darling. I'm sorry. It can't be as easy as it looks."

I slung another sip into my mouth. "I wish I were different."

Edie reached up to fluff the hair at the back of my head, waking up the fall of the curls a little. She held a hand out for my drink, which I passed to her.

"You are far from the first to wish that for herself," she said, roving her thumb along the beveled edge of the glass. I watched the passage of her lacquered fingernail and told myself I could stand to be Margaret Shoard. I could live like this. I could just be Wesley's wife.

Edie took a sip and grimaced at the taste. "God. How do you stand this shit?"

"I hate myself."

"You're awfully good at that."

I took the cup back from Edie and finished the rest of it. "Why do you think I wanted to be an actor?"

7

᠀᠀᠀᠀

1956
Vivian and Harry Faulk's dining room

I STILL WENT to parties with Wesley, but I didn't have to like them.

Arm candy to a more capable man, just as I'd been with Hollis—except now I wasn't even getting roles out of it. I was simply listing along down a lazy, aimless river. It was revolting.

Vivian Faulk invited us to dinner along with three other couples on a miserable, drizzly night at the end of January. She was an aging mezzo-soprano who sang with the Metropolitan and used just enough kohl around her lashes to make her burgeoning crow's feet work for her. I used to think we had some affinity, her also being married to a man who preferred the company of men, but the more time I spent around her the more I realized she was less of a sister and more of a cat who liked to toy with mice before eating them.

"And you, Margaret," she lobbed across her ugly mahogany table with the center leaf installed to make it long enough for ten, "what are you up to these days?"

I paused with my soup spoon halfway to my mouth and looked at her. She had laced her fingers together and propped her chin on the lattice of them. The rock of her engagement ring was digging into her cheek. If the light in her gaze hadn't been so delighted to watch me squirm, so ready to dig in and hold me under her paw, I probably wouldn't have snapped.

I was a big girl. This far away from it, I could take it on the chin that Ezra Pierce shelved me like chipped dishware. It was business. But Vivian was a known gossip, and I hated to be someone else's social meal ticket.

I set my spoon down and dabbed gently at the corners of my mouth with the hideous powder-pink napkin in my lap. "How do you mean?" I asked, genteel as possible, feigning innocence.

Wesley's toe prodded at my ankle under the table. *Leave it.* I ignored him.

"Oh, well." Vivian mocked careful concern, frowning gently at me over the misshapen centerpiece. "You were really on the rise, weren't you?"

"*Great* review in that one paper with the opener, before the whole . . . business," piped another guest, a woman whose name I had forgotten, who worked as a consultant at Bloomingdale's and fancied herself a patron of the arts.

I furrowed my eyebrows and played dumb. "What business?"

The woman shrank under my attention. Wesley cleared his throat. I glanced at him. "What," I muttered at him, "is it too heavily spiced?"

He cut me a warning look through the corner of his eye. "Don't," he whispered.

"I only think it would be difficult," Vivian said, her voice pitched perfectly to drag the attention back to her with dramatic gravity, "to return to a *simpler* life after all that. It must be horribly depressing."

She sat back in her chair and waved a hand. The men were judiciously silent.

I stared at the middle of the table—that centerpiece really was awful. When I glanced up, I noticed the Bloomingdale's woman angling a look at my arms, as though trying to see past my sleeves. I held her nervous gaze until she looked away and hid in her soup.

Tipping my head genially, I beamed at Vivian. She gave a disarmed smile right back, perplexed beneath its practiced ease.

"It certainly is," I said.

Vivian's gaze flashed. She raised her dark, drawn-on brows. "So what is it you do with your days, Margaret?"

I pretended to mull it over through a steady sip of wine. The table was tomb-silent beneath the polite clatter of silverware against the Faulks' fine china. I might not have ignored the prodding of my righter mind, but I always did sip my drinks too quickly at parties— I'd had two cocktails as aperitifs in the sitting room after we arrived, and now I was on my second glass of chardonnay.

Wesley was drawn tight as a bowstring beside me. I hoped I wouldn't send him into catatonia.

I set down the crystal goblet Vivian had gone on about holding in their laps on the airplane from Venice three summers ago. (*Or was it four? Harry, when was it your friends invited us?*)

"Oh, you know," I said airily, flashing my most charming smile. "Mostly I've just been daydreaming about climbing to the top of the Chrysler Building and being done with it all."

Bloomingdale's dropped her spoon with a clatter. Vivian's eyes bugged. Wesley nearly choked on his mouthful of soup as the most delectable hush fell over the table.

"That's our cue," he announced, balling up his napkin while he hurried to his feet. He tapped me urgently on the elbow to bid me stand as well. Wesley cleared his throat with a tight huff and bowed stiffly to Vivian's end of the table. "Thank you so much for having us."

With my pulse roaring adrenaline-hot, I snatched up the centerpiece under one arm. "I'll just—relieve you of this," I said, and led the way to the door with Wesley's hand firm on my lower back. The other couples watched in stunned disbelief.

"*Honestly*," he hissed, glaring at me and my lifted door prize. He jerked his chin back over his shoulder. "Give that back."

"It's so ugly," I whispered, unable to suppress a manic giggle as Wesley crammed my hat on my head.

Vivian rounded the edge of the hall. She looked unsteady on her feet, as though the apartment had begun to tip. A petrified stare struck me from the back of her gaze. "You're leaving?" she said in an oblong way that sounded to me like she really meant to ask, *Just who the hell do you think you are?* She stared at the bundle of flowers in my arms, which I realized now were all fake.

"I'm so sorry, Vivian," Wesley said briskly, and tossed my scarf around my neck before yanking my coat from the hanger by the front mirror. "We'll get out of your hair. I'll call Harry next week, those tickets for—"

"No, no. It's alright," she insisted, stiff and cordial. Vivian held up a hand and held her ground several long strides away from us. She took a half-step back, like there was some contagion in the air between us and her. "You're indisposed, we understand."

Wesley's nostrils flared. He swallowed and ran a hand over his slicked-down hair before putting his own hat on and nodding once. "Of course. Thank you again for dinner."

"You hardly ate half of it," Vivian said in parting, ichor-sweet, and turned on her heel to hurry back to the table.

The locking chain bounced against the inside of the door when Wesley yanked on the knob. He gestured sharply for me to exit first. I clutched the centerpiece to my chest. "Are we—"

"*Go*, Jack," Wesley ground out, and didn't look me in the eye.

We hailed a cab from under the front awning of the building, its edges dripping miserably in the rain. I glared at the downpour over the edges of the fake flowers sticking up in front of my face.

We shuffled into the next car that pulled to the curb. "Let's hope this lets up soon," Wesley pitched briskly over the front seat once he'd given the address.

Our driver grunted. "Hasn't let up all day, why start now?"

The city blurred in an angry, fluorescent wash through the dark smudge of the window. I suffered the tension for as long as I could bear it, running one of the fake, waxy leaves between my thumb and forefinger.

"Vivian is a bitch," I announced. I turned in full this time to watch Wesley shut his eyes in brief mortification.

"Later," he muttered.

"Sir," I asked the driver, "do you mind if my husband and I have a marital spat?"

"Go right ahead," he said, monotone. "I'm not even here."

I turned back to Wesley and glared at him. "I shouldn't have come."

"Don't be ridiculous, she explicitly invited you."

"Only to pry gossip out of us. I should have played sick."

"You played sick last time."

I scoffed. "Please. As if she's keeping count."

Wesley leveled a look at me that said Vivian was most certainly keeping count. I rolled my eyes.

"Well, just . . ." I trailed off, shaking my head and slouching back against the seam between the seat and the door. "I don't know, Wesley. Go to these things without me."

He snorted. "Please. You know the sorts of things they'd start saying if I showed up without you."

"Like what? 'Looks like Margie finally got the job done'?"

Wesley stared at me. "You're my *wife*, Margaret."

"Which was never supposed to be my only identity!" I snapped.

Sitting forward in his seat, Wesley's low-wrought anger turned incredulous. "You think it comes terribly naturally to *me*?"

I leaned in and dropped my voice to match. "What the fuck do you expect me to do now that I can't call myself anything else?"

"*What?*"

I closed my fist around the fake flowers. Plastic bit toothlessly into my palm. "I used to be able to say I was Margaret Wolf and that was *enough*. But the longer I stay offstage, all I can say is that I'm Wesley Shoard's wife. That's all that means anything to anybody!"

Wesley flinched. That had dug in to wound. "Is being my wife really the worst thing in the world?"

"I'm not cut out to be *anyone's* wife, Wes!"

"Adapt!" Wesley cried.

I let my eyes fly wide, patronizing and daft. *"Adapt?"*

"All you can do—all *any* of us can do—is adapt!"

I stared at Wesley. An ill, pitching feeling wrenched hard in my gut. I touched the driver's shoulder lightly over the seat back. "Pull over, please."

Wesley pinched at his forehead and shook his head. "Jack."

"Here is fine," I said. The cab rolled to a stop, and I shouldered my door open. The rain's spattering leapt up like sudden applause, ushering me into its muddle.

"Jack!"

I staggered from the cab and slammed the door shut behind me before chucking the centerpiece to the wet, frigid sidewalk. As I hurried across the street to stop under an overhang, I clenched my fists and shut my eyes and tried to ignore the swirling, throbbing noise doing devilish work against my skull.

I had completely lost sight of who I intended to be. I would never find my way out of this.

I looked up at a car door slamming farther down the block. Smeared by the rain, Wesley jogged up to me with the blue shoulders of his coat jacket sodden to black and his hair dripping lank into his face. He'd left his hat in the cab in his haste and probably overpaid the driver by at least five dollars.

"Come home," he panted. "Alright? We'll forget about this whole mess. I won't drag you to any more of Vivian's parties."

I gave a friable sniff of dark humor. "Forget it. I meant it about the Chrysler Building, you know."

His face fell. "Jesus Christ, Margaret. You think I *like* seeing you like this?"

"Exactly! If I remove myself from the equation, no one will have to see me anymore!"

Wesley looked so taken aback I thought his knees might buckle. He came forward carefully and took both of my hands in his. "You are the only person alive who knows me," he said, his voice trembling with low intensity. "Every—every part stacked up to make me who I am. I've never trusted *anyone* like that."

I averted my eyes to the pavement. "I know."

"Do you, really? I don't think you do, I don't—I don't think you understand how much I want you here, beside me, all the way to the end of it." Wesley angled to catch my gaze, unwilling to let me hide from him. "Even your most insufferable bullshit is less of a chore to me than imagining you gone, how do you not see that? I don't know how the hell else to say it to make you understand, Jack."

I stared at him. I couldn't say anything that wasn't just more noise, railing uselessly at the sky.

"You protect me," Wesley whispered, barely pleading, "and I protect you."

"How do you protect me from myself?" My eyes began to leak. "Crack me open, reach in and rearrange me, sew me back up again? I already tried that, Wesley, and it didn't work. I'm so . . . *tired*."

"I want you to see a doctor."

"What the hell's a doctor gonna do?"

"The kind that can reach in and—and rearrange you, without cracking you open."

I would sooner go back to Kentucky than become yet another has-been diva with an analyst. But Wesley was looking at me with such toothsome grief, such *guilt*, that the ugly concrete pylons under the boardwalk of my resolve began to crack.

Goddamn it.

"Say something," Wesley begged me. He was still holding my hands. I set my jaw.

"Fine. A doctor. Whatever you want."

◆　◆　◆

"AND HOW ABOUT your marriage, Mrs. Shoard?"

I re-crossed my ankles under the overstuffed divan to which I had fused myself the instant Dr. French invited me to take a seat in his office. He was a serious man, gray-haired and scrawny with a pointed chin that made him look like he wore the bleached head of a praying mantis. He watched me with small, close-set eyes behind a pair of lenses a mile thick. I gave him a flinching smile.

"What about it?"

"Are you content? Is there anything amiss, any arguing? Does he lay hands on you?"

My brows twitched together. "My husband would never hurt me."

"That doesn't answer my question."

I itched for a cigarette, but there wasn't an ashtray to be seen in the tidy office. "I'm very content. I *should* be content. Wesley never hits me, no."

"'Should be content.' Elaborate on that."

Elaborate on that. It was very clear, even only knowing the man for the past forty-five minutes, that Dr. French was keen on asking me to pick out the threads of every statement I made in front of him. I had woven my adolescence for him like a lumpy blanket: my early childhood in Cherokee Park, the absence of my father twinned with the presence of my stepfather—the rabbit hole Dr. French tried to run around Mr. Matthews took up half the time so far—then the flight to Richmond, my worship of Jensen, the folly of my attachment to Hollis, and now to my marriage. *Elaborate on that.*

It was the fifth time Dr. French had said it. I supposed that was his job.

"Well." I wound the empty finger of one leather glove around my thumb in my lap, over and over in a nervous rote. I pursed my lips. "We're not often . . . predisposed to intercourse."

Dr. French hummed shortly to himself and scribbled something into his notes. I wondered at the shape of his handwriting, whether his lettering was cramped or elegant or particularly aware of itself. "Does that bother you?" he asked without looking up at me.

"No, not really."

"Not really?"

"I suppose I don't think about it very much."

Again, his pencil harped quick along the page. "That's normal," he said after a moment.

"Is it normal that I daydream about being dead?"

Dr. French's pencil stilled. He looked up at me over the top edge of his glasses. In my lap, my glove creaked under the pressure of my clenching fist.

Dr. French let out a meditative, low-bellied sigh through his nose. When he set his notes aside, he removed his glasses and gave me a steady look that slid straight between my ribs. I tightened my jaw.

"The human psyche is misty. Correlation and causality tend to blur when it comes to emotional regulation; libido aggression can be a bell in the fog."

I blinked at him. "So my brain is falling apart because my husband isn't getting me between the sheets."

Dr. French's bushy eyebrows went up—it was as though his hair, steadily taking its leave from his head, had decided to stay its migration when it found a comfortable place above his eyes instead. "I wouldn't put it quite so crudely, but yes, it may be a contributing factor."

"What," I huffed through a humorless chuckle, "do I get a prescription to take home to my husband that just says 'sex'?"

"Mrs. Shoard." Dr. French gave me a dry look. I looked right back, my own expression tart. "I think it more prudent to treat your melancholia at the root."

"Melancholia," I repeated aloud. Dr. French replaced his glasses and rose from his desk, where he hunted a stout pad of paper from one of the drawers.

"Depressive tendencies."

"It sounds prettier the first way."

"Most poets would agree." Dr. French scrawled on the top leaf of the tidy white square. "Do you have any aversion to inhalant medicine?"

"I don't know."

Dr. French tore off the paper with a tidy ripping burr. He crossed the office to bring it to me. "I'm prescribing you an amphetamine powder. You sniff it."

"You're giving me pep pills?" I took the prescription from him and squinted at his pen strokes, inscrutable glyphs.

"Stronger than those. It goes straight to the nervous system, takes up to about a minute to hit. You'll take a dose whenever you feel that craving to hurt yourself, or sense any thought patterns that make you fear for your safety. The medicine will, hopefully, interrupt those patterns and give you the space to steer yourself away from the impulse. Near-immediate action. *Not* a party drug, don't mix them up."

He was looking down at me like an intractable child. I stood and pulled my gloves back on before tucking the prescription into my pocketbook and holding out a hand for him to shake. "Good thing I don't get invited to parties anymore."

◆ ◆ ◆

THE PHARMACIST AROUND the corner didn't blink twice at my prescription.

"Do you need a consult?" he drawled, handing over a little sachet of powder.

"How much should I take per dose?"

He considered that as I turned it over in my hands. He was fairly young, his mustache sparse and the corners of his eyes unlined. "No more than a fingertip at once. Most ladies press it into a compact to keep it with them, like cosmetics." He shrugged. "It's fashionable."

I passed a tidy fold of bills over the counter and made for the train back home, the sachet tucked like a secret into the inner pocket of my jacket. It thumped softly against my chest with each stride. I was to come see Dr. French twice a month, and then return home to my little nothing-life as a little nothing-wife.

No. I turned up my collar against the wind and dug my fists into my pockets as I took the steps to the train back home. It was cruel to think of it like that. This wasn't Wesley's fault. The least I could do was be a good sport.

I had agreed to this.

I would live.

I would protect him.

The train screamed in through the tunnel. I held myself back from opening my mouth and screaming right along with it.

Seated at the end of the car, nobody paid any attention to the woman in a green wool trench fumbling with a pouch of white powder. I tugged off one glove with my teeth.

The train lurched around a bend in the track as I regarded the medicine on the end of my little finger. I held it to my left nostril and sniffed in sharply.

It burned with a sudden smack through my sinuses. I touched tenderly at the tip of my nose with the back of my hand and glanced around—still safely couched in anonymity. Nobody cared. The great boon of a faceless city: With so many people about, it was easy to overlook a stranger.

God, but it burned. I pinched lightly at my philtrum and sniffed again, gently, with the tang of metallic brevity high in the back of my throat. Blinking quickly, I looked up through the window across from me as the train shot out from the tunnel to slow for the next platform.

A single thought struck me like a javelin through my spine as I stared, pinning me to the chilly vinyl cushion of my seat: Had the hard, yellow underground bulbs ever before been this beautiful?

I marveled at the window, the scuffed edges of its glass, how the spidering scratches caught and threw the light like a string of beads from the neck of a whirling cabaret girl. My breath filled my lungs rich and rare and precious. I swallowed, and that, too, eddied like silk.

I looked down at my lap. I gazed at the toes of my shoes. I traced the edge of my jacket cuff with my bare hand and sat in awe at the way it dragged softly along the grooves of my thumbprint.

A flickering in the door to the adjacent train car caught my attention, and I looked at it with my gaze dragging like sweet molasses. A woman was watching me from the middle of the aisle: her expression hard, her wild auburn hair done up in dozens of combs, her white nightgown more vibrant than the rest of the world falling dull around her.

For several sprinting strokes of my pulse, I stared at her. She watched me right back.

Lady Macbeth, queen of Scotland, was standing on the southbound IRT and staring all the way down to the engine of my being.

I collected my purse and stood up without telling my legs to move.

The track screeched underneath the joint between the rails as I stepped from one car to the next. Riders jostled gently around me, *Pardon, I'm sorry, Excuse me,* as I slipped between them.

I didn't know what I would even do if I caught up to the Lady. Would I embrace her? Hit her? Shout in her face? Kiss her? What would she do to *me*?

A white sleeve fluttered to my left. Without thinking, I grabbed it.

"I *beg* your pardon."

Embarrassment flooded red-hot under my skin when it turned out to be nobody but a stranger. I made an apologetic mumble at her and turned away to stare at my washed-out reflection in the window.

My face looked more familiar to me in the dark mirror. I forgot about being embarrassed. A flood of bliss oozed like pierced egg yolk across my brain.

I looked down at my hands and studied them, one covered and one bare. The faint threads of the scars on my arms were covered by my sleeves, my glove, every other inch of my skin made secret with winter. I wondered why I had ever obeyed the compulsion to destroy myself—a thing so capable of change, a thing so very lovely.

The train dragged to another stop, and it was my station approaching. Even the squeal of the brakes had a hint of melody to it.

When I mounted the stairs to the street, all of me light on my own carriage as though my limbs were held by pigeons pulling marionette strings, the sun stung and dappled the air in the sweetest way I had ever seen.

I smiled at absolutely nothing.

8

Shoard Downs

WITH WESLEY GONE to call without me most evenings, the bruisy blooms of lonely sunsets found me running old scenes with myself.

It was the least I could do for my sanity. Our apartment used to be alive with it, the chatter of practice—Wesley would amble through the rooms, fiddling with his dailies as he decreed his own lines with easy grace, and I would reply from my usual spot pacing tightly at the end of the corridor: between the bathroom and the bedroom, inwardly counting my steps along the runner, able to watch myself in my old gilt mirror hung up in the hall.

"Your face, my thane," I recited, staring hard at my own steely expression, "is as a book where men may read strange matters."

How have you been feeling about not working? Dr. French asked me at our last session. I had the sense he was particularly intrigued by my case, given that most of the other women in his waiting room looked like housewives whose origin point of a mental break had been motherhood.

What do you mean by 'how'?

Has the medicine been helping?

I would have been a terrible mother. I'd had enough of my own horror show already.

"To beguile the time, look like the time; bear welcome in your eye, your hand, your tongue. Look like th' innocent flower, but be the serpent under 't."

I haven't tried to hurt myself in a long time, I'd told Dr. French, careful not to lie. I was boring myself numb with inanities like shopping, coffees or drinks with Edie at places with names like Saffron Sugar and Brother's, the nail and hair salons, and walks through the parks—it still hurt too much to sit and see a production. The closest I got were cabarets, where at least the immersion wasn't so complete.

Dr. French had nodded sagely. *Good. That's good.*

"He that's coming must be provided for: and you shall put ... shall put— *Damn it!*"

I tore away from the mirror and pressed both fists to my eyes until blotches bloomed at their edges. My breath was shaking. It felt as though I had lived six thousand lifetimes in the distended stretch of these past several months. The unknowns of my future made me shy away from thinking of it.

What awaited around the next hairpin turn, the next veer in the road I wouldn't see coming until I was careening head-on into it?

Wesley was out, and would be until morning. I made for the bedroom to seek my medicine compact in the front drawer of my vanity. As though tucking a saintly bone into its reliquary after pilgrimage, I always put the powder back amid my hairbrushes and bottles of perfume when I returned home.

I stopped when my fingertips met the bare floor of the drawer.

It was gone.

A ringing started at the root of my skull and rose to a thumping whine. My veins beat hard against themselves with each pulse.

It was gone.

It couldn't be *gone*.

I needed it. It wouldn't have just disappeared, it—

Nobody could have taken it. Wesley never touched my vanity, and he told me when I first showed him the medicine about how the pep pills Andrew used to feed him made him want to climb the walls and crawl out of his skin. He didn't touch drugs anymore, only drink.

So then it was still *gone*, but how? Walked away on its own two feet? Forgotten in someone's bathroom as I stole away to soothe my nerves, pretending to use the toilet? Slipped out from my purse and dashed to the street?

A steady whimpering built to join the buzzing in my head as I tore apart the vanity—drawers out, bottles scattered, liners peeled up to check if anything slipped underneath. Nothing. I ripped open every drawer in the apartment, even in the spare room; I slammed that nightstand shut again at the sight of a jar of oil that was *not* Wesley's hair pomade.

Still nothing.

The whimpering was *me*.

I barreled into the bedroom closet and stood amid the rows of clothing like the hollowed-out corpses of every woman I used to be— the dresses, the tennis skirts, the slacks, the blouses—waiting to be filled.

I feared for my safety in earnest in that moment for the first time since my dressing room.

My purse. I had taken a different purse to dinner last night, to match the teal of a new skirt.

I tore at the wicker basket beside the laundry hamper where I stored my clutch bags and pawed through the shucked shells of them until I found last night's slid down to the very bottom. My hands were shaking. A cold sweat built at my temples.

I let out a sob of relief when I pried at the clasp to find the powder sitting there, like a giddy child jumping out from a well-picked hiding spot—*Found me!*

I bullied it open with a trembling thumb and stared at the powder, glimmering white, pressed and flaky and taunting me with its assured peace. "Found you," I breathed, and measured out a dose.

It burned. I shut the compact, slipped it into my pocket, and stared numbly across the closet at Wesley's clothes.

A jacket he had worn two or three nights ago to a party was hanging against the dark battery of his other blazers and sport coats, waiting to be taken to laundry. The sleeves were still rolled at the cuff as he tended to ruck them after a few glasses of wine, baring the firm lines of his forearms and lending his habit of talking with his hands a sense of effortless grace.

What must it be like to be him?

He had told me one night not long ago, when I was keeping myself awake with my own shortcomings, that there were six words for love in Greek and they all meant different things. I had teased him for sounding like Ezra, and he had hugged me close.

Which one would we be? I asked into his chest. He was pulling a hand through my hair with slow, roving movements. It was finally putting me to sleep, but I so loved hearing him murmur low.

Philia, he whispered. *A soul-bond, wrought on the battlefield. We know each other as we would know ourselves, in mind and body alike.*

Do I know your body? I teased him lightly, and he had sniffed a chuckle and kissed me on the crown of my head.

Enough to count.

Enough. Was it really enough, to adore him through the glass like that? Was it enough for him to adore me? I crossed the closet and took his jacket from the hanger. It slid easily over my arms, broader in my shoulders where it tapered so neatly against Wesley's.

Tell me another, I'd said against the knot of his throat.

Philautia.

What's that one?

Love of the self.

I had scoffed lightly and wrestled the side of my head briefly against his chest at a more comfortable angle. As I stood in the closet and stared at myself in Wesley's husk in the mirror, I lifted the collar to my nose and found his cologne and the threads of someone else's smell persisting alongside it.

I don't know how to love myself, I had whispered into the bend of his neck.

Of course you do.

How?

You're still here, aren't you?

I leaned back into the billow of my Technicolor dresses with Wesley's jacket wrapped around me. Pillowed in cottons and silks and taffetas, I watched in the mirror the incongruity of it; the divergence of my very self.

The powder began to work with a soft fizz. It blurred across the back of my mind like a thumb smearing lipstick from the corner of my mouth. I pressed the heel of my hand to my forehead and forced myself to breathe.

The soft bleed of the drug billowed upward, from the soles of my feet to the rushing tingle of my temples. I blinked rapidly and took my time; in, and out.

I gathered an armful of skirts on either side of me. I drew them in close and inhaled: laundered, textile, lightly camphored, and, even lighter still, the soft animal scent of my own skin clinging to them just as Wesley lived in his jacket, between every little stitch.

He lived.

We lived.

I owed it to both of us to do the same.

♦ ♦ ♦

THE SENSIBLE HAT and brown oxfords by the door I noticed as I came in from the grocer the next day did not belong to Wesley. I stared at them for a moment as I stepped out of my own shoes and hung up my hat on the hook above the umbrellas. I had worn one of Wesley's old sport coats out like a chic ladies' blazer, unbuttoned and pinned neatly along the midline to tailor the waist.

I tried to imagine what the man who wore the oxfords might look like. I didn't often meet the men Wesley courted. Only occasionally if we were out together would I notice a friendly acknowledgment across the restaurant or nightclub, angled at my husband from all manner of serious-looking types. In those moments, I saw his personal life flickering into view like the vague shapes of yards shooting past behind fences along a motorway.

After I set both armfuls of paper sacks on the kitchen counter, sure to be courteously quiet, I leaned out into the side hallway to see the spare bedroom door securely shut. I put away the week's sundries on tiptoe, opening and closing cabinets in silence, and prepared a pot of tea.

Bringing a small tray of cream and sugar to the sitting room, I placed it on the settee and curled my knees up under me to settle in with a book. Right as I dropped my second sugar cube into the cup, the bedroom door opened down the hall. Soft socked feet walked into the bathroom—not Wesley's gait.

The sink ran, a low voice whistled a light and pleasant warble, and then the toilet flushed. The sink ran again. A short silence. I took a sip from my cup. The bathroom door opened, and the man came out again, this time making for the sitting room.

"Wes," called an unfamiliar voice—he was rounding the edge of the hallway, coming closer, "I think I'll— *Oh*."

Frozen like a brown mouse in the middle of a snowbank, the visitor gawped at me. He was perfectly handsome, studious, and—of course—professorial. I guessed that he worked at one of the universities, perhaps lecturing on things like fate and purpose and mankind's place in the universe. He looked suited to the activity of pondering.

I set my teacup down in its saucer and smiled at him. He was mostly dressed, save for his shoes, which were still by the door. "Would you like some tea?" I offered.

The man cleared his throat and fussed at the neat part of his hair. "I'm so sorry, I—"

"Cream or sugar?"

"I don't . . ." the man foundered, glancing wildly over his shoulder at the bedroom as though bidding Wesley to come rescue him from his mortification. I stood up and smoothed my skirt before sticking out a hand.

"I'm Margaret," I offered. He stared at it for a long moment before taking it and shaking once, distracted and firm in a businesslike pump.

"Thomas. Tom. Uh, Dr. Hunt."

"Pleasure to meet you. Medical doctor?"

"It's, ah." Dr. Hunt rubbed absently at one elbow and did not meet my gaze. "Yes. Ophthalmology."

"A good specialty. Everyone has eyes."

He glanced away from my smile. "Quite. I, um, you have a. Beautiful apartment . . . Mrs. Shoard."

"Thank you! I didn't used to think I had an eye for decorating, but it's just like any other habit; keep practicing, and suddenly you have strangers complimenting your choices. Do you like the wallpaper in there?"

I nodded down the hall at the spare bedroom. Dr. Hunt cleared his throat and gestured at the door. He refused to meet my eyes. "I'm going to . . ."

"Oh, of course. Don't let me keep you. Lovely to meet you, Doctor."

I sat down and turned back to my tea when he mumbled something that sounded like *You, too.* As he fumbled with his shoes and crammed on his hat, the bedroom door opened again.

"Here, Tom, you— Oh. You're back?"

I looked up from another steady sip of tea to find Wesley stopped at the edge of the sitting room with a tie in his hand. He was shirtless, his hair tousled, and his belt was gone. He looked at me without accusation, only light surprise.

"I didn't have to go across town, after all," I said, "they had the perfect size roast at the closer butcher's."

"Oh. Good."

Wesley still seemed to be calibrating, standing there with the tie in his hand. Dr. Hunt stalked over and snatched it from him, fastidiously slinging it around his throat and wrestling it into a knot. Wesley blinked, coming back to himself, and ushered Dr. Hunt by both shoulders to the door. I curled my legs up under me and peeled the book open again.

I stared through the page and sipped steadily at my tea as I listened to the low patter of their hurried conversation. Dr. Hunt seemed rattled, as was his right—Wesley was speaking in the dewy tones of someone trying to diffuse a delicate tension. Ultimately, the door shut. The apartment fell quiet.

Wesley dragged a hand along the back of his neck as he came back into the sitting room. "That drink I had with the director in Midtown got moved up," he said, as though I had asked a boy to explain how a crayon doodle got all over the wall. "Tom's Thursdays are always . . . odd. So. We seized the moment. I thought you'd still be out, obviously. I'm sorry."

"You would have kept it all very tidy if I'd stuck to my plan," I said, still staring at the pages I held open in one hand. "No fault for trying."

Wesley gazed past the couch, out the window and over the city. The leaves in the park had turned a particularly virulent green lately with the deepening of springtime, visible between the buildings. "Was he terribly awkward about it?"

"Only gently mortified."

"Hell. Sorry."

"Oh, please. That was the most fun I've had in days. Met him at a party, did you?"

Wesley looked at me and let his hedging break with a soft smile. He shook his head to himself. "Yeah. Met him at a party."

When I stuck out my foot to prod him companionably against the knee with my toe, Wesley reached down and patted my ankle before returning to the bedroom to dress again.

He seemed jittery, so after I finished my first cup of tea, I decided to give him some space. I dumped the rest of the pot down the sink and went upstairs to see Edie.

She was making a very tall pour of gin for herself when I knocked twice and let myself in. I stopped in the atrium of her sitting room, and she raised the glass to me.

"What's the occasion?" I asked.

Edie made a carping sound. "It was once a beautiful girl's birthday. Would you like one?"

"No, thank you. Was she a ballerina?"

Edie smirked dryly at me and mocked a toast. "To love," she said, and drank down half the glass. She scowled at herself, her eyes fixed to the middle distance of the carpet. This wasn't her first drink.

"I'm sorry," she said, glowering. "I'm being miserable."

"You're not miserable." I drew up close to rub companionably at Edie's shoulder. "I know miserable, and you aren't it."

"Distract me. What's the latest on the fifth floor?"

"Wesley was having a tryst with an ophthalmologist who didn't know I was home."

Edie laughed. "How was he?"

"I offered him a cup of tea, but he didn't want any."

"He always falls in with such tight-asses," Edie said. She pulled a humorous face to herself. *"Well."*

I pinched benignly at the back of her arm as Edie chuckled. She fixed me with a look that was much brighter than before. "Here's hoping he might branch out a little in New Mexico."

My expression twitched to confusion as I felt the sudden lurch of being left out of a joke. "What's in New Mexico?"

Edie blinked at me. "Shit." She took another wide sip. "He's still deciding whether or not to take the job, then."

"What job?"

Edie mulled something over to herself for a moment before giving up. She sat down on the fine paisley of her sofa and patted the cushion. "There's a director based in Jersey, Vaughn Kline—fancies himself a Renaissance man, more money than he knows what to do with. Old associate of Ezra's. He's hosting a festival at some . . . lake in the middle of the desert. Big tract of land, new theater space, all of it. Two hundred dollars a week for the actors, board included. I've been helping with the logistics." Edie swirled her glass and seemed to consider something, staring through the window. She didn't say anything else.

"A lake," I said slowly, "in the middle of the desert."

Edie shrugged. "Your guess is as good as mine. It would be something new, that's for sure."

I stayed standing. "Has he said anything to you about whether or not he was going?"

"Last he told me, he was trying to find a graceful way to tell you about it. They're doing *Titus*."

"Graceful, how?"

Edie sighed. "He wants to go, but he doesn't want to leave you alone here."

"I wouldn't be alone. You'd be here."

"I don't know, Margaret, he's very particular about you."

Affection stung in me, welling liked a pricked finger. I picked up a glass and began to throw a cocktail together for myself in lieu of examining the feeling too closely.

"Did you do much summer stock?" I asked her as I chipped ice into my glass from the block slowly melting in its filigreed bucket.

Edie snorted. "I did *plenty* of summer stock."

I took the opening for a distracting conversation. We shared two drinks and fond, old memories of our separate summer days, and I tried not to think about Wesley leaving me behind for a job.

When I caught sight of the time and hurried to get myself back downstairs, Edie took my empty and followed me to the front door.

"Where are you headed tonight?"

"The cabaret on Eleventh, Chap hosts there now."

Edie air-kissed me goodbye on one cheek. Her sandy perfume

wafted close, enveloping me briefly in the acute smell of her. I could always think more clearly when I was near Edie. "Tell him hello for me if you see him after the show, won't you? He owes me twenty dollars."

Inside our apartment again, I heard Wesley bustling in the bathroom. He was whistling "Some Enchanted Evening," which meant he was shaving. I approached the open door and stood there to watch him in the mirror, until he noticed me over his shoulder and smiled. The left half of his chin was still lathered white.

I stepped over the threshold and slid my arms around his waist. Holding him from behind, I pressed my cheek between his shoulders.

We stood together for a moment. The faucet in the tub had taken to dripping again.

I smoothed my hands up, passing over the firm strength of his midsection, and squeezed him gently. "Are you happy, Wes?"

Reaching under his arm, I took up his razor and peered over his shoulder to carefully shear off an inch of shaving cream from his cheek. He smiled at me. "Very," he murmured.

I had to believe him. What other option did I have?

9

Ezra Pierce's apartment, Hell's Kitchen

EZRA INVITED ME over for lunch later the following week—which meant I left messages with the front desk of his building until he finally called me back at two in the afternoon on a Monday.

"You're worse than the IRS," he snapped before I could even ask who was calling. "Come over tomorrow at one."

I smiled, smug with victory. "Anything I should bring?"

"I'm low on good booze," Ezra said, and hung up.

The next afternoon at ten to one, I stood on Ezra's doormat and held out a bottle of his preferred cognac fresh from the shop around the corner. "Tell me about the festival in New Mexico," I demanded.

Ezra took the bottle and gestured with it to invite me over the threshold. "Hello to you, too."

He shut the door behind us and took my hat first, then my jacket. He peered at the lining as he hung it up. "Is this new?"

"I have more time to shop these days," I said.

"With whose money?"

"Yours," I said, kissing him hello. "By way of Wesley's wallet."

Ezra led the way to the kitchen, where he'd set a spare but quality spread of cold meats and cheeses. He didn't have a dining room, nor did he ever have need for one as a flighty, terminal bachelor—and even if he had, the space in it would just have been taken up by more books. What Ezra lacked in meaningful human companionship, he made up for in volumes of novels, biographies, bound plays, loose folios, and stacks upon stacks of ancient sheet music for the upright piano tucked into the corner by the only visible window. The young men he fancied only ever saw him as a stepping-stone to the next rung of the show business ladder, but Ezra's true love was literature. He was never terribly wounded when his young men moved on, for there was always another book.

I sat in the chair Ezra pulled out for me. He uncorked the bottle and poured mine first.

"It was Bishop who spilled, I presume," he said lightly.

"She does tend to be the most reliable source of news."

Ezra poured his own glass and sipped with a tight frown. "The old adage used to be that one should only fill her teakettle with secrets if her spout was too distracted by another chorus girl."

"So it's supposed to be a secret?" I hummed. I began to serve myself, starting in on a delicate rosette of pastrami.

"It's supposed to be a very intimate gathering."

I frowned as I paused in the middle of spooning capers onto my plate. "Ezra, Wesley and I are *married*."

"A tabby to a terrier."

"I would have found out."

Ezra shrugged, blowing off the fact like unwanted input on his casting decisions. "They'll be getting paid."

"Is it some barn-in-the-woods shit that nobody's going to come to?"

"Concern yourself only with the fact that Wesley will be coming home with more cash than you've seen all year," Ezra said. "You can buy as many chic blazers as you'd like."

I flattened a look at him across the table. "I just want to understand what he would be getting himself into."

Ezra regarded me coolly and took a slow sip. His plate was empty. "Are you his keeper, or his agent?"

"Is there a difference?"

"What's a wife, if not both?"

I snorted. "I don't make commission."

"The jacket begs to differ."

I looked at him until his eyes began to sparkle with mischief. "It's a favor," Ezra admitted, embittered by the performance of his weakness against my obstinance.

"When is it not. To whom?" I asked.

"An old colleague."

"You have colleagues in New Mexico?"

"I do have a private life, you know."

I raised my eyebrows at the water cracker onto which I'd folded a piece of Swiss cheese. "An enigma, I'm sure."

Ezra held out his plate for the slab of roast beef I offered him. "One of my lenders is calling in a very old IOU," he said.

"To do what?"

"He's in need of a theater troupe, and the compensation is obscenely good for three months of work regurgitating *Titus Andronicus* for a parvenu in the desert."

I made a face at the tabletop. "Nobody does *Titus*."

"Exactly."

I watched Ezra assemble a small plate. "You've signed the company up to do your dirty work," I said. Ezra gave me a tired look.

"Don't be crass. It's just work."

"Looks the same from here."

Ezra propped his elbows on the table and leaned his chin on one hand. He peered at me, cataloging, and said nothing for several long seconds. I chewed uneasily.

"What?" I finally muttered, reaching for a small dish of pitted olives.

"How are you feeling lately? I forgot to ask."

"Don't. Not unless you're going to give me my job back."

Ezra looked vaguely impressed. "The Sumner outfit isn't *dangerous*. You don't have to worry about Wesley."

I snorted. "Outfit! What are they, cowboys?"

"Near enough." He popped an olive into his mouth and stared at my hands, briefly distant, before he resigned to some inward faltering. "If you must know, Margaret, I promise you nobody will get into trouble. My lender is in hot water and appeasing someone higher up the ladder—think of it like a summer season in the Hamptons, being put up by rich patrons."

I cast him a doubtful look. "Of course, the Hamptons—famously located in the desert."

Ezra smirked. "They'll all have a lovely time with the coyotes, I'm sure."

We finished the rest of the lunch with the usual chatter— who's-whos, what's-whats, and did-you-hears in surplus—and I tucked away all my questions about exactly what kind of man it was whose pockets Ezra had gotten himself into; deep down, somewhere in the marrow of the years before Richmond, I already knew the type.

I had met loads of them at Mr. Matthews's church once he married Mama, where they shook his hand after service and accepted thick envelopes from Mr. Matthews at his rectory desk. They were well-dressed men with shiny shoes and nice cars, and they always chucked my chin as they passed me, bent over my Bible at the edge of the room after I helped count the money. *She's gonna be awful pretty,* they'd call over their shoulders as they left, *ain't she, Charlie?*

I took the stairs back to the ground floor of Ezra's building after lunch and stopped in the privacy of the second floor landing to steal down a sniff of powder.

In the lobby, lined with long mirrors to throw the shapes of us in hundreds of shivering figures, Lady Macbeth walked beside me through my periphery on my way back out to the street.

I caught her gaze. She smiled at me. I ducked around the corner into the mail room, where the reflective wall gave way but a small mirror hung above the outgoing postbox. The Lady stood at my shoulder, giving me an appraising look through the glass.

"What do you want?" I whispered sharply. The Lady raised her thick, dark brows.

"You were me, for a time. You tell me," she said, her voice like clattering river stones.

I glanced over my shoulder to ensure I was alone and drew closer to the mirror with my voice dropped low. "I was acting. You aren't real."

The Lady looked impassive. She wasn't buying it. "What I want is the same thing you always have."

"And what would that be?"

She smiled. Every angle of her face came alive with smug conviction. "Power."

I turned from the mirror and hurried out to the street. I focused not on the chill of the word—*Power*, sticking to the back of my neck, echoing through the heart of me—and stepped into the glittering sun.

Summer was coming. I would face it fully, on my own terms.

◆ ◆ ◆

AFTER HOUNDING THE truth out of Ezra, I watched Wesley move through the ensuing week without saying a word about it. I didn't want to come off as the helpless, mewling damsel who always needed her husband near, so I was patient. I waited for the right moment.

I wanted to go with him. I needed a break from routine, to spend time with the company again. But the last thing I intended to be was dead weight on his career. I had to be tactful.

Wesley approached the den on his next free afternoon looking charged, driven by a fretting anxiousness. "Did you have plans for dinner?"

I looked up from my book. I had worked my way twice through Wesley's collection of crime serials. He liked stories about jaded, gray-moraled heroes with strong jawlines and very specific taste in women, so by proxy now I did as well.

"Takeout," I suggested. "Any preference?"

"I was rather thinking we could go see a show somewhere."

He was bursting with a sharp energy of the unsaid. I stood and took my time smoothing my skirt. "Sure. I could wear that new shirt-dress."

Wesley put his hands in his pockets. "I was hoping a little more . . . to-do, than a shirtdress?"

"You want to go *out*, out?"

"Why not? It's been a little while."

He looked sheepish, but his eyes were full of nervous hope.

"Give me an hour," I said, closing the book and brushing past to kiss him on the cheek.

"Two hours it is," he sallied over his shoulder as I made for the closet.

I exhumed a magenta A-line I hadn't worn since before we got married and a pair of mostly matching silk gloves. I laid them out on the bed to stare at the empty shape waiting to be occupied by a body, and frowned—Schrödinger's savoir faire, both myself and not at once.

"Chin up, woman," I grumbled, and slipped into the bathroom to tease some life back into my hair.

We left the apartment just over an hour later, with no small amount of self-satisfaction from me.

Wesley helped me out of the cab to the curb outside of the Stork Club. He led us down to the good seats inside, deep in the roar of a crowd at full bray.

"You didn't have to splurge," I muttered at his ear, as he pulled out my chair for me.

"Who said I splurged?" he muttered back, and pointedly shared a thankful look with the waiter setting a fresh tea candle on the table between us.

"If there's anything at all I can do for you tonight," the waiter chirped, "don't hesitate to let me know."

Wesley tried to slip him a ten, which the waiter smoothly slipped right back into Wesley's breast pocket as he moved to the next table. I dug a cigarette from my purse and held it out for a light.

The performance tonight featured a few newer talents. Wesley and I ordered drinks and food as the show began, and we dished about what we did and didn't like in low voices between each act—someone's sense of timing in the band was off; the dancer with the stoned tights had the tiniest waist either of us had ever seen; the comedian who came on after the dancer with the heart-shaped pasties put himself across as everyone's favorite gentleman, but off the stage he was an absolute dog with a penchant for dope; we both had stories about him.

I was enjoying myself. Thank God. I missed picking apart a

production with Wesley. It had been a long time since I'd felt so comfortable in public.

Amid the applause at the end of the first act, the crowd still laughing at Chap's last quip about tipping the waitstaff, I realized I couldn't remember the last time I'd scratched my arms to ribbons.

The lights went up for intermission. Wesley smiled at me with a moony grin I hadn't seen from him in months. The surprise of its reappearance made me return it reflexively. "What?" I asked, halfway laughing.

"I missed this," Wesley admitted. He reached across the table and took my hand. "It's nice."

I hid in a sip of my drink. "Sorry I've been a drip lately."

Wesley waved off the idea and leaned back in his seat. He lit a fresh smoke for himself, offering the flame before he doused it. I demurred and smiled at him again, more subtly. He peered at the empty stage, awash in the sound of the milling crowd again. As usual, Wesley wasn't going to be the first to broach an uncomfortable truth.

I waited until he tapped out the cigarette. "I know about the summer contract, Wes."

He set off into a minor coughing fit. "What?"

"The new company, the job in the desert. Edie told me. Are you taking it?"

Wesley wiped at the watery corners of his eyes. "Damn it," he wheezed. "Well, I'm not sure."

"You love *Titus*, and nobody ever does it these days. You'll kick yourself if you don't go."

Wesley peered at me strangely across the table. I leveled a look at him.

"I would have found out eventually," I said.

"I know. I just—well."

"Well, what? It's money, and apparently a lot of it. Why even think twice?" I sipped from the shallow dish of my martini glass and watched Wesley, who seemed to squirm lightly under the scrutiny.

"I want to be very . . . careful," Wesley said with clear evenness, "not to jar you. You've been doing so much better lately, really moving in a—a good direction, and I don't want to disrupt that."

"And that's very sweet of you. But you know what would help more than worrying about me?" I looked pointedly at Wesley, who returned the look. "An obscene amount of money."

Wesley snorted. "It *is* obscene." He fussed with the lay of his jacket lapels. "And I'm not *worrying* about you, I'm looking after you."

"Same thing."

"Patently not."

I shook my head. "I want to come with you."

Wesley stared at me. He ground his back teeth ever so slightly, the angle of his jaw bending.

"Is that really what you want, Jack?"

I turned the foot of my glass around atop the tablecloth and managed not to look away from him—those bright, quick eyes of his weren't difficult to look at, but the gravity of them watching me with such keenness woke a fire in my core.

Power.

"I need some time outside the city," I said. "I haven't had an open space to . . . relearn how to *breathe* since this whole business started. I want to come with you."

Wesley's gaze softened. The tenderness worked in between my organs like a knife. I looked away.

"If it's not possible," I amended, "if the director is stingy, that's fine. I only—"

"No, you're right. It isn't fair. It hasn't . . . been fair." Wesley turned his hand over, palm-up under mine. "Of course you'll come. I'll make it happen."

I sent him a conspiring smirk and hooked the edges of our thumbs together. "Are you sure I won't be invading on your plans for a sordid summer fling?"

"Just look the other way if you don't think he's handsome enough."

Wesley stood up and held me close by the waist for an extra moment when I rose to make for the ladies' room, passing behind his chair. I kissed him in keeping on the cheek.

"We'll figure it out, Jack," he murmured low at my ear.

"I don't doubt us for a second," I mock-whispered, and went to fix my face before the second act.

I slipped into a stall to draw out my powder and take a quick sniff, to assure myself I could get through the rest of the evening without any hiccups. I avoided looking at my scar as I pulled off my glove, like an old acquaintance crossing on the opposite side of the street with whom I had nothing of substance to talk about any longer.

I flushed after shutting my purse again, just to keep up appearances.

A small gaggle of women were gathered at the mirror. We said nice things about one another's dresses and jewelry and hair, and when I was the only one left primping, I looked around to make sure I was alone before smiling a glittery practice smile at my reflection.

It looked happy. *I* looked happy.

As I turned away to leave, the briefest flash at the corner of the mirror clung to my periphery—the feeling of being watched, sized up from a distance through my own reflection.

Power.

I returned to the table as the lights went low once more. Wesley took my hand with the band's wailing introduction, and as the curtain flew upward, he kissed my palm.

A feeling of falling very slowly plummeted through me at once. It was nothing. Only the powder hitting.

I settled in to watch the rest of the show. By the time we were standing backstage with Chap and a few of the dancers, sharing some hash and listening to Chap tell the stories the owner of the club wouldn't let him tell onstage anymore since he got slapped with a nasty fine, I was entirely apart from myself. Wesley's arm was around my shoulders. He was solid and warm, and we were going to go on an adventure together. I could be there. I could support him. It wouldn't hurt me at all.

I looked over at him and smiled, the one I had practiced earlier in the mirror, and loved myself when he smiled right back.

10

The Port Authority Bus Terminal

AFTER OFFICIALLY SIGNING his contract for the summer festival—the Sumner Summer Shakespeare Soiree, which looked more like a series of printing mistakes than a bona fide production—Wesley and Edie both assured me it was legitimate. They'd met the impresario and deemed him real, if eccentric; he'd given the actors handsome advances ahead of their regular weekly pay before they even left Manhattan.

But *legitimate* hardly meant *comfortable*. We found that out the hard way at six o'clock in the morning, bags in hand, standing before a fleet of battered Volkswagen Transporters ready to cart us across the country on a thirty-hour drive.

"You're kidding," Wesley said, his trained-in smile only faltering partway. He adjusted his grip on his suitcase and shifted to keep the other under his arm in place. "I had assumed we were only going from here to the airport."

One of the men leaning on the driver's-side door of the nearest van gave him an appraising look. He seemed constructed from choice cuts of beef stacked together in the vague shape of a man, corded and over-muscled. He said nothing, but another one came forward to take my suitcase and hitch it to the nearest roof rack.

A small, compact man approached me with his hand stuck out. "You must be Margaret Wolf."

I took the offered greeting, my stomach lurching at the rarity of my stage name. "Shoard," I said. "I've married."

He was shorter than me by an inch or two, shy of five-and-a-half feet, but he carried himself like a giant. His hair was combed down in an oil-slick part that barely covered a balding spot on the crown of his head. He led with his shoulders, which were heavily padded to a se-vere line under a sharkskin jacket.

"Vaughn," he said, grinning so broadly I could see three gold fill-ings in his premolars. He churned my hand like a water pump. "Vaughn Kline. Director and general upstart."

I flashed my own smile at him, the most obvious I could make it despite my doubts. "A pleasure."

A sharp, weaseled glint in Kline's deep-set eyes caught my reluc-tance. "I've heard about you."

"Have you?" I hadn't let go of his hand. He didn't have a terribly firm handshake—Kline seemed to me the sort of man who didn't need to be intense; if he saw himself as the brain, then this armada of strongmen did the literal and less-literal heavy lifting for him. All he had to do was be smart.

Smart could be dangerous.

He regarded me without lechery, simply sizing me up. "You plan-ning on gracing the boards with us, too?"

My resolve shuddered. I withdrew my hand and pretended to fuss with my purse. "That's kind of you, but no," I said, avoiding his gaze. "I leave that to my husband."

Kline glanced over his shoulder to where Wesley had given up trying to help the driver load our trunks onto the roof. He tarried back with his jacket draped over his arms, terribly out of place amid the collarless shirts and cigars, and tried to hail the working men to no avail with his questions—*Excuse me; are we really driving all the way there? That would take what, a week? Do we have that kind of time? . . . So you're all from Jersey?*

Jerking a thumb at him, Kline raised an eyebrow at me. "I've heard about him, too."

With my hand still inside my purse, I found my powder compact and closed my fist around it like a security blanket. I gave Kline another wooden smile. "He's plenty marvelous for the both of us," I said, and excused myself to secure a seat by a window.

I climbed into one of the empty vans and peered around: two rows of bench seats behind the driver, cracked leather and yellowed detailing from eons of smoking stains, the persistent smell of spilled coffee. I prepared a dose from my compact on my finger and sniffed it down, absently licking off the last of it.

Wesley climbed in after me, scowling. "Lovely hospitality so far," he said under his breath.

"I met Kline."

"Isn't he a riot?"

Lisette stuck her head into the van, wearing the sunglasses that meant she was staggeringly hungover. "Room in here for another?"

We helped her inside, and as though we were sitting at a bistro for a bit of hair of the dog instead of preparing for a cross-country caravan, she launched into a story about a dinner party last night in

Gramercy Park that somehow turned into a scavenger hunt along the East River. She kept her sunglasses on.

As we left the city—trundling through the Lincoln Tunnel, blinking in the sunlight after exiting on the other side of the water, shifting with a wince as the van's chassis bumped hard and often over potholes—Wesley slept heavily against my shoulder. Our driver drank a steady march of beer cans cracked open as he followed the route westward, smack-dab in the middle of a five-long caravan. Three newcomers to Ezra's crew had taken the other seats. I knew them only in passing from other corners of the Village, and their names slid off my powder-fogged brain when Lisette and Wesley introduced them to me. They smoked a sweet-smelling herb and didn't offer any to us.

It would be three days of driving crammed tight with this cobbled-together company. I kept up a low buzz with quick sniffs of powder every few hours and watched the scenery bleed from busy urban density into rural blandness. It was more than I usually used in a day, but I told myself it was a temporary measure. Once we got to Sumner, wherever it was, I would find plenty of other things to stay busy and pull myself back down to baseline.

We stopped for gas several times along the approach to the Midwest. Lining up to wait our turns at the toilets made me feel like a schoolgirl again. I averted my eyes from the mirror, knowing I looked like hell but not wanting the confirmation, and scoured my hands in each measly sink despite knowing I wouldn't feel clean until I could get a shower at the motel at the end of this first day's leg.

On our third stop, I climbed back into the van and considered for the first time whether or not I was making a mistake coming along. What was out here for me? What had I signed up for by asserting myself—a summer of slow wasting while Wesley was constantly away doing his job, just to catch a whiff of it from beside him?

I couldn't think of it like that. I had to believe it would be worth it. It was either this, or fritter away three months on my own.

I stared through the window and searched the feathery clouds hanging above this stretch of highway north of Pittsburgh. With the van door hanging open, the air swam sharp with the smell of gasoline. Our vans took up both fill pumps, idling in a line like the lot of us using the restrooms.

One of the rust-flecked toothpaste-colored beasts was stacked to the limits of its roof rack with huge boxes bursting with skeins of fabric—costumes. The man at the pump beside the open driver's-side door stood out against the droll gray daylight as though he'd stepped from the pages of a men's fashion catalog.

He sported a head of copper-red hair in a perfectly pomaded coif. His nose, straight and long and ending with a flick like the tail of his face's signature, arced down above a firm mouth pursed with vague derision. He held the stern set of his expression as though keeping in a scathing remark to everything at once, the graceful jut of his chin just the delicate side of square.

He looked up and found me through the window, past the black impasse of his round sunglasses. I couldn't look away from the casual acuity of his unseen gaze while he peered at me, one hand in his pocket and the other steadying the fuel nozzle at height with his hips.

Before I could drum up the muster to let my attention flit away, the man smiled. It was subtle, nothing more than a quirk of his lips.

I turned quickly in my seat and stared through the opposite window at the endless roll of Pennsylvania blandness. I dug out my compact and, still dizzied with my last dose, clenched my fist around a tube of lipstick Edie had lent me before leaving the city. *I can't wear this color here*, she'd told me easily, waving a hand; *don't know why I even bought it. Go give it some new life in the middle of nowhere.*

The untouched wax stick was a deep, earthy red. I applied a fresh coat along my lips, careful and practiced, and found it perfectly balanced to my skin tone in the hand mirror.

I felt the itch again—the weight of eyes. I shut the compact and looked up at the man at the pump, but he was gazing out at the horizon past the vans. He was stunning.

As I shut my purse again, Wesley came out of the gas station with a paper cup of coffee. He passed the costume-stacked van with the red-haired man and, turning to catch his eye, offered a wave. The man returned it.

"How much fuel do these monsters guzzle?" Wesley asked. He patted the rump of the van.

"Too much," the man said, and gave him the same keen smile. "But it's Kline's money, so I feed the bitch as much as she wants."

Wesley laughed, carrying the notes of interest I could hear in him like fine partials of ringing glass.

Well, if he really was interested, this man seemed quite the departure from Wesley's usual type of oh-so-particular and mannered. I watched the stranger rack the fuel nozzle and tug a kerchief from his pocket to wipe tidily at each finger in turn, peering along the stretch of road rising into the distance. He tucked away the kerchief before pulling a strike lighter from inside his jacket, and crossed to the gaggle of drivers cutting fresh cigars to offer them the flame with the ease of belonging amid their grit.

Maybe not Wesley's type, but certainly mine.

◆ ◆ ◆

WE STOPPED AT a deflated motel outside of Columbus, Ohio, as dusk pulled in tight. There was a restaurant down the street, and Kline announced we would be breaking bread together there. I had a headache from one too many doses of powder and looked forward to a drink to soften the dull throbbing.

"Don't worry about your things," he said over his shoulder, leading us across the empty street like a foolhardy mother duck in monk shoes. "The boys have 'em."

I looked backward at the vans parked in a row outside the rooms we had rented. The glow of several cigars persisted in the dark. Wesley touched my elbow.

"Ready, Jack?"

A streetlamp caught a hard angle of his face in oxidized off-orange. I took his hand. "After you."

The place across the street, Dizzy's, was sleepy at best. Kline hailed the owner, who was hunkered in an office in the back, while the rest of us milled at the bar and pretended not to overhear the chatter through the half-open door about an eye-popping sum of money for some hot meals and an open bar tab.

I peered at the rows of solemn-looking bottles along the back of the bar. The other patrons, a scant combination of locals and freight drivers, eyed us as though we'd dragged the circus into town.

A harried waitress with a pile of limp brown curls tied back in a bow herded us to a row of tables hastened together into one long plank. Amid the chorusing of chairs scooting out and all of us taking a collective load off, wincing for cramped legs or sore backsides, I took stock of the company.

I was the only one in attendance who didn't have something to do with the production. I knew a little more than half of the others from the Bard Players or various corners of the theater circuit in passing acquaintance made at one party or another—Lisette and Chap, the dancer-née-songbird Oliver Langham, and several other people I could only call friends at a surface level.

Well. It was something to do. Hopefully I'd get back home with a good story or two.

I carved into the same rubbery steak slathered with ketchup the rest of the table had been served and glanced around the restaurant.

"Who was that man at the gas station?" I asked Wesley, low at his ear. He glanced at me as he sipped his drink—at the very least, the bar here was stocked more than well enough to satisfy the road-weary. After the first few rounds, we would forget to be fussy about the trip still ahead of us.

"Who?"

"The man, the one with the sunglasses and the beautiful suit."

Wesley's eyes flashed. He glanced up, nodding his chin at the bar, where the drivers not on van-watch duty were perched. "Felix?"

I looked up and found the man from the fuel pump dropping a couple sugar cubes into a cup of coffee. He sat with poised tension, as though all of him had been sewn and tucked and primped exactly into the picture of man he now presented.

I bit down around my fork and chewed at the gristle, nodding shortly to Wesley. "What does he do?"

A small smile flicked up onto Wesley's mouth. "Costumes."

I narrowed my eyes at him. "You know him?"

Wesley nudged me with his elbow. "What," he muttered, "are you keen?"

When I looked back up at the man, Felix, he was sipping from the cup with a distant frown, soldiering through the taste of roadside sludge. He set the cup down and added another cube—and looked over at us, where he caught only the scrap of my gaze before I looked quickly back down at my plate.

"I don't know him well," Wesley said with an air of fond teasing, smiling directly at him, Felix, while he spoke to me. "But he *is* handsome, isn't he?"

I nudged Wesley right back. "I *knew* it, you dog."

When the waitress cleared our plates—much more cheerily now, with a fat wad of tips in her apron pocket—we did as all theatrical folk tended to do and began to tell stories.

Wesley was a wonderful storyteller. He did voices with uncanny accuracy and could arrest a room with the recitation of a shopping list. When it was his turn around the table, he told one about the time Ezra tried to cover a dance call himself in the absence of our choreographer. Wesley paced the length of the table as he gestured, snapped, and bitched with perfect mimicry, reducing the lot of us to stitches.

He closed on a cheap pun about curtain legs and a low, graceful bow. We applauded, and I looked up to find Felix standing by the jukebox watching Wesley.

It was a familiar look where Wesley was concerned. He was a dazzling specimen, particularly in his element, and I knew well the ways hungry men made eyes at him.

I excused myself from the table and crossed to the bar under the auspices of topping off my drink. Felix caught my eye on the single look I gave him as I stood, and he appeared at my side as the bartender scraped a cloudy glass through the ice bucket.

"Your husband is quite the character," he said, drawing up to lean an elbow on the bar.

His voice was oddly liquiform, oak-barrel soft and bending as though his accent had been molded into too many different shapes to recall which one it was meant to hold. I watched him in my periphery, keeping my attention on the drink coming together for me on the bar top. The sunglasses from earlier had been clip-ons, fixed to the narrow brass frames of his spectacles, whose lenses reflected the garish indoor neon signs like shimmering soapsuds.

"Would you like to meet him?" I passed a bill of my own across the bar and turned to face the man in full. I stood as high as his shoulder. He looked more put together than anyone should be allowed to after a full day's road trip.

The left hand he put out in the narrow space between us was unwavering and well-manicured. "Felix Haas," he said, his eyes flicking over all of me at once. "Master tailor and costume designer."

I ignored how aware of my own dress I had become, how frumpy I felt after not being able to freshen up in earnest. I took his palm with the intent to shake it, but he lifted my hand to his mouth and pressed a kiss to the back. I smiled at him over the rim of my drink. "Margaret Shoard. Margot. Wesley's wife, erstwhile actor myself."

Haas's lashes behind his glasses were thick and pale, with dramatic herringbone curves. He peered at me, cataloging my body with a surveyor's eye. "Of course. Did I see you in the Bard Players' Scottish play?"

I sipped and took a moment to meditate on the medical sting of the cheap whiskey coating my tongue. "Only if you came to the opener," I said breezily, and flashed my most disarming smile—Felix looked at my mouth, his gaze sticking for a moment. "Do you know Ezra? Were you also drafted by him to come out here?"

Haas returned the smile as though matching an ante. "My accord for this parody lies elsewhere, but I do know Ezra Pierce—somewhat against my will."

I furrowed my brow, still smiling. "Parody?"

Haas's poised mouth twitched with distant amusement. "Of course. It's summer stock."

"Margie! Come help us with 'Sixteen Tons'!"

I looked over at the table and found Lisette waving me over. I shot back the rest of my drink and touched Haas's arm. "Good to meet you, Felix."

"And you, Mrs. Shoard," he said, nodding politely at the table to usher me back over to them. He looked pleased with himself. "Or do you prefer Margie?"

I grimaced with levity and earned a warm chuckle from him before returning to my chair. I didn't help much for singing, but I kept time with my hands on the tabletop as several others spun half-drunk renditions of their favorite standards.

"Does he even know the first thing about theater?" I asked, nodding toward Kline, once we gave up the busking and commandeered the jukebox—someone had cued up the same doo-wop single for five songs in a row. I had lost sight of Wesley.

"Who cares?" Chap crowed. "We're getting paid our weight in gold to take a fucking break from Manhattan. I'd recite the Gettysburg Address to a barrel full of raccoons if he told me to."

A minor headache had started to settle in at the back of my neck. I collected my purse and excused myself for the restroom to take another dose of powder in private.

Just one. Just one last hoist to my mood, and I'd be done for the day.

At the back of the restaurant, two narrow doors with chipping paint stood under a measly hanging fixture with a satin glass shade. I tried one handle and found it locked, so tried the second one and found it open. The door groaned inward with a rusty heave.

"*Get*— Oh. Shit. Hi, Jack."

I froze in the doorway staring at the tumble of two bodies: Felix

Haas, lounged backward against the chipped porcelain edge of a dripping sink, and Wesley on his knees before Haas's open belt. I blinked. Haas tipped his head slightly to one side.

"Jack?" he asked with lilted curiosity.

Jogged back into the moment, I looked away and hurried to cover my eyes.

"You should lock the door," I blurted, scrambling for the handle again. "I'll— Jesus, Wes, at least put a towel down, the floor is filthy."

I yanked the door shut again and pulled until the latch engaged. Haas muttered something that made Wesley chuckle, and the gentle rattle of shucking open a pair of very finely made trousers continued.

I returned to the table and finished the last sip of a drink that might or might not have been mine. "The toilets are a mess here," I said to any of the company that was listening. "If you see Wesley, could you tell him I went to the room?"

I hurried back across the empty highway and fetched our room key from the front desk attendant, who looked halfway asleep on his feet, latched like a baby to the nipple of a baseball game on a portable television frizzling with static.

The hot shower I summoned for myself was most welcome. The tiles had a suspicious off-brown luster to them, the water smelled heavily of lye, but *I* was clean.

I put my hair up in a towel and pulled on a slip that didn't smell of the van's stale upholstery. The television leapt to life as I switched it on in passing, and listlessly I watched it through the mirror as I set my curlers for the next day.

Power, I could still hear like an echo now that I was in the relative silence of privacy. Or was it *Devour*? The shape of the sound was too muddled to tell. I turned up the volume on the television by a couple clicks to drown it out and burrowed under the covers of the single bed furthest from the tightly shut curtains of sickly yellow velour.

Wesley returned a little under an hour later. He slid the chain lock home on the door and came over to kiss me on the forehead.

"I'm sorry you—"

"No apologies," I said gently, not looking away from the television screen. "Tell me you washed up."

"Of course I did, you goose," Wesley muttered with an impish grin mashed against my temple. "Rinsed off with toilet water, though, couldn't be helped."

I rolled my eyes and swatted at him. He made for the bathroom, and in my periphery I marked the looser pitch of his gait; mellowed, as though Wesley had been unfolded, ironed out, and reassembled by attentive hands.

He showered with the door open, singing idly to himself under the steam. I watched his back as he combed his hair and pulled on a pair of clean cotton shorts for sleeping.

"Scoot," he said, slipping under the covers beside me and leaving the second bed empty.

I leaned into him, my cheek pressed hard to his bare chest. All of me ached from so many hours of sitting. I loathed that there were two more days of this ahead.

"Promise me you'll be careful," I said gently. He drew one hand down the length of my arm.

"About what?"

"Just be *careful*, Wesley."

Tenderly exasperated, Wesley gathered me more fully in his arms and squeezed. "He likes you, too, you know."

I made a neutral sound, ducked close to the soapy scent on

Wesley's skin. "He's very handsome," I said through a yawn. "I'm not exactly looking the other way, but . . . you know. Don't get blinded by the flash."

Wesley sniffed a chuckle to himself. I shut my eyes.

"He is that," he murmured, resting his cheek sideways on the crown of my head.

"What was it he said when I shut the door?"

"That 'Jack' seemed pedestrian for someone so beguiling."

My face flushed. Wesley laughed again, feeling me fail to hide my smile in the sure, unflagging thud of his heartbeat.

When Wesley rose later to switch off the television, I turned over and doused the light. He settled back under the covers beside me, curling up to hold me close and sigh mightily into the space between my shoulders.

No matter how hard I tried not to listen to the dark, the absolute silence of this place was deafening.

Power.

Devour.

When sleep caught me, it was sudden and black and entirely dreamless.

II

Who the hell knows, Missouri (outside of Joplin)

OF COURSE, IT wouldn't have been a proper cross-country journey unless we ran into mechanical issues.

The van holding the costumes swerved, flagged, and limped to the side of the road as we all slowed in the middle of Missouri's sprawling emptiness. The drivers pulled the vans off to help assess any damage, and Kline decreed the unexpected stoppage the perfect time to begin rehearsing.

"What'd the old queen say," Kline announced to the milling actors over a gust of flat prairie wind, "all the world's a stage, or some shit?"

He gestured broadly at the highway, the rolling grasslands hefting the lonesome pitch of the horizon. The company milled to the far end of the shoulder, where Kline shepherded them through a gap in the roadside fence. They spread out as he began to opine loudly and entirely incorrectly about the origins of *Titus Andronicus*.

I hung back at the end of the caravan. Still in the thick of my last dose of powder, it felt as though my eyeballs were floating in their sockets. I could hardly wait for the drive to be over. Keeping myself obliterated like this was exhausting.

I stared at the torn-up carcass of a rabbit in the middle of the road. It had been split open to the crude, hot eye of the sun and baked on the asphalt. I counted its ribs, dried-out and bleaching, wondering whether the vultures had already come to take their share of it.

What do you want?

You tell me.

I blinked myopically, shook my head, and turned to the men unloading the costumes so they could jack up the van and check the tire. They lifted boxes and stacked bare mannequins on the road shoulder. Thick layers of fabric sat in scattered rows of carefully folded bolts, bins, and reams in the midday light.

The draw was impossible to ignore. I craved to be close to some part of the work again, and if I couldn't join the scene-making, I would have to be content with perusing the armor of artifice.

The dresses, box after box of them, were some of the finest I'd ever seen. Unnoticed in the milling of the men hurrying to get the van road-ready again, I ran my hands along crushed velvet and flat beading, stitchwork so particular I nearly had to cross my eyes to see the individual threads.

I was roving my thumb along the edge of a heavy purple skirt when a shadow touched me—I looked up to see Felix Haas with his sunglasses back on, regarding the same garment with the critical eye one could only apply to his own creation.

"That one is old," he said simply. Haas held his cigarette out to me without looking away from the dress.

I accepted it between two fingers. "Old or not, it's beautiful."

"It's one of my few early pieces still intact. I lost much of my best work to a theater fire in London several years ago."

I took a wobbly sip of smoke. The taste of his tobacco was foreign, lightly toasted and earthier than what I was used to. "Did you have to make them all new?"

"Hardly slept for weeks to do it in time." I passed the cigarette back. Our hands brushed lightly with the transfer. "Mostly I played Victor Frankenstein on older pieces with a few rentals no one had picked up and the scraps that weren't so badly damaged."

"Did it feel like you'd never climb out of your own pit?" I asked without meaning to, not looking at him, still halfway stuck in my own head.

Haas pursed his lips and hummed shortly. At the edge of the ditch, the drivers began to lever up the van by the chassis. "At first," he mused. "But then I set my hands to the work, and it got done."

He regarded me sideways, appraising me from behind the dark, round lenses of his glasses. A smile persisted on his mouth, the subtle pink of his lips. "Am I to believe you've found yourself in a pit, Mrs. Shoard?" he asked lightly.

"Please, call me Margaret."

Haas reached out to me and, just as he had on the dress, drew his hand with a measuring touch along the shoulder of my blouse. "You're so very put together, Margaret, even amid the dust of the interstate system."

My heart made a fluttering turn in my ribs. I hoped the flush on my face wasn't half as bright as it felt.

We watched two men patch the tire—*Fuckin' piece of glass*, one of the drivers called up from beneath the undercarriage, while another two standing by traded a handful of money for betting on the reason.

"I used to be those women," I admitted. I gestured at the box of dresses. "They used to be me."

When I looked over at Haas, he cast a very subtle, encouraging smile at me. "I'd call you far more alluring than half those tragic windbags."

I barked a laugh, which made my headache pulse. I reached out for another sip on the cigarette. Haas passed it to me without hesitation. We stood in silence and watched the drivers lower the van back down, kicking shallowly at the tire to make sure it held air again. One of them gave a sharp whistle at Kline when he deemed it road-ready.

Wesley approached me and Haas with an arm raised as the rest of the company broke apart and began returning to the vans.

"Trading secrets about me?" he needled with a grin. Color had risen in his cheeks from the sun. Haas plucked a fresh cigarette from his pocket and lit it for Wesley, who accepted it with a charmed smile.

"How was the baptismal rehearsal?" Haas asked. Wesley chuffed a laugh and wrapped an easy arm around my waist.

"Kline doesn't know the first thing about any of this." He shared an exhilarated glance with Haas.

Haas peered out at the road spooling away ahead of us and smiled to himself. "Kline is all hunt and no shot. Only listen to him when it benefits you," he said, and moved off to oversee the repacking of the van.

From the van's side mirror past Haas's shoulder, I could see Wesley and myself reflected back against the pale, endless blue of the sky. We looked haggard but whole.

Haas peered back at me as though drawn by the weight of my sticky, lingering attention left clinging to him.

I wasn't *not* attracted to him.

Back on the road again, I realized the exact pitch of the feeling burrowing low in my belly: desire, and the magnetic pull of being wanted in return.

◆ ◆ ◆

IN THAT NIGHT'S motel, I was cataloging my belongings through a buzz-eyed haze as I did at the end of each day to make sure nothing was getting pinched. I counted my stockings and underthings first, and the tidy fold of emergency money secreted into one corner of the lining second.

Wesley was divested down to his undershirt, shining his black wingtips on the edge of the bed. I sat on the rickety vanity bench that smelled of old dust and regarded him with a lazy cigarette as he worked. I could hardly concentrate on one thought for longer than a handful of seconds. It felt like my teeth were going to leap from my jaws.

"I can hear you thinking," he said without looking up. A small smile was pinned to the corners of his mouth.

I gave him a twitchy smile. "What am I thinking, then?"

Wesley winked. "That you adore me *so* very much," he minced, pleased with himself.

I blew a mouthful of smoke in his direction. "That's cheating."

The radio was broadcasting the patter of someone narrating the last of spring training. I watched the quick work of Wesley's hands, so practiced with the blacking polish to avoid getting even a jot of it on his fingertips.

"You're enjoying his company?" I asked, not looking up from the glossy, sludgy streaks Wesley was scrubbing into a smooth shine over the leather. He paused.

Felix Haas had taken to orbiting me and Wesley at a wide but constant berth. He intrigued me, and I knew he and Wesley had started up regular rendezvousing at gas stations and any stopover longer than a handful of minutes. Wesley rode along with him in the costume van after the men patched the tire when I convinced him I would be fine on my own—I managed to sleep for a few hours and woke with a crick in my neck without Wesley's shoulder, but it was worth it to see Wesley with a specific lightness of being in him.

"I suppose so." Wesley didn't have to ask for a name.

"He's . . . nice, then?"

Wesley angled a look at me. I raised my eyebrows in a silent *What?* "You don't have a habit of being . . ." He searched for the word somewhere along his back teeth with the prodding tip of his tongue. "Curious, about them."

I considered that for a moment. Tracing the end of my cigarette with the edge of my thumb, I stared at the pattern of the filter smudged with the last of today's lipstick. My head felt thick and obscure as Wesley's shoe polish.

"He doesn't seem very much like your usual type. And he intrigues me," I said.

Wesley snorted. "You don't have to be coy. You *intrigue* him, too."

I frowned gently and took a steady drag of smoke. "I'm not being coy," I said, but doubted the words as soon as they left my mouth. "Seriously, Wesley. Do you even know the first thing about him?"

Wesley dipped into the tin and scoured at a persistent scuff where his left foot tended to turn in a bit more than his right as he walked.

"I don't want you to stumble into another Andrew situation," I said before I could stop myself.

Wesley stilled. He set his shoes down and wiped his fingers off on the kerchief in his pocket as he rose to stand beside me. "I'm being careful," he said, looking straight at me in the glass. "I promise."

"Are you?"

Wesley's expression begged companionable judgment. "Most of

the ones in New York have a whole host of complexes. I'm showing them some bright spots to a side of living they're all so fucking *scared* of. Men like Felix, they're—you know. He's artistic, he's bold, he says exactly what he's thinking. I've missed being close to that."

He put a hand on my shoulder and hesitated for only a moment before leaning in and kissing it, a light and encouraging peck. "It's just a summer crack. Andrew took much longer than we have out here to show his true colors."

I made a pale sound, shrugging weakly, and turned back to organizing my things scattered on top of the vanity. Wesley sighed.

"We're all under someone's thumb for the season anyways," he said. "How out of hand could anything get?"

I didn't look up at him. "I don't know," I said lightly, lining up a few tubes of creams and paints in tidy rows while I steered wide around what I knew about the festival.

Wesley was quiet until I looked up at him. His gaze had softened with sympathy. "I'm not wandering around in the dark here, Jack," he murmured. "I know the sorts of circles Ezra runs in."

I held in a rude chuckle. Sure, he knew the sorts, but he didn't *know* them. He hadn't grown up right alongside the rank and file. I could still remember the loud laughter and acrid aftershave hanging thick in the air at the dinner parties my mother used to host for Mr. Matthews and his chums in those few years before I fled to Richmond, and I didn't want Wesley anywhere near that sort—they would eat him alive. Felix Haas didn't seem in-line with the worst of them, but still. I worried.

"I just don't know him," I said, which was true. Wesley smoothed his hand over my hair, stroking his thumb along my nape.

"You should *get* to know him. He would probably like that."

I ashed my cigarette in a smudged porcelain dish. "Would he?"

"He's got diversified taste." Wesley examined himself in the mirror, peering at the sides of his jaw with the particular angle of his gaze that meant he'd go for a shave soon. "Who knows? Could be nice to have for the summer."

"Mr. Shoard, are you proposing we *share*?"

Wesley shot me his most roguish smile. "What's mine is yours."

I laughed a breathless little huff, more flustered than I would have expected.

Across the room, the radio cut away to a syrupy jingle advertising a new grocery store.

"Would you even want to share?" I asked.

Wesley leaned a flat hand on the vanity top and gave a genial shrug with one shoulder. "Who would I be to stop you? I say again, he likes you. And you're curious about him."

"Well." I peered at the edge of my slip and ran the tip of my finger along the scalloping. My heart had begun to beat more quickly. "I don't want you to think I'm loose. And you saw him first. Didn't you?"

Wesley leveled a look at me, the look that always made me go soft. "The only thing I'll ever think of you," he said, quietly emphatic, "is that you're brilliant, and wonderful, and one hell of a good-luck charm."

I hid a smile in my collar and glanced up into the mirror to look at him there in the glass. "Maybe he can make room for me in his schedule," I muttered. "We'll see."

Wesley pushed off from the table and kissed the shell of my ear before returning to his shoes—picking one up, he turned it in the bilious halo of light from the single nightstand lamp.

I set to pinning my hair ahead of bed. On the radio, the crack of a good solid bat and the roar of the crowd was swallowed by the transmission fuzzing briefly.

When he finished with his shoes, Wesley set them by the door and strode into the bathroom. As I listened to the shower valve groan open and sputter down, I stared into my reflection.

I emptied my purse onto the vanity and took out the paper sack I stored in my suitcase between my least-titillating layers of clothes to dissuade further prying. Dr. French had sent me off for the summer with a few extra rations of powder.

It was a finite supply. I'd been overdoing it for these past few days to keep sane throughout the caravanning. But there was still plenty to last through August, and I could make do. I *would*.

I stole down a short sniff to stop my temples pounding and began to pack it all carefully away again.

It would be enough. Especially if there were other entertainments to distract me, to make me remember what it felt like to want.

12

Lake Sumner, New Mexico

OUR FINAL DESTINATION was, as I'd feared, a nothing-place.

The country was filled with them, these yawning spaces. Whether they were purposeful, by way of the government playing keep-away with resources from the hands that needed them most, or simply the accidental way in which nature made room for itself, creating abscesses in the vast swaths of Western openness, these places were like vacuums for reality. We had been seeing them in small ways throughout the journey, but here now we landed on the emptiest place of all.

And we were to pass the entire summer here.

What the hell had I gotten myself into?

As I stared through the window at the sleepy outskirts of town scrolling past, disappointment tried and mostly failed to burble beyond the surface of my last dose. The buildings were all small and low, as though they were embarrassed by having been built. Whitewashed slabs of adobe and sad plastic siding lined the narrow, empty roads like chipped and scattered shards of bone. I counted more buzzards

on the electrical wires than I did cars parked outside of shabby, unre-
markable buildings.

And they were courting an audience for Shakespeare? *Here?*

I sank lower into my seat and held my sides with crossed arms. I
practiced breathing very steadily: in through my nose, out through
my mouth. The vans weren't stopping.

"In what part of town are we staying?" I called up to the driver
over the rumble of the engine.

"There's a motel on the main drag," he grunted to my curdling
chagrin. "We'll pass the theater on the way."

I shut my eyes and tried to remind myself this wasn't about me.
This wasn't forever.

Besides, a few months of boredom might be *good* for me. It might
force me out of my own head.

I might get t—

"Oh, Jack, *look.*"

I had drifted off. "What," I said, fighting to open my eyes against
my fluttering lashes, "a tumbleweed?"

"*Look.*"

Wesley's voice was so full of awe from the other side of the seat
that I couldn't help but follow his stare. My jaw dropped.

I had only ever seen illustrations of the Globe in the endpapers of
Shakespeare folios, and in photographs of a replica building from
Edie's scrapbooks—before stepping back from the stage, she had per-
formed in what she deemed the only real American production of
Richard III during the Great Lakes Exposition in Ohio twenty
years ago.

Another clone of the hallowed place towered in the middle of the
desert, alone and ecclesiastical.

A wide, glassy lake bled like a vast puddle over the empty ground.

Low scrub trees traced its edges, clinging to the only evident mois-
ture, and on an islet in the water rose the theater. It was as if someone
had sliced the real thing directly out from the beating heart of Tudor
England and airlifted it here in one piece.

The caravan slowed, but nobody got out. Only one door from the
leading van opened for Kline, who stumbled out onto the dirt and
began to speed-walk at an awkward, self-conscious clip to the lake's
edge. The line of vans started up once more toward the motel as soon
as the door shut again.

I stayed glued to the window, marveling at the theater. A sunset-
colored Corvette was parked under a cottonwood by the lakeside, on
which a skinny-hipped man with a cowboy hat was leaning with his
arms crossed and the brim angled low over his face. He kicked into a
stand with a palm stuck out in greeting, and before the dust cloud
from our retreating tires obscured the last of my vision, I saw Kline
eagerly take his hand.

We decamped at the motel—the sorriest of all the places so far,
but at least the couple's suite was vacant. In addition to two double
beds, Wesley and I got what passed for a kitchenette with a single-
burner hot plate, a sink, and one narrow cabinet filled with mismatched, lightly chipped dishware.

The cramped bathroom left much to be desired. The carpet had a
questionable stain worked in by the foot of one bed. The bedclothes
didn't look *that* itchy.

Home, for the next three months.

"I'll unpack in a bit," I said briskly to Wesley as he laid out his
clothes. I hurried out the back door with my purse in tow.

An open field sprawled beyond the motel, patchy with yellow
grasses and the occasional sprig of insistent wildflowers pushing up
through the cracked earth. An empty, dilapidated swimming pool

baked in the sun like a discarded Bundt pan. With the main road stringing along past the front of the motel, here at the back there was nothing for as far as I could see in the interminable miles beyond.

The shard of my reflection looked back as I prepared a dose in the compact. The sky hung with a vivid, choking blue above and around me.

"Afternoon."

I flinched at the call from the next door over, carrying easily through the still air—I nearly dropped the dose but managed to hurry it into my nose before turning to greet whomever was also out here, taking it all in, perhaps also deeply regretting their own choice to join the company.

Felix Haas stood in shirtsleeves with a hand raised in greeting. I fussed the compact back into my purse and swiped subtly at my nose. "Settled in already?" I called back.

He sauntered over with that long, easy bearing. He wasn't much taller than Wesley, but the archness with which he viewed everything around him lent a peremptory pitch to his carriage. Haas nodded at my purse. "Analyst's chalk?"

I sniffed. "For my nerves. You know how it goes."

Haas's collar was open to the third button and color rose faintly under his fair, high cheeks, likely from unloading boxes of costumes. A spray of freckles decorated the bridge of his nose. I tried not to stare at the divot of his throat. He smiled, a supple tip of his lips. "If you're ever in need of a more effective fix," he said, his voice low and conspiratorial, "please know you need only ask."

I raised my eyebrows. "And what might *that* mean?"

"Is Wesley inside?" Haas glanced at the door behind me, through which the low muddle of the radio persisted—Wesley had found the daytime channel.

"He's unpacking."

The roots of my teeth began to tingle. The tension in my shoulders ebbed, ever so slightly. I sighed gently, easing into the familiar feeling, and tried not to think of going without this relief if I ran out.

I couldn't think about that—fear reared hard in me, bidding me away, away, away from that thought. I couldn't be without it.

Couldn't I?

Haas was eyeing me when I focused back on him. "I mean it," he said gently. He lifted a hand to the seam at my waist, where my skirt met my bodice, and ran his thumb over it with the unassuming rote of familiar work. "Anything you need, anything at all; I'm right over there, room six."

I was keen, of course. I would have to be blind not to be piqued, at the very least to pick up the innuendo he was dropping for me like breadcrumbs for ducks in the park. But I reached down and removed his hand with a gentle push, letting my thumb linger ever so slightly on the fine ridge where the heel of his hand met his arm. "You're a very good salesman, Mr. Haas, I—"

"Felix," he cut in gently. He slid both hands into his pockets and looked me over like several good yards of fabric. "Call me Felix, I told you."

I smiled. "Felix. You're astute, but I don't think you want to get involved with my mess."

"Mess?" Haas's expression flashed with amusement. "Au contraire, Mrs. Shoard—"

"Margaret."

Haas peered at me, the intention of his gaze lifting yet another layer of fascination. "How about Jack?" he asked lightly.

My chest tightened with a brief and subtle squeeze. "Only Wesley has that privilege."

We watched each other through a long silence, broken only by the faint sound of the radio inside the room behind me and the faraway whistle of wind I swore I could hear slipping across the mountains as the drug made soft the border between reality and illusion.

Haas dug into his breast pocket with one long, fine finger and thumb to produce a small silver tin the size of a pack of playing cards. He proffered it in the air between us. "You can say no," he said.

"Is that the more effective fix?"

"It could be."

"Maybe another time," I said, and held out a hand between us. "I still need to unpack."

Haas took my hand and shook it this time instead of kissing it—but with the heat in his gaze, he might as well have put my fingers in his mouth.

I stared after him on his return to the room next door. He moved like a mountain lion, svelte and sure-footed and proud of his own shape.

I slipped back into our room. Wesley looked up at me from the fold-down ironing board with a smile. "Want to leave your dress for me?"

"Oh, no, it's as sweaty as the others. I'll find a Laundromat to-morrow."

I turned to present my zipper to him, which Wesley peeled down for me. He kissed the back of my neck before I wriggled it from my waist, stepped out of my skirts and slip, and retired to the bathroom.

I ran the water as hot as I could get it. I peered at myself in the mirror, dimpling and nudging my flesh and lightly judging the juts of my bones and joints from every angle out of habit as the edges of the mirror fogged gently. No longer was I the scrawny, bug-legged child with the freedom of a flat and sexless body, but I certainly wouldn't have said no to a more shapely figure.

Under the shower, I let sensation wash over me as the water scourged away the days and days of travel. The nudging impulse twisting in my gut had evolved beyond my brief exchange with Haas from simple curiosity to an insistent arousal.

The sense of my body as a thing with an appetite was not something I tended to focus on very often. Looking on my own wiles from the inside out was a dangerous game; there was too much buried in the loam that made me Margaret, and to dig my hands into it could unearth hideous bones I feared classifying. In me were too many scabbed-over hurts I couldn't risk picking at lest they bleed again—the old nausea from feeling Mr. Matthews leer at me as I helped him embezzle from the collection plates without realizing what the work really was; the burning shape of Hollis's hand squeezing bruises into my flesh, which I still felt sometimes without intending to remember at all.

And yet here on my own, in the privacy of my thoughts far away from home and held aloft by my medicine, my body *wanted* with briary persistence that would not be quieted by anything besides facing it.

I shut my eyes and summoned up the sight of Haas with his shirt open, and then with no shirt at all. I did away with his shoes, his socks, his belt and trousers and shorts; I imagined him bare in the sun, kissed with a reddish tan; the way he could take me by the hand to lead me into the vastness of the field beyond the motel—how he might strip me bare with tender fastidiousness, lay me down gently on the dusty ground, or in the basin of the empty pool, and then hold me down for my own good, because maybe I'd ask for that; open me up, press my name into the side of my face as he knelt over me, and I would all but taste the way he fell in thrall to me, my—

My hand slid flat along the shower tiles as my knees buckled gently, stumbling forward to catch my weight before I slipped.

I looked at myself in the fogged mirror, sodden and wrung out and alone, my eyes bright as anything amid the sulfurous mist of the showerhead.

Devour.

The hot water ran out with a groan from the pipes—I yelped as I jumped away from the cold and shut the faucet with a hasty slap.

I stood dripping, returning to myself, and tucked away the mystery of my desire on the same deep shelf that held my ambition.

◆ ◆ ◆

I TRIED TO find the pattern of decent living in Lake Sumner.

As much as I hoped it would be a freeing retreat—to suddenly find myself awake, as though doused in the lake itself; dragged back to my surface, gasping for a wide and full-chested breath of dry, clean air—it was nothing of the sort.

The first few days passed in one great blur. I found the Laundromat a ten-minute walk away and spent two hours watching a couple loads thump and tumble and blur with my perception smeared like the sudsy wash. Next door was a sleepy salon that only did cuts. No color. No set and shellac. I did my own hair from scratch each morning, but that only took up meager half-hours at a time—a full sixty minutes if I really took pains with a new style, but there was never any reason to dress up or look particularly nice.

There were too many goddamn hours in the day.

It was deeply lonely even despite the dinners and drinks and evening chatter I spent with Wesley and Haas, both together and separately. Otherwise the company went up to their rehearsals at the lake, and I stayed behind like a bird unable to take wing through the open door of its cage.

I was confined to the motel and the paltry offerings in town—the bar, the sorry excuse for a grocer, and the endless emptiness that surrounded us. I was stranded. At least in the city if I went stir-crazy, I could jump on the bus and go spend money on things I didn't need.

Here, I was alone. Completely, utterly, and entirely.

The motel had no name or title to speak of. It simply stretched low and off-white for twenty room-lengths, lined with uniform red doors that sported each number with rust-rimed plates. The cantilevered roof, extending flat as a cap brim, sagged faintly between the angled wooden beams that braced it.

Every one of us, the actors and the outfit and any in-between attached to this peculiar venture, had been flattened here into the same class: boredom. There was a certain poetry in it. Had I the patience, the general sanity, I might have found rare charm sewn in along the edges of what was happening here. But as it stood, I was desperate and fraying. The immediate present, charged and burning, was the only thing I could stomach holding in my hands.

Wesley was taking an afternoon with Haas next door. I had been lying around in my slip after we got a drink together at the bar—Haas had invited me, Wesley had encouraged me, but I still didn't feel comfortable inserting myself into whatever was blooming between them. I made a silly little excuse as we parted on the breezeway, and I'd been staring through the weak signal of the television for nearly an hour now with nothing but frustration buzzing around under my fingernails. I was ready to start peeling the wallpaper with my teeth.

I stood up without ceremony and pulled on my robe before stepping into my house shoes.

I knocked briskly on Haas's door. There was silence within, but soon the soft rattle of the chain and the lock flipping open.

"Margaret," Haas said, squinting in the blanched slap of sunlight that carved into the cool, low light of the room through the door's vee. He sounded pleased to see me. "Have I kept your husband past curfew?"

He wasn't wearing a shirt. A cigarette hung casually from the corner of his mouth. I wasn't staring. I blinked quickly and made a twitchy gesture. "I only wanted some company."

Haas nodded backward over his shoulder and opened the door a fraction wider in invitation. "He's washing up. Come in, if you'd like."

Inside, my eyes took their time adjusting—all of the shades were drawn, and the first thing I saw with any clarity was the tossed riot of sheets on the bed. I hadn't heard them at all through the shared wall.

Haas offered me a smoke, but I held up a hand. He indicated the single sun-faded armchair before crossing to a tidy collection of bottles on top of the sagging dresser, where he began mixing up a drink.

"So, what do you think so far of our lodgings?" Haas asked over his shoulder, heavy with sarcasm. I sniffed dryly and prodded at my forehead as though I might dispel my constant headache.

"Do you want the pretty lie or the ugly truth?"

Haas mocked a thinking face as he turned and held the cup out to me. I took a deep-throated sip, savoring the smooth bite of it— bottom-shelf, but still whiskey. "Is there a pretty truth?" he asked.

I thought for a moment and jangled the remelted-together ice in the belly of the cup. "I've lived in worse places for longer," I said tightly. Haas made a commiserative grunt. He crossed his arms and leaned easily back against the dresser, peering with a lingering glance at my bare legs crossed at the knee under the hem of my robe.

"I, for one, hate this fucking tomb," he said starkly and gave a flat smile.

I chuckled. "Have you been here before?"

"Once." He didn't elaborate.

The water in the bathroom stopped with a shallow shudder. Haas took a slow suck on his cigarette, still watching me. "I'm one of Kline's associates," he clarified, as if taking mild pity on me.

I gave him an expectant look. "Which means . . . ?"

Haas flicked his eyebrows up, pleased with himself. "Details are reserved for my paramours, and only if they ask nicely."

I pursed my mouth around an avid smile as the bathroom door opened—*shit*. I had wanted to ask for a taste of that more effective fix he'd mentioned the other day, but it felt too abrupt now with Wesley stepping fresh into the room, his hair combed back wet, drying himself off briskly with the same threadbare blue towel as in our room.

"Well!" The light in his eyes flickered, just barely. He beamed at me and unconsciously made to cover his nakedness with a smooth flick of the terry cloth. "Alright, Jack?"

"I'm fine." I stood up and tossed back the rest of the drink Haas made me. "I just needed company."

Haas was watching me, attempting to pry down past my surface as I stood and set the cup on the dresser beside him. "Two's company," he said lightly, "but three; are you sure you weren't looking for a crowd?"

"Give her a crowd," Wesley said with his back to us as he stepped into his shorts and hunted the rest of his clothes from the floor, "she'd give them a hell of a show."

"Would she," Haas said, not looking away from me. His gaze made a persistent heat beg up under my skin, a restlessness that didn't know how to free itself.

"You should have seen her in *Twelfth Night*," Wesley carried on. He tossed his shirt around his shoulders and turned to us as he buttoned it. He winked at me. "Looks better in a pair of buckskins than anyone."

"Oh, I don't doubt that for a moment." Haas's gaze crawled up me from the root; ankle, calf, the bend of my knee, my thigh, nestling—

Haas jogged me from my imagination when he leaned forward, one hand on my hip, to kiss me on both cheeks. He had the faint scent of Wesley about him. "Good afternoon, Mrs. Shoard," he said brightly. On drawing back, he felt the sash of my robe between two fingers as though testing its thread count. He made a gratified sound and gestured at the flash of my slip past the bottom hem. "Perhaps I'll see more of you like this."

He crossed the room to kiss Wesley goodbye as well, on the mouth—I looked away in automatic propriety, but I caught sight of them in the mirror fixed to the wall. Wesley looked more centered in his skin than I'd ever seen him before.

He deserved this happiness, and more.

And me; what did I deserve?

Wesley finished tucking in his shirt and smiled at me. "Shall we?"

He was happy.

I looked at Haas again, set to tidying the bedclothes with fastidious ease. He glanced up and caught my gaze in the low, simmering heat of intrigue.

Why should I not be, as well?

13

The Lake Sumner motel breezeway

I TOOK THE arm Wesley offered as Haas ushered us out of the room. The sunlight stung my eyes after the cool dimness, and I was quiet as we returned to next door.

Wesley had a spring in his step. I nudged him genially in the side. "Cat got the cream?"

"He *really* likes you," Wesley muttered, singsong. We stopped at number five, and he dug into his pocket for the key with a self-assured smile hitching up one corner of his mouth.

"When did he tell you that," I muttered, "was it while you had him on yo—"

"*Stop*," Wesley scoffed, laughing, wrestling an arm around my waist to hurry me into privacy.

In the silence of the door falling shut again, I didn't let go of him. I turned to hold Wesley from the front, and I buried my face briefly in his collar. He smelled of shampoo, with no evident trace of Haas.

"I'm still thinking about it," I muttered against his skin.

"What, sharing?"

I nodded. Wesley rubbed my back briskly. "Take your time, Jack. We've got all summer."

Edie would have sound advice. I collected my clutch and made for the phone booth sticking up at the side of the empty main road. As I waited for the line to connect from the collect exchange—which was more expensive than I'd expected—I stared at Haas's door and turned the sensation of his weighty gaze over and over in my head like a worry stone.

"Hello?" Edie said, sounding exasperated.

"Edie, it's Margaret."

"Oh good, I was wondering whether you'd fallen into a sinkhole somewhere."

"Do you have time?"

"I've got five minutes."

"That's fine." I crowded myself up into the corner of the booth and shut my eyes. "Heading out?"

Edie made a suffering sound. "Meeting over drinks with some visiting upstart from Illinois. How is it out there?"

I regarded my thumbnail, the chipped pearl-pink paint I'd reapplied the other afternoon in an effort to cheer myself up. It hadn't worked. "I'm so bored I'm going to turn to dust."

"Your excitement is absolutely infectious."

"Wesley is having a *wonderful* time."

"Is he now? What sort is it this time, an actor who thinks he's Gregory Peck or one of the crew?"

"Crew, with a Gregory Peck garnish."

Edie made an amused sound. "Good for him."

A quick silence fell between us.

"I can tell when you're miserable even without looking at you," Edie said gently. "What's got you, poss?"

I opened my mouth to tell her about my spiraling attachment to the powder, how it was starting to scare me that I could hardly go an hour without feeling peeled-back from my own body, but asked instead, "How do you tolerate being off the stage?"

"Oh, I don't know if 'tolerate' is the right word." The clatter of cosmetics rattled softly on Edie's end. I imagined her daubing her cheeks with rouge, dragging a thick mascara wand along her lashes. "Do you really miss the work so much?"

"I do. I didn't think it . . . well." I scowled at the faint shape of my face warbling back at me from the glass across the booth. "I always knew it had a hold on me, but not like this."

Edie paused for only the briefest moment. "Are you going to be okay out there?"

I swallowed. "I should go."

"Margaret."

"I'll be fine, Edie," I said evenly, and waited to find whether or not I even believed myself. I couldn't tell.

"I can't tell if you're being honest, or if your penchant for lying is getting rusty without practice."

"Give Ezra my regards."

Edie sighed. "Let's catch up when you're back in town," she said. "Alright? You'll be fine. We'll figure out what comes next."

"We will," I said, and gave her my best before hanging up.

I could get through this summer. I had chosen this, I had asserted myself to get here, and I would be just fine.

I would only need a touch of help.

In the pocket of my robe, digging for a cigarette, my fingers bumped against a foreign object. I lifted it out and found a small plastic sachet of fine white powder.

Haas—when he kissed me goodbye, that hand light on my waist. *Stronger stuff.* Crafty of him.

I held it up to the threads of sunlight pushing in through the phone booth and examined it: finer than sand, more like powdered sugar, light and so white it was nearly blue.

Later. I would save it for when I really needed it.

If. *If* I really needed it.

Very carefully, I scraped a half-measure of Dr. French's powder from my compact. I recalled how I used to ration my sardines in the early days of the Christopher Street apartment. This wasn't much different; sustenance could be many things.

I lingered in the phone booth until it hit again. When I returned to the room, Wesley was dozing as he watched the daytime news. I settled down against him, curled up on my side, and let him pull me close with a cloudy, pleased whuff against the back of my neck.

I stared at the shape of us in the vanity mirror across the room. I wondered if it was Wesley who held Haas, or Haas who held Wesley. I wondered how affection might stretch to hold three instead of two, and whether or not that was something I truly wanted.

Sliding my hand into the pocket of my robe, I ran my thumb along the secret gift from Haas and promised myself I would be patient with all of it: myself, my time, my medicine.

◆ ◆ ◆

HUNCHED IN FRONT of the vanity, I was alone in the room. Wesley was at a morning rehearsal. We would get lunch together in town when he was back, but until then I was on my own.

The persistent headaches wouldn't chase themselves away without more. The highs lasted for less and less time. I presented an unbothered mask, but on the inside I was a jittering wreck of jellied, sandblasted nerves.

I tried to take less, which made me feel sick. So I took more to feel normal, and more, and further more. I was staring over the edge of a chasm with no foreseeable end, and for what? To languish in my own stale sweat in nothing but my underwear, hoping I would feel better?

I'd given up on getting dressed and was instead staring at what was left of the powder, trying to estimate how much I had to supply my current pace. I tallied and re-divvied the last of it out to six more days—eight, if I stretched it.

And beyond that, nothing but my own misery.

Except: the small packet of Haas's product.

I'd kept it sandwiched in the pages of my pocket calendar in my suitcase, like an ornery dog that didn't play well with others and needed to be kenneled separately. And still it beckoned with a desperation I could feel in the root of my tongue. I wanted to hold off. I wanted to save it. It was a last resort.

But I'd been made weak by loneliness. If the only person I had to watch after me was myself, I knew how that would end.

I flipped to the sachet in the agenda book and stared at the drug. It looked harmless.

Easy.

Haas seemed to know exactly what I needed, without my even asking. It felt nice to be looked after.

I took half the sachet.

It hit with stunning immediacy. Soft as silk, far more distilled, the tingling euphoria of being vaulted farther from my own body than ever before rushed up through my head. My eyes fluttered, and I stumbled back into the vanity seat. I pressed the heels of my hands to my eyes.

It had *never* felt this good before.

This was amazing. This was— Did everyone but me feel like this? If the drug was an interruption of my own bullshit patterns, at least by Dr. French's definition, then was Haas's product what a truly happy person felt like all of the time?

When I looked up again, blinking rapidly in the mirror, I was no longer alone. The Lady was perched on the foot of the bed, peering at me curiously.

I gasped, a flat hand flying to my chest in automatic shock. The Lady didn't flinch. "Jesus. What are you doing here?"

"Observing."

"I thought you— Why didn't you stay in New York?"

I'd figured my brief sightings of her were a figment of direct aftermath, a sad manifestation of me missing the role too dearly and the sharp pain of recalling my breakdown. I had hoped with distance she would have faded.

The Lady cast a dry look at the vanity top, where the compact and the unused rest of Haas's sachet sat like half-finished hors d'oeuvres. "Why have you allowed them to remove you from your own presence?"

Self-conscious, I tucked the powders away in my clutch. "You had your remedies, I have mine," I muttered. I blinked owlishly. *God*, I could feel *everything*—my pulse had dimension, and my thoughts ran in sprinting byways like liquid mercury, and there was nothing on this earth that made sense anymore if I could feel this endless and not wake up dead at the end of it.

The Lady gave me a curious look. "That was practical witchcraft. An honorable art."

I stared at her in the mirror. I drew myself up by a fraction, heightening my posture to match her own commanding stature. "It helps me."

"By blunting your teeth?"

"I'd rather them blunted than use them to gnaw off my own leg," I said.

The Lady regarded me coolly. "And who set the trap in which you've been snared?"

"Who?"

"An animal does not bite unless it has been made desperate. It is not in the nature of wolves to hunt men unprovoked."

I stared at her, unblinking. "I'm not a man."

"And yet here you sit, filled with bolder humors than they."

A chill ran through me—not unwelcome for the prickling sweat that had come up along my skin. "You and I are not the same," I whispered.

The Lady's gaze flashed. "Aren't we?"

We stared at each other for a long while through the mirror. Neither of us blinked—until my lashes stung with dry impatience, and I broke the moment. The edges of my vision blurred to a soft pink with the sun coming through the red curtains.

"You are more like me than you care to acknowledge," the Lady said.

"Why, because we've both taken the blade to someone?" I spat. Dizziness pitched me softly. I gripped at the edge of the table and managed not to swoon. I shut my eyes. "Leave me be. I don't want to think about you right now."

The Lady said nothing else.

When I opened my eyes again, she was gone.

I stared at my reflection for a long time, finding new amusements in my face to which I hadn't been privy before the revelation of Haas's drug—the alluring little mole at the very edge of my top lip, the prettiness of my nostrils curving where they met my cheek, the shape of my mouth half-parted with desire.

An urgent pulse of need lit up between my legs. I pressed my thighs together and considered addressing it. I looked toward Haas's room, and thought *perhaps*—well, he was still at the theater, but . . . nothing. No coherence. I couldn't keep a thought together. All I could feel was my own swollen pulse.

I went outside, through the back door, the ground only dotted spare with anemic little sprigs of grass along the edge of the concrete basin. The sun had baked the earth to a hard and unyielding crust, but it was warm to the touch. I lowered myself down onto my back, my face tipped up to the sun, and felt held for the first time since before I knew what to call myself.

When a full sheen of sweat had bloomed across my body, clinging my clothing to my skin, I rose carefully to sit on the edge of the swimming pool with my feet dangling into the yawn of the diving end. I juggled my lighter from my pocket and smoked a cigarette before returning to the room.

I shed my dress and stepped into the welcome shock of a cold shower, shivering with a feeling like champagne bubbles moving along the back of my neck, the sides of my jaw, the backs of my eyes.

Damp and sated, I wrestled into a clean slip and switched the television on. I sprawled across the bed and stared at the flickering picture, some talk show with a spirited guest who had a lot to say about nothing, and felt myself return to tangibility in slow, small increments.

Wesley returned however long later—I looked at the clock on the bedside table when the lock rattled. It had only been forty-five minutes since I took the dose. It felt as though years had passed. I was entirely chemically different.

And yet here you sit, filled with bolder humors than they.

"Well, th— Oh, Jack, are you ill?"

Frowning, Wesley came over to the side of the bed.

"I'm fine. I took a nap," I rasped. I stared at him and wondered if he'd ever seen the edge of the earth like I had. Honesty took me before I could stop it: "Let me come to rehearsal tomorrow." I shut my eyes. "I can handle it."

Wesley plucked blithely at a flake of stale mascara stuck to my cheek. "It really is stunning; they got the construction dead to rights. I think you'll like it." He searched my face for a moment as I levered up carefully into a seat, rubbing at my eyes and fussing uselessly with my hair. "Why didn't you say something earlier?"

"I didn't want to bother you. You're having a lot of fun, and—"

"You come first, Jack," Wesley cut in gently. He smoothed his hand over my brow, as if checking for a fever. "You *always* come first."

I said nothing, but I gave him a sleepy smile. I searched inside for anxiety, fear, anger, and found nothing. Only silence.

He peered at me, looking distantly amused. "You sure you're okay?"

"I'm fine." I kissed him on the cheek and buttoned up the last button he'd forgotten on his shirt. "I promise."

14

En route to the Sumner Globe

INSTEAD OF PARTING from the company after breakfast the next morning, I stayed on Wesley's arm and piled into the vans to head to the lake. I felt like a girl riding the big yellow school bus for the first time—but instead of a lunch pail, I clutched fast to my purse and reminded myself I had my medicine if it became too much to see a theater at work again.

I'd mixed Haas's powder in with the rest of Dr. French's, which gave me another week of safety. I was unstoppable.

At the lakeshore, the drivers ferried us to the theater islet on pull-cord metal dinghies. As we carved through the water, I peered down into its murk. It was at least deep enough to get the engine rudders through, but otherwise I couldn't tell how far it went.

Wesley helped me from the boat onto a rickety dock, and smiled at me when I was on solid footing. "Ready, Jack?"

"Don't let me fall in," I said with a breathless huff of laughter. I followed after the company threading through the doors flung open at the rounded edge of the theater's outer wall.

I stood in the middle of the house and turned in a circle to take it all in, the open eye of the endless blue sky above, the peaked roof over the stage itself, the benches lining the packed dirt here in the middle, and there, the tiered rows of seats stretching up to the heights of the building. It smelled of fresh pine from the bare timbers. I was enchanted.

"Are you alright to explore?" Wesley asked, shedding his jacket.

"Can I?"

He smiled at my eagerness. "Of course. Just don't get lost."

"I'll turn back if I hit water."

The company settled into the familiar bustle of pre-rehearsal habits. Kline bumbled his way in across the apron, gesturing with a rolled-up folio in his hand at the stage crew and their half-finished set pieces scattered along the boards around a long feast table for the fifth act of *Titus*.

While they rehearsed, I ambled through the ascending levels of the house and sat periodically to watch the pell-mell practice from various vantage points—they were good, if stretched a little thin. The house was one great ring. All the seats angled forward to look down at the actors like gods watching their mortals at play.

A hard lance of daylight poured in through the open roof to soak the stage. I went from row to row to row in a slow progression, running my hands over the empty seats. I took a narrow staircase back down to the ground floor, steadying myself with a hand along the wall.

I sought the back halls, the true veins of the theater. I crept through the skeletal wood of the trap space, where I found a pit for instrumentalists that didn't exist. I skirted wide of the direct wings but climbed carefully up a ladder that let me peek into a loft above the main level—made for actors to portray deities, or ghostly visions, or the spirits of the west wind.

The rows of dressing rooms back on the ground floor were little more than broom closets, and in that regard, it was very familiar. Backstage magic, the charged current of it, filled me wholly. God, but I missed it.

There was music in the muffled thump and ramble of footsteps across the boards. If I shut my eyes, I could imagine there was an audience out there. I could imagine I was simply waiting to go on; ready for my cue.

My eyes welled up. "Shit," I hissed, pawing at my lashes, and hurried to find a bathroom.

A lone toilet, a sink, and a hangdog mirror waited back the way I'd come. At least the door locked. While I sat, I stole down a sniff of powder that helped me believe the watering in my eyes was from the sting rather than frustration.

I washed my hands in sputtering, rusty water and clenched my teeth together until the back of my mind began to fizzle apart. Wagging the dampness from my fingers, I leaned forward to rest my forehead on the mirror.

"Chin up, woman."

I stepped back and looked up, unmoved, to see the Lady standing behind me in the low, oblong light. I dabbed at the edge of my nose with the back of my hand. "I'm fine."

I put my compact away and sniffed as I stepped back, regarding her fully. She was giving me a calculating look.

"You are not a delicate liar."

"Well, I'm *fine*. Thanks for asking."

"Come now." She appraised me, keen eyes looking for flaws in a skein of weaving. "You spent so much time mired in the bogs of other women's tragedies, and now the only one you have left is your own. Is there no familiarity to be found?"

I frowned. "I wouldn't call this a tragedy. It's life."

"Are you happy, Margaret?"

I touched up one corner of my lipstick before drawing my shoulders back. "Of course I'm happy," I said, breezy, and smiled my finest smile. "Are *you* happy?"

The Lady leaned in to peer at the both of us from over my shoulder. I could swear I felt the brushing of her hair against the side of my face, the layers of her braids below her gold circlet. "Only because I learned of how to snap the chain that held me."

I flinched away from her, fumbling for the door handle, and sped from the bathroom down a back hallway that was still very much under construction. Long plastic tarps hung down from the ceiling, and I almost turned around again but for the sound of a voice carrying with fulsome intent: *"Well, that's a damn shame, ain't it? I'd be ever so keen to know why in the hell you figured that would work out in your favor."*

The sound of a dull *thwack* and a barely muffled wheeze of pain shuddered up from farther down the hall. I froze. The voice came again.

"You'll probably wanna start talking, or maybe I'll consider you a lost cause. Huh?"

Curiosity snared me the same way it used to when I peeked in on the meetings Mr. Matthews held in my mother's sitting room with strange, well-dressed men. Up on my toes to keep my shoe heels from clicking, I moved silently to a hole in the wall scaffolding where yellow light leaked from a small alcove. It shivered with passing shadows—pacing boots moved slowly along the floorboards, circling.

I put my eye up to the wall and looked in on the moment: Two of the drivers stood back with their corded arms crossed, flanking a man tied to a chair with a dirty gag in his mouth. He looked panicked, peering up at the pacing passage of someone else I couldn't see properly.

"I'll ask one more time," came the same voice as before. It was sweet as pie, smooth with unhurried purpose. "Are you gonna talk, or will we have to find a nice deep hole outside of Mosquero with your name on it?"

The man tied to the chair breathed hard through his bleeding nose but stayed quiet. He fixed his stare forward, glaring at nothing, and finally the speaker came into view: the mustachioed cowboy with the orange Corvette who had greeted Kline when we first arrived. I hadn't seen a wink of him since, but now here he was in the belly of the theater doing ugly work. His hat was off, his silver hair slicked back. He wore fine boots on his feet and had an easy lope to his long legs.

He sauntered up behind the man in the chair and rested a tender touch on the crown of his sweating, stringy-haired head. "You know," the cowboy said gently, peering down at the trembling man with what looked like true concern, "I have to respect your conviction. I really do. You've got integrity, and I gotta think there's something worth keeping in there."

The cowboy reached into his pocket, and the light winked gently from the red enamel of a folded knife handle. "But maybe," he cooed, leaning down to hover at the man's shoulder, "maybe not your tongue. What do you think?"

The cowboy looked up, the sharp flick of his eyes cutting straight through the gap and meeting mine in an instant—his gaze flashed, invigorated. "What do you think about that?" he repeated with a grin and flicked the blade out with a twitch of his wrist.

I hurried backward as the man shouted against the gag and began to buck—the heavy thumping of the chair legs rattled against the floor, and then the sound of him choked off.

I turned and sped back down the hallway, careful to stay silent even in my hurry.

He saw me.

What did that mean for me? What was this place, really?

That was a knife with a mean-looking blade.

I leaned against the wall and shut my eyes, catching my breath back. I sagged and focused on the steady centering exercises Dr. French had taught me: In through the nose, out through the mouth. In through the nose, out through th—

"Margaret?"

I jumped, my eyes flying open, and found Haas standing in the mouth of his workshop. A half-manic chuckle chuffed from my chest. "Oh, God. Hello. You scared me."

"Are you alright?" Haas glanced with steely eyes over my shoulder, down the hallway I'd just come out of.

"Yes. I'm fine, I'm—I just got lost. I was exploring, *completely* turned around back there. All that construction . . . it's silly. I panicked over nothing. I'm fine."

I gave him the winningest grin I could manage. Haas came over and put his arm around my shoulders.

"If you intend to wander in this place," he said easily, steering us back toward the winding hall that fed into the house, "tread lightly."

"Why's that?" I fussed at the edges of my hair for something to do with the last of my nervous energy. "Loose timbers?"

"Unpredictable men."

The simple clarity of the warning jammed me into silence for a moment. I cleared my throat and lifted my chin slightly. "What do you mean?"

"Some men are like land mines," Haas said, half-wearily, as though having to impart a lesson to a younger student. "Tread on the wrong part of his pride, and it all goes up in smoke."

Haas gave me a dry, perfunctory smile and gestured ahead of us, *After you.*

Onstage, it seemed the entire cast had been doused in sugar blood—the scene was a mess of dramatic slaughter, the climax of the tragedy at its fever pitch. Haas put one hand on his hip as he pawed the other down across his mouth. He growled a low oath to himself in German, and then flashed me a wry look. "I'm going to be scouring those godforsaken doublets until my fingers fall off."

"Do you want help?" I asked.

"That's kind of you. I wouldn't want you to ruin your manicure."

I snorted, held out my cracked cuticles, and looked up to find Haas smiling at me—truly smiling, and I glowed with the sense I'd caught him in unexpected pleasure.

The company broke for the afternoon, the bloodied ones among them wagging strings of thick, syrupy crimson from their limbs. Haas held up a hand to hail Wesley. He bounded from the stage to the floor with his buttons open to his undershirt, blood-soaked with a syrupy smell hanging heavy in the air about him. Wesley grinned, a hearty flush under his cheeks.

"I haven't fenced like that since university," he said, panting. He kissed me on the forehead, smearing a small track of red at my ear, and cast a private look at Haas.

"What say you get cleaned up," Haas offered, nodding his chin at Wesley, "I lend you some fresh weeds, and we three find some lunch?" He drew a set of van keys from his pocket and nodded over his shoulder. "There's a place further west down the highway that knows how to salt their food."

Wesley beamed. I couldn't help but mimic him, despite the brackish churn in my gut from what I'd seen backstage—*What do you think about that?*

Haas caught my eye. He quirked another brief, knowing smile, and led us out to the lakeshore together.

◆ ◆ ◆

WESLEY WORE HAAS'S clothes well. Where Wesley's palette was full of slates and blues, cooler colors against his complexion, the warmer-toned finer fabric of Haas's wardrobe lent a summery flair that brought him a certain radiance—or perhaps that was just him being near Haas, the juvenile flush of adoration mixing well with liquor.

We were forty minutes outside of town at a cramped cantina where nobody spoke English, but we'd been able to pantomime enough of what we wanted that we found ourselves pleasantly tipsy and filled with food as the sun hung swollen and high in the sky.

I had never before tasted spices with these sharp, earthy flavors. Haas ordered a tequila for himself after we finished our food, and it arrived plainly poured on an earthenware dish with two small piles of salt and cinnamon on the edge. I couldn't help but watch each sip he took—casual as anything he would lick the pad of his thumb, press it into the salt and cinnamon, stripe that off on the tip of his tongue, and then finally take a sip from the tiny cup; savoring the flavor, dragging his lips across his teeth. Haas caught me looking more than once. I was intimately aware of my own tongue darting out against the rim of my glass to catch the salt stuck there.

As the men collected their hats after paying the bill, Haas looked pointedly at me. "Margaret," he offered, "would you care to join us for an aperitif in my room?"

Wesley looked amused. "Aren't those for before the meal?"

Haas's eyes crawled briefly, hungrily over me, as though the empty plates on the table meant nothing. "Precisely."

I glanced between the both of them. Wesley pulled an expression of neutrality, *Your choice, Jack*, and fit his hat down over his brow.

Looking pointedly at Haas, I made the same gesture at the front door of the restaurant he'd made in the theater house earlier—*After you.*

We crossed the wide gravel lot back to the van. "Don't you have another rehearsal?" I asked.

Haas hefted open the door to the van and tossed the keys to Wesley, who caught them easily in one hand. "Not until evening," Haas insisted. "Plenty of time." He held out a hand to help me into the seat.

Wesley rounded the flat nose of the van to get to the driver's seat, and Haas climbed into the back after me. He hauled the door shut, tucked his glasses neatly into his breast pocket, and rounded on me with a starved kiss as the engine growled to life.

I hardly had time to react but for a sharp inhale—my body surged immediately with the instinct to turn toward desire. I crushed Haas's lapels in two messy fists as Wesley backed out onto the main road, tires jostling, and Haas arranged me easily along the seat. He kissed his way down the open expanse of my neckline and painted his hands up the curve of my waist. Sitting back on his heels, both of us flushed, Haas hunted in his inside breast pocket. He proffered a neat envelope of paper, which was filled with white powder when he tipped open the edge with one finger.

"Did you enjoy the sample?" he asked, brisk with appetite.

"I was going to ask for more after you drove us back," I admitted, giddy and addled by the foreign rush of being touched so ravenously.

I leaned up and took my usual measure of Dr. French's powder without thinking to pare it down for the strength of Haas's product. He took a sniff and offered it to the front seat without looking away from me, his expression terribly pleased.

"None for me, thanks," Wesley said, glancing up at us in the rearview. Unbothered, Haas finished off the rest of it. He pinched shortly at his nose and blinked several times, before licking his thumb and swiping it over the dust left on the paper to streak his gums.

He offered his thumb to me. I took it into my mouth, holding the sear of his eye contact as I sucked, and tasted the lingering salt and cinnamon still left behind in his fingerprint. I tugged him back down by the end of his tie.

The overwhelming presence of everything took on a plush, soft volume behind my eyes—a thick droplet of blood, breaking into meandering threads in water. The rush was exactly as I remembered and more.

It was better than any feeling I'd ever believed could find quarter in this body.

Wesley parked in the spot outside room number five. Clamoring out of the van, my skirt rumpled and my stockings in disarray, the men steadied me between both of them. We stumbled to Haas's room, and I glanced at Wesley—he was making his smug *I told you so* face, the one that made me break during rehearsals when one of us forgot or flubbed a line, so of course I lost the battle against the giggle that broke hard from the edges of my teeth.

By the time we made it over the threshold, I was guffawing into Wesley's neck as he caught me with barely enough time to keep me from going sprawling. I stumbled inside as Haas crowded in neatly after me.

Haas shut the door behind him and wasted no time catching Wesley in a kiss that firmed him back up against it, fumbling to slide the safety chain into its latch without looking.

I sat at the foot of the bed and pried off my shoes. My head had flown far away from me. Every sensation puffing and wisping through the air was concentrating itself in my chest, my throat, my pounding skull, and all of it trickled steadily down to pool around my hips.

Haas pulled back just enough to shuck and toss his jacket over the edge of a desk chair, switch on the lamp, and tug his tie knot apart to slip it off over his head. Wesley kept himself busy with his mouth along the cords of Haas's neck.

"Come here," Haas rasped, looking right down to the very heart of me.

I laughed again and sprawled backward on the bed, laying my arms out long above me just to feel the stretch, and lolled my head sideways to look at them both urgent and half-bare. "You come *here*," I sang.

"Felix," Wesley hummed against the ridge of Haas's jaw. He was fumbling with both of their belts. "Be sweet."

"You want sweet?"

Wesley grinned through another kiss. "Sure. Why not."

Haas nodded his chin at the bed. "Then go sit and watch."

Wesley came to sit on the bed with me, briefs and sock garters still on. Haas took his time stepping out of his own fine clothes—cuff links unclipped, shoes toed off, laces neatened, trousers into a crisp fold, shirt stays unclipped, shirt shrugged off and smoothed over the jacket across the chair. With his undershirt tugged off from the back of his neck before folding it with automated precision, Haas brought himself elegantly bare, down to nothing but undershorts.

"Dress off, Margaret," he said, kneeling before me and running his hands along my calves.

I spread my knees. "Why don't y—"

"Dress," Haas cut in smoothly, his grip tightening gently into the give of my flesh. "Off. Margaret."

That soft heat coiling in my belly tightened like the jolt of acceleration out of a starting gate. I sat up as Wesley worked down the zipper. It hissed from my shoulders to the lower curve of my back, where he and Haas slid it off me.

"Is this alright?" Wesley murmured at my ear. I was several light-years away, merely observing the unfolding like a diorama as my pulse ran, ran, ran—I nodded and hummed.

Wesley reached down and unclipped my stockings. Haas rolled them away and tucked them neatly into the toes of my shoes.

With two fingers hooked around the elastic, Haas slid my shorts down to my ankles as I did away with the clasp of my brassiere. He put a hand to my flank and kissed me high on my hip, and when I laid back down again peeled to nakedness, I rested my head companionably on Wesley's thigh.

I looked upside down at Wesley and smiled dreamily at the blush staining his face. "I think I might like it here, this way," I told him.

"I figured you would," he whispered. I shut my eyes and laughed again with a freedom I hadn't believed for years could be mine.

The wet heat of Haas's tongue pressed into me without warning.

I choked on a sharp, ecstatic gasp. My hands, flailing softly, flew down to knit themselves in his hair.

"Oh, shit," I breathed up at the ceiling. Wesley skated his own fingers up the back curve of my head, combing softly down to my scalp.

I squeezed my eyes shut and gasped at the concentrated feeling—more intimate than a kiss.

Breathless laughter hitched low along my ribs and pulled, punching itself up with a throaty leap as Haas's mouth worked against me. I flexed my fists against his roots and drew an attendant groan from him, the hot burst of air from his nose fluttering against me.

What *was* this? This—the feeling was foreign, almost violent with insistent pleasure. Profane. Glorious.

Haas ministered until I was nothing but a melted wash of sensation. The building of my limit was sharp, harrowing, more sudden and far denser than I'd ever been able to cause on my own.

When I pitched over its edge, my body jumped and seized with live-wire tremors as I tried not to make too much noise. Wesley whispered encouragement into my temples, my hairline, the corners of my eyes, where thrilled tears had built. I was endless, one with everything for just a moment.

Haas sat back in a kneel with a victorious look in his eye, wiping at the corners of his mouth with the edges of one hand. The sight of him beholding me with my taste on him lit a primal hunger of my own in my gut.

He crawled onto the bed and let Wesley do away with the maroon satin of his shorts. His body was lithe, wiry with control and fine training. He was hard and brazen in the half-light. Floating in my afterglow, I watched him sprawl out long.

Leaning down smoothly, as Haas combed a guiding hand into the sweat-damp waves beginning to coil at the back of his head, Wesley took Haas easily into his mouth. "Go on," Haas said, feather-light and yet brooking no argument, and groaned his low approval as Wesley reached down past his own waistband and obeyed.

The immovable cleaving of Haas's eyes latched into mine as Wesley worked intently on him. His pupils were huge and dark, swallowing me whole, and I watched with my restive heart in my mouth to fear losing even a moment of the sight by blinking.

They were wondrous, the communion of them, in that same urgent and fundamental way Haas's tongue on me had been.

I was looking out over the precipice of my own belonging, fearless of the plunge, and could not look away.

Haas losing his composure was quick and subtle—he made a hurried fist in Wesley's hair, pulling an encouraging grunt from him as his own pace picked up, and those long, pale lashes fluttered once against Haas's cheeks. His mouth fell open with a soundless gasp, and he looked away from me to the soft edge of where the light fell to shadow against the carpet.

In the collapse of his expression came to me a knowledge I hadn't thought to seek: Men, just as weak to the pull of the self; that same obligatory need which pressed us hard against the line of madness.

Hysteria.

Haas caught his breath. Wesley had pulled off, panting against Haas's hip as he rose toward his own point of no return. He let out a hitched, damp gasp when Haas's hold in his hair tugged again.

"On Margaret," Haas said, and looked directly at me as he reached to light a cigarette from Wesley's case on the nightstand.

Wesley went up to his knees with his eyelids heavy and low, unfocused. His frame trembled with the tensile stress of need. I reached out and cradled him where the back of his thigh turned into the curve of one buttock, staring unblinking at Haas.

Wesley made a bruised cry as he broke like a stone from a sling across my stomach.

The three of us returned to ourselves in the long stillness of frayed endings. Haas gave Wesley a sip of the cigarette, who passed it to me, and I sat up carefully to take a short draw before handing it back to

Haas. He was staring with a bone-deep satisfaction at the sight of us before him, absolutely sated.

Wesley was the first to stand. He laved a spent kiss to Haas's shoulder and staggered to the bathroom to fetch a washcloth.

We tidied one another, pastoral and careful. The bed was hardly habitable with three of us, but for the moment it would hold—I shimmied up between the two of them and shut my eyes when they each slung an arm around my waist.

Tucked there, my heart beat over-present with such richness I feared it might swell out from under my skin and run away. I stroked my hands over each body flanking me: the sturdy trunk of Wesley's leg, the dark fur of him curling softly on the ridge of his knee, and the mussed slouch of Haas's once-orderly hair so fine I could barely feel it sliding through my fingers.

"Alright, Felix," I murmured, "I think I qualify now: Who's pulling your strings?"

Haas sniffed an amused chuckle and leaned into my touch. "Fine. Are you good at keeping secrets?"

"Masterful."

"Kline and I have a side project," Haas said. "We sell product for a volatile sort, but we skim and cut a portion of it with my own home brew that nets pure profit. You're feeling it right now, you tell me. It's good, isn't it?"

I thought only fleetingly of the cowboy backstage before the drug snatched away my concern, tossing the idea to the wind of aimless pleasure. I groaned happily, stretching long through my back to arch sweetly along his side. "Better than what the doctor ordered."

"I'm being kept on a very tight leash," Haas whispered at my neck, kissing me slowly, "for having such thrilling ingenuity."

"Poor you," I breathed.

"Not to interrupt," Wesley said lightly, reaching over me to set a gentle hand on the bend of Haas's hip, "but we have another call in an hour."

"I'll drive us," Haas said against my throat. "Don't worry. Lie here for a while, won't you?"

I reveled in the aftermath of us. The promise of sex was alluring, but so was the fevered fascination of men keeping secrets; a temptation toward which I had been conditioned, touching it but briefly as I came to understand the man who refused to call himself my father but still insisted I behave like a daughter—or the man who cleaved me to his ego, and only bound me more tightly once he realized I had no intention of making that easy.

This was the closest I'd ever come to holding agency in my own hands.

Here, I was a solid thing, thick and vital with purpose.

15

The Lake Sumner motel, room number five

A TIDY TAPPING at the edge of the storm door woke me the next morning like a small bird pecking at a tree to check for breakfast.

I blinked in the early light pushing through the curtains and sat up before remembering Haas had come over to our room after dinner, where we eventually fell asleep on the floor in a nest of blankets and pillows pulled down from the beds after more of his product and the blitz of pleasure.

Behind me, Wesley was in the middle. Haas had an arm thrown across him, and Wesley's nose had been nuzzled against my neck. They were both still out cold.

Taktaktak.

I stood up before the noise could wake them too. Dragging at my cheeks to tug my consciousness to the surface, I shrugged my robe around my shoulders and unfastened the safety chain to slip outside and shut the door softly behind me.

"Can I help you?" I held in a yawn and looked up as I crossed my arms over my chest. The pale sun was still eking its way up from the endless, flat horizon smattered only distantly with the heavy hips of mountains.

The cowboy from that backstage alcove removed his hat and nodded at me. He was wearing a plain white undershirt beneath a tan jacket and a matching pair of trousers, held up by a belt buckle studded thick with lapis stones. A pair of mirrored sunglasses over his eyes showed me my distended reflection. "Morning, ma'am."

I frowned and angled myself away from him ever so slightly. "Morning."

"Pardon the hour," he said, gesturing humbly with his hat. "I was wondering if I might make a small request, as you haven't the particular mantle of responsibility as the rest of our fine company."

Tread on the wrong part of his pride, and it all goes up in smoke. I nearly shrank further into myself for just a moment, but held my ground and looked the man directly where I assumed his gaze was meeting mine. "And what might that be, Mr. . . . ?"

The man ducked his pepper-haired head and put his hat back on with practiced ease. "Jesse. Nothing serious at all, Mrs. Shoard. I'd only appreciate it if you'd keep those lovely brown eyes of yours peeled here among the rabble for any, shall we call it, subterfuge."

He held out a hand. I took it, prepared to give him a farewell and ignore the strange request—then balked when the feeling of tightly rolled dollar bills met my palm. I peered at him, our hands still clasped. "I don't make a habit of taking hush money, sir."

"Please," he said with a smile, charming to the bone, "call me Jesse. And that's not for keeping quiet."

"Then what's it for?"

"Consider it an advance."

The sunlight glinted from the edge of Jesse's sunglasses. I took my hand back without taking the money and crossed my arms again. "I don't snitch."

Jesse's grin twitched, as though picking up an unexpected scent. "Perish the thought," he said. "I only value knowing any information to which my attentions might not be directly privy from a little higher up the mountain."

"Then make your own way down every now and then to look for it yourself."

Jesse made a wry expression and spread his hands. He glanced pointedly up and down the empty breezeway, silently asking, *What the hell do you think I'm doing out here?*

"I've known dozens of men like you," I said.

Jesse looked pleased, like I'd done a card trick for him. "And how's that?" He set his weight back on his heels and rested his thumbs on his belt. He didn't have a holster strapped to it, but I wouldn't have written off the high possibility of a shoulder harness under his jacket.

Dozens of men like him.

"Pardon the assumption, but you look like the sort of lady who'd rather cross the street if you saw a 'man like me' coming your way."

"Well maybe you aren't one of 'em, then." I raised my eyebrows. "They usually sweep in without bothering to ask my preference first."

Jesse regarded me keenly. "Where you from, Mrs. Shoard?"

"Grew up in Cherokee Park, in Lexington." The name still bit at my tongue on the way out.

"No shit? One of the guys in the outfit is from thereabouts."

"You think we had homeroom together in junior high?" I said tartly.

We watched each other in a long stretch of silence. Far away—the desert was flat enough that the sound might have carried from clear across the county—a dog barked with a quick, asymmetric report.

"Any of the other boys know any of this about you?" Jesse asked. He had an easy tone for speaking everything as though we were having any old conversation between friends, the texture of it like well-worn denim. It had dropped to placid secrecy, as though he trusted me differently with this new knowledge.

"As far as I'm concerned, they don't even know my name."

"Good. Keep it that way."

"So you *are* that kind of man."

Jesse tipped the brim of his hat at me and pocketed the money. "Not always myself, but some of the others never quite learned their manners."

"Noted," I said, shifting to cinch my robe more tightly around my waist.

"You have a lovely day now, Mrs. Shoard," Jesse said.

I watched him lope to the Corvette. The tapered legs of his pants revealed brief flashes of rich brown boots crunching over the dust, the block heels and pointed toes wrapped in hammered silver. Jesse vaulted over the convertible door into the driver's seat and saluted me in one last farewell as he gunned the engine. Dust peeled behind him in great clouds as he steered northward, toward the lake.

I leaned back against the motel façade and slipped my cigarette case from the pocket of my robe. I lit and smoked one down with brutal efficiency.

Glaring into the distance, the empty silence of early morning, I tried to unshoulder the incessant pressing of old memories clawing against the walls I had very purposefully built to keep them out.

When I slipped back into the room and safety-latched the door, I found Haas had risen. Wesley was still heavily asleep—he had kicked free of the sheets twisted around his body, and his arms held a pillow in a chokehold with his face pressed fast to the lumpy down.

The soft clatter of preparing coffee came from the kitchenette. Haas, awake and industrious.

Haas, who had become a conduit in the low light and long shadows of the bedroom lit only by a single lamp; his mouth on me, his hands gripped hard to my hips, the communicable patter of sex working its way up his body as Wesley ministered to him like another limb from the same body.

I blinked. *Coffee.* I needed coffee.

I sidled through the pocket door to the other half of the suite and pulled it shut behind me. Haas had the percolator going on the hot plate, three of the mismatched cups on the counter, and was smoking the last of a tidily rolled cigarette.

"Good morning," I said.

Haas turned to me with a small, tired smile. Despite the minimal sleep we'd all gotten, he looked shoddily immaculate: hair parted, a shirt hanging open over his shoulders, satin shorts hitched back up over the subtle severity of his hips. The easy line of his freckled torso twisted, lithe, as he leaned back against the counter.

"Morning. Did you sleep well?"

I yawned behind the back of one hand. "I did, yes. Deeply."

Haas made an amused sound around another peck of smoke. I recalled the sight of him looking up from between my knees with a similar look, an angle of victory. "You enjoyed yourself, then?"

I peered at him for a moment. "Yes," I admitted, the whole and simple truth. "I did, very much."

"Good."

Haas turned back to the hot plate. I fiddled with the flyaway hairs at the back of my neck. "How long have you been up?"

"Oh, not long," he said as he rummaged through the paltry cabinets. "Is there any sugar?"

I hunted the box I'd bought the first day here and passed it to Haas. Our thumbs brushed. "Do you know a man called Jesse?" I asked.

Haas glanced at me with a frown. "Jesse?"

I considered the truth for a moment. "The—one with the hat, and the boots. And the convertible. He offered me money for information."

Haas's cheek flexed ever so slightly as he clenched his teeth, staring at the stovetop. "Jesse Malus," he said crisply—his gaze went a touch faraway for a moment. When he came back to himself, the light flaring across the back of his gaze, he gave me a brittle smile. "You'd be smart not to take whatever it is he offered. He isn't the sort to be trusted."

"How do you know him?"

Haas sized me up keenly before measuring out two dinged-up spoons of sugar into his own cup. "I could ask the same of you."

"I haven't the faintest. If anyone knows the first thing about this outfit," I said, frowning, "it's Ezra. And he isn't in the habit of giving details—he tells his company to jump, we ask how high."

"Ezra." Haas sighed knowingly. He glanced over his shoulder to find me still frowning. "What?"

"You said it yourself, *Ezra*—what's the connection?"

Haas rolled the tip of his tongue across his top teeth under his lip and tapped out his cigarette in the chipped crystal dish beside the burner. "Less than legal lending sources," he said steadily and gave me a wan grin. "That's about the sum of it."

"Then what about you?"

Haas tipped his head ever so slightly. "What about me?"

He was still smiling, but with a sharpness; diversion. I raised an eyebrow and nodded backward over my shoulder at the bedroom. "Call me old-fashioned, but if we're going to make this a regular thing, I'd like to know a little more about you besides the fact you're dealing drugs for someone who offers hush money. My husband has been burnt before."

Haas pursed his lips and crossed his arms loosely over his chest. "And you haven't?"

I said nothing.

"I was born in Austria," Haas recited, as though ticking through a mental list, "came up as a tailor's apprentice, moved with my mother to New York between the wars, and found a haven of particular taste in the theater, as well as the American privilege of supplementing my income with discreet dealings for Jesse and his ilk through my workshop. Anything else you need to file away for your records, Mrs. Shoard?"

I watched him and thought back to the first time Wesley had told me of Andrew. "Does Wesley know any of this?"

"He knows exactly what I just told you," Haas said, turning to shut off the hot plate as the percolator came to a soft, growling boil. "As you've seen, it hasn't stopped him getting on his knees for me, so I would say he at least marginally approves."

I didn't love his tone, but I couldn't begrudge him finally being forthcoming. He swirled the percolator, turning the handle of each empty mug to face the same way.

"Come, Margaret, don't be silly." Haas glanced up at me as he set to pouring three coffees from the spotty urn. He took up the sugar box again and wagged it jauntily at me before putting it back in the cupboard. "Das Leben ist kein Zuckerschlecken."

I made a doubtful face. "Which means?"

"Life is not all licks of sugar. But we make the best of the hands we've been dealt. Don't tell me you wouldn't do the same to look after yourself; I see you, Margaret, there's fight in you."

I regarded him with measured patience. Perhaps that was why I was so drawn to him—deep down, I could feel the current of danger in him and longed to spark my own skin by drawing close.

"How are you so sure of that?" I asked.

Haas's brows drew softly at their middle. "How do you mean?"

"You hardly know me."

Haas gave me a soft, knowing smile. "I saw you in *Othello*, have I told you that?" he murmured. "You are a truly extraordinary actress. But you knew that."

The particularity of his body, the liquid iron of his limbs, seemed to soften while he beheld me. However brief the moment, it intoxicated me entirely. I swallowed.

"I *used* to be." My voice was pale, no contrarian left in it.

Haas took up two of the coffees. "We will pass a very fine summer here," he said brightly, "you'll see. Steer wide of Jesse and his ilk, and it will be a very sweet lick of sugar."

He moved past my demurring half-step out of his way and drew so near I could smell the sylvan whiff of pomade still clinging to his hair. Haas leaned sideways and caught me lightly with a kiss on my cheek.

The thought hit me gently, like the wafting scent: "*Othello* was *years* ago," I said.

"Was it?" Haas hummed blithely. "Time flies."

I stood there peering at a peeling corner of the kitchenette linoleum and listened to him go—soft steps along the carpet before setting one mug on the nightstand and kneeling to wake Wesley with a murmur.

I took up the third coffee. The first sip scalded the tip of my tongue.

◆ ◆ ◆

LATER THAT WEEK, I knocked on the open archway of Haas's workshop in the theater and waited for him to look up from his sewing machine. Under the yellow halo of light from the bulb above him, its wires running like exposed veins along the bare wooden beams, he looked like a fastidious saint of rich fabrics and hand-stitched pockets.

"Are you using the van?" I asked.

I hadn't stopped to think until then how many hours of work Haas must have put into the costuming, all on his own—Kline didn't seem to have any other tailors in his file that he could convince to come along.

Haas's glasses were perched low on the tip of his nose. He peered at me over the frames and didn't stop the pedal, the *chatta-chatta-chatta* of its rhythmic, hurried churn.

"Right now?" he said flatly, with a wink of humor behind his eyes. "I don't know, perhaps I might be."

I gave him my most enticing smile. "Could I trouble you for the key?"

"So you can abscond into the untamed wilderness?" He looked back down at the needle, steering the fabric in a smooth arc around an edge. I strolled into the space and drew up beside him to peer over his shoulder.

"So I can get my hair done properly before I go insane," I said lightly, bending down to flirt at his ear.

Haas made a neutral sound but didn't stop working. I waited, hovering at his shoulder, the warmth of his cheek in the narrow space between us as I watched the fine stitch run under his dancing needle.

"Who taught you to drive?" he asked, not looking up.

"My mother," I said. She'd taken me to the empty parking lot of the liquor store the first Sunday after my thirteenth birthday. My feet only just reached the pedals.

"How terribly modern," Haas said breezily. "The key is in my left front pocket."

"And which of us is going to reach for it?"

"Which of us indeed."

I pressed up along his side to reach my arm around his back, creeping my fingers brazenly, slowly along the ridge of his waist. Inside his pocket, warmed by his body, I closed my fingers around the key and took my time sliding it back out.

"Do you need it back anytime soon?" I asked, my teeth barely teasing his earlobe.

Haas reached the end of his stitching and snipped off the end of his thread. He slid his right hand under my skirt and squeezed high up on the inside of my thigh—I flinched, twitching closer to him and leaning heavily on his broad shoulders.

"I'll let you determine how quickly you need to return," he said around one end of the thread held between his incisors, still not looking at me, and neatly tied off the stitching with one hand. His grip persisted, intensifying for a moment that nearly bordered on pain—I bit my lip when he let go, sensation rushing back into my flesh.

"Run along." I could see at the edge of Haas's lips that he was smiling to himself, so subtly it only barely lit the corners of his gaze.

I straightened my dress and took a few steps back. The flush on my cheeks had a hot, cottony burn to it. "Tell Wesley I'll be back before sundown," I blurted, and hurried to the dock for a ride back to the shore.

◆ ◆ ◆

THE TOWN OF Santa Rosa was a single step up from Lake Sumner in terms of liveliness. At least here, wrestling with the gear shift and steering wide around every turn, I saw handfuls of people on the sidewalk going between storefronts or driving alongside me.

The salon I found was called Connie's, on the corner of the only road I could hazard to call anything close to busy. I manhandled the van into a parking spot, did my best to touch up my makeup in the side mirror, and went inside to see what passed for a salon this far west.

Salons in the city were an ecosystem all their own—the ultimate bastion of femininity, the germinated seed of status and the ground floor of the social climber's starting ascent. Hair, nails, tweezing and plucking and bleaching and waxing: one of the only realms in the world we could truly call our own.

The bell above the lintel chimed as I pushed the door in. A few heads turned toward me, some lined with curlers under the massive hoods of dryer chairs, others with their legs crossed only sparing a glance up from a glossy magazine. A young woman behind a front desk with a wedge of cardboard under one of its legs gave me a once-over.

"Cut or color?" she drawled.

I gave her my least obtrusive smile. "Just a set and shellac."

The woman looked down at the wrinkled agenda book in front of her. "Appointment?"

"No, walk-in."

Turning in her chair, peering around the shop, the woman called out, "Darla!" When she turned frontward again, it was straight back to the crossword on her folded-over newspaper without another look at me. "Third chair," she said, and licked the tip of her pencil.

Darla was a woman with a broad, pretty smile who looked like she'd been made from still-proofing dough by a very attentive, affectionate sculptor. Her fingers against my scalp were warm and quick as she asked me what I was doing in town.

"We don't get many unfamiliar faces," she said, smiling through the mirror.

I adjusted my smile, watching the edges of my top teeth come into view with the angle Edie tended to call my *I Promise* smile—as in *I really am fine, I promise, now quit asking.*

"Just passing through," I said.

Darla pulled a brush from the apron around her waist and began to section my hair. The narrow-faced woman letting bleach work at her roots in the chair beside me glanced up from her magazine. The cape draped over her shoulders swallowed the rest of her body into an amorphous, off-red blob. "Heading east," she asked, "or west?"

"West," I said, making nice through the mirror. The woman hummed around the plastic end of her long, yellowed cigarette filter.

"You going to Albuquerque?"

I thought of Wesley. "California."

She hummed again, knowingly. "Could have guessed. You're too glamorous for Albuquerque." A cloud of white smoke pistoned up from the corner of her thin, creped lips painted beet red. I tried to divine how old she was—either younger than expected for her leathery suntan, or much older and aided by the lightness of her hair. The bleach tickled at my nostrils.

The blonde woman didn't look up from her magazine as she slowly turned the page, her gaze tracking it lazily as though she hadn't quite finished reading it yet. "My brother lives in Albuquerque," she appended, sucking on the plastic filter again.

I made a vaguely interested sound of acknowledgment. Behind me, Darla chuckled.

"The idiot or the Casanova?"

Both women shared a laugh—Darla's throaty and rounded, the blonde's brittle as a crow's cackle.

"The idiot," the blonde said. "I tell you he went looking for work with those wiseguys?"

Darla, who had begun winding my hair into rollers with swift and tidy habit, scoffed in response. I watched all three of us through the mirror. The blonde woman shifted in her seat and looked at me as though stooping to give an aside to the audience.

"All those *families* out east," she said, her voice pitched to mock-lowness, "a few of 'em tried to burrow into those Italians who set up shop in Albuquerque before the war."

"*Lots* of Italians there," Darla muttered as though it was a secret. They both said it with a long *i*, *eye*-talians.

"You know Sherry, with the baby?" The blonde woman asked. Darla nodded. "She told me once her uncle-in-law and a few of his old friends stood watch at the train station out there when they got word a bunch of bosses had hitched a car to come and try staking their claims. Whole row of 'em with their big mustaches and bowler hats, standing on the platform in Sunday best with their rifles! Train car rolled open, wiseguys found themselves cross-eyed looking down the barrels; stay on the train, they said, keep moving."

The blonde paused for another long mouthful of smoke, her tobacco wrapped with pink paper the color of stomach medicine. Darla was already more than halfway done placing the rollers in my hair.

"Few of 'em turned around and dug in here instead—didn't want to go home empty-handed," Darla supplied, like a human footnote. "Their gals are pretty as anything, all gussied up—dumb as bricks, bless their hearts, but sweet as can be. They tip real good, too."

"All that to say," the blonde woman sighed in conclusion, turning back to her magazine with an air of finality, "my brother's a real character. I told him if he wants work, it should be honest work. Set him up with a mechanic instead."

Darla laughed again, with the surprised gusto that indicated a long-standing inside joke. The blonde woman looked pleased with herself.

I chuckled gamely to play my part as the amused out-of-towner. If nothing else, it was heartening to know there was still gossip outside of the city. Darla herded me to one of the open dryers and indicated a stack of magazines from 1954.

Staring through an old spread of Lambert's "Best Dressed Women," I realized I felt more centered amid a gaggle of chatty strangers than I did anymore in a theater. I didn't trust myself enough to turn that revelation over without a dose of powder—I was still trying to be good with my rations. I didn't want to ask for too much from Haas. He was already fucking me. Wouldn't want to get greedy.

When my hair was done, I looked fresher than I had in weeks. I tipped Darla real good.

Two scattered blocks away from the salon, a phone booth baked in the sun. I waited for an old man inside to vacate it. When he came out, three nickels later, he jerked a thumb at the machine.

"My mother's a real piece of work," he said. He nodded at my hair. "You go to Darla?"

I glanced up from digging in my purse for change. "Yes, I did."

"Darla's a real piece of work. Have a nice day, sweetheart," he said with a pinched frown and shuffled down the sidewalk.

I watched him go as I thumbed my own coins into the slot. The exchange connected me to New York, and I waited for the line to pick up.

"Bishop."

"Margot again. I have news."

"Oh, *do* tell—the well is dry as a dowager here without you all."

I told her about the shady men of the outfit, Jesse and his ilk, how I'd been offered money for open ears and loose lips. Edie sounded unaffected.

"Of course they're shady," she said. "When has anything Ezra Pierce touched not been at least halfway tainted? He used to be a mess with gambling."

"Did he?"

"His only taste of it now is pissing away whatever time he's got left with those snobbish imps of his—although I suppose hinging his hopes on a man who drops him once something more exciting crosses his path is less embarrassing than a losing streak at craps."

"At least he's getting exercise," I said flatly.

Edie made a doubtful sound. "I've always preferred thinking of him as sexless, like an eel."

"Eels don't have sex?"

"What time is it over there, one in the afternoon? Are you drunk?"

"No." I peered at my nails. "I've been having some very good sex myself."

I could hear Edie's demeanor light up like a hound to the scent. "With Wesley?"

She sounded in awe. I snorted. "Not just."

I told her about Haas, just the essentials—Austrian, handsome, undiscerning, and eager to show off. Edie laughed when I told her nobody had ever used their mouth on me before, her disbelieving laugh, as though a punch line had caught her off guard.

"God, you *are* getting an education. Well, as much as I wish I could stay for more," she said, clearly bustling with the phone cradle in one hand to cart it with her through the apartment, "there's a luncheon I've already rain checked twice and really can't miss again. You *must* call back with more details later."

"So long as you don't take dictation," I said, grinning into the mouthpiece.

"Oh, you know I can't type. Ooroo, darling. Do keep having fun. It becomes you."

Back in the van, I turned on the radio. I glanced at my purse before cranking the gear into drive—I could do with a dose, but I felt fine.

I looked at myself in the rearview mirror as the engine grumbled and gave my most dazzling smile: hair neatly done, nerves set back to rights after a good cackle with Edie, all of me right where I should be.

I would be fine.

As I steered back toward Lake Sumner, I turned up the foggy planging of a slide guitar on the fuzzing radio band.

I would be *fine*.

16

ৎৎৎৎ

The Sumner Globe, Felix Haas's workshop

I TOOK TO joining Haas at the theater when I tired of watching *Titus* rehearsals—there was only so much I could take of the same dramatic mess unfolding over and over again on the boards stained red from all the sugar blood.

The company was doing a fine job of it. Wesley played a brilliant Marcus, but it was purely my own exhaustion that soured me on the show. I much preferred privacy with Haas, where I could watch him work and peruse the costumes and daydream about some of the better memories from my early days.

Before Jensen deemed me fit to go onstage with the Richmond Revue, when I was still just an errand girl sniffing after him like a lost puppy, helping the costumers had been my favorite job—assisting with the whirlwind of a quick-change; fetching this or that piece from the storage closet; hiding backstage during performances, mouthing along with the players onstage and imagining myself wearing every costume in the shop.

I was wandering through the mannequin rows and trying to recall if Ezra's rentals had ever been so fine as Felix Haas's handiwork. The sewing machine across the packed-tight room whirred at a steady pace, where Haas was finishing some hemming on several layers of skirts.

"Do you prefer comedies," I called over the chattering, "or tragedies?"

"Indifferent," Haas called back. "The costumes are the same."

"Not true."

"Oh?"

I peeked over the top of a rack at him, and the machine paused—he angled back to regard me in full. He looked doubtful.

"They're completely different," I insisted with a grin. "Costumes for tragedies should be terribly uncomfortable. If the actor is miserable, their character will be, too."

The sharp chips of Haas's eyes dug at me, not so much biting as they were seeking. "Is that what you needed to get into character? A costume telling you what to do?"

I ambled along the row of brocaded jackets, running my hand over their shoulders. "A good costume is *always* telling the actor what to do."

Haas pushed his glasses up his nose and looked at me without saying anything for a moment. "You haven't lost any of the love for it," he asked, "have you?"

I gestured broadly at the workshop, the theater, the discipline itself. "How could I ever?"

"You'd be surprised."

"It's worth it. Every inch of misery I've ever put on myself, the theater has made worth it."

"What do you consider misery?"

Haas held my gaze when I leveled a look at him.

I tipped my head at the sewing machine. "Don't you have work to do?"

"It's just hemming. I could hem in my sleep." Haas stood up from his workbench and began tidying it idly. "You seem more highly strung since yesterday."

The supposition hit me from left field and made me frown—although he wasn't wrong. I hadn't taken a dose yet today, as a secret little challenge to myself. Just for fun.

"I'm not highly strung," I said.

Haas mimicked my look right back at me. "You've been pacing the workshop since you came in."

"I've always paced."

"And your doctor prescribed you an upper?"

"Felix Haas," I teased him lightly, "you're more than a bit of a bitch when you want to be."

Haas shot a small, private smile at me and shut the light clipped to the top of the sewing machine. He crossed the room and drew up close, corralling me a single step backward against a rack of muslin dresses, and took my face gently in one hand. "Allow me to ask again," he murmured. "Is there anything I can do to help quiet your mind?"

I didn't have the willpower to look him straight in the eye. If I met his gaze, I would have him right here in the workshop. I swallowed. "I might be in the market for another bit of medicine," I said as casually as I could make it.

Haas made a small mouing sound, clicking his tongue. He stroked his thumb along the soft hollow below my jaw, the root of my tongue on the underside of my chin. "You wound me, Margaret. I told you, you need only ask. And you know exactly where to find me, don't you?"

"Room six," I said lightly, trying not to melt entirely into the dresses parting like petals behind me.

Haas smiled at me before tucking his lower lip neatly under the very edges of his top teeth. "Is this you asking nicely?" he murmured—and I might have had some modicum of resistance left if not for the lightest lope of melodic teasing bending the ends of each word.

"If *nice* is what you're wanting," I said, handpicking the words.

Leaning down, angling my mouth gently to seek his, Haas sensed my brief hesitation—his eyes flashed at the shudder of misgiving, and he proceeded with closing the distance.

His mouth moved with rangy awe as though each time he kissed me was the first, a barely reined thrill that stoked my ego to its very foundation. I was helpless against it, the idea I could render someone so wanting, so eager for the person I was *now*. He had only known me as Margaret Shoard, never Wolf, but his attentions kicked up the pieces of who I used to be, left behind in the silt deep in my spirit's reservoir. He made me want to dredge them up and don them again.

Haas pulled me to him and roved a slow path of filthy kisses down the sloping side of my neck. With one hand, he drew another square of paper from his pocket. He slipped the envelope open and licked his thumb before coating it thick with powder.

"Here."

I swallowed and bent my head sideways to give his mouth more room. "I'm curious, what is it, exactly?"

"Paradise."

I let him push his thumb through my lips to slowly trace the roots of my teeth along my gums. I didn't blink, watching him—he stared at the passage of his finger, as though greedily tracking the pull of a thread through the hole made by the tugging point of his needle.

"Good girl," he breathed.

I shut my eyes. "Don't call me that."

My mouth dropped open at the sharp tug of Haas's hand in my hair. "Aren't *you* the one who likes to be told what to do?" he cooed.

An airy laugh kicked shortly from my chest. "Who are you, my director?"

Haas's grip stung at my roots with just enough intent that it made my breath catch again. "Go ahead," he said—and roved his other hand under the hem of my skirt. "What was your favorite monologue?"

I laughed again, but it died quickly as Haas's fingers found me wet past the gusset of my shorts. I fell against him briefly and drew a steadying breath, clinging to his arms.

In the fitting mirror across the workshop, a rickety stand-up of five secondhand full-length mirrors pulled out of someone's dump pile, I caught my reflection and held my own gaze over Haas's shoulder.

> Come, you spirits
> That tend on mortal thoughts, unsex me here,
> And fill me from the crown to the toe top-full
> Of direst cruelty. Make thick my blood.
> Stop up th' access and passage to remorse,
> That no compunctious visitings of nature
> Shake my fell purpose, nor keep peace between
> Th' effect and it. Come to my woman's breasts,
> And take my milk for gall, you murd'ring ministers,
> Wherever in your sightless substances
> You wait on nature's mischief. Come, thick night,
> And pall thee in the dunnest smoke of hell,
> That my keen knife see not the wound it makes,

Nor heaven peep through the blanket of the dark
To cry "Hold, hold!"

I returned to myself with the fishtail darting of urgent pleasure quickening from my toes to my brow, rolling outward on its own tide. The instantaneous release of heavy tension broke with a hitch and made me sag, strings cut, into Haas's near-trembling chest. He breathed against my neck and worked me through the burn-off.

His eyes were bright and pleased with himself. He still held me fast by the roots of my hair. "You're stunning, Margaret."

I clung to the dresses behind me. Before I could gather myself to respond, the twisting progress of the drug persisted to drag me far, far away from myself.

I lost time.

Next I could recall, I was perched on the end of the workbench. The sewing machine was thrumming again, back to hemming. The only evidence of our brief entanglement were my mussed curls, and a few errant strands from the razor-sharp part in Haas's hair.

"I'll take care of you," Haas said without looking up, bent close to the stitching. "All you ever need do is ask."

I was staring at myself in the mirror. Something in me was different, but I couldn't tell what. I fussed with a few of the bobby pins at the back of my head. "Wesley takes very good care of me," I said airily. I smiled.

Everything felt good from here.

"Does he?" Haas hummed, loosened in his frame, and angled a smirk at me. I tried to bite my lips shut around my smile splitting wider, but I couldn't help it. And Haas didn't laugh, exactly—but he was smiling, and when I nudged his hip with my toe, he leaned down to kiss my knee.

◆ ◆ ◆

A LITTLE OVER four weeks before *Titus* was set to open, Kline called the phone in my motel room to bid me come meet him at my earliest convenience.

I frowned at the handset. "Do you mean Wesley?"

"Is Wesley's name Margaret?"

"No, but—"

"One of the boys'll be there to drive you up," Kline jabbered. "Knock twice when you arrive."

When I got there, the actors were milling in the house on a break between scenes. Wesley hailed me from a gaggle sharing a lighter and deposited a kiss on my cheek.

"Summons from Kline," I said by way of explanation as I returned the kiss, distracted.

"He should give you secretary wages," Chap sallied. I shot him a cheap smile punctuated with my middle finger to indicate I understood perfectly well he was joking and refused to let it wound me.

Kline's office was marked by an off-center nameplate on the door that read BOSS. I knocked twice.

"Come on in, sweetheart."

I stepped inside and left the door ajar. Behind a large desk, Kline was sitting in a high-backed red leather chair that looked as though it had been reclaimed from a landfill. To my surprise, Haas stood beside him.

"Glad you could join us," Kline said. He made no motion to stand. Haas stepped around me and put one hand lightly on my waist as he leaned to shut the door.

I put on my most unbothered air and drew my shoulders back to look Kline in the eye. "What did you want to discuss?"

Kline put his hands flat on the empty desk before him. "Brass tacks! I like it. We're changing the program. *Macbeth* instead of *Titus*. Congratulations."

I stared at him, his smarmy little ferret smile. I blinked. "What?"

"We're pivoting. Goodbye, Titus-what's-his-nuts; hello, Mr. Macbeth."

Still struggling to catch his intent, I opened my mouth once before pausing to try again. "With all due respect, it—this is a theater, you really shouldn't say that."

"Say what?"

"The Scottish play."

"The *what*?"

"It's a superstition," Haas cut in smoothly. "To say the name of the new production is considered bad luck. It's cursed."

Kline scoffed. "That's ridiculous. Macbeth, Macbeth, Macbeth." He raised his eyebrows and looked between me and Haas. "See? Nothing t—"

I cried out as one of the lightbulbs above burst with a flash and a snap.

In the silence, Kline looked annoyed to have been humbled. He pursed his mouth and drummed his fingers lightly on the desk in the longer shadows of the new lighting. "Goodbye, Titus," he repeated tightly, "hello, Scotland."

I shook my head. "I don't think—"

"It works perfectly," Haas said, peering at his own shoulder and brushing at glass dust from the burst bulb. "We can reuse the sets and almost every costume, but none of the women we brought in for *Titus* are right for the Lady."

Congratulations.

Oh, shit.

Oh, no, no, no.

"Felix, that's very—"

"Very what?" His eyes flicked immediately up to mine. "Very astute of me? Of course it is. You're a wonderful actress, Mrs. Shoard."

I stared at him. My brain was noise.

"*None* of the actresses could do this," I said evenly, narrowing my eyes at both of them; "none of the other women who signed a *contract* to perform this summer, who are expecting to be paid for it, none of them would be a fit?"

Kline pulled a *You're telling me* face. Haas didn't blink, only twitching up one edge of his left eyebrow as if challenging me to step up to the plate.

"Why me?" I asked. I wished my voice didn't sound so breathless.

"Top brass heard you never got a chance to finish the production in New York," Haas said, straightening his sleeve by the cuff and digging his cigarette case from his breast pocket. He pulled out a hand-roll and took his time lighting it. "Is that right? It was the opening night at which your . . . accident . . . occurred?"

I clenched my jaw until it sang. The smoke from his mouth smelled deep and herbal with a promise of quiet nerves. "Who told you that?"

Haas smiled at me, perfectly genial. "Your husband and I are very good friends."

We stared at each other for what felt like an eternity. "If I accept the role," I asked Kline without looking away from Haas, "will everyone else still make their money?"

"Handsomely," Kline said. "With bonuses, for the trouble."

I turned to face him and led with my hand stuck out for dealmaking. When he went for it, I yanked mine barely out of reach and redoubled the intention of my stare. "*I* will be the one to tell my husband," I snapped. I looked between the both of them, challenging any pushback. "Do you hear me? Not a word of this gets out until Wesley knows. From *me*."

Kline raised both hands in surrender. "Whatever you gotta do, sweetheart. I just need a Lady Macbeth."

Both Haas and I failed to hold in a wince.

"Seriously?" Kline looked between us, baffled by the rules to a game he didn't know he was playing. "That one counts, too?"

"They all count," I said through my teeth and shook his hand.

She was mine again.

Haas ushered me to the door with a hand on my back.

"Can I speak with you?" I asked lightly, and didn't wait for a response as I led the way down a side hall.

I rounded on Haas as soon as we turned a corner out of view. "How did this happen?" I hissed.

Haas finished another mouthful of his hand-roll and extinguished it neatly on the sole of his shoe. He tidied the burnt-down half and tucked what was left back into his cigarette case before giving me a blank look. "I don't pretend to know the whims that drive Jesse. You'll really do it?"

I scowled. "I said I would, didn't I? Felix, if you knew h—"

"You look peckish," Haas cut in easily. He furrowed his brow. "Could I buy you lunch?"

I ground my jaw. "You can buy me a very stiff drink."

He drove us to the restaurant across from the motel, which had become the company's regular haunt—our tabs were infinite, straight from Kline's coffers. I beelined for the bar and ordered a whiskey, neat. Haas hailed a coffee with two sugars.

I knocked back one sip, reconsidered the full glass, took the whole thing, and raised the empty for another from the burly bartender.

Haas was either playing perfectly innocent of my dressing-room incident, or truly didn't understand how badly taking this role might rattle me. He said nothing and waited for me break the silence.

"What do you have to do with any of this?" I asked, cutting a sideways glance at him.

"I'm Vaughn's dramatic advisor. He trusts my taste." Haas sipped from the edge of the cup, grimaced tidily, and dropped another of the sugar cubes in. "And you're to my taste. Obviously."

I glared down at my hands, fiddling with the empty cup. "It was . . . messy, the last time I had that role. I don't think this is a good idea, Felix."

"What if it wasn't Kline asking? Would you do it for me?"

I sniffed. "For *you*." I dragged a finger along the rim of my glass. I wanted to itch at my arms and shoved the impulse away.

Haas took another steady sip, peering at the rows of bottles in front of us. The record that was spinning skipped with a shallow scratch, stumbling over its own twang.

I ran the tip of my tongue along my lower lip. "Last time I did it for *me*," I said slowly, "it nearly killed me. It *is* cursed, you know."

In my periphery, Haas's gaze roved along my profile. "I told you," he said, "I'll look after you."

Our scattered reflection in the mirror wall behind the bar showed me the way he cataloged me, picking at my seams. How far into my depths could he see? Were there private pieces of my shortcomings I had left visible at the surface this whole time?

"That's sweet of you," I muttered. "Although your only other reference point is the world's most disappointing Desdemona."

Haas gestured at me with his cup, mocking a toast. "I've seen more than enough of you here to know you need something of your own life back—something you can control. You seem . . . troubled. Purposeless."

I simmered on that thought. He wasn't wrong.

It rankled, that my struggle was so obvious.

Haas sipped down his coffee in pensive silence as I stared through the wood grain of the bar. I tried to imagine what it would feel like to inhabit Lady Macbeth again, if I even *could*—deep down, I really did want to. A significant part of me still ached, hanging open with the unfinished run of her.

But was wanting enough?

"I don't like feeling as though I owe anyone," I said with a low voice. "Not a *thing*."

Haas peered at me again until I met his gaze. "Who were you, before your adulthood?"

I measured him up. If there was anyone who might understand—uprooted from his own home, thrown into the wilds of the city to find his own way—it was Haas. "Why do you want to know?"

"I'm curious about you."

Curious. A low warmth bloomed in the cradle of my hips. I drew a soft breath and gave him the short version, as short as I could get it without leaving holes in the story.

My biological father: gone before I was born. Who knows. Mr. Matthews: a savior new to the pulpit of Mama's favorite First Baptist. My mother threw parties for him, the men he considered colleagues, and their glamorous wives. He passed off thick sheaves of money to the men every Sunday after service, money I helped him count from the collection baskets, and I ran away from home just past sixteen when I caught wind of a man high up on the ladder in Biloxi fixing to propose a marriage arrangement to my mother and Mr. Matthews—a union of the houses.

Then, Richmond. Jensen. I skipped broadly over Hollis, embarrassed at having been bridled. I didn't want him to think of me like that.

And now I was here, Margaret Shoard, of Wesley and Manhattan and a thousand ruined women in the roles I'd left behind.

"How lucky we all are to have you here then, Miss Wolf," Haas hummed when I had finished. He pushed aside his saucer and stood with an air of casual ease. Checking the watch face on the inside of his wrist, Haas caught me looking. I was still half-slumped on my bar stool. He smiled. "Besides, you're much brighter than all that petty depravity. Care to go for a drive?"

17

Route 84, northbound

"ARE YOU NOT eager to at least consider Kline's proposal?"

I glanced over at Haas as he broke the thin silence between us. We were driving aimlessly along the unending ribbon of the highway, carving out into the distance where the horizon had no discernible edge. *Proposal.* "I don't trust myself with that role," I admitted. "Not anymore."

Haas drove with one hand holding the wheel steady at eight o'clock and the other readied on the stick shift, lazily perched with inaction for the interminable stretch of flat land. "You sounded confident enough in the workshop the other day. What of it do you not trust?"

I gave a dry sniff and leaned my forehead against the passenger window. The chaparral blurred with the sagging barbed wire strung along stretches of the shoulder as we passed, and passed, and passed. "My sanity."

"Sanity is a myth," Haas said, smiling to himself.

I frowned. Carved against the impenetrable sky past the window, his profile stood against the lowering afternoon sun reaching red through heavy iron clouds. "Why are you so keen on getting me on-stage again?"

"Would you like another dose?"

"Of what?"

"I believe I called it 'paradise.'"

My heart fluttered. I stared at Haas for another moment. The engine heaved as he wrestled it into the next gear.

"You didn't answer my question."

Haas dug into his pocket without looking away from the road and offered me his tooled tin case over the center console. "I can give you a full brick of it if you'd like, no charge."

"Why are you trying to champion me, Felix?"

His jaw flexed briefly. The speedometer ticked up a few miles per hour. "Because it's clear to me nobody has taken the proper care to stand up for you in a very long time. Do you want some or not?"

I stared at him for a moment before taking the kit. I pried it open to balance on my knees. There was an enamel straw inside, and a mirror under the sachet of powder. I poured out a slim line and nudged it into a neat row, and recalling parties from the Christopher Street days, I lined up the straw at my nose.

Because why not? Here we were, nowhere as far as the eye could see, and I had unearthed things for Haas I hadn't let myself think about in years. It would be silly not to give myself the comfort.

"There you are," Haas murmured. He kept the van impeccably straight in the road. I shut my eyes and tipped my head back, and I winced when I touched the edge of my nostril and felt a wet trickle of blood on my knuckle.

I put the kit back together and flipped down the passenger visor to peer at myself in the mirror. I swiped the blood away, just a jot of it from some weak blood vessel giving up, and examined myself before shutting the flap again.

Haas glanced at me when I passed the kit back, his eyes bright. "You are quite the fascination. I never would have guessed you came from such simple beginnings."

I smiled bitterly through the windshield. "That's very kind of you," I said.

Haas rolled to a stop on the side of the road. The desert stretched around us, still and infinite. There was pointed intent in Haas's eyes for a moment as he turned to look at me—but a wash of softness chased it away.

"I'm 'kind' to you," he said gently, "because you deserve somebody in your corner who sees you as you really are. Not what you're expected to be." He placed one poised, warm hand high up on my thigh. "Where to next?" he asked.

I stared ahead at the road, where a hand-painted mile marker bleached numberless by the sun swayed in a stiff breeze. Wesley was the only other person who knew me to my cells, but this was . . . different. Somehow. This was pressing a handprint into snow that hadn't yet been sullied by the slurry of dirt from the curb. This was a claim on a good, pure thing. Haas hadn't known me at my lowest.

It was nice, to be seen as whole.

When I put one hand down to close gently around Haas's fingers, I squeezed just firm enough to make sure he knew I meant it: "I'd like to take you home."

Haas sped back toward Lake Sumner with his guarding touch on my leg. He parked at the rear end of the motel and wasted little time tugging me forward by the waist to kiss me across the gearshift.

"Shall we?" he asked against my jaw.

"That depends on what you mean by 'we.'"

"You and I find ourselves in your room." His hand roved easily along one garter strap. I leaned into him, puttied. "You let me help you clear your head."

I probably said yes—the details hazed. He concocted a *very* good drug.

We hurried inside, and I was already unclipping my stockings as I tossed my key onto one of the beds. Haas locked the door and came up behind me to nose another heady kiss to the curve of my neck. He staggered forward, steering blind, and roved us over to the vanity.

My knees knocked gently against the front of the drawers. Haas rucked up my skirts and wrestled my shorts down to my ankles. "Up," he panted, his hands firm around my elbows. A fresh current of awareness ran under my skin, white-hot, and punted sensation itself onto an entirely different plane. I was afire, all of me, and I wanted to obey Haas's direction with desperate wonder.

He hoisted me up onto the table and went to his knees, pushing the chartreuse crush of my hem aside with one hand.

I clutched for his hair and the tight bundle of his fist holding my dress. When I looked down to behold him, the high holding me aloft to let reason only batter like mooring frantic against a storming dockside, I was watching bliss happen to some desperate body that could have been my own. What ecstasy, to be so unmade, to be treated like a tender animal that knew only the pleading scraping up my throat: *Yes. More. Just there.*

I pressed forward to Haas's mouth. His brows twitched with concentration. He had removed his glasses at some point—tucked in his shirt pocket, they winked at me when one lens caught a flash of the gauzy light slicing in from a thin gap in the drawn curtains.

He stilled suddenly and huffed a misfire of a gasp against me. He pulled his mouth away with a gutted sound and groaned against my inner thigh.

"Wait," I rasped. All of me was dancing, my nerves in a tizzy. I slid my hand up to dig my fingers into his hair at the root. Haas's voice skipped and cracked. His breath was hot on my skin, muffling himself and shivering all over. I tightened my grip and spurred him between the shoulders with a nudge of my bare heel. *"No*, keep—I'm not—!" My head met the mirror behind me with a dull thud as I arced my neck backward.

"Here," Haas growled, dragging two fingers along his tongue, and before I could ask what, the slick nudge of them entered me in tandem.

His touch was everywhere. When he staggered into a stand, his left hand closed gently around the sides of my neck—he hushed me softly when I made a tight sound at the pressure, pressing his mouth to the side of my face.

"There you are," he panted, hoarse and airy. "Calm. *Calm*, Margaret."

He held me, pinned and helpless. Haas's hips pressed at the back of my bare thigh as he leaned in, crowding down into the space between our mouths. I felt the evidence of his release through his trousers.

I had rendered him that helpless.

Power ripped through me, ruby-red and violent. I possessed something of him now to have cracked him in half over his own fulcrum.

Devour.

I broke with a wounded cry at a soft squeeze of his fingertips at the cords of my neck. Haas hissed a sharp jag of German into the bend of my cheek.

The air was foggy as I came down again. Haas let go of my neck and opened the silver clamshell of his kit again, biting his lips around his teeth to pluck free a tight hand-roll and flick at his strike-lighter.

The first puff of smoke scored the air with a fetid burn, and he turned it to slip the end into my lips like I'd watched him do to Wesley.

I stared at him as I took a languorous mouthful in the unsettled sparkling of refraction. Haas was unstuck, his edges peeled up with frenetic hunger.

I had done that to him.

He took the cigarette back. His hands were trembling. The borders of my vision danced with Christmas lights. I shut my eyes and dissolved into breathless, giddy laughter.

I slid down from the vanity to stumble into the bathroom without another word. I ran the faucet and stripped down to my slip without feeling anything but the pleasant, persistent buzz zinging through my teeth and the backs of my eyes.

I was alone in my reflection. I stared at myself in the rattling hiss of the water.

Haas was lounging naked on the settee at the mirror when I came back out, tidied. His clothes were folded neatly on the foot of the bed and his shoes squared on the carpet. I sat beside the tidy little pile and felt absently at the fine linen of his shirt.

"You certainly know your way around," I joked lightly. I looked up at him, latching my eyes to his in curious fondness. "Have you been married before, or are you just a quick study?"

"We should probably keep from walking on each other's biscuits," Haas murmured, offsetting the intensity of his voice with a playful smirk.

"Another idiom?"

"You'll find I'm full of sayings that make little sense, to you."

We shared a dry chuckle. A bird twittered from somewhere past the back screen door.

"Did you know," Haas said, his voice tightened by a deep draw on his herby smoke, holding it in, "a thing that confounded me when I was first learning English is that the word 'marital' is not the same word as 'martial.'"

I stared at his bare feet, his high arches and the elegant jutting of his ankles. "Was it."

"Experienced in or inclined to war."

I gave a tart sniff. "And to which of those does this apply?"

"Precisely."

Another several heartbeats of unflinching staring ticked past.

"Are you in love with him?" I asked. My tone was sharper than I intended. Haas's gaze softened. He took a draw that bent his cheeks, his mouth supple and easy.

"I'm deeply drawn to him," he said, letting the smoke curl up aimlessly from his lips. "Your husband is very kind."

"What am I to you, then? Masculinity insurance? A challenge?"

Are you happy, Margaret?

I glanced at the mirror behind Haas. Only myself and the lithe muscle of his shoulders easing into his spine looked back.

Haas regarded me steadily. "On the contrary. I'm drawn to you as well. Quite obviously, I would say."

He watched me for another moment before rising to cross to the bed. He bent at the waist and combed his fingers through my hair before kissing me on the forehead.

"If I'm not a nuisance," I asked, still staring at us in the mirror, "martial in what way?"

Haas leaned back to search my face. "How do you mean?"

"Marital. Martial. Which of them the war?"

"I'd no idea a philosopher's heart lived alongside the thespian's."

"Only when I'm loaded."

Haas drew his thumb over the shell of my ear. His hand still rested at the crown of my head as I looked up along the fine length of his body. "Why take up arms in the first place," he mused, "if not to protect some sanctity of hearth and home? Of one life charted against another?"

"You *have* been married before," I said plainly.

Haas gave me a very patient look, a forthright smile. "We were quite young. Certain truths, when they emerged, became untenable."

"Like what?"

"We were misaligned, regarding the future I believed we deserved together," he said. "She had no sense of compromise."

Haas took one last slow drag, meditative, and felt the strands of my hair between his fingertips as though examining the luster of gilt thread in the sunlight.

"Your husband is avoiding me lately," he said.

I chuckled. Wesley always got distracted with an opening approaching. I had no idea how I was even going to begin to tell him about *Macbeth*. "He's in a mood. He'll work himself out of it."

Haas made a vague sound, tinged slightly with regret. "Whatever are we going to do when we have to return to the land of the living?"

I stood up and put a hand on Haas's shoulder, rubbing it absently with my thumb before kissing him there lightly. "We don't have to think about that right now."

Haas peered at me as though unwilling to look away. I realized for the first time we had the same eye color, an impenetrable earthen brown.

"Are you truly going to do it?" he asked. He lifted his hand to one strap of my slip.

"What, the role?"

He said nothing, but his eyes flicked up to mine and held me there with the same bolted ferocity of his grip at the sides of my neck. Heavy and viscid through the haze of the drug, arousal welled in me again with a hard lurch.

"Of course I am," I said, because I wanted to. I would. There was no other option. "Especially if you garnish me with a lot more of what's making me feel so good right now."

This was what I wanted.

"Good girl," Haas murmured as he laved a kiss into the divot of my throat.

Don't call me that—but no, too pedantic. I let it be.

Over his shoulder, the Lady looked on through the mirror.

The sleeping and the dead are but as pictures, she spoke in the distance of my mind. *'Tis the eye of childhood that fears a painted devil.*

"On your back," I breathed, turning to steer Haas to the foot of the bed. I faced away from the mirror, putting myself firmly in the present, and dragged my hem up past my naked waist. "Don't shut your eyes. Look at me this time."

◆ ◆ ◆

THE NEXT AFTERNOON, Wesley was running a fencing call on-stage with Kline in absentia. I hadn't told him about the Lady yet, and I knew the longer I waited, the more I risked someone else starting a rumor that accidentally walked and talked into truth.

To his credit, despite his unannounced spats of absence and general (complete) lack of knowledge of the craft, Kline hadn't let any inkling of the role change slip. They knew it was *Macbeth*, the men had already been recast, but there was no mention of who would be the Lady. *We're still running the numbers*, Kline would snip whenever someone asked.

None of the other women particularly cared. They were still getting paid, regardless. But my nerves had ramped up—and I couldn't tell if it was just the runoff of Haas's product still knocking around in my system.

I had to tell Wesley. I watched him lunge and flèche and dart across the stage, the very picture of grace, and so badly wanted him to be proud of me.

If he didn't believe I could do it, a part of my spirit would always doubt. I loved him as I loved myself.

Philia.

A hard clatter of metal on wood jolted me to the present.

Wesley had dropped his foil, rolled up his sleeves, and stalked across the stage to throw a mean right hook into poor Oliver Langham's gut.

It happened so quickly I could hardly mark it. One instant they stood en garde, and the next they were struggling on the floor in a furious grapple.

"Wesley!" I abandoned the script I was secretly looking over at the back of the house and ran up onstage, where I got Wesley by the back of the collar and pulled. He stumbled backward, still clinging to Oliver's sleeves, and I shook him by the scruff as one of the stagehands hurried over to haul Oliver backward, too.

"Wesley, *stop it!*" I snapped.

Spitting a jot of blood to the rust-red stage, Wesley rounded on me. Eyes wild, he pointed furiously at Oliver—he'd pinned the man so fiercely there was a broad, angry scrape across one cheek from the boards. "We have three weeks to pull the Scottish play from our asses," he snarled, "none of these idiots can keep from being soaked drunk long enough to take a goddamn fight from start to finish, and *none* of this shit even matters, because we're going to be performing it for *fucking ghosts!*"

Wesley's voice flew up into the eaves and warbled several times in echo through the empty theater.

I closed my hand around his elbow and cast a hardened look at him. "Let's take some air. Yeah?"

Wesley scowled. He raked a hand through his hair, shook his head, and wrapped an arm around my shoulders to skulk us both at a quick clip down the apron, through the aisles, and out to the dock.

Wesley helped me into the boat and pushed it roughly from its ropes before ripping the engine cord with a tension in his shoulders I knew better than to comment on. Instead of peering warily at his disquiet, I squinted into the harsh throw of sunlight against the water's glassy surface.

When we reached the middle of the lake, Wesley cut the propeller and let out a heavy sigh. I turned to regard him again and took stock: his rumpled collar, his lower lip bleeding, his hair tumbled down out of its neat coif. He was staring at his dusty shoes as the water rippled in endless circles from the boat's edges.

"Are you alright, Wes?"

He glowered up at me through his lashes beneath the draw of his brows. "Do I look alright?"

I pretended to appraise him. "The split lip looks terribly butch."

He didn't laugh. The light caught his gaze at an angle that made his irises fade almost completely into the whites of his eyes, leaving only the pinprick pupil in his gaze.

We floated for a while in the stillness. Wesley's temper abated steadily—he scrubbed at his jaw with a flat hand and licked absently at the cut on his lip, testing its sting.

"I'm happy you've been spending more time with Felix," he said after a spell, stilted and awkward and clearly trying to change the subject. He wasn't looking at me.

I played along, prodding his knee saucily. Wesley shot me a piquant little grin that didn't reach his eyes. "Truly, you're night and day from when we arrived. Is that really what's doing it?"

"You have him regularly enough," I said, blushing despite myself. "You know how it goes."

Wesley shrugged. "He likes you best."

"Oh, I don't—"

"It doesn't bother me. God knows you deserve a good time. And I'm used to them coming and going."

I raised my eyebrows and sniped a joke so bawdy it made Wesley laugh my favorite laugh: the one that caught his top lip just so, rollicking and hitching it up over one eyetooth. But it died more quickly than I'd hoped and left Wesley silent again, distant.

He leaned back in his seat and tipped his face up to the sky. His eyes were closed against the sun. "This role is hard for me, Jack," he admitted. "It really is. I wish they hadn't changed it."

"What, you've forgotten it already?"

"I don't— I can't see anything but you . . . bleeding out in your dressing room when I'm playing him."

I watched him without breathing for a brief spell.

"Kline offered me the Lady," I finally said. "I said yes."

Wesley stared at me for a long time, unblinking. The water knocked at the metal siding of the boat.

"Are you sure?" he asked, very gently.

"Yes."

"Are you *sure.*"

"You said it just now, I'm doing much better. I trust myself, Wesley. I do."

We stared at each other.

"Say something," I said. "Please."

". . . I don't want to be the asshole bothered by my wife having a career."

"You aren't. You've never been."

"It gives me pause. Can you blame me? I wish it didn't, but it does. Things are—they're different now."

"I know." I angled for his eyes as he tore them away again, looking sourly into the water, and put a hand to his cheek to keep him with me. "Hey. Look at me. I know. Things *are* different now. I have medicine. I can manage this, and I'll tell you the moment it feels bad again. If it even does."

Wesley peeled my hand down from his face and held it in his lap. "Even the *whiff* of it, you let me know. Promise?"

"I promise."

I leaned in and kissed him square on the forehead. Before sitting back, I thumbed the lipstick mark from his sweat-tacked brow.

Wesley searched my gaze for a moment before coming to sit beside me on the bench plank instead of the rudder seat. I wrapped an arm around his waist and tendered his head down to my shoulder, where he leaned into me and finally, truly settled.

"I'm sorry you had to see it," I said.

Wesley sighed. "You're too good of an actor, Jack. Damnably good. Congratulations."

The breeze came occasionally to check on us like a nervous chaperone as we floated under the indiscriminate sun. Regardless of what came before, the *if*s and *should have*s and *wanted to*s, we were together.

18

The Lake Sumner motel

"BISHOP."

"Me again. Lots of updates."

"Oh, *good.* I don't have any bothers going on today, I'm all yours. Start from the top."

I was smoking the back half of a cigarette in the phone booth with my hair in rollers and my good girdle on under my robe. I'd already done up my face for the party we were all invited to later that night. Handwritten notes had been delivered under our doors that morning: *Be ready at 8, don't be late!!! Party outside town. Vans leave 5 after.*

"They switched the show. It's not *Titus* anymore, we're doing the Scottish play."

"Oh, dear. How are—"

"I'm doing the Lady again."

"Oh, *dear.*" Edie paused and let the weight of silence settle. "Are you . . . ?"

"I'm alright with it," I said briskly. "Truly. I'm—excited, and nervous, sure, but it's been nice to relive it. Our folios are all different editions, they had to go four towns over to find a bookshop with enough copies."

"Do you trust yourself?"

The sun was too low to show me a whit of my reflection in the booth siding, so I stared out at the faraway mountains and thought about that through another mouthful of smoke. "I do."

"Well, you certainly are having an eventful summer. How's the Austrian?"

"Athletic."

"Rehearsing feels good?"

"It feels great."

"Maybe the secret to getting you back on even keel really *was* just getting yourself regularly stuffed."

"You could be an analyst." I tapped out my cigarette on the side of the telephone unit and smeared the end on the ground under the toe of my shoe. "And tonight, *finally*, we're going to a party."

"With whom, the coyotes?"

I snorted. "I know. We got invitations this morning written on napkins from the bar across the highway. Lisette said she heard the house it's hosted at is positively vulgar."

"Is that a good thing? How does the beauty queen of Wisconsin know that?"

"I think *she's* been getting stuffed by one of the caravan drivers."

"Good for her." There was a smile in Edie's voice. She had a soft spot for Lisette.

"They have more money than God out here," I said. "Would you believe it?"

"Of course I believe it. Money is the national religion, and you're playing among its most devoted."

We chatted for a few more minutes, until the line pinged its hunger for another nickel. I groaned. Edie laughed.

"Go have fun, poss," she told me. "Thanks for checking in—let me know how it goes, will you? The whole of it." She paused. "I'm proud of you."

Warmth bloomed through my chest. "Thank you. I'm proud of me, too."

Returning to the room to finish getting dressed, I felt more like myself than I had in ages.

We drove out to a sprawling ranch about an hour north in another prosaic patch of empty desert. The massive, hyper-modern slab of a house rose from the night as our caravan approached.

All of us were dressed to the nines. Kline had told us the hosts for tonight were *fine people*, so I was wearing a black silk cocktail dress and a pair of shoes nice enough that I cared to avoid any mud on the winding walkway up to the house.

I'd been to my fair share of parties, and maybe more than that. But apparently, *fine people* in Western parlance meant *unhinged libertines* by New York City standards.

As the company stepped over the threshold, a petite woman in a pink negligee and little else proffered a silver dish. Instead of appetizers or glasses of champagne—which I could see elsewhere, offered by handsome men in crisp shirts and vests—an array of pills and tidy hand-rolls were arranged for the taking.

"Jesse hopes you all enjoy your night," the woman said with a dazzling smile.

Jesse. The elusive cowboy. As Wesley and I politely refused anything from her tray and he led us into the churn of the party, I peered around for a glimpse of the pepper-haired man and his boots, the wink of the silver rings encrusting his fingers.

The wide walls of the house were decorated with avant-garde spatters of art. Low, sleek furniture sat packed with carousing bodies, and the crowd was so eclectic I wouldn't have been surprised to discover they had all been living in a bunker under the clay on layaway to simply attend parties. The fact this many people existed out here baffled me.

My nerves started humming at the back of my neck. Wesley passed me a glass, and I quaffed it in one go without even tasting it.

"I was wondering when you'd arrive," Haas said from behind me—I turned to find him cutting in smoothly between us. He kissed me hello, and then Wesley as well without a single care of being seen. Safe company, then.

"Have you been here long?" I asked. Haas lifted a glass from a passing tray and plucked away my empty to replace it in one fluid movement.

"I was on setup committee," he said breezily, steering us forward. "Come, there's fun to be had."

It was almost like being back in a warehouse party. If I shut my eyes, the noise was the same—music, chatter, laughter and raised voices, all the pressing sweat of human abandon. I marked a massive set of plate-glass doors thrown open to the night, and a long hallway disappearing into low light where a number of rooms sat ready for stealing privacy as the night unraveled. Several were already occupied.

Haas took us around on his arms through the ocean of splendor—rich men, beautiful women, escorts, and eccentrics; the full gamut of privilege under one roof, and I wouldn't have known it from three miles off. This was ten times the outfit I had known in Lexington, all of whom could fit at my mother's dinner table.

I realized for the first time that summer the kind of freedom that existed in a nothing-place: I thought we lived quite openly in the city, but in comparison we were practically puritan. Here was the real abandon, the true American underbelly amid the dust and rust and the empty cry of the country's parched throat.

When Haas offered me a hit of his powder, I took it without thinking. Wesley raised his eyebrows.

"You sure you should be mixing that stuff?" he said, low at my ear, more amusement than concern. I patted him on the shoulder and straightened the lay of his collar.

"It's all the same from here," I said, and planted a friendly peck on his mouth.

I tried to settle into the rhythm of the debauchery as we moved through it, but my social tolerance had been weakened by the weeks of solitude. After emptying my third glass, I set it on another passing tray and excused myself neatly to find a quieter spot.

The kitchen was at the end of the house, still bustling but certainly less crowded than most of it. There was chrome everywhere, with sparkling-clean tiling on the floor and bright yellow cabinetry stretching across one whole wall. It was spotless. This wasn't a kitchen made for use.

"Well, fancy meeting you here, Mrs. Shoard."

I looked up from tracing the sleek, modern edge of the refrigerator to find Jesse, hatless, leaning on the island counter behind me. He gave me a smile. I pointed a finger at the ceiling and twirled it in a wide circle.

"Is all of this yours?" I asked.

Jesse shrugged. "Most of it."

He was making himself a drink. He offered me the first pour after jostling the shaker, but I demurred and leaned back against the cutlery drawers. "I suppose I should have brought a hostess gift."

"What do you get the gal who has everything?" Jesse mused. He poured over the ice in his glass and set the shaker in the sink without emptying it, among a scatter of other used glasses and plates.

"Are you the gal?" I asked.

Jesse smirked and raised the glass at me. "Ask me after a few more of these."

We watched each other as he sipped.

"I saw you up on that stage the other day," Jesse said, perfectly conversational.

I frowned. "You watched a rehearsal?"

"I've watched several. That's the beauty of owning the only theater in these parts, I can show up anytime I please." He grinned at me. "Learned that one from our pal Ezra, although I don't like to make such a fuss about it as he does. I prefer to observe—just let the top spin after dropping it."

Unconsciously, I drew my posture up slightly. "And what do you think of it so far? The pivot?"

Jesse's sharp, gold gaze flashed, pinning me to the spot. "You make a hell of a leading lady. You got hungry eyes in that head of yours, you know that?"

"Is that a compliment?"

"Absolutely." Jesse sipped from his drink again and smacked his lips. "What do you think of Vaughn?" he asked, swinging broad.

I snorted. "He's a piece of work," I said without thinking. The drugs and drink had set me apart from my own shame.

Luckily, Jesse laughed. "You think this dog and pony shit is enough penance for him losing track of two hundred thousand dollars of my product?" My brows shot up. Jesse mocked a wince and nodded. "Yep. Been trying to track it down since Christmas. Ho-ho-ho."

"I wouldn't trust him to look after a half-dozen eggs," I admitted.

Jesse grinned and sipped again, eyeing me over the cup. "I like you, Cherokee Park," he said, pointing at me with the hand holding his glass, his grip easy.

"Is that why you pivoted the play?" I asked.

"What do you mean?"

"From *Titus* to *Macbeth*. Is that why you changed it, because you like me?"

Jesse furrowed his brow, pleasantly baffled. "Kline's the one who changed it."

I looked down and fussed subtly with the wire of my girdle digging into my waist. "Does Kline change his mind very often?"

"Well, he's got a spine made of milk. He's an easy son of a bitch to persuade."

"So you persuaded him?"

Jesse finished off his drink and put the glass in the sink as well. "I dunno what he changed it for, but I gave him free rein to do whatever he sees fit to give me *one* good show of Shakespeare out here." He held up a single finger with a huge chip of turquoise on his knuckle and grinned. "I don't mind the difference. I happen to love the Scottish play, all that delectable superstition."

"Jesse?"

A young man I recognized from the stage crew stood with polite hesitation at the entrance to the kitchen. I didn't know him by name, but he was always sure to give me a *Hello, Mrs. Shoard* when we passed in the wings. He was holding an empty beer bottle in one hand, peeling at the label with a nervous thumb, and looking at Jesse with the reined heat of bravery drummed up by way of several drinks swimming around in his big blue eyes.

I gave Jesse an expectant look, which made him smile slyly at me.

"Shit, I said I like *you*, Margaret, not your skirt." Jesse sketched a bow. "You enjoy your night, won't you?"

He retreated with his arm slung easily around the stagehand's waist, melting back into his party. I took up the bottle of liquor on the counter and stole down a mouthful. It was a fragrant, with a label in Spanish and a bite like a mouthful of smoke. I kept it with me as I went to find Wesley.

I wandered until I'd explored the entirety of the house, sipping occasionally from the bottle in hand—expensive trinkets, shiny furniture, room after room packed with life and finery—and finally came to the hallway of doors. I ambled down the narrow corridor and peeked into rooms that weren't shut all the way, cadres of people split off from their cavorting to sit in a quieter place; some still holding conversation, and others done with conversation entirely.

"There you are."

I looked away from what seemed to be a card game attended by six women and two very drunk men. Haas leaned on an open jamb at the end of the hall. His jacket was gone, his cuffs unbuttoned, and his eyes bright in the low, ochre light.

Behind him, Wesley was sitting on an armchair across from a wide bed. He looked rumpled and upset, his face mottled with angry flush. I frowned and looked past Haas's shoulder. "Are you alright?"

"Everything is fine," Haas said in Wesley's stead. He took up a drink already on the dresser and held it out to me, switching it for the bottle in my hand. "Will you join us?"

I accepted the cup but angled still for Wesley's eyes. Haas shut the door behind me, and I sipped at the drink without thinking.

When Haas slipped a hand around my hip from behind, I turned to stop him gently with my shoulder. "Whose idea was the switch?" I asked, still stuck on my conversation with Jesse.

Undeterred, Haas reached for my garters under my dress with one hand while the other tipped another sip of the cup into my mouth. "What do you mean?"

I swallowed reflexively and swiped at a droplet on my chin. I twisted away from Haas and tried again to meet Wesley's eyes, but he looked tired and faraway. Haas unclipped my stockings. "The—changing the plays," I said, and blinked owlishly as my words slowed. I stalled. My thoughts began oozing through their own grip. "Lady Macbeth, it—who was it?" I pushed my hand softly, uselessly against Haas's chest. "Kline, or—was it Jesse?"

Haas kissed me as I fell away from myself, into complete and utter darkness.

It was just like falling under that afternoon in Haas's workshop: one moment, here; then gone in an instant; and then back up again, as though simply blinking my eyes.

I was only aware next of my own feet, the sight of them blurring into focus as I stumbled carefully down the front walk.

Wesley had me stabilized against his side, his mouth drawn in a thin line.

We stepped carefully down the spooling driveway. One of Wesley's hands was at my back. The other held gently to my arm as though I was an invalid again. He called over his shoulder at someone, maybe Chap, who was asking about his bow tie, something about picking it up tomorrow at rehearsal.

Haas was standing ahead of us beside a sleek-looking Ford I had never seen before. It had rained while we were inside—the air smelled heavy and metallic with a damp, persistent cling. I was exhausted.

"Are we met?" Haas asked brightly. I reached around in my own head for a moment to remember how to respond but came up dry. I made a soft sound as Wesley opened up the door and bent to crank the front seat forward.

"I have a headache," I grunted.

Haas reached into his pocket and flashed his kit. "Care for a pick-me-up?"

Wesley's head was bowed in the shadow of the car, working at the seat lever. I swiped an errant fall of hair back from my forehead. "Sure."

I lined up a dose and sniffed it down before handing it back to Haas. Wesley avoided my eye as he helped me into the back seat.

Haas keyed the engine, and Wesley settled in beside me. He let me rest my head back on his leg. The car was a much smoother ride than the vans as we made our way down the main road back to the motel.

"Wesley, are you sure you don't want more?" Haas offered from behind the wheel. I watched from my backward sprawl as the streaks of rainwater on the windows traced themselves into long threads.

I glanced up at Wesley and his uncharacteristic silence. He was staring out the window as well. I wondered if he could find the same patterns in the raindrops.

"No, thank you," he said delicately.

I reached up to pet a hand along the back of his neck. His hair was always so baby-soft there, so I made my touch as gentle as I could.

"Did you have a nice night?" I asked him.

"Of course I did."

He didn't sound like it, but what did I know? I was tired and stoned and needed to sleep. My body ached faintly as one singular organ. I wound a lock of Wesley's hair around the tip of my finger. He looked rakish and unbound when he let his hair grow a little longer. It suited him.

"I'm proud of us," I said. A yawn stole away most of the last sylla-ble. Wesley reached up and pried my hand from his hair with patient tenderness before carding our fingers together. He rested our hands over my heart, nestled in his lap.

"Yeah," Wesley murmured.

He was avoiding Haas's gaze. It was purposeful, wide as the swing of a turning freighter.

I took stock of Haas in the driver's seat. There was a mild smug-ness in him, and his gaze was clear and virile.

You got hungry eyes.

I tightened my grip on Wesley's hand in mine. "Tell me how much you love me," I said over the car's rumbling, intent on bringing a smile back to his pretty face.

Haas's gaze flicked to mine through the mirror. I shut my eyes.

"I love you as I love myself," Wesley murmured, which I felt more than heard in the shape of his mouth pressed to the back of my hand, running one knuckle over and over the bow of his lips like the edge of a well-loved security blanket.

◆ ◆ ◆

OUR *MACBETH* SCRIPTS totaled up to three different editions with varying pagination. The rest of the cast did the best they could. I still had the entire text memorized.

"... Thou wouldst be great, art not without ambition, but without the illness should attend—"

The front doors of the theater heaved open, stopping me mid-sentence. The prop letter in my hand fluttered gently with a swirling breeze. Daylight streamed in through the doors as Kline stood up from the front row of benches, turning with tightly wound fury to shout at the interruption of our run-through.

"Vaughn Kline?" called a voice before he could erupt, and two silhouettes made themselves known: the broad hats and shiny badges of two lawmen.

Kline ran a hand along his comb-over and strode confidently down the center aisle on his stocky legs. The rest of the cast, scattered in the wings and the house, stared in pin-drop silence.

"Welcome, gentlemen!" Kline gestured broadly at the empty theater and offered a hand to shake, for which neither of the men took their thumbs from their belts. "How can we be of assistance?"

The taller of the officers gawped subtly at the playhouse like he'd been transported into a different layer of reality. The shorter one, an older gentleman with a walrus mustache, peered at Kline. "We'd like to speak with the proprietor."

Kline bowed with a flourish. "Speaking; Vaughn Kline, at your service. If you'd care to step into my office—would you like something to drink? Parched out there, isn't it?"

"It's been a rainier summer than usual."

Clearly on the back foot, Kline led the officers toward the wings. I wondered idly if he was taking them to the place I'd first seen Jesse, and whether they would emerge again. "Take a ten!" Kline called over his shoulder before disappearing.

The company broke to mill into the house. I remained onstage, fussing with the prop letter. I was still drained from the party.

Wesley drew up beside me and pawed his cigarette case from his back pocket. "It'll probably be at least a twenty," he said, and pulled out one for each of us.

We sat down in the first row of benches. Neither of us said anything for a long stretch. The rest of the company looked just as scoured to the bone as I felt—trounced by a night out, bleary-eyed and slow. Wesley had the stares. I jogged his heel with a few taps of my foot.

"Are you alright?"

Wesley blinked and ashed the long tail of his cigarette to the ground, grinding it away with his heel as he pinched at his eyes. "I'm fine. Fucking exhausted."

"I know."

"I shouldn't have taken that shit."

"What, from Felix?"

He hummed the affirmative and took a deep, punishing draw that burned down the paper quickly and bent his cheeks. Wesley shook his head. "Figured I'd see if I could stand it, he made it sound like— fucking lollypop land." With a dry widening of his eyes, still staring at nothing, he heaved a shallow sigh. "Did *not* agree with me."

"I wonder why it affects you so much," I said, not quite looking at him.

"I don't know how you do it. You're sure it's good for you?"

"What, his medicine?" I nodded at the stage and met Wesley's gaze. "You see me up there, you tell me."

Wesley sagged. The fight was gone from him. He shrugged with one shoulder. "I know. I just . . . worry."

"About what?"

"I don't know, Jack," he said lightly. "A little bit of everything."

I patted his hand on the bench between us. The soft, church-like muttering of the rest of the company killing time floated up and broke apart in the air along with the ghosting smoke at the ends of our cigarettes. Lisette was toward the back of the house flirting with her fling. Chap had made friends with some of the stage crew, and I noticed the blue-eyed looker from Jesse's party in a small group standing with him just offstage. They all chuckled at one of Chap's jokes with a muted, hungover cadence, and for just a moment I could have shut my eyes and been in any given bistro on a Sunday morning in the West Village.

"I'll be glad to go home," Wesley announced.

I sniffed in commiseration. "I know. I miss getting bumped into on the train."

"If I hadn't gotten blasted out of my own skull last night, that party would have *healed* me."

"What do you miss the most?"

"The noise," Wesley said without having to think about it.

"Really?"

"The quiet out here is . . . unsettling. Spend more than a few days on a submarine, you can't help listening for silence like an ending."

I nudged our knees together. "I miss the food."

"*God*, I miss the food. I need a hot breakfast from the Old Chelsea."

"I need a good bitch session with Edie."

"Don't you get those on the phone?"

"They're not as much fun if I'm paying for it, hemorrhaging nickels makes it feel like I'm talking to Dr. French in drag."

Wesley bit off a tart mouthful and gazed up at the sky through the roof as he exhaled. "I could do with a doctor or two of my own."

I leaned into Wesley. He looped his arm around my shoulders and briskly rubbed one before leaning down and smudging out his spent filter in the dirt. "Oh, Jack . . ." He sighed, yawning, pinching at his eyes. "It's certainly been a summer."

"It's been fun. Hasn't it?"

Wesley crossed his legs and leaned forward, curling up to prop his cheek on his fist facing me, smeared up against his knuckles. "It has.

I'm ready to be done, though. I don't know. It was nice, but it's a chapter I can't say I'll be sad to see closed."

I gave him a sympathetic smile. He kept looking at me.

"You still feel okay with the role?" he asked.

"I feel good," I said, nodding to myself and staring at the splotchy stage, its leftover bloodstains like spilled wine. "My mind is quiet."

Wesley's smile pushed against his hand. I stood up and kissed him on the crown of the head as Kline emerged from backstage with the lawmen in tow, laughing through the end of an adage about blondes. He ushered them to the back of the house, bid them a good afternoon, and shut the doors behind them with a firm bang.

"Jesus Christ, you'd think I had Vincent fucking Mangano shoved up my ass," Kline groused, stalking back down the aisle to the stage. "Bastards wanted to sniff through every little nook and cranny in this shithole. *Places!*"

I pulled Wesley back up to his feet when he offered me a hand. "You can ignore his direction if you want," he muttered, angling a surreptitious nod at Kline. "He hasn't even read the play, so he won't catch it if you just make your own choices."

Wesley helped me up onto the apron, and I held his hand to steady him up after me. "Direct myself?" I said briskly. "How modern. Ezra would have a conniption."

"Just do what feels right," Wesley said, and crossed to take his place for the top of our interrupted scene.

Do what feels right.

From the back of the house, I noticed the lithe shape of Haas enter and seat himself on one of the benches. His lighter flared. I met his gaze even far from the reach of the long shadows cast by the tall, curved building. I tried to think of the party. I tried to remember what the three of us had done last night after I'd spoken with Jesse, and came up dry. That handful of hours had tripped away into nothing, like they never even happened.

Haas smiled.

We were set again for the top of the scene. I lifted the blank prop page once more.

It all felt perfectly fine.

19

⁓⁓⁓

The Lake Sumner motel, room number five

WE RETURNED TO the motel after rehearsal. Wesley and Haas went ahead with the rest of the company to dinner across the street, and I stopped in our room to freshen up first. I realized as I was buttoning my only unwrinkled shirtdress that I hadn't bled yet that month.

I paused and stared down at my stocking feet. I counted the weeks backward.

I was late.

My pocket agenda was tucked in my suitcase beside the pile of delicates I had recently hand-washed in the sink and hung up to dry over the shower curtain rod. I crouched back on my heels and peeled it open across my knees, paging to last month and scouring the grid of weeks for the little pencil-dot I put beside each day I bled.

There, the last one: a month and two days ago.

I hadn't been off my own very punctual clock since after the rescue surgery—the doctors told me the general anesthetic could throw my body's schedule for a loop, and it certainly had. Aside from then, I was always regular to a fault, to the very day.

Yet now here I was. Late.

I shut the diary and sat on the floor for a moment with my knees drawn tight against my chest.

I was *late*.

It could be either one of them. The mechanics of the three of us sleeping together had become an unsolvable tangle as we'd spent more and more time together. It was impossible to point to either of the men with conviction.

Late.

Slowly, stiffly, as though obeying a tiny pilot in my head and not my own volition, I stood up and replaced the little book back in my suitcase. I sat down carefully at the vanity and prepared a dose of powder.

I couldn't tell anyone.

I waited very patiently and stared through the brittle hollow of my own shock until the Lady entered the edge of the mirror as though she had simply been taking air out of sight.

"Did you ever have a child?" I asked her, very softly.

For a long beat, she looked at me with an unshakable stare.

"Do not ever ask me about my child."

I looked away from the indomitable heat of her eyes. "We were careful," I blurted.

"Were you?"

I glared and pointed at her in the mirror. "Don't do that. *Don't* make me doubt myself."

"Is it yourself you doubt, or one of them?" The Lady pointed at the bed.

"It can't be them."

The Lady barely raised an eyebrow. "And whyever not?"

I shook my head. The compulsion to scratch at my arms prickled through my mind for the first time in weeks. I prepared another dose of powder. My hands were shaking. "It—I don't want this," I babbled. "I don't want to, I can't—"

"Don't be daft, girl," the Lady said coolly as I sniffed it down and winced, pinching at my nose to keep the stinging at bay. "You cannot unmake what's been made."

Girl. Once, she had called me *woman.*

My lip curled up in a snarl as I glared at the Lady. "I take my pills!" I snatched up the plastic circle of round pastilles in their neat rows from beside my lipsticks to wag them sharply in the mirror.

"And ingest as well a gallimaufry that would cross the eyes of Hecate herself," the Lady snapped, her voice banded with steel. "You mix your magicks."

She spat on the floor at her feet.

I stood and clamored my purse back to rights. "I don't need you." I glared up at her, watching me through the reflection, and tasted the bitter tang along the back of my tongue. "I don't need your lectures."

I slammed the hinged sides of the vanity shut, putting away the glass. The room fell into a thick, sudden stillness.

Alone.

I stood in the middle of this empty, silent place and caught my breath.

I glanced at the face of my cocktail watch. "Shit," I hissed to myself, stumbling into my shoes and hurrying from the room without another thought.

Wesley and Haas were at our usual table. I slid into the booth and gave them both my most charming smile. Wesley passed me the rest of his drink, which I chugged in one quick go.

"Christ, Jack, no reason to rush catching up. We have all night."

Wesley grinned at me. Under the table, Haas's hand slid warm and possessive around the curve of my thigh. My grin faltered, only barely.

We ordered and ate. Haas didn't quit touching me. My skin prickled meanly, even through the mask of the powder. I excused myself to the restroom with only half my plate finished. Wesley stood as I did. "Are you alright?"

I patted him on the arm. "I'm fine. Just—a little woozy, need some cold water on my neck."

I darted a disarming grin at Haas. He was watching me. "Hurry back," he said, smiling as well.

I couldn't tell them. Not either of them. I could hardly bear to tell myself.

In the bathroom, I paced and paced and paced in front of the mirror but repeatedly found myself the only figure in my reflection. Even leaned close to check the edges of the glass, as though the Lady was hiding just around the bend—nothing. She had left me alone, like I'd told her to.

As I washed my hands, I found the pink marks of unconscious scratching alongside my scars—shallower, brief in their bright anger, yet stinging all the same.

◆ ◆ ◆

THE FINAL DRESS rehearsal for *Macbeth* arrived three days later. I still hadn't bled.

I couldn't bear to be on my own in my tiny, cluttered dressing room. It rang with far too much portent, the past rising up from in-side its own mouth—I hurried down the bustling backstage hall to Wesley's dressing room, dodging actors and set pieces with only my paint left to do, and knocked briskly.

"Can I come in?" I asked at the jamb.

Wesley opened the door with a smile, which faltered when he saw my face.

"Lock the door," I whispered as I moved past him.

Wesley wedged his chair under the door handle before turning to look at me. "I'll stop this dead if you need me to, Jack. Say the word and it's done. We can just go home."

I could see it in him, too; the memory like thick smoke dimming the light behind Wesley's eyes. I wrapped my arms around myself, pinning my hands down under my elbows to keep from scratching.

"No, not . . . I think I'm pregnant."

Wesley went very still. The quick work of backward calculation danced over every little twitch of his body: the brief flare of his nose, his lashes blinking rapidly, the slow intake of a breath he let out and then drew again before speaking. "Should I be congratulating you," he murmured, "or helping you come up with a plan?"

"I don't know, it—all I know is that I can't tell Felix. I *can't*. He doesn't need to know."

Wesley swallowed. "Do you think he's the father?"

"Regardless of whose fault it is, *you* would be the father. *You're* my husband." The sudden, ugly prickling of tears made me look away. "You're my husband, Wesley."

With a careful lulling sound, Wesley crossed the small space be-tween us and held me close with a tight, centering embrace. "We'll figure it out," he said into the high pile of my hair pinned up at the crown of my head. "Do you want me to tell Kline to pull the plug?"

"No. I'm fine. I want to do it."

"Then get ready in here, could you? I don't want you to be alone right now."

Wesley held me for a few more moments before stepping back to arm's length. He searched my bare face and leaned over to his make-shift dressing table, where his paint kit was laid out. I had interrupted his ritual.

"I'll do yours," he said lightly, uncapping a liner pencil and taking up his lighter to heat the end of it, "if you'll do mine."

Together, we drew each other's faces to dramatic attenuation. I painted his lips. He tinted my eyelids. I powdered his neck. He blushed my cheeks.

We beheld ourselves in the spotty mirror when finished, standing side by side. I gave him my best, most valiant smile, fully seated in the Lady. "I'll be alright," I insisted and squeezed his hand in mine. "It will be wonderful."

I could feel my eyes tearing up, but I forced them to hold. He'd done such a fine job on my tight-line.

Wesley didn't look away from the glass, as though to turn from it would ruin the moment. "I wish there were an audience here to see you do this again. You're sensational."

"It doesn't matter. The only person I care about seeing it is you."

The call for places went up.

Wesley lifted our hands and kissed the heel of my thumb so softly the red hardly transferred. He looked at me with a heady mix of pride and sorrow. "Break a leg," he said, with all the weight of *I love you.*

"Toi toi toi," I said—a tear tripped down from my lashes as I pressed the smile wider onto my face.

I did not steal down a dose of powder as I crossed to the other side of the stage.

For the next five acts, I would be in full communion with myself. I would face the curtain entirely lucid, in all my own miserable splendor, and I would live.

20

The Sumner Globe

THE DRESS REHEARSAL was, unfortunately, flawless.

I couldn't bear to open the show in its aftermath. Even without an audience, the old superstition held fast: A perfect dress rehearsal spelled disaster for anything that followed. I couldn't do that to myself.

The company was given a rest day before opening. I left Wesley to sleep late and dodged an invitation from Haas to get breakfast together, electing instead to convince one of the drivers to take me up to the theater—I'd left a tube of lipstick behind in my dressing room, you see, and it *really* was my favorite one.

If Kline agreed to table the show, I would get out of this place alive. I had to try. It was me who was going to fight for my own sanity for once.

I knocked on Kline's door and didn't wait for an answer before testing at the latch. It opened, unlocked, and I stopped in the jamb.

"Afternoon."

Jesse was bent to the task of measuring out several bleach-white bundles of product on Kline's desk, wearing a black undershirt with a fringed suede jacket draped over the back of the chair.

I averted my gaze as though I had walked in on the man half-nude. "I'm—so sorry to interrupt, I was looking for Kline. I need to speak with him."

Jesse nodded me into the room. I stepped inside and shut the door behind me. None of my warning lights lit up, no hackles raised; the primitive instinct of my body was just as at ease here with Jesse as it was in Edie's apartment.

Jesse made two tidy lines and sniffed them both down. He nodded to himself and sat back in the chair, swiveling idly with both hands on the arms.

"What needs discussing?" he chirped. "Kline's probably back in town seeing to his girls, might be a little while. Anything I can do to help?"

I crossed my arms tightly and shook my head at the floor.

Jesse tipped his head at me with genuine concern. "Everything alright? Anyone giving you shit?"

It sounded earnest, which made me soften a little before I realized it. "I'm fine," I said automatically, but stopped myself. I swallowed. "I need to go over some—character notes, for the show."

Jesse sighed, full-bodied, like a shaggy dog settling down to rest. He looked at me for a moment. "I knew you juniper New Yorkers were gonna take this whole thing too seriously," he said to himself. He off-set the strange observation with a roguish smile. "Isn't it enough to just make art?"

I frowned at him. "What?"

Jesse's grin broadened. "What do you mean, what? It's theater, the great human pastime. Relax. Not everything has to be so fuckin' ideal."

He leaned back, his long body in repose, and crossed one booted ankle over his knee on top of the desk. I stared at him. Looking pleased with himself, Jesse leaned forward and prepared another two lines.

"Where the hell'd I put my manners—ladies first!" He deftly cut and pushed with the edge of his ruby-red pocketknife. From up close, I could see the handle was shaped like a showgirl's leg: knee, stocking, calf, punctuated with a heeled shoe at the end. "Propriety's sake, in case my grandmother's still watching over. Won't take it personal if you'd rather not."

Jesse held the tray out to me.

It was fine. Not nearly as strong as Haas's, but smoother. Kinder, if the word could be applied. I stepped back and watched Jesse take his, pinching briskly at his nostrils.

"I see a man's life is a tedious one," I quoted from *Cymbeline*—testing him, if only for my own diversion. "I have tired myself, and for two nights together have made the ground my bed."

Jesse laced his fingers together behind his head, his bandy elbows out wide. He had a rangy collection of home-brew tattoos along his bare arms and chest, the crawl of them like glyphs rambling foreign and storied, disappearing beneath his undershirt.

"I should be sick," he quoted back at me, crisp and twanged, "but that my resolution helps me."

I watched him for several seconds, sizing up the stack of Jesse's eclecticisms. "Why Shakespeare?" I asked.

"Shakespeare, Marlowe, all those uppity punks hunkered down in their taverns and talked of kings the way we knock back a few and harp about politicians. It's timeless." Jesse reached into the back of his mouth with one pinkie nail, picking at his teeth, and prodded the spot briefly with the tip of his tongue in thought. "Only they had the balls to put 'em onstage; give those kings stories, dramas, all that private bunk exposed. Helped us small folk understand that power can bleed just like us—and if something bleeds, you can kill it."

We watched each other for a silent stretch. The desk chair squeaked softly with each pass of Jesse's lazy swiveling.

"Why an entire theater?" I asked. "Why not just hire people to perform at that . . . giant fucking house for a summer?"

Pressing another stretch into his shoulders before sitting forward again, Jesse set back to meting out his product with the peaceful rote of a housewife folding laundry. "It's mighty quiet out here," he said with vaulted gusto, "and I wanted to have myself an eventful summer before I get much more seniority under my belt, which'll mean I've got more 'n a few people ready and waiting to stab my back."

I stared at him. "Should you be telling me this?" I asked lightly.

Jesse smirked. "Not like it's any surprise, is it?" He glanced up at me, his gaze humored. "Between you and me, a coup is more likely to get me than age. My mother lived to be a hundred and nine." A fond smile lifted his side-hitched mouth. "One of the boys, that wily little stagehand you saw the other night, he said I should have done *Julius Caesar*."

"Does your outfit plan on making a habit of hiring theater companies from the city?"

Jesse laughed. "No, ma'am, once is enough." He peered at the scale, dabbed a bit off the top, and scrubbed it onto his gums before standing and drawing up to his full, sway-hipped height. He nodded his chin at the ceiling rafters. "Built this beauty over land we don't want getting *developed*, if you catch my drift. Crowbait."

"You *really* shouldn't be telling me this."

"Shouldn't I? I dunno. This shit gives me motormouth." Jesse gestured at the desk.

"So there's . . . what, just going to be a replica of the Globe sitting empty in the middle of the desert?"

Jesse whelped another laugh, spiny and cracked as the coyotes I could hear beyond the motel walls most nights. "Sugar, there are much stranger things out there. We aren't even at the *beginning* of the middle of the desert. We're still within spitting distance of the feds." He winked at me and gave a quick, sidewinder grin. "Just barely— only if you really hock it."

I worked my jaw, my mouth dry, and ran a hand along my cheek. "What do you even do out here?" I asked without looking at him.

"She's *curious*," Jesse mused.

"Call it a reminder of my upbringing."

"Thespianism aside, I like to consider our branch somewhat of a concierge service for the rest of the gents. You take a little heat back east, or fall into some trouble in Vegas, you cool your heels here with my fine folk. Everyone tends to forget what ails them after a little Southwestern hospitality." He gestured with a spin of his wrist at the drugs. "The house special helps, too."

A light cotton fuzz had taken its time pulling up along the back of my mind. It was a sweeter dive than Haas's, less urgent and more sure of itself. I fixated on the way the light spangled against the sparkling alloy of Jesse's leg-shaped knife—the second bulb still hadn't been replaced. Jesse glanced up at me and caught me looking.

"You can have that if you'd like," he said. He licked his thumb and counted through a few sheets of blank cashier's checks in a binder open beside him. "Pretty thing like you could probably use it more than me. I only keep it 'cause it's cute anyhow—my real muscle is a little less flashy."

I gave a dry chuckle and raised an eyebrow at him. "Cute?"

"You heard me, Cherokee Park. Take it. I like giving gifts."

I stared at the knife. "I can't open the show," I said without looking away.

He paused. "Now why's that?"

"A good dress rehearsal is a bad omen."

When I glanced up, Jesse's eyes were unmoving but not cold. He smiled at me with a distant wistfulness. "You sure? You look like you become someone entirely different on that stage. I've never seen anything like it."

"I have a bad history with the role. I don't think she'll let me out alive again if I do another opening night."

Jesse watched me for a tenuous silence before he shrugged, unbothered. "Never could say no to a Bluegrass lass. I'll see about throwing another party instead, how's that?"

He made a small baggie of powder with the knife before shutting the blade and gesturing casually at me with the offering like a backward olive branch. I took it—the handle was warm and surprisingly dense. I tucked it into my skirt pocket.

The door opened. Both Jesse and I turned to face it. Haas stood in the jamb with his face creased in stony concern.

"Morning," he said coolly, giving a curt nod to Jesse and gathering me hastily by the shoulder. Haas made to steer me from the room, but I pushed against him and held out a hand to Jesse.

"You have a good day," I said.

He grinned at me and tipped the brim of his hat, his gaze moving between us. He gripped my hand with a brief but fierce clasp. "You do the same, Mrs. Shoard. I'll be in touch."

Haas shut the door firmly behind us and started a quick clip back down the hall, pulling me after him. "He'll be in *touch*?" Haas said through his teeth. I glared at him, digging my heels in to stop us there in the hall.

"Why do you care who I have business with?" I demanded.

Haas's stare hardened. He looked up and down the length of the hall, ensuring we were in privacy, and still took a step closer to drop his voice. *"Business,"* he spat, as if I were a child skiing around in her mother's good pumps. "What did I tell you? You shouldn't ever find yourself alone with men like him."

"I can look after myself, thanks very much."

"Can you?"

I opened my mouth to rebut that, but nothing came out besides a wounded scoff when I saw Haas's eyes flick down to my arms, my scars and the chapped-raw scuffing of my bad habit come back to life. When I found my voice again, my pulse pelting up to a furious sprint, it matched Haas's steel. "He's fucking harmless," I hissed, and turned to make my way back to the house.

"So are wild dogs when they're looking for someone to give them scraps," Haas snapped. "Why were you in there, anyways? His product is *shit.*"

I made to keep walking without him—but Haas darted out and snatched my wrist, holding me fast with a stinging zing where his grip twisted my skin.

Devour.

I ripped my hand away. *"Don't* grab me."

The air shuddered between us, tension crackling like the greasy lick of an oil fire leaping to life. Haas's stare burned behind his spectacles. His jaw flexed.

"I think I'll have dinner with Wesley alone tonight," I announced. I hesitated for only a moment longer before hurrying at a brisk clip toward the front of house.

"Margaret," Haas called after me. It was a command, but I didn't stop or turn to look at him.

The daylight sliced in harsh over the theater's east wall. I returned to the docks, where a driver took me back to the shore and then helped me into a van to get back to the motel.

I watched the lake grow small through the back window. There were so few things in my life that I had been able to call mine in earnest—I had wanted the Lady to be one of those things, and now Haas to be another for as long as I could keep him.

Maybe he'd calm down. I'd talk to him in the morning.

I slipped Jesse's baggie from my pocket and examined it. I dug my compact out from my purse and peered at the colder, blue-white shade of Haas's powder.

I latched the clamshell shut again and tapped out another sniff of Jesse's onto the edge of my hand.

◆ ◆ ◆

I WRESTLED WITH whether or not to tell Wesley about closing the show for the rest of the day. As we got ready for dinner that night, I stood at my jewelry pouch and ran my fingers along a slippery string of pearls.

"I don't think Felix is joining us tonight," I announced.

Wesley poked his head out of the bathroom, dragging pomade through his hair. "Things go sour?"

Did you tell him? asked the soft fever in his eyes.

I played my thumb over the pearls in my hands like prayer beads. "I went up the ladder and closed the show."

"What?" Wesley set down his comb on the edge of the sink. "When?"

"I went to the theater this morning. Jesse was there—the one who runs things. I told him I wasn't comfortable after such a good dress. He said we'd have another party instead."

Wesley stared at me in stunned silence.

I looked down at my hands and hurried the pearls around my neck, shaking my head miserably as I fumbled with the clasp. "I'm sorry," I muttered, "I should have told you, it—"

"I haven't been this relieved since you woke up in the fucking hospital."

I turned to look at him and dropped the loop, catching the necklace against my chest. "Really?"

Wesley came over and helped lock the hook and eye together. He bent to nuzzle me gently at the back of my neck. "Let the past lie," he murmured. "We'll get back to civilization, and we can figure out what comes next. Be patient with yourself, Jack. These things take time."

I shut my eyes and reached back to hold him briefly by the back of his head.

As Wesley finished knotting his tie, I peeked surreptitiously at my pocket calendar again. I stared at the empty days where there should be a mark. I longed for proof that I wasn't doomed to another unintended fate. To bleed was to remain my own.

"Ready?"

I hastened the cover shut, stowing it hurriedly under my clothes, and gave Wesley a sunny smile as I offered my arm.

The food tasted better than it had in days. Wesley and I told stories and jokes and laughed together in a way we hadn't since before my accident, and my heart beat warm and vital in my chest. *This is the life I want to keep*, I thought, as Wesley fixed me with a tender smile across the table. *This is the life I must keep for myself.*

After ordering our postprandials, Wesley and I settled in at the bar with a few others of the company, who had confirmation we were off the hook for the summer—paid in full, and all of them happy to be going back to the city with a few good stories alongside the cash in their pockets.

"Are you disappointed you won't get to open?" Lisette asked. I waved her off and shot back the last of a whiskey Wesley and I had been sharing.

"Are you kidding? Now I have something to hold over Ezra's head when we get back," I said with a grin.

I excused myself to take some air. A meditative cigarette on the front porch of the restaurant had me staring out into the dark, rolling the role over and over at the back of my mind. In playing to the empty theater as Lady Macbeth, even for just a single rehearsal, I had put her to bed for good. I gave up the best work of my life to the ghosts and then let go of it, willingly.

Healthy detachment, Dr. French had discussed with me once. There was a time I considered that phrase completely useless. Oxymoronic.

In that, the strangest idea of all: Perhaps I really could grow beyond it all.

I tapped out my cigarette on the wooden railing on which I'd been leaning—but before I could return inside, the flare of headlights from one of the company vans veered up and parked at an off-angle so close it nearly rammed the edge of the porch.

The driver's side door opened. Haas stumbled out. He looked rumpled, unglued, his eyes flashing with strange purpose.

"Margaret," he barked, coming straight for me. He crossed into the light, and I saw he was thoroughly ripped on his own supply.

"Felix." I made to sidle past him in tidy farewell, nothing beyond acknowledgment, but he caught me hard around the waist and held me fast to the spot.

"You killed the fucking production?"

I set my jaw. "I didn't *kill it*. I made a request, and Jesse agreed. We get back to the city a few weeks early, no money lost. We all win."

"You've wasted my work!" Haas pointed furiously into the ink-black night in the direction of the theater. "You're dashing *everything* we've done here, like a selfish child!"

Fury boiled over, hot and roiling between my ribs. "Eat shit."

He surged forward and seized me by the shoulders, his fingers digging deep enough to bruise.

"You aren't playing by the rules!" Haas cried. He was fuming. I hadn't seen a man so angry at me since my days with Hollis— *No.* That was then. This was now. Let it lie.

"Whose rules, Felix?" I demanded. I shoved against his grip, but Haas didn't budge.

"You signed a contract!"

"*I* didn't sign anything."

"Your fucking husband did! I could *ruin* you!"

I had to laugh at him. I spat a sharp jeer in his face—Haas flinched, and my defiance flared. "*Could* you! Let's check the fine print, shall we?" My voice rose, and my old Kentucky patois with it, as though the wounded little thing I'd been when I was there wanted to say her piece as well. "Oh, look, contract's written by the fuckin' *Dixie mob*, I'm sure that shit'll hold up *real* nice in county court!"

Haas's mouth trembled and curled with derision, showing his teeth. "You uppity, bumpkin slut."

He crowded me with a swift and hideous grace. I could hardly recognize the shape of him from so near.

My yell for help died in nothing but a reedy squeak as Haas's hand closed hard over my mouth.

Panic flooded me with a tidal heave. Glass-eyed with fury, Haas moved like a man possessed and shoved me against the support beam of the bar's porch at my back.

He could kill me, right here—he *would* kill me, if he wanted to. Right here.

He could kill me, and he wanted to, and he was going to get away with it. Right here.

But—no.

That isn't how it goes.

Art thou afeard to be the same in thine own act and valour as thou art in desire?

I bit down and didn't stop until the skin broke.

The snap of flesh parted and burst around my teeth. Haas yelped and reared back, leaving his gore behind in my mouth, before he swung hard against my cheek with a closed fist.

The pain was secondary. Haas was panting. He was going to tear me apart with his bare hands, those tightly wound and nimble hands.

He was going to kill me, because he wanted to.

DEVOUR, the Lady's voice shouted into the webbing of my brain, overtaking everything at once—I was her, and she was me, and we had always been the same person, hadn't we?

"Jack?"

I turned to see Wesley coming out from the small crowd of the company that had been playing dominoes inside. He wore concern beneath the rosy flush of a nice night out. As he looked between me and Haas—the unsettled seat of Haas's shoulders, the way I was nursing my cheek—I spat a mouthful of Haas's blood to the ground.

Wesley's anger bloomed. "You *bit her*?" he snarled, advancing on Haas.

"Wesley," I snapped, "don't."

"You and your beard can hop in the mud and make waves," Haas spat.

Wesley was on him with momentum. This time, I didn't step in to call him off.

"I asked you a question, Felix," Wesley snarled, a knee driven between Haas's shoulders, shoving him hard into the dirt after a brief, messy struggle, "did you lay your fucking hands on my wife?"

Haas's bitten hand was pressed hard to the ground where he was pinned, trapped against his chest and smearing his sport coat. He turned his face with a mighty wince, scraping hard against the dirt, to rear up and glare at me. Fury leapt hot along the snarling straits of his upper lip, and he leered at me through the flash of his skewed glasses catching the lamplight.

That stare was a curse. My insides went frigid as a familiar rush of queasiness rankled along the underside of my deepest shame; the look of all before him who'd seen me as nothing but a tool to be used.

Had he been wearing it the entire time? Was he just that good at covering it?

"Well, I wouldn't have to if you deigned to do it on your own, you fucking poof," Haas sneered.

Wesley hauled him around and hit him square in the jaw, holding him by the collar, and didn't stop until blood from Haas's nose began to stain his cuffs.

Staggering finally to his feet, furtive in the dark to keep the rest of the company inside from seeing, Wesley delivered a final, solid kick to Haas's midsection like the exclamation point at the end of a damning sentence. "If you so much as *look* at her again," Wesley warned, his voice as low and placid and unknowably black as the water at the deepest part of the lake, "you are a fucking *dead man*."

Wesley steered us quickly back to the motel, hurrying across the empty highway. I went, willing and wrung out and grateful.

I didn't look back at Haas. I didn't want to see him dragging himself back up. Part of me hoped he would stay there, laid out in the dirt, to rot under the indiscriminate sun forever.

21

The Lake Sumner motel, room number five

WE SLEPT LIKE hell.

I made toast on the hot plate around sunrise, because I couldn't think of what else to do with the morning. I could hardly focus and burnt it before changing over to brew coffee.

When Wesley came out of the bathroom and shuffled to the kitchenette, he stood behind me with his arms around my waist and his cheek resting on the back of my neck. Sunlight was finally starting to feather into the room with slim, pale fingers. I turned to look at him over my shoulder, and Wesley examined my cheek.

"Does it still hurt?" he asked. He'd sat with me in silence last night at the rickety wooden table; as I tended my bruising with a hefty chip from the crusted-over icebox wrapped in one of the bath towels, Wesley took a kerchief soaked in club soda to his shirt where Haas's blood had touched him.

"Not really. Is it still red?"

Wesley's lips drew into a thin line. "A little."

I shrugged. "Makeup."

"Christ." Wesley sagged his face into my shoulder. "I'm sorry, Jack," he said against the lower slope of my neck, "I shouldn't have left you alone."

"How could we have known?" I shrugged again and moved to shut off the hot plate when the percolator began to rumble. There were only two cups on the counter. "I've been alone with him before, we both have. We couldn't have known."

Wesley's gaze was unfocused, fixed to an unseen middle distance for a long moment. He finally blinked. I turned to pour us each a cup.

"I just feel like—"

"If you're about to blame yourself," I cut in immediately, "don't."

Wesley took the second cup from me and searched my gaze before I let go of the mug's edge. "I feel like I should have . . . felt something. I've known men like him before. They're all the same."

"So have I. It's not your fault, Wes. We'll be back home in a few days and can pretend he never happened. We don't have to remember him if we don't want to."

Wesley frowned as I made for the table, where I laid out the toast and the spreads on one plate. "You're better at shrugging off men than I am," he groused.

"Of course I am. I'm married."

My reward for the teasing came as an edgewise thing: a smile, barely there at the corner but there nonetheless. I sat down and took up the butter knife to scrape with unintended violence at the butter dish.

Wesley pawed a hand down his face. His unshaved chin rasped across his palm. "God," he said and sighed, aimless into the morning.

Silence sat thick and ill-fitting between us. As I mulled over a bite of toast bright with stale jam, I watched Wesley drag his butter to the edges of his bread with tightly sewn concentration.

"He was so fucking *selfish*," Wesley said suddenly to his plate. "Nitpicky. I didn't think anything of it before, but he always took, never gave."

"Even when it was just the two of you?"

"Especially then. Trust me."

I thought of the times Haas and I had had sex alone. He found a masochistic rapture in denying his own pleasure as far as he could stretch it every time, fixated on delivering himself to near delirium with delay. I turned the shape of the word around at the back of my mouth. *Selfish.*

Like a selfish child!

"I do," I said, and focused on my sad little breakfast instead of the primal fear of disappointing someone.

"You should call Edie," Wesley suggested. He took a tidy bite of toast. "She's good at picking the shit from the Shinola. She'd find a silver lining here."

I snorted. "I wouldn't even know where to start."

"Start from the beginning. She's a good listener."

I took a ruminant bite of my own toast.

"Do you ever wish you could un-fuck someone?" I asked, and felt the barest inch of weight lighten on my shoulders when Wesley finally chuckled.

◆ ◆ ◆

THE FAREWELL PARTY was to be later that night. Slapdash invitations—handwritten again, this time on scraps of motel letterhead—were shoved under our doors around midday: *Party, No Show. Caravan leaves motel 9 sharp. Late? No Party. REMEMBER: Leaving sunup Monday!!!*

Our room was a mess. I was doing my best to get some preliminary packing in order, and I had lost track of my pocket calendar. There were piles of clothes, both laundered and unlaundered, scattered shoes and makeup in disarray, both of us tired of this place and grown sloppy in its upkeep. We had two days to get our luggage ready to go. It made my teeth itch to be surrounded by chaos.

I had to call Edie. I didn't *need* the agenda book, her number was memorized . . . but it rankled me to be missing it.

No matter. I would find it later, doubtless under a dress I'd neglected to hang.

I hunted the little sachet of Jesse's powder in the vanity drawer. I had hardly left the room since the episode with Haas, and I was doing my utmost to conserve it and not just tear through it all in a stir-craze.

Only enough to stave off the worst of a splitting headache—I put on my sunglasses as I slipped from the room and made for the phone booth at the far end of the motel.

I dialed long distance.

"Operator; number, please."

It wasn't the usual switchboard girl. I gave Edie's number. The woman made a doubtful sound.

"That isn't local."

I frowned. "This is long distance."

"You'll have to connect locally from here."

"Right. Fine. Could you send me to the New York exchange?"

"That will be twenty-five cents."

I jammed a quarter into the machine.

"Hold please." The switchboard gave a cloudy click. I crossed my arms and shrugged up into the corner of the booth, examining my nails. They were a wreck. Thank God we'd be done with this place soon.

New York picked up, a sleepy-voiced woman—"Operator, how may I help you?"

I gave Edie's number again.

"Thank you," she all but yawned. "Hold please."

As the line hissed and cracked, I chewed on the tip of my tongue.

"Bishop," Edie said breezily.

"It's me. I need some advice."

"Margaret?"

"Have you ever had a tryst go belly-up?"

"Slow down."

"We're coming home early."

"Margaret."

I shut my eyes and took a deep, slow breath. I held the handset away from my mouth to let it out in one great huff. "Hi, Edie," I said, forcing myself to evenness. "How's your day going?"

"Not nearly as eventful as yours, by the sound of it. What's going on?"

"Do you want the short or the long?"

"It's collect, save my money. Short is fine."

I shut my eyes and rested my forehead against the glass siding, made warm as a wheel well in the baking sun. "Dress rehearsal went great, I got gun-shy, and we *aren't* opening the Scottish play at all, but we all still get paid, we're coming home early because there's no run, and the tailor Wesley and I were fucking is an asshole, so that isn't happening anymore."

Edie was quiet for several long seconds in the ensuing silence.

"Happy summer stock," I deadpanned.

"You're alright?" Edie asked lightly.

I stared and stared and stared at the very edge of the mountain far against the foot of the sky. "I don't know. I might be pregnant."

There came then the deepest cruelty in a phone call: the silence of a machine speaking its own volumes—the stillness of Edie hearing me, processing my secret, fluttered and clicked ever so faintly like a living, jeering thing.

"By the belly-up tryst," she finally asked, her tone very careful, "or by your sweet husband?"

I shook my head, smearing my forehead against the glass. "I don't know."

"You don't *know*."

"It's been a long couple of months, Edie."

I stared along the stretching shadows growing tall toward me across the dirt, reaching with their slow infinity.

"Well, Margaret." It wasn't a chiding reply but held liminal concern. "Do you even feel equipped to . . . be someone's mother?"

I made a doubtful sound, warbling and manic. "I haven't been very good at being someone's daughter in the first place."

Edie was quiet again. Edie Bishop thinking before she spoke meant she really was taking it seriously. "Worse things have happened to less capable people," she said gently. "We'll figure this out. Don't worry."

"I'm not worried. I'm just . . . *done*." My shoulders sagged. I stepped back and rubbed the pressed-up spot on my forehead.

"Everything will be fine. I promise. I have a good doctor; I'll get you in to see him. Alright?" Edie insisted.

"I have a doctor."

"Not like this one. We'll get you sorted, Margot. I promise." Edie made a cagey sound. "I'm so sorry, I need to go."

"I always call when you're on your way out. Sorry."

"What sorry? You're no bother at all, my darling. Break a leg."

"I told you, we're not opening the show."

"I know. But you've got a lot of life to figure out right now. It feels cheap to wish you good luck. Keep your head on, poss."

Ka-klik.

I went back to the room and stared at my suitcase. I wanted to find my pocket calendar. I wanted to be back home *now.*

I pawed around at my vanity, its drawers and clutter and half-done work of returning me to where I belonged. I needed more bobby pins.

"Hey, Wes?" I called up, still poking through the mostly emptied drawers. "I'm going around the corner for more pins."

Wesley emerged from the bathroom freshly groomed and fragrant with aftershave. "Want me to get some for you? Chap and I are about to head to the tobacconist."

"No, it's fine. I'd like the walk." I examined myself in the mirror, the careful makeup covering the angry red stain under my eye, and practiced a smile in the glass. Good enough.

Keep your head on, poss.

◆ ◆ ◆

AT THE GENERAL store, the shopkeeper grinned as he rang up my flimsy card of hairpins and a pack of Marlboros—my usual Benson & Hedges were impossible to find out here. "How much longer are y'all in town?"

"We're leaving in two days," I said. My sunglasses were still on, even in the sleepy half-light of lowering afternoon barely pushing through the dusty windows.

"It's been a wild summer for us with that motel all full, I'll tell you what," the old man said. He sounded a little wistful. The register pinged as he tallied my total.

"It certainly has been that," I said, watching his bony fingers pluck at the summing keys. When I passed him my change, I looked at the endless lines of his palm and wondered at the doggedness of life; to grow old out here where nothing much happened—but then with nothing happening, every day must have been its own monumental miracle.

It's called an affirmation, Dr. French had instructed me early on, soon after our appointments began. *Think of it as the mental equivalent of easing your foot onto the brakes of a speeding car.*

What if I don't believe it?

I put my sunglasses back on and left the shop. The sun beat down on the empty, cracked sidewalk with a vengeance. I found that I missed the feeling of Dr. French's exacting stare, reaching down into me to knock politely on doors I didn't even know were there.

He had watched me in silence the day we created my "mantra" for a long moment with cool, professional obscurity. *The human mind is shockingly easy to dupe, Mrs. Shoard. If one tells herself something for long enough, it only takes enough times before one will believe just about anything.*

I returned to room five to continue getting ready. Room six was shut tight. I forced myself not to rush, or fumble the latch, or drop my keys.

"Every day of mine is a gift," I said to myself under my breath, praying to my own sanity, and was met with only silence in reply.

22

Another glamorous monstrosity, beyond Lake Sumner

THE CLOSING PARTY was hosted at a different house, just as modern and decked out as the last.

The sense of a season's completion put a charge in the air. The mix of the company plus the stage crew and Jesse's impressive strangers had turned into a real riot. I took the rest of Jesse's powder in the bathroom after twenty minutes.

At a sweating lope, the party carried into the small hours of the night—and caught in the soaring fever pitch of refusing to let go of a good time, I found my vision spinning as I became startlingly aware of myself. I was crushed hard in the middle of a nattering circle of conversation. Someone had just delivered a punch line I forgot to listen for.

My head felt like it was full of cotton balls. I'd lost sight of Wesley after slipping away to touch up the makeup around my bruised cheek a few minutes after midnight, and now here I was. I excused myself for the sprawling back patio; it was drizzling outside and I could take a cigarette in peace.

I would wait for things to die down a little before going back in to find Wesley—I was well and truly done. I wanted to go home.

The dark mountain shoulders shrugged up against the night seemed to watch me in return from their abstract relief. I found with a soft panging behind my breastbone that I would miss them, the stretch of a horizon unfettered by buildings. I looked up at the small patches of stars showing through the smudged, swollen clouds, more numerous than I ever could have imagined. They were illuminated from behind by a moon three-quarters heavy with silvery light.

Something closed hard around my elbow. My cigarette fell to the ground with a hiss.

I wrenched against it, but the hold gripped down more tightly. It hauled me into the dark, and all I could do was stumble down the muddied path.

"What—?"

"Quiet."

The hand around my arm was fierce and tense with certain fury. A hand, it was—a hand, Haas leading me at a clipped stride. Haas.

I dug my heels in, the ground scuttling uselessly under my party shoes, and tried to stop. It didn't work. I pried at his iron grip.

"Felix, you—"

He squeezed me harder, and my flesh protested as he shook me tightly. "I said *quiet.*"

My fingernails scored his hand as I struggled against him, but he didn't relent. His unsettled gaze roved with a paranoid intensity. I scrabbled at his sleeve as he hurried me into the emptiness—I looked wildly over my shoulder at the lights of the house retreating in the distance, slipping away, but nobody was there. I had stepped alone beyond the safety of my flock, like a stupid lamb.

"Stop!" I shouted and wrestled harder against him as my voice disappeared into the night-heavy sprawl of the desert.

Haas took me by the other elbow to steer me violently, the hard bite of it making me cry out. "Get in the fucking car," he snapped.

He shoved me into the same Ford that had taken us back to the motel from the first party. My vision swam. My breath came short, and as I fought to calm it, I realized a low litany of *no, no, no, no* was dribbling from my mouth.

Haas's expression was restless, his jaw grinding, his stare bright and horrific in the throw of the headlights leaping to life—I jostled messily in my seat as he tore into third gear and gunned it onto the main road, speeding in the opposite direction of town. When I yanked at the door handle, it was already locked.

"Who do you think planted the seed in Kline's empty fucking head?" Haas shouted, as though resuming an argument he'd already been having with himself. His knuckles clenched white around the steering wheel. "'Talk to Margaret Shoard, I saw her in Ezra Pierce's last farce, she and her lily of a husband were the only good part!' I *gave* this to you! I gave this to you with both hands!"

"What the hell are you talking about?" I cried around my heavy tongue. "Let me *out*."

"He wasn't going to bother when he heard Ezra had dropped you, but I told him to take Wesley anyways, he was still passable on his own," Haas spat, barreling onward. "I gave you back *exactly* what you wanted and now you have the audacity to think you'll—what, go home again to your kitchen, and a nursery, give *all of it* up? I brought you back to life, Margaret! You were unspoiled! Where did you misplace your *fucking gratitude*!"

I kept at the door handle, but it wouldn't budge. Haas accelerated.

It was useless. I would be dashed on the asphalt if I tried to leave the car at this speed.

"You want to throw everything away, FINE!" The persistent growl of the engine ticked upward. The odometer crawled past eighty. I plastered myself to the seat and tried not to panic. "You're chaining yourself to a fairy who knows *nothing* of how to handle you! If you want any future at all, the best thing you can do for yourself is drink a capful of bleach and leave him!"

"This is about *Wesley*?" I shouted, nearly laughing. "You knew we were married from the start!"

"I thought it was a fucking act, but look at you!" Haas pitched something hard at me, and I cried out as I tried to duck it—my pocket calendar thwacked with a sting against my shoulder, falling open in my lap. "Fucking *PREGNANT*! You think I never let myself off in your cunt for the fun of it?!"

What?

He'd been through my things, he'd found my calendar, he'd— *read* it, deciphered it, and stolen the most basic knowledge of my own body from me.

This violation sparked a new and more bone-deep terror, as though Haas had crawled inside me to squeeze his hands in between my very organs. "How the hell did you get this?" I breathed, afraid to touch it lest the pages burn me after being in his hands.

"You're a stupid, selfish, shortsighted bitch," Haas seethed.

I shook my head as terrified tears began to pour from my eyes. "I'm a good wife."

"You've gotten by on batting your eyelashes and spreading your legs! I should have known you weren't any different!"

"I am a *good. Wife*," I insisted, unable to find any other words.

"You're a common fucking whore!" The car purred at near ninety miles an hour, the engine whining. "The second your *husband* gets a taste for having this kind of money again, he's going to leave you for some uptown fop and you will have *nowhere* to turn but me! Be grateful I'm still willing to bear the sight of you!"

I flinched, full-bodied, and could do nothing but bawl. *Be grateful to me, Margaret.* It was Hollis all over again.

How had I let this happen? Mama said it all the time, only stupid girls invited bad shit to roost.

That was all I ever had been, then, from the very beginning: a stupid girl.

Haas flexed his hands on the wheel. "We'll solve this nasty fix of yours and forget this ever happened, or I will *make* you forget it. Now shut up. Quit crying."

Rolling my head to the side, I clawed my stare out, out, out along the basin of the desert as though any of it might reach in and pull me to safety. Heavy clouds churned in the distance over the jut of a mesa illuminated in a hard shaft of moonlight. The rain came down in heavier sheets.

"I want to go home," I sobbed.

"I said *shut up*, Margaret."

"Fuck you!"

"SHUT UP!"

His voice boomed like a cascade of thunder rattling the claustrophobic interior of the front seat. I shut my eyes and tried to hold in the cry that still slipped out.

"I've seen better women than you piss away every opportunity in the name of the mewling whelps they claimed to want," Haas roared. "I will not let it happen again!"

"I don't want to," I babbled, shaking my head wildly, clinging to the door handle and begging silently for this to be a nightmare. I wanted to wake up. I wanted to find myself in a cold sweat in scratchy, starch-stiff sheets and pile into a van that smelled of ancient tobacco leaves and leave this place. "Felix, please, I want to go home, I—"

"I don't believe you! This is all your fault! You threw yourself at me, you *begged* for this! And for *what*, so you could have an excuse not to put yourself back onstage!"

He slammed his hands on the wheel, which made us fishtail shallowly down the empty road—I vised my grip to the door and screamed through my tears.

"NOBODY can be more than one thing at once!" Haas bellowed over me.

"STOP THE FUCKING CAR!"

Haas slammed the brakes and peeled violently off the road, only narrowly avoiding the pit of a ditch opening up ahead. I caught both of my hands on the glove box and barely kept from smacking my forehead on the dashboard.

The windshield wipers danced in the sudden, sickening silence— *thup-thup, thup-thup, thup-thup.*

"You want so badly to find a villain on whom you can blame *everything* wrong with you." Haas's voice dropped to a horrific murmur as he glared at me in the dark, the headlights illuminating him in their watery reflection glancing from the hood of the car. I had never seen a man so angry in my entire life, not even with the worst of Hollis's benders. "You want me to be a villain?"

Incredulous and terrified, I could hardly make out what he was saying. Reality whined around me like the filament in a lightbulb about to burst. I fought to take control of my breathing again.

"What the fuck is going on?" I wept.

"If you want me to be a villain," Haas said through his teeth, his mouth trembling and his eyes wet, "I'll show you a villain."

I tried to plead.

Truly. I did.

Sometimes I turn this moment over in my mind to wonder at it. Did I really kick my feet at him as hard as I meant to? Did I shout at him and bite at his fingers and wrists with as much feral abandon as I could have?

I think I did.

I think I did everything a desperate creature can do, but when a monster is intent on peeling back his skin to show you the truth of his bones, there isn't any amount of fight that can remove the decision he's made to do harm.

The dirt bit into my knees. The air was cold on the backs of my legs, the ground wet and unforgiving against the side of my face as Haas pinned me and did what he willed.

It was horrific.

I had thought I knew how terror lived in a body, but not like this. Never like this.

I went very far away.

All of me became a muddy throb, like congealing blood pushing up through a wound. I couldn't say for how long it lasted—it might have been seconds, minutes, hours, or years. It was an aberration of existence, a cystic tear so violent that it separated itself from the plane where real things happened.

Haas left me for a while in the rain when he was done.

Still face down, staring sideways across the ground as I labored around oblong scrapes of breath, I watched as he staggered into the shafts of the headlights and leaned on the hood of the Ford to catch his breath. He put his head in his hands not with shame or regret, but with the sense of stilling himself after a very difficult and artistically rewarding performance.

My stomach turned. His shoulders rose and fell. The pelting breeze tugged at his clothes and the ends of his hair.

I had never before hated anything so much as I hated Felix Haas in that moment. The ferocity of it burned through me, barreling along my veins in one great cauterization.

I hated. I would never again be ignorant of hate so intimate. I was, all of me, hate.

A shallow puddle sat beside me, catching the upside-down reflection of the sky. I wished I could dive into it and never return. I wished I never had to feel anything ever again.

The Lady was there with her hand held up to the surface. Her palm was clean and unwavering, and I lifted one trembling and filthy hand to meet her there. The water broke cold around my skin.

"Devour," I croaked, and flexed my fingers into the wet earth to try to cling to her—but nothing held me in return.

◆ ◆ ◆

I WAS EMPTY.

All that filled me was a searing absence, which hurt far more than anything of the act that had stolen my peace for good.

I was nothing.

I still had a fistful of mud clenched at my side. Haas and I had ridden back into town in a stiff, unspoken silence. There was nothing to speak of. We had seen each other down to our very natures, and in seeing I had unearthed from his depths the monster. This was him, Felix Haas at his very core: his blood, and his bones, and his choice.

It was done.

"You behave as though nothing is the matter. The morning the rest of the caravan goes back," Haas finally said, parked at the far end of the motel lot, "I am taking you to Juárez and we are *fixing this*. Is that clear?" His voice crackled with fatigue, raw from all his shouting.

I heard him, but I couldn't make sense of it. I couldn't make sense of anything. "What about Wesley?" I said distantly, my own voice just as ruined.

I flinched when the back of Haas's knuckles skimmed my cheek. I shut my eyes and prayed he was through with me.

I didn't dare look at him. If I looked at him, I would be sick. In my periphery, Haas peered with distant curiosity at the mud on his fingers. I must have looked like I'd crawled from my own grave.

"Not a word to him," Haas murmured, and then paused. I could still feel him looking at me. "I told you, I'll take care of you."

This was a lie I'd been told for years. Wesley was the only one who had ever meant it.

My eyes were leaking. I couldn't have stopped them if I tried.

"Let me out of the car, please," I said lightly.

Haas leaned close, and I cringed away from him on instinct—he reached across my lap and pushed the door open.

Haas lingered over me. Every ounce of bravery left in me activated at once as I flicked my eyes to his and found him peering at me with concern; as if realizing for the first time he was, perhaps, pushing me away from him by having done his. "I swear it, Margaret. If you tell your husband what you made me do," he whispered with the lightest tinge of desperation, "I will teach you what it means to cross me again. Is that clear?"

The cool damp of the night met me as I hurried into the washed-out light of the breezeway.

It's as if I am nineteen years old again, and I am afraid of everything.

The world was not made to love me, and I know this—and still, I am afraid of everything.

I recall, somehow, the way to unlock the door. I shut it behind me. It takes a moment for me to register that this place is the motel. Lake Sumner. Not Richmond. Wesley is here, standing up from the foot of the bed. We are in Lake Sumner, together.

Margaret? Margaret.

Someone is saying a name, the name my mother gave me. *Margaret!*

I stare at Wesley. Wesley Shoard, my Wesley—he looks frightened. I look past his shoulder. He is my husband. I, there, me in the mirror, I am his wife. *Margaret*—is that name still mine? I look monstrous.

I shudder. Mud in my hair, my clothes a mess, am I truly—

"Jack!"

I blinked; came to. My eyes filled with tears in a great heaving rush.

"What happened?" I breathed.

Wesley watched me with alarm hastily covered at the back of his stare. He made no move to reach out to me or touch me at all. "I don't know," he said carefully. He looked me over with a quick pass of his eyes, and I felt his gaze like a flaying scrape. "Are—are you hurt? Was there an accident?"

I . . . had been. I was. Many and various times, but did any of it matter? Was this an accident?

I sat down on the edge of the bed. In my lap, I clutched my purse so close I could feel my pulse in my stomach, the pocket calendar stuffed inside, thumping with each heartbeat.

"Did I ever tell you about Hollis?" I asked him distantly, staring at the wall across the room. I couldn't bear to look at the mirror again. "Michael Hollis?"

Wesley was silent as he knelt in front of me. He still didn't touch me, but he seemed so shaken I figured perhaps he was confused.

"He was a—a director," I offered, clarifying, hoping he might quit looking concerned if he knew what I was talking about, what I was trying to talk about. "He took over after—after Jensen was arrested; Jensen was my favorite, he took such wonderful care of me, but Hollis. Hollis was a monster."

Wesley nodded slowly. "Okay," he whispered. "Jack, can I . . . ?" He held out a hand, hovering it over my knee. I watched the edges of his hand shake. I nodded. When he rested it there, over the dirt and the raw skin with small pieces of gravel stuck to the stinging scrapes through the hole in my stocking, I shivered. But it was a tender touch, and it didn't make me want to snap his wrist in half. So I let him leave it there; I stared at his fingers, the fine shape of his hand so gentle by its making, and kept on.

"I did nothing without his approval. I was his pet project, he—he *made* me, but only in his own image. He took what he said I owed him in return whenever he saw fit." I drew a deep tremor of a breath and let it out again in a quavering rush. Wesley did not move his hand or attempt to soothe me with any petting or patting. He simply was.

"I was so good for him," I said, and it sounded as though I was begging—bargaining. "I was such a good girl, and I—all I wanted was to be loved, what could be so wrong with that? How could he have hurt me? I'm not a girl, but I still—I still want to be good, Wesley, I want to be . . . I want to be so good for *everyone*, why did he hurt me?"

I looked my husband directly in the eye and abandoned my purse to cling to his hand with both of mine so fiercely my tendons stood up like roots. "Why did he hurt me, Wes?"

His eyes, so dark in the low light they were almost violet, flickered with a reluctant, aching recognition. I begged him silently to know me, to love me as himself in this moment.

"Was it Felix?" he asked, gentle as a moth's wing.

I stared at him until my eyes filled again. Wesley blurred into a wash of color.

"He was so—*angry*," I gasped as a sob worked thick and sticky up through my chest. I pulled Wesley's hand forward to hold it against my chest as I fought for breath.

Words left me. I began to bawl like an animal, reduced to my lowest self.

Wesley pressed his cheek to my knees and let me keep his hand clutched desperately to my heart as though holding back my vile insides from spilling out. Beneath my sobs, I could hear the sound of him lulling me with patient repetition—*It's alright, Jack. You're safe. I'm here. I'm so sorry.*

I cried until there was nothing left, all the way down to my fumes.

I am nineteen years old again and I am staring at the fuel gauge of a Hudson Hornet that does not belong to me, ticked nearly all the way down to EMPTY.

I am alone in the middle of a night that was muggy in Richmond, but here at the bus terminal farther north there's a certain briskness. It is almost autumn. I have always liked autumn best.

I am nineteen years old, and I buy a bus ticket to New York City with Michael Hollis's money. *Name?* The attendant asks, not looking up at me.

It is a privilege to name myself. There is perverse victory in seizing one's identity back from the hands that have molded it in one's stead.

Margot, I say with my best enunciation, claiming Jensen's nickname for good. *Margot Wolf.*

I am nineteen and I am afraid, but fear makes me a hunter; a better, more dogged chaser of the things I must take for my own from this unkind world.

I am nineteen and I am afraid of my woman's body. Mama never talked about how any of it worked because mortal bodies were temporary, the spirit was all that mattered, and I thought my blood coming in when I was twelve meant I was dying.

I am nineteen and Hollis has taught me that desire is also something to fear, because to desire means to be touched, and being touched is horrific. Being touched makes me go very far away.

I am nineteen and I am twenty-nine and I am Margaret, I am Margot, I am Jack, I am a beast with blunted teeth that has become tired of being denied my nature.

I will open my jaws.

I will devour.

I will become.

23

The Lake Sumner motel, room number five

WESLEY HELPED ME to my feet and into the bathroom.

"Do you want me in there?" he asked when we stumbled upward, his voice rough with tears.

"Please." I turned to offer him the zipper of my dress.

He opened the shower and took off his shirt as I peeled out of my dress, my underthings, my ruined stockings. The pain was there, but I could feel none of it.

Wesley tested the water with his hand before steadying me in ahead of him. He scrubbed carefully at my skin—working the dirt away, rinsing the blood from my knees and elbows and heels of my hands in small, steady passes. When he turned me to face him so he could start rinsing my hair, I found he had a few bobby pins in his teeth.

His eyes flicked up to meet mine, raw and miserable. The water had gotten him just as wet. It wouldn't have mattered if he cried, but still he insisted on holding himself together.

"I want him to die, Wesley," I said, without knowing I was going to say it.

"So do I," he said around the pins, lathering a dollop of shampoo between his palms.

"I want to kill him."

With his hands stilled in my hair, cleaning me of the horror I would never be able to shake from my body's memory, not entirely, Wesley stared at me; into the awful hunger in me, awakened.

Over his shoulder, I found the Lady watching from the mirror above the sink. Her hair was unbound and her nightgown stained red by the pathways of her bloodied palms. Conviction lived deep in her eyes.

Devour.

I closed my eyes and sank into the feeling of Wesley gentling the mud from my scalp.

Devour, sang my racing pulse, my shuddering breath, the awful rhythm of defiance. *Devour. Devour. Devour.*

We dressed in our pajamas. I pulled Jesse's knife from its place in the vanity drawer without ceremony. Wesley balked at the sight of it.

"Is that yours?" he asked lightly, tinged with alarm.

"It was a gift," I said, and levered it open before setting it on the floor to sit vigil beside it.

I pulled my legs in to my chest by the shins and settled back against the side of one bed, in the alley between them. The red enamel of the knife's handle shivered each time I blinked.

"Come sit, Wes," I said without looking up, my chin balanced on both knees over the slippery silk of my nightgown.

"I don't—"

"You promised." I looked straight at him. "'Say the word and it's done.' Did you mean it?"

Wesley stared at me, wrung out and dog-tired in a fresh undershirt and shorts. From the floor, the shadows cast longways across his body made him look carved from fine-veined marble. He didn't blink for a very long time.

"You swore," I whispered. "Our wedding night, Wesley, you swore—"

"You think I can do it?" he cut in, the hint of a manic chuckle making him pause. He put a hand over his mouth and stared at the knife. "Jesus, Jack, you think I can even— Can *you*?"

He gestured broadly at me with a flat hand. I stared at him.

"Who do you think I am, Wesley?"

He swallowed, his throat sticking wetly to itself. "I don't know what you want me to say."

The heavy silence compounded with each passing second.

Reluctantly surrendering, Wesley sat down next to me. I gathered him up against my side and began to imagine.

I rambled aloud, softly—the theater, late at night, just the three of us; a chance to seize back from him what he'd taken from me. It moved through me like a current, not of my mind but of my instinct. My spirit.

The spirit was all that mattered.

I went silent when I reached the end of it and dwelled on the bloody dream-shapes making space in my head.

Wesley was a heavy, mortal weight on my shoulder.

"Alright," he whispered. "It's your show, Jack. Whatever you need."

I let the silence settle overtop of us again, sealing us in together with the decision made.

"You ever dream up a way to do it before?" I asked.

Wesley made an ironic sniff. "Sure, plenty of times. But I never made a plan."

I stared at the knife, the arch of the shoe, the liquid sex of the handle's calf curve. "Not even Andrew?"

"I don't have your conviction."

"Nonsense." I elbowed him gently. "You got plenty of conviction, Shoardie."

He gave me a miserable smile. I searched his face.

"Do you wanna go over it again?" I asked. The crown of dawn was threatening outside by now. Not even the coyotes were still out yipping.

Wesley dragged both hands down his face. "Sure."

"You'll invite him to the theater," I said. The pocketknife really was beautiful. "For dinner. Dessert. I'll put on my best face, pretend all's forgotten."

"You're *sure* you're okay to do that?" Wesley asked.

"I've played harder roles for less important reasons."

Wesley drew his knees up and ran a thumb over his lower lip. "How will we get away with it?"

"The stage already looks like someone's been slaughtered."

Staring at me, Wesley's brow twitched. "Jesus," he said.

"What?"

Wesley didn't look away from me as he swallowed. "Nothing," he said. "Nothing, I just. Thought about it again."

I gathered him back to me with my arm around his shoulders. "You don't have to think."

"Good," he murmured, staring at the blade as though the answers to every question he didn't know how to ask were etched onto it.

I kissed him on the forehead. "Good man," I said into his hairline.

◆ ◆ ◆

IF I'D THOUGHT my nails were a mess before Haas's violence, they were a wreck now. I sat on the floor in the center of the room and filed them as I waited for Wesley to be done with his errands, put on his breeziest, most unassuming air, and stop by Haas's room to invite him out to the theater that night for one last private romp.

We were leaving for New York tomorrow morning. I had tried packing to distract myself, but all I could do was stare at my hands and be reminded.

I didn't want my body to be a mirror in which I only saw its horrors.

I looked up at the vanity. Only my head and shoulders reflected back, my hair dried in a wavy riot from leaving it wet last night. Wesley and I had hardly slept, but we managed.

The vague formants of speech burred in through the wall our room shared with number six. I put down the nail file and crept to press my ear to the faded wallpaper.

Tonight, I heard, unmistakable in the clip of Wesley putting on his shy-but-pretending-I'm-not-trying-to-be smile. *We're . . . to go . . . off without you.*

I clenched my jaw and did my best not to vomit as I heard Haas's voice, low and intrigued.

I couldn't bear it. I stalked back to the opposite side of the room and glared at the wall in silence.

The door opened two, three minutes later. I watched Wesley latch the deadbolt and the safety chain, and then I went over to examine both locks myself to ensure they were done to my liking.

"Is he going to come?" I whispered.

Wesley took his time sliding off his shoes and rubbed fiercely at his eyes with the heels of his hands as he sighed heavily. "We're taking him to a picnic at the theater tonight as a last hurrah," he murmured, not uncovering his eyes. "Well after dark, just the three of us. He asked if you agreed, I told you loved the idea. He has a key to the front of house."

There was still a snarled piece left at the edge of my torn thumbnail. I chewed at it with my front teeth for a long spell of silence. "Does he know you know?" I asked around my knuckle.

Wesley ran a hand through his hair. The bags under his eyes were bruised and sallow. "About what, last night?"

I nodded, still chewing.

"No. He seemed perfectly unfazed, although he *definitely* had a hangover. Offered me some hair of the dog."

"*Prick*," I spat, wanting to yell but keeping it soft.

"Understatement," Wesley said, and rooted into his bags to hunt out whatever was left in his own flask.

With nothing else to do before dark then, I set back to packing. We moved in silence, not even the radio buzzing along, and separated our things from their muddled piles—his clothes from mine, my toiletries from his, packing our lives back into our separate bags.

"If nothing lets to make us happy both," Wesley announced out of the blue with his stage voice, shaking out a pair of my slacks, "but this my masculine usurped attire, do not embrace me till each circumstance of place, time, fortune, do cohere and jump that I am Viola."

I gave him a tired look. "Those are my lines," I said. Wesley raised his eyebrows and pitched the trousers at me. I barely caught them.

"Which to confirm," he continued, digging through the dresser drawers, "I'll bring you to a captain in this town, where lie my maiden weeds; by whose gentle help I was preserved to serve this noble count." He carefully exhumed my folded underthings. "All the occurrence of my fortune since hath been between this lady and this lord."

I watched him flatly for a long moment before Wesley glanced over his shoulder at me and gave a *go on, then* look.

"Be not amazed," I said, assuming Orsino's role with my voice weary-weak; "right noble is his blood. If this be so, as yet the glass seems true, I shall have share in this most happy wrack." I pulled one of Wesley's ties from the back of the armoire and crossed over to flick it up and around his neck. "Boy, thou hast said to me a thousand times thou never shouldst love woman like to me."

Wesley flashed a tired smile. "And all those sayings will I over-swear," he insisted, "and all those swearings keep as true in soul as doth that orbèd continent the fire that severs day from night."

I pulled one of my wrinkled dresses from its hanger and examined it briefly—one of the first I'd worn here in Sumner, a bright linen blend that knew nothing of what awaited. I returned to Wesley and held it up to his body. "Give me thy hand," I said, pretending to ap-praise the fit of it, "and let me see thee in thy woman's weeds."

Wesley raised his eyebrows and twisted his face up into a saucy look that had never failed to make me laugh.

I tried to, truly, I did; but there was no quarter inside me for joy. Where I wanted so badly to do nothing but laugh with my dearest friend, all I could do was hold in another weary tide of tears.

Wesley held me, pressing the dress between us, and let me collect myself with the last of my dignity. I relented to my sorrow only briefly, one last time, in the perfect privacy of our safe haven.

24

The docks at Lake Sumner

I HELD THE flashlight as still as possible on Wesley as he deftly untied the boat from the dock. My hands so badly wanted to shake.

Wesley glanced up at Haas. "Did you have the Boy Scouts in Austria?"

We'd made an artful escape from the farewell dinner while the rest of the company celebrated, filling up on vices before packing back into the caravan to return home come morning. I could hardly hear myself think for the high, nervous ringing in my ears.

"I preferred football clubs," he said breezily, and continued watching Wesley free the boat from the dock.

I stood at Haas's shoulder. I wasn't looking at him. If I looked at him, I was sure I would act on the plan before we even got him onto the stage.

Haas leaned close—I managed not to flinch. "We have our fun tonight," he said in a low, private voice, "and we leave at first light. Are you packed?"

I managed not to laugh, or scream, or bite a bloody chunk out of his neck in one fell snap. Instead, I stilled him with a touch to the inside of his wrist and, in my finest and most subtle act of theater, angled my softest doe eyes at Haas. "Not now," I whispered, barely above a breath, only for the two of us to hear. I pointed my chin subtly at Wesley, as though afraid to let him see us scheming. "This is for him."

"Are you—"

"*Yes*. I'm packed. Now give him a good time, would you? It's the last he gets of either of us."

It felt like spitting ashes to say it, but I watched the light shift behind Haas's gaze. My bravery compounded. I steeled my will to the neck and let him hand me into the boat.

I watched Haas from the opposite end of the skiff as Wesley steered us toward the theater in the deep dark. He looked pleased with himself. His collar was open, his sleeves rolled up tidily, and his hair tossed.

He had to suspect something. How could he not?

"What is it we have to eat tonight?" he asked over the burring of the engine. Wesley had packed wine and some apricot tarts from the grocer in a spare handbag of mine as a makeshift picnic basket.

"Dessert," I said, digging out a cigarette and lighting it.

Haas reached into his inner jacket pocket and extended the silver kit to me. "Here. I figured you could use it more than me."

I stared at the offering and exhaled steadily into the air, the smoke snatching itself away with the passage of the boat.

Call it old time's sake—I clicked open the container and peered at the contents: two hand-rolls of hash, three pills, and a fresh sachet of his powder.

"If you're done with Jesse's placebo," he said.

When I looked up at him, he gave me a smile that showed the edges of his teeth.

I snapped the kit shut and passed it back. "I'm taking a break."

"Oh?"

"It's been giving me a headache."

Haas watched me with a slightly narrowed, calculating gaze as he returned the kit to his pocket without taking any for himself.

Wesley pulled the skiff up to the empty dock and threw a loose tie onto one post. I flicked my cigarette into the lake.

We had a plan.

But Haas had to know. Look at him, watching me like that; he absolutely had to know.

I feared his knowledge far more than his ignorance. If he knew, it meant he was prepared.

How deeply I hated my weakness; my fear.

Haas disembarked first and walked ahead of us. He jangled a ring of keys from his pocket, unlocked the lobby door, and disappeared inside. Wesley helped me from the boat.

"I don't want you to be collateral damage," I whispered—Wesley hushed me.

"Nonsense." He led me over the threshold and pawed at the wall for the work lights. "It's the both of us as one, or nothing at all."

The red-stained boards were lit with an out-of-focus wash. Haas hoisted himself easily onto the apron. Wesley joined him and set out the bag of desserts. Haas proffered the little cakes in their crackling cellophane, poured wine in mugs lifted from the motel, and sat back on his elbows with his long legs crossed as he popped a tart into his mouth. He watched us.

He had to know.

Wesley was downing wine almost as fast as Haas could pour for him. I sat beside the basket with my knees drawn up, mug clutched in both hands. When Wesley finally crawled up the length of Haas's body and slipped him into a kiss, I forced myself to pretend I was just as interested as I'd always been. Wesley was a brilliant actor.

"Impatient?" Haas asked against his lips.

"Hungry," Wesley mumbled, and began to pry open Haas's belt.

The empty theater, the lake and the desert outside; all of it was so quiet I was sure my racing heartbeat was audible in the dark. But Haas gave over to Wesley with a proud sneer. He buried a hand in Wesley's hair to steer him and looked up at me.

"Come watch from here," he purred.

I didn't want to watch. I wanted to chew off my own fingers. I swallowed the taste of pennies in my mouth and tried at a smile that didn't flinch too badly. "I can wait my turn," I said.

Haas tightened his fist in Wesley's hair and yanked, making him grunt with a flash of pain. Fury lashed in me, and I scrambled to keep it down. Haas's eyes flashed. "I didn't ask for *patience*, Margaret. Get over here."

I didn't meet Wesley's gaze. I would not lose my nerve too early. I would not leap before the window was open.

Carefully, slowly, I knelt behind Haas and put my mouth at the nape of his neck. With the ghost of my breath pretending at teasing a kiss, I reached one hand into my bodice.

The handle of Jesse's pocketknife was warm from my skin. Very slowly, behind Haas's back, I opened the blade.

"Look at him," Haas breathed.

I breathed very carefully through my nose and shut my eyes. "I'm looking."

Haas reached back with his free hand and grabbed my hair, just as he had Wesley's.

The bright sting of his fist against my scalp rocketed me back—back to the dirt, the rain, the mud.

I had the knife in the side of his neck before I was aware I'd moved to strike.

As I tore it across his windpipe, I reached up and clamped my other hand over Haas's mouth to keep in his ragged shout.

Wesley acted quickly, just as we'd rehearsed: Hold down his legs, wrestle his arms to his sides, immobilize him completely—we would let him bleed like bound swine.

But *Jesus*, the play had it right; who would have thought he had so much blood in him?

It spewed with arterial force. I could smell it, see it, hear it burbling so near to me I might as well have been tasting it. He shouted uselessly against my hand, gnashing and biting, and his thrashing soused Wesley red and slick—"*Jack!*"

Fuck. *Fuck*, he was slipping. Haas's frantic instinct to survive seized its second wind, and I shouted wordlessly as he bucked Wesley off. We hadn't planned for this. Goddamn it, we hadn't *planned for this*.

I should have known. I had felt this before, hadn't I? All dying things struggle. It's in the nature of something that has tasted living to want to continue. I scrambled to hold Haas down on my own, but I was frantic with dread. He lurched and knocked the knife from my fist.

I screamed. Haas's bloody hand came down hard to clamp over my mouth. He tackled me backward and loomed above me, eyes feral and distant, the vitality speeding out through the ragged, weeping hole in his neck and compelling him to fight with abandon before it bled out entirely.

"NO!" Wesley roared. He shoved hard at Haas's body, punching his kidneys and hauling uselessly at his trunk, but Haas had a murderous grip on my jaw, my neck, his fingers squeezing and closing—

The knife. All I could think to do was grope for the knife. My hands were soaked, everything slipping in my grip, but I found the handle with one wild flail and struggled to close my fist around it as my vision began to tunnel. Haas threw an elbow that caught Wesley hard in the gut—reeling and coughing, unable to hold on, he staggered.

Blood, everywhere and in torrents. Haas was going to take me with him.

What pride, what arrogance, what appalling vanity, to believe I could be more than this, more than the borrowed time of my own mistake-making?

Yet it wouldn't just be me.

He would end both of us, as one.

I threw every bit of my weight into my pinned-down shoulder and swung. The knife sank full to the hilt into Haas's ribs.

Stabbing him again and again and again until he let go of me, I threw my weight forward with a holler so ragged around its edges I ceased feeling entirely human. The din of us grappling must have been from a distance like the shrieking coyotes I'd heard so many nights in the unseen desert.

Straddled atop his hips, I jammed the blade back in his neck. Haas made a wet, bubbling sound. He gaped up at me, accusatory with disbelief.

There, finally he knew it: He was dying.

"Did you think I wouldn't do it?" I seethed. My arms were trembling. I put my face directly in his, staring all the way down into his petrified stare. My voice was a wild wreck. *"Did you?"*

I put one hand in his hair and tilted his head back. "I am what you made me," I snarled.

Haas's body heaved with resistance. His eyes rolled frantically, baring the flashing whites of them in panicked desperation. I held on. I had never known power like this.

Finally, miraculously, he was still.

I took a shaking breath and sat back on my heels. With the edge of my hand, I pushed a lock of hair from my face. A red, sticky track smeared in its wake. My left fist remained vised in Haas's hair. His skin still felt alive, warm against my fingertips.

Yet he lolled there, finished. Dead weight. His eyes were still open—the fear frozen in them made him look more like prey than I had ever seen him, pared back to his truest self in death.

Wesley was leaning over the apron, vomiting.

I was done. Exhausted. Wrung out.

Here, too, though: purpose.

Happiness.

Are you happy, Margaret?

At the edge of the stage, Wesley sat down heavily and began to weep.

"If something bleeds," I marveled, "you can kill it."

The night sank back into place in death's wake, like a curtain falling shut again behind the final exit. I stared at Haas's eyes and dared him to lurch upward and drag me away with him.

I had seen it once, the blank space at the end of everything.

There was nothing there—no paradise, no hell, not even the misty gray of a featureless in-between; just emptiness, forever, no company but one's own self shed from its flesh in infinity.

It was what he deserved.

Wesley stumbled twice while staggering to his feet, white as a sheet under the spattered coating of blood. "Fuck," he wheezed, striding unevenly upstage. "Fuck. *Fuck*. What the *fuck* did we just do!"

I swiped the blade clean on one of the only unbloodied spots along the hem of my skirt. Wesley's breathing was so hurried and constricted it had a pitch to it, but as I looked at Haas's ruined body under me, I could find only a washed-clean sense of quiet in every hollow of my being.

I smudged the worst of my hands off on the rest of my skirt in long, red spears before slipping Jesse's knife back into my bodice. I stood up carefully—first one foot, then the other.

Delayed, as though my mind was sending messages along the rusting length of a telegraph wire, I finally looked up at Wesley and away from Haas. He had both arms hugged tight around his own waist, cowering in the wings.

"It's alright," I said, holding out a slow, careful, red-streaked hand. "It'll be alright, Wes."

He sucked on oxygen with desperate heaves and kept staring at, through Haas sprawled motionless on the boards. "I'm—" He cut himself off with a wet sob. "God! How is there so much blood!"

Wesley seemed unable to even blink, unwilling to look away.

"Quit looking at him," I said.

"I *can't*."

"We need to get rid of him."

"Jesus Christ, Margaret! Do you feel *nothing*?"

My temper flared white-hot—I pointed viciously at the body. "You KNOW what he did to me!" I shouted. The ghost of the syllable rang upward into the night through the broad column of the theater's throat—*me, me, me*. "I feel *everything*!"

Everything. All of it. So intensely it folded back in on itself into nothing.

Nothing at all.

My hands were shaking.

Wesley put his face in his hands as his shoulders jumped in full-bodied, arrhythmic sobs. He dragged his fingers across his eyes and swiped at his nose before reaching out to cradle my cheeks as if handling glass. He swept his thumbs along my lower lashes, petting away—tears? I was crying as well. We were both soaked and body-warm, sopping red.

"I'm sorry," he whispered, "I'm so sorry."

I reached up to hold him by both wrists and leaned our foreheads together. "Don't apologize. 'Screw your courage to the sticking place,' right?"

Wesley sagged with sorrow. Our skin and strands of our hair smeared together where we touched. He stayed there for a moment and caught his wet breath.

"Bricks," he said eventually, as though the syllable were a labor.

I nodded and made for the steps that would take me to the trap space. *There's a pile under the stage*, Wesley had suggested last night, both of us leaning on the other as we stared at the knife. *We can sink him, after.*

"Bricks," I replied.

Wesley tied his fine, quick knots after we hauled cinder blocks and rope with grim determination. He averted his eyes well away from Haas's face as he worked. Before we dragged the body back out to the skiff, I plundered Haas's pockets and stole every red cent from his wallet.

It was horrid progress. And yet it calmed me, as though a hidden part of me had been waiting for this and already knew exactly what needed doing.

We set our hands to the work and got it done.

Wesley steered out to where the lake looked deepest. The weighed-down heft of the body gave an oblong splash of ink-black water when we pushed it in together, the ripples disappearing almost as quickly as they came. His long, fine fingers were the last of Felix Haas to slip into the murk.

I stood up in the boat, balancing myself carefully on Wesley's shoulder, and began to unfasten my shoes and stockings as Wesley started on the buttons of his shirt.

We wrapped everything but our underclothes around the last of the bricks. Wesley tied off the bundle, and we sank it into the water on the opposite end of the lake.

Back to the shore then—we kicked and scuffed at the dirt to smear away the dripping traces of blood as best we could.

The van.

The long ribbon of the road, both Wesley and I as silent passengers to the other as I drove.

The rest of the company was still making merry at the restaurant. I stared at the glow across the highway as we pulled up to the motel and hurried into our room. I yanked the curtains shut, locked every entry, and struggled out of my underwear as though I would catch fire if I wore them any longer. Wesley started the shower.

We scrubbed ourselves in silence, so frantic to be clean we didn't even pull the curtain shut. Water pooled shallowly on the tiles over the spotty lip of the tub. Wordlessly, Wesley bid me scour his hair and then did mine for me in return just as he had last night.

The suds threaded at our feet with each round of soap, red then pink then finally clean. We examined every inch of each other's skin, and when we were finally washed of our deed, I sank against Wesley with the fight well and truly sapped from my body. He tucked my head under his chin and held me as though he wanted to crawl into my ribs and hide there forever.

"Are you happy, Jack?" he murmured against my wet hair, just barely audible over the hiss of the shower. It was the first either of us had spoken since departing the theater.

I looked sideways and stared at the desperate shape of us in the steamed mirror. In the fog we were of the same body, fused together in irrevocable sin. I nestled my nose into the warmth of his neck and inhaled the mineral scent of the water as I shut my eyes to the pace of his pounding pulse. He was shaking all over. He was alive. So was I.

"I will be," I whispered, and held him until the water went cold.

25

Hattie's Quik-N-Go

WESLEY AND I shuffled into our travel clothes at dawn and trudged to the twenty-four-hour diner at the edge of town for breakfast before getting on the road.

After cleaning away any and all evidence of blood in the motel room, I'd stuffed our ruined undergarments into the paper grocery sacks left from last night's desserts. We packed them at the very bottom of Wesley's trunk. I would burn them in the basement furnace once we got back home.

The bell on the lintel rattled as Wesley opened the door, escorting me into the little truck stop. We sat heavily in a two-top vinyl booth, made tired smiles at our waitress as she poured us two mugs of burnt coffee, and said nothing to each other as she bustled off.

We must have looked like twice-churned shit. Nobody was saying anything sideways about it.

I leaned down to sip from the lip of my mug. Wesley reached across the table and added exactly the amount of sugar I liked. I shot him a wan smile, picked up the cloudy spoon, and shined it on the side of my skirt before stirring.

Wesley ordered a breakfast platter with his eggs scrambled. I ordered plain toast. Neither of us touched much of the food, pushing it to and fro as we stared through the plates.

"Would you ever want to do it again?"

I looked up at Wesley's question over the edge of my sunglasses—*Kill someone?*

Wesley's eyebrows twitched, barely recoiling. "No . . . Sharing."

"Oh." I prodded the corner of one stiff slice of bread. "Sure. It was fun. Until it wasn't. You know."

"Good. Not—good that he . . . you know. But good. Me, too. Maybe someone else. At some point." Wesley looked up at me, his eyes bruised by fatigue. "If you can. I mean . . . you know."

I took another slug of coffee and nodded distantly. I didn't much feel like talking.

Another long stretch of silence; Wesley took a single bite of his eggs, regarded one of the measly breakfast sausages, and sat back in his seat. He stared through the spotty tabletop. "So what's the plan, Jack?"

The angle of the sunlight coming through the window illuminated the edges of his eyes, dull and hollow. Neither of us blinked.

"We live," I said.

Wesley considered that for a moment. He slurped from his cup, regarded it mutely, and pushed it aside.

"Are you going to try sleeping on the way back?" he asked.

"Try," I said. "Operative word."

Wesley grunted in agreement. "Chap has sleeping pills. Might ask for one."

"I'll bet there's a fucking pharmacy in the glove compartment of any one of those vans if you ask nicely." I stood up to make for the ladies' room and dropped a kiss on Wesley's head as I passed his side of the booth.

Wesley stood up and collected his hat. Both our plates sat almost entirely untouched. "I'll pay. Meet me at the counter."

I used the toilet, washed my hands, and did my best to wake up the edges of my face in the mirror. I froze as I reached instinctively for the medicine compact.

I looked at what was left of it—two or three more doses at most. Nothing remained of Haas's work but the bruises under my skin and these scant fingers of powder. The prickling taste for it, that sudden and inconvenient wanting, the same thing that had made me turn toward Haas in the first place, itched at the back of my head.

I turned back to the toilet and scraped the powder out into the bowl. It floated miserably on the surface, crumbling slowly into the rust-rimed water as I watched it drown.

I tugged the old pull-chain flusher and let it spiral away, gone with the shit.

◆ ◆ ◆

KLINE CHECKED HIS watch and squinted through his yellow shades at the motel breezeway.

"Taking his sweet fucking time, isn't he?" he groused.

Beside me, Wesley was practically humming with fear. I squeezed his hand and tucked it into the pocket of my skirt. He glanced at me, brief and nervy, and pulled his hand back to cross his arms tightly under his elbows.

We were packed into the vans, ready to leave, and waiting on Haas outside his room.

"I say we go without him," one of the drivers called from the leading van. He had his elbow propped on the rolled-down window, a cigarette between his fingers. "Burning daylight, Vaughn."

A muddled chorus of assent went up among the company, antsy and ready to get back to the city.

"We'll give him another ten," Kline said, toeing meanly at a pebble on the ground, "and then I'm getting that big motherfucker at the desk to give us his key."

Wesley heaved a tight sigh and went to bum a cigarette from Chap. I caught my reflection in the window beside me as he moved off, but I knew I probably looked a piece: exhausted, frayed—just like the rest of us, and lucky I could simply pin it on a hangover.

Not a word to anyone, I had said last night from our desperate huddle in one bed. *Like it never even happened. Alright?*

Like it never happened, he hummed, running his fingers gently, gently, gently through my wet hair.

Ten minutes crawled past. A shard of unshakable anxiety lodged in my gut told me everyone could tell that I had done something horrible just by looking.

But I hadn't made the first strike. I had been hurt in small ways for many long years, and Haas's blow to my armor against such common violence had birthed a hideous creature made desperate from the snares of past transgressions.

His death was on his own shoulders.

Kline and several other drivers took turns hammering on Haas's door. Good thing we had been the only guests at the motel—this racket would have woken the dead.

Shit.

I froze, my fingernails gnawing fresh and hungry into the inside of my forearm. I swallowed. Smoothing my skirt, I glanced subtly over each shoulder.

Kline came out from the front kiosk brandishing a key. He muttered to himself the whole way back to room six, going on about balls on a spit and shoving bolts of fabric in orifices, and wrenched open the latch. My heart, squeezed tight in my mouth, had quit its beating.

"The fucking idiot's packed," Kline cried from past the doorway, "so where the hell'd he get off to!"

I blinked quickly, drawing a belated breath in through my nose.

Kline stalked back out, waving a page of motel letterhead crumpled in his fist. "Slippery cocksucker went to Mexico and left all his shit behind. Goddamn it."

Haggard, furious, Kline looked at his watch. It was forty minutes past when we were supposed to have left.

"Let's go," he announced, his voice rocky and afraid, and hustled to the caravan with his short, clipped stride. He gestured blindly at the vans. "Sunny, with me; south. Rest of you to the city, we'll catch back up in Newark. *Goddamn it.*"

Wesley did not meet my eyes as he helped me up into our seat. The engine turned over with a heavy, trundling growl. Our driver heaved the door shut, and then we were off.

Hunched up in the back corner, Wesley brooded out the window and gently refused to make conversation. I stared out at the sun still low against the mountains—the boundlessness of a nothing-place, where I had been so reduced to my barest being that the animal within me was finally given the chance to run free.

I imagined it as a separate creature sprinting loose and four-legged, streaking through the desert along the side of the road and howling, howling, howling, into the endless blue of the watchful sky.

There was no room for it to follow me home, but I could not unlearn what I had become here. That, at least, I knew.

26

Shoard Downs

THE FURNACE ROOM used to terrify me.

I stood in the basement back in New York, staring down the long, dank hallway that took me into the belly of our building.

Doing the laundry was the chore I loathed most about keeping house. Whenever I had to come down here, I'd get the strangest inalienable chill. The clicking pipes, the damp air, the lightless churn; even children know there's a reason to fear this place.

I clutched the paper sack closer to my chest. I'd wrapped the parcel in an old, stained towel.

The roar of the furnace built to a low thrum that made the edges of my vision shake the closer I drew. I cast about for the crook I could use to pull open the mouth of it.

I shielded my face from the heat with the lump in my arms and stretched out long with the crook, fixing it around the handle and heaving it open with a clumsy lurch. The hot, bright breath of it washed over me with a hissing belch and the shriek of metal.

I took two quick steps forward, hurled the bundle into the fire, and hauled the belly of the burner shut again. I set the crook back against the wall and caught my breath, setting both hands heavily on my hips as I stared at the flames eating away the last of my most damning secret.

"Every day of mine," I panted very softly, "is a gift."

I turned on my heel and hurried out of the basement.

Up in the apartment, I scoured my hands in the bathroom. When I sat down to use the toilet, I ran my mental list of what still remained to be done to resume life here after Lake Sumner: Burn the clothes, done. Collect the mail that was forwarded to the post office, Wesley was doing that now. Restock the groceries, whenever; we'd get takeout until one of us felt un-rattled enough to cook. Get a drink with Edie, Fridays were her busy days; I'd probably see her on Sunday at the earliest.

Go to the doctor, too. I'd have to make an appointment. I'd have to . . .

I stopped short in the middle of my list when I noticed the gusset of my shorts. The familiar surprise of a dark stain stopped me cold.

I blinked.

Well, that would come out with a cold-water soak.

Or I could just go back downstairs and throw it in the furnace.

I started laughing before I could stop myself, a sick sense of exhaustion and relief and the briefest kick of true regret swirling through me. I doubled over and pressed my forehead against my knees.

"Easy," I hissed. I slapped myself once on the side of the head, sucked in a shaking breath, and soothed my hand back over it as I let out a breath. "*Easy*, Jack."

It hadn't amounted to anything, all that grief and wretched anger. I'd just been late. Simple as. Back now to square one.

Like it never happened.

I sat up, shuddered, and set myself back to rights.

When I stood, I stepped out of the shorts and washed my hands again. I looked up, just over the edge of my shoulder, and found the Lady leaning against the small white tiles of the opposite wall. She was still in her nightgown, but the blood was gone.

"Welcome home," she said.

I opened the cold water tap and splashed it shallowly against the sides of my neck. "I thought you were through with me."

"I figured you—"

"You figured I, what," I said, not looking her in the eye, "didn't have the courage to do it? That I'd have botched it like you did?"

The smallest shudder of surprise twitched into the Lady's carriage. Her gaze fell flat, empty with unexpected hurt. I had wounded her. "I did what I did to protect myself," she hissed, "my *kingdom*."

I shut the faucet and wrung my hands dry on the towel ring, cutting a sharp glare up at her. "So did I."

I snatched up my underthings and left the bathroom without another look in the mirror. Rounding into the kitchen, I stopped to find Wesley home from the post office. He had left the piles of envelopes in messy stacks on the kitchen table and made us both a drink without even taking his hat off first—straight pours, neat. He held mine out to me but hesitated when he saw whatever had written itself on my expression. "What's wrong?"

Without ceremony, I held up the bloodied shorts.

Wesley frowned at the incongruence, but quickly put two and two together. He shut his eyes and set the glass on the counter. When he opened his mouth to speak, the soft draw of air clicked wetly in the silence. "Goddamn it, Jack." He paused, swallowed, and shook his head. "I'm sorry for all of it."

"So am I."

I hunted the bottle of Wild Turkey from the cabinet above the sink. Only three pulls were left, and I ripped off the cap to suck down two of them straight from the neck.

Wesley stared at me, his eyes dark and heavy with sorrow as though the distance between us was an endless, fallow tundra. "Are you?"

Instead of answering, I drank the last mouthful of the bottle and dropped it noisily into the sink.

◆ ◆ ◆

THE CITY WELCOMED us back with the affection of not having skipped a single beat in our absence. There was strange comfort in knowing a place could persist so steadily without us.

A friend of a friend was hosting a salon on the far end of the East Village, which promised to be perfectly avant-garde and at least middlingly entertaining. I was looking forward to distracting myself, diving fully back into the churn of currents that had absolutely nothing to do with me, and hoped Wesley would find some solace in it as well.

Unfortunately, the gossip well had been a bit dry of late. Everyone and their mother at the party wanted to hear stories about the summer directly from the horses' mouths so they could compare notes on what that place had been like.

I was better at shaking them off than Wesley. This time, for the first time in a very long time, I was the one flitting through the party like an overeager pollinator—practically drunk on the welcome influx of strangers, and questionable art, and even more questionable cocktails. I felt more and more like myself with each passing conversation.

Whenever I glanced at Wesley, he was tarrying by the bar cart, only halfway engaged with whomever was trying to bend his ear.

It was different than usual, but it was fine.

Until it wasn't.

The specific sound of Wesley's voice yanked me from a blessedly mundane discussion about Pomeranians with a modern dancer— *"You've got to be fucking kidding me!"*

Shattering to silence, the pleasant thrum of chatter stilled.

I excused myself and hurried in the direction of clattering glass and the polite yet urgent tones of bystanders not wanting to get involved with a tussle that was clearly developing into a brawl.

Wesley had some poor man with a waxed mustache by the collar, his fist drawn back, and evidence of the spilled drink that likely started the row splashed over one elbow. I threw my hands around his arm and held it firm before he could swing—he whirled on me, and for just a moment I saw a blinding flash of how horrifying it was to be on the receiving end of Wesley Shoard's combative streak.

My breath caught in my throat. Wesley realized it was me and overcorrected so sharply he nearly stumbled backward. I was still holding on to his jacket and only just kept him standing.

He caught his breath for a moment. The crowd was staring. I glanced around and did my best to look apologetic for the both of us.

"Is this *your* husband?" the man with the mustache demanded. He was tidying his bow tie and glaring at Wesley—one of his eye sockets had a pink mark in a circle around it, and I saw the shattered monocle on the floor at his feet.

"We were just leaving," I said. I made to pull Wesley after me.

The man snorted. "You'd do well to keep that hound on a shorter leash."

Wesley surged forward to lunge at him again, but I already had a better grip on his arm. The man stumbled out of the way, his face blotchy-red and his jowls trembling.

"We were just *leaving*," I repeated through my teeth, and hauled us to the foyer.

At the coatrack, Wesley snapped my jacket out flat with a touch more furor than he probably intended. He didn't look at me when I angled for his gaze, averting his fevered stare to the far corner of the wall.

I didn't push the issue until we were halfway down the eight flights of stairs back to the street. I turned to stop him on a landing and glanced around to make sure nobody else was about to hear.

"Honestly, Wesley," I hissed, "our first night back?"

"It's not our first night," Wesley growled. He leaned heavily against the wall. I scoffed.

"That isn't the point, and you know it."

"I can't do it, Margaret!" Wesley blurted. He stared at the peeling plaster across from him as he made a flailing gesture with one hand in front of him. He dropped his voice to a fevered whisper: "I'm not— I'm—I'm not built for all this fucking *guilt*!"

I held my ground and stared at him until he turned to look at me, miserable and angry and so hollowly sad I wanted to look away—but I held it.

"We did it together, didn't we?" I asked, pitched low.

Wesley hesitated for a moment, then nodded. I reached up and tidied a lock of his hair bounding down over his brow.

"And we'll live with it together," I said gently. "We'll *live*. Won't we?"

He chewed on the edge of his tongue and still wouldn't look at me. I slid my hand down to his cheek and held it there, not pushing but simply holding him, until he sighed with a long defeated sniff and his gaze swung listlessly to meet mine.

"Won't we?" I whispered.

I watched the quivering, subtle flicker of his eyes tracing my face, the high thrum of his pulse in his neck.

"I'm going to ask you a serious question," Wesley said under his breath.

"Ask away."

"Where did you put your conscience?"

"I tied it to a pile of bricks and drowned it in a lake."

Wesley's pupils widened softly, unblinking. He wet his lips with a shallow drag of his tongue and shook his head. "Who are you?"

"Your wife."

Wesley scowled to himself and stared at his feet. I stared at him until he turned his face to kiss my palm.

"Come on," he muttered, and took my hand to lead the rest of the way down the stairs.

We hailed a taxi. It had begun to spit a meager rain, the kind so weak it was little more than a simple mist hanging in the dark.

We said nothing the whole way back, staring out opposite windows as the city smeared to nothing but light and dark.

27

Shoard Downs, *again*

IT WASN'T THE same agony as Wesley's guilt, but a craving madness ruined me in the ensuing days.

Without a regular fix of Haas's product, I was a wreck.

I told no one.

I stayed at home as often as possible, and I could write off my cold sweats and sheared nerves to Wesley as anxiety. But the greatest boon of being Edie Bishop's neighbor was just as much the only negative: She could drop by any time she liked.

I was laid out on the sofa with the television on the lowest volume setting I could get it, staring through the dull wash of the studio audience laughing along with *Feather Your Nest* on NBC. A cold compress melted slowly on my forehead. Wesley was at a lunch meeting with Ezra.

"Knock-knock," Edie called from the front door.

"In here," I deadpanned, and made no move to get up.

She came in and stopped, looking between me and the television and my unstockinged legs. "Are you ill?"

"Something like that."

"I remember those summertime kissing plagues." Edie sat beside me on the long side of the couch. "I'm sorry I've been so hard to get ahold of, everything is always such a mess this time of year. How was it, how are you?"

"Not pregnant."

Edie looked at her lap for a moment. She nodded once. "Is that why you look like shit?" she asked lightly.

"I ran out of my medicine."

"Oh." Edie looked surprised. "Are you still seeing that doctor?"

I shut my eyes. "Once a month."

"Good. That's good, I'm glad you'll keep doing that."

"Why, because it makes you feel like the sane one?"

She pulled an exasperated expression. "Please. It's . . ."

Opening one eye, I stared at Edie and waited for her to find the right words. She examined me with her regular, exacting ease.

"You look better," she finally said. "Cold sweat aside."

"Thank you." I reached up and pawed the damp cloth off my forehead. "I'm worried about Wesley."

Edie's frown twitched. "Why, is the Committee prodding again?"

"No. He had a rough time out there."

Edie was silent, clearly waiting for me to fill in the details. On the television, a cheap joke about newlyweds got a laugh it definitely didn't earn.

"He does seem . . . distant," Edie managed. She scratched at her nose and didn't meet my eye. "Did something happen, with you two and that tailor? The bad tryst?"

I shook my head, rumpling the silk scarf around my undone hair against the pillow under me. "It was nothing."

"You'd tell me if it was serious?"

"Of course I would."

"Blink twice if it's divorce."

I shot Edie a look. She raised both hands in defense and made an innocent face.

"We're fine, Edie," I insisted gently. "Promise."

"Are there at least any juicy bits left over?"

I sat up slowly and took my time getting back to my feet. I mopped at my forehead, plucking at my hair, and crossed to the television set to switch it off—it was making me nervous. Everything made me nervous lately. I wanted to be through with this.

Facing away from Edie, I put my hands on my hips and stared out the window. "He's gone," I said without turning around.

"Gone?" Edie sounded impressed, if not confused.

"He went back across the pond. He had an atelier in London."

". . . Oh. Will you miss him too badly?"

"Not in the slightest."

Edie's dress rustled gently as she stood up and came to stand beside me. She put a hand on my shoulder. "Just because one person leaves doesn't mean someone else won't come right along and fill the same spot."

I crossed my arms and leaned sideways into her. "He hurt me, Edie," I said very, very softly.

She turned to look at me, perhaps to tease me for being dramatic—but the lowering afternoon light caught my face through the window, and of course Edie saw it. Her gaze quickened to the yellowing rind of a fading bruise under my eye, which I hadn't been covering up so fastidiously because seeing it in the mirror centered me more than the powder ever had. The only thing keeping me in my right mind was the reminder, the *proof* that I was the victor—the one who came out on top. Alive.

Edie moved her hand down to find mine, and she held me there with a tight, unshakable squeeze. It was the ferocity of a shared burden; a touch made soft by the horrible tenderness of experience. I clung back with double my strength, shunting every bitter ache into our affinity.

"It's alright. He's gone."

We held each other for a quiet, knowing moment.

I moved away and fussed at the edges of my hair as an excuse to blink past the prickle of emotion. "I'll have to go find something for dinner," I said with an air of moving on. "We haven't filled the refrigerator back up yet."

"I'll go with you," Edie said briskly, touching the corners of her eyes. "I was coming down anyways to ask if you needed an excuse to take a walk."

♦ ♦ ♦

I ARRIVED BACK to the apartment with a brisk flush in my cheeks, taking the stairs instead of the elevator simply for the lather. I had a paper bag of takeout in my arms, and I found Wesley already in the kitchen staring through the open newspaper as I set to unpacking it.

"They gave me extra piroshki," I said over my shoulder. I gave the silence a few seconds, shuffling the mail out of the way and fetching a pair of dishes for us.

I glanced at Wesley. "Edie says hello. I saw her earlier. How was Ezra?"

Another silence. I stopped and turned around.

"Wesley," I said, and waited for him to acknowledge me.

He took his time turning the newspaper page. He was in an undershirt and a rumpled pair of slacks, with one untouched cigarette burning down at the lip of the ashtray and another growing a long leg between his fore and middle fingers.

I let him pretend he hadn't heard me for another few heartbeats. I would *not* get angry at him. I would be the very fucking picture of patience.

"Wesley," I said again—and flinched when he closed a quick fist around the paper and turned sharply in his seat to face me.

"What."

I glared at him. "I'm trying to have a conversation."

"Can't you see that I'm busy?" he snapped with a sharp gesture at the crumpled paper in front of him.

"If I can't talk to you when you're busy," I said, forbidding myself from raising my voice, "when do you expect me to do it? You're always making yourself busy lately, I can't—"

"Well what the hell else do you expect me to do?"

I stared at him, my mouth drawn in a tight line. He shifted in his chair to face me more fully, sucked on a shaking mouthful of smoke, and extinguished the end with a hurried, ashy smear in the dish.

I licked my lips and raised a hand in deference. "I don't—"

"No, Margaret, if you want to *talk*, let's fucking talk."

I stared at him. My pulse ticked up with a lurch along the side of my neck. "Are we going to talk," I said, "or shout?"

Wesley glared at me. "You're leaving me *completely* out with the wash here."

"What's that supposed to mean?"

"You're carrying on like it doesn't even bother you!"

"Say the word," I said, raising my voice to match his, "and it's done. Who told me that?"

"Don't make this about us, Margaret—"

"I'm not making it about us! Who told me that, Wesley?"

"You made the fucking call!"

I threw out an open hand at him. "You could have said no!"

He stood—the chair under him clattered backward and just barely failed to topple. Wesley pointed a finger at me so accusatory I swore I could feel it break the surface of my chest. "Tell me you believe that, Margaret! I can *never* say no to you!"

"Don't pin that on me!" I shouted.

"I was trying to protect you! I made you a promise, I kept my word!" Wesley gestured at the window, as though any direction outside the apartment led westward. "What he did to you, I mean, Jesus Christ! But every fucking ounce of this guilt is falling on me alone! How can you just ignore it? Do you not see what this is doing to me!"

I stared at him as a film of tears sprinted up over my vision. "If you weren't entirely sure you could handle it, you should have said no," I said starkly, and shook my head as I jabbed my own finger at him just as violently. "*You* could have said no!"

Wesley sat down heavily on the table behind him. He covered his eyes with one hand, collecting himself. "I'm a mess. I'm a fucking *mess*, Margaret. First it's Andrew's blackballing, then this—this constant fear I'll come home to find you dead any time I leave the apartment, and now we *kill* someone? I mean, who *are* we!"

"*Hush*," I snapped, glancing toward the shared wall as though someone would suddenly burst through it to take us away.

"Oh, come off it, they'll think we're practicing our lines."

"I'm done having this conversation," I snapped. I returned to unpacking the food.

"You're going to pretend you don't want to talk about this?" Wesley cried. "I *see* the way your fucking eyes light up whenever you think about it!"

I slammed down the serving spoon in my hand and rounded on Wesley. "Fine! Let's dig it all back up again! You tell me there isn't a part of you that feels satisfied at having done it!"

"That's the worst part, it felt *right*!" Each word came from his teeth tight and miserable. Wesley grimaced as though the very thought had a taste.

"He was a monster, Wesley, of course it felt right."

"So what does that make us?!"

I said nothing.

Wesley's eyes were wild and feverish. His mouth twisted with vile, bitter disappointment. "I try so hard for you, Margaret." He raked both his hands into his hair, rustling all of it to a flyaway mess. "I'm trying *so hard* for you, I—"

"Well, I'm sorry I'm such a fucking inconvenience!"

"I never *said that*, it's not the *point*!"

"Then get to it!" I shouted.

"I feel *FILTHY*!" Wesley roared. "All the time, every day, I feel rancid and evil and—and unworthy of *anything* good, I can *never* be washed clean of this!" He paused to suppress a thick catching at the back of his throat and looked at me with such anguish I could hardly see him past the shape of it. "I can't quit my mind from—from running around this endless fucking track of thinking about how we got one of two outcomes: Either he was ready to kill both of us and be done with it, or he intended to kill *me* and drag *you* off to Mexico for God knows what, and I can't decide which of those scares me more!"

"It's done, Wes!" I shouted. "You can't be scared of what can't happen anymore!"

"Well welcome to the show, Margaret, I'm scared *all the time*! Christ! It makes me *sick* to let you out of my sight anymore!"

We stared at each other. My eyes welled up. I wanted to hate him.

I wanted that hatred so badly, for it would have been easier than loving him this thoroughly.

I shook my head and didn't let myself look away from him. "How can you let yourself think for a *moment* that I could ever bear to be apart from you?"

Wesley buried both eyes in the heels of his hands. He schooled himself, drawing hard and haggard breaths, until he finally looked up at me the way I'd been wanting him to since before Haas raped me—with his full heart in it, like he wasn't afraid anymore of breaking me by saying the wrong thing. "You bring out the parts of me I'm most afraid of," he said very carefully, flayed and stinging. "It—you always have. You always *will.*"

I sniffled hard and pinched messily at my nose. "'I love you as I love myself,'" I said, and shrugged. "You're the one who married a fucking basket case, Wesley, you gotta learn to look at me and face it."

Wesley nodded distantly but said nothing.

I pointed down the hall at the bathroom. "I'm gonna go in that bathroom," I said, "and I'm gonna lock that door, but I need you to know I'm not gonna do anything stupid. Okay?"

Wesley looked at me for a long time. "Alright," he murmured.

"I wanna live, Wesley."

"I know."

"I really wanna live. I do."

"I know. I do, too."

Wesley's eyes welled up with a rush, and he hid his face in his arm as his expression collapsed. I gave him his privacy and went into the bathroom.

I shut the door behind me and locked it. I held a flat hand out in front of me.

Nothing. Not hardly a twitch, not even the barest hint of a tremor.

Free.

I breathed in.

Free.

I breathed out.

I'm free.

I stared at myself in the mirror above the sink. I smeared at my eyes and wagged my wrists, breathing rhythmically to push out the present the way I did in the wings before making an entrance onstage.

The thought hit me as I turned, examining the bruise along my cheek: My hair had gotten too long.

I dug through the kits under the sink until I found a pair of manicure scissors. Without ceremony, I held up one slouching curl and snipped it off.

I did the same with another.

And another.

I cut away each lock like slicing ballast from a sinking ship.

When it was done, I looked at myself in the mirror—really *looked* at myself for the first time since returning home.

I had been changed. For the worse, probably. For the better, certainly.

It could be both.

The downy piles of hair in the sink fluttered as I ferried them into the wastebasket before running the hot tap to let it warm. I rinsed out the basin and lathered the half-gone cake of soap between my hands to wash clean.

I had cut them all away, every other woman in my aching body. I was free of the countless selves I used to be.

I unlocked the door and returned to Wesley.

He had righted his chair and was slouched backward in it, sitting low with one hand in a loose stranglehold around the neck of an open bottle of port. He was staring blankly at the paper with a miserable, tearful emptiness.

Gently, approaching as I would tender a struck dog, I pried the bottle from his grip and balled up the newspaper into the trash. I set the port beside the takeout and continued portioning out our plates in silence.

Wesley remained where he was. If he noticed the jagged mess of my hair, he said nothing. His eyes were heavy, thick and rubied by the tears that had ripped themselves out of him.

I set two places, one for Wesley and the other at the diagonal beside him. I lit the stubby candle between us and put my napkin in my lap before I began to eat in silence.

Finally, he sat forward and picked up his fork. He fussed half-heartedly at his plate.

We ate in silence. Wesley pushed his food aside after only a few bites, but he sat with me until I was finished.

I packed up the leftovers and stowed them in the refrigerator. I scraped off our dishes and washed them. I peeled away the rubber gloves and took a stilling breath over the sink before returning to the table.

At Wesley's chair, I knelt steadily behind him and wrapped my arms around his waist. I pressed my lips to the back of his neck, holding in a bolt of emotion at the familiar smell of his cologne, and remained there for a moment.

We were two creatures pared to the quick, our only comfort lately the solace of wounding each other. To sink our teeth in was pure instinct, the product of feeling nothing for the sake of getting on with it.

But we had found ourselves in each other, somehow, and here we stood: together, bound, facing the bloody maw of the unknown because it was not only a mantle, but a duty to persist. An act of victory against those who would see us ground to dust.

"I miss you when you don't call me Jack," I whispered.

Wesley slid his hands down over my arms and squeezed me close.

I held him. There was nothing on this earth I was meant for more than simply to be there and to hold him.

28

Home

AFTER DINNER, I found an old brick of ice cream in the freezer and plonked it onto the table with two spoons. We hashed through more wounded admissions, even more wounded apologies, and I assured Wesley I would keep seeing Dr. French. He promised me in turn that he would be alright—it would only take time.

I kissed him good night on the cheek and slept alone in the bed that night. Wesley took the chaise. He would return to our usual comforts when he was ready to do himself the kindness of wanting them again.

These things, all of them, would take time.

The next morning, I saw him off to a regular appointment with a fair-weather beau.

"You need some normalcy back," I said lightly, handing him his hat in the front hall. "*Your* normal."

Wesley leaned his head down to let me put it on for him. "I'm not going to be much fun."

"I don't believe you." I snugged his brim down against his brow and searched his face. "Anyone outside this door only knows the Wesley you want them to know. It will be good to go put on your best face."

Wesley didn't look convinced, but he didn't take the hat off. "I'll be back before lunch."

"I'm going to the salon later. I can bring something home, if you'll be hungry?"

As he touched lightly at the ragged ends of my hair, Wesley hummed vaguely. "Probably won't be, but I suppose I should."

I left him to his business. When the door closed behind him, I picked up the phone and dialed Ezra's home number.

If Ezra's ironclad routine was still the same, he would be making pot of thick Turkish coffee on his wheezing gas range right about now. The line picked up with a clatter.

"Hello?"

Not his voice. I leaned against the counter and twirled a finger idly along one end of my dressing gown's sash. "Good morning, is Ezra Pierce there?"

The young man put the receiver to his shoulder and called for *Ez*. I raised my eyebrows. At least the nickname had lasted longer than Benjamin-Not-Ben.

A soft rattle of handing-off, Ezra clearing his throat, and then a gruff greeting of "What."

"Hello, Ezra, lovely to hear from you as well."

He gave a cloudy, half-asleep groan. "Margaret."

"Did I hear correctly," I said, "or did your latest call you *Ez*?"

"He's new," Ezra deadpanned. The scrape of his hand scratching along his chin punctuated a yawn. "Someone had better be on fire or dead if you're calling me at this hour."

"I just wanted to ask if you'd have time this evening for a drink?"

"I always have time for a drink. With whom? You?"

"Anything wrong with that?"

Ezra sighed. "So long as you don't beg me for work, and you're buying."

"I just want to catch up."

"I'll hold you to that."

I tipped my head to balance the receiver against my shoulder and examined the end of the robe sash—I'd need to mend it soon, the edge was fraying. "Great. Six o'clock at the Edison. Who's the new one?"

Ezra grumbled something about tenors, told me he'd see me at six, and hung up without a farewell. I stared at the handset for a moment, vaguely proud of myself, and made for the closet.

I found the hat that hid my hack-job best and built an outfit around it. As I put on my face in the mirror, the roots of my back teeth itched madly for more medicine.

There had to be a solution for this aimless hunger. "Patience," I whispered, and looked at myself to say it again. "*Patience*, Jack. Every day of mine is a gift."

I would solve this. Somehow, I would stanch every oozing tributary left dangling from the hole I'd torn in my own life, and it would all be fine. It had to be. There was no other option.

I walked to Chelsea and reveled in the warm greeting at the salon. When I took off my hat, the ripples of intrigue at the sight of my hair tickled me absolutely pink.

"I singed it over the range," I said to the ceiling as the shampoo girl worked fastidiously at my scalp. "Snipped off the worst of it, but thank *God* Sheila had an opening."

Everyone stole looks at me as Sheila made quick work with her shears and rollers. I smiled into the mirror, draped in the bright green cape and born anew. Here I was, entirely myself. The other women were fascinated—lightly horrified, intrigued to the last. The thrill of being beheld filled me with another dram of proof that I was here; for at least another day, I was among the living.

These things would take time.

◆ ◆ ◆

THE EDISON THAT evening was awash with actors seizing their night off. I arrived early and installed myself at the end of the bar with my purse on the seat beside me, sipping only sporadically from a neat pour while I watched the door.

Ezra arrived in a brown velvet suit and a new pair of pince-nez. He kissed my cheeks before sitting down, and he looked at me sideways after placing an order for a gin sling.

"What on earth did you do to your hair?"

I primped at the edges of it, shorter than I'd expected to go but more than happy to embrace the cooing comparisons to Audrey Hepburn that Sheila and the other salon ladies made as she clipped shorter and shorter. "I made a decision."

Ezra flicked his eyebrows up and smiled dryly at the bartender when his glass arrived. "You do tend to do that with aplomb."

"How have you been?" I asked.

"Busy, with the good and bad alike. As always. You look well, hair included."

He sipped off the edge of his glass and kept eyeing me.

I smiled. "The time away gave me some perspective," I said with as much sincerity as I could muster without making it saccharine.

"Is that what they're calling it these days?"

I leveled a look at him. "I'm trying to apologize for being so difficult."

Ezra snorted. "We're all ridiculous creatures, Margaret, don't waste your breath being sorry about it." He twirled his stirrer between two fingers and kept on watching me, as though searching for something he expected and couldn't quite find. I smirked at him.

"What?"

"Nothing, you're . . ."

I pulled an expectant face. Ezra scowled.

"You seem *happy*," he said, and stole down a wide sip as though the word needed a chaser.

"Good," I said, "I am."

I asked about the company's goings-on from the summer, and Ezra gave me the highs and lows. I told him about the empty theater, the strange dynamic of performing to almost nobody, and steered wide around Felix Haas. When I told him about *Macbeth*, the cutting-short of the odd season and the outfit pulling its long purse strings, I found an avoidant light flickering around behind Ezra's sharp, pale eyes that I wanted suddenly to chase down.

"About that, by the way," I said in a brief lull, pitched for secrecy under the dull roar of the bar crowd.

Ezra's lines tightened subtly. "What, that?" he bit out, his old bitching tone lashing just as keenly as I'd remembered.

I plucked up the cherry sticking to the ice in his glass and bit it from the stem. I watched Ezra and took my time chewing.

"I want to call in a favor," I said.

Ezra scrutinized me with his fist against one cheek. I mimicked his posture until he realized what I was doing and shifted instead to drape his elbow over the edge of the bar top.

"You have *one* left to exercise," he said.

"You're keeping count?"

"Of course I'm keeping count, I've built my entire fucking career on the economy of favors."

"I need to speak to someone. Does the name Jesse Malus ring any bells?"

Ezra stared at me for a long while. If I didn't know better, I would have called the look a novel brand of respect.

"What did you get yourself into?" he muttered.

"We're all ridiculous creatures, Ezra," I volleyed right back. "Mind your own. All I need is a phone number."

He eyed me before shaking his head. He raised a hand to hail another drink and let only the slightest smile emerge at the edge of his mouth. "Have I told you lately how deeply I loathe the soft spot I have for you?"

"Can I take that as a deal?"

"I'll ask around. No guarantees."

"I don't need a guarantee. Just an attempt." I swirled my glass and finished down the last of it. I turned the empty around against the bar top. "Wesley's nerves are shot. He had a rough time out there. I want some assurances from someone I can trust."

Ezra made a sympathetic grunt. "He's a sensitive one, isn't he?"

"He is. But I'm looking after him."

"It's strange. If you'd asked me the sort of person who would put Jesse and the word 'trust' in the same conversation, I wouldn't have pointed to you."

I slid from the bar stool and took up my purse, flashing a grin at him. "And I wouldn't have thought to place you in his pocket, but here we are. I'll be right back; grab the next round?"

Ezra made a suffering sound, but I could see the mirth shining at the far corners of his eyes. I ducked into the restroom and began freshening up in the mirror.

"Look at you, shorn like a lamb."

I looked up from pressing my lipstick along my lower lip and found the Lady over my shoulder.

"Everyone has something to say about my hair," I said, reaching for a tissue to blot.

"It suits you."

"I'm sorry."

"Be not sorry for your own choices. Only be honest."

"About what?"

"You cannot ignore the sins you carry. You must bear living with them, lest they claw through the walls to make their own room."

I shut the clasp of my purse and moved slightly sideways, so we could stand beside each other at the counter. "Have I been ignoring them?"

"If you choose to live, you choose also to change." The Lady reached up and brushed a hand along the baby-soft hair short at the root of my skull. A sweet, chilly shiver chained down my body. She smiled distantly, trailing her fingers against the back of my neck. "To change is to remain. Grow like a tree around the stone stacked alongside it—let your roots find new paths in the mortar."

I stared at her. "How do I do that?"

The Lady leaned forward and kissed me lightly at the top knuckle of my spine. She looked me straight in the eye through the mirror. "You play the part."

The door behind me opened. I turned hurriedly to smile at a young woman in purple chiffon, the flush of a few drinks high in her cheeks, as she made for one of the stalls.

I straightened in the mirror and gave myself one last look over. I could still feel the bright fizzle of the Lady's mouth against the back of my neck. *Play the part.*

It was all a show.

Life was just the same story being told over and over again with different endings, and each of us had a role.

I smiled.

For the first time in months, I meant it.

29

~~~~~

Dr. French's office, uptown

DR. FRENCH GREETED me warmly from his desk when his secretary showed me in, and ushered me to my usual armchair. He'd acquired a touch of a tan over the summer. When I asked, he spoke briefly of his wife convincing him to follow along to Mallorca before winding his desk timer and fixing me with the scrutinizing gaze I didn't realize I had missed until then.

"Enough about me," Dr. French said mildly, the tip of his pen poised over his notebook. He gave me a quick, professional smile. "How was *your* summer, Mrs. Shoard?"

I started from the beginning, as far as I could recall it: the caravan, the emptiness, the motels, the boredom, the hard right turn of reassuming my role, the ache of it all. I left out any implicating details of Kline, or Jesse, but I did mention Haas. I told Dr. French about our arrangement, the three of us, but not about the drugs. Or any of what came after.

Dr. French watched me, occasionally jotting down a note.

"You seem reluctant," he said finally, speaking up for the first time in the middle of a brief silence. I had just told him about sitting down across from the mirror after the dress rehearsal in Sumner, terrified to even remove my makeup lest I release the Lady permanently from my body.

"In what regard?" I asked.

"In letting yourself believe that you taking these . . . creative steps, to forge closeness with yourself again—and your husband, too, by the sound of it—was a good thing."

Creative steps; a very tidy way of putting it. The truly good thing for me had been taking back what was mine with the mean end of a knife that didn't belong to me.

I turned that over in my head—I was a murderer.

Play the part.

"There are—people," I said haltingly, staring at a blank spot on the carpet. "There have *been* people, who tried to . . . put me in a box they built. Make me into what they wanted. And I followed them, I've been so ready to just . . . follow them. Every time."

Dr. French's brow was drawn with curiosity. He jotted quickly on his page. "And is your husband one of those people?"

"No, I think Wesley is the only person who's ever cared enough to stand back and let me decide for myself."

Another silence came, a thinking sort. Dr. French let it play out— I was steering this conversation.

It's your show, Jack.

"I don't think I knew how to be happy before I met him," I said very quietly.

To change is to remain.

I was free.

"Does that scare you?"

Dr. French watched me keenly across the finely woven Persian rug between us. I took a moment to interrogate this foreign clarity, my feelings in rare order where they sat inside me.

"It doesn't scare me," I said gently. "It makes me sad, that I've been . . . starved of my own peace for so long, without even realizing it."

The desk timer chimed. Dr. French made several lines of quick notes, flipped back through a few pages, and looked up at me. "How are you on the amphetamine prescription? Was it helpful while you were away?"

I looked down at my hands and spun my wedding band idly around my finger. "I've been going without it since we came back to the city," I admitted.

Dr. French's fine white eyebrows went up. "Nothing at all? Complete cessation?"

"Why, is that dangerous?"

Dr. French removed his glasses and buffed them gently on the lapel of his sport coat. "Withdrawals can be somewhat concerning, if not managed properly."

"I want to know I can get along without help."

"There is a risk, Mrs. Shoard, that you *can't*."

I nearly bit back against that—I'd survived overindulgence just fine, I could weather my way easily through temperance—but I stopped. I re-crossed my legs and pointed my gaze avoidantly through the office window looking out over uptown's tidy splendor.

Dr. French sighed through his nose. "Would you be disappointed in yourself for using a crutch if you had a broken leg?" he asked.

"This is different."

"How?"

"It makes me feel weak." The idea of taking more medicine made me think of Haas, and I couldn't bear to let him remain even in memory.

"Needing help is human nature, Mrs. Shoard. We aren't made to go at it all alone."

Dr. French stood up and neatened a stack of papers beside his desk lamp. "The simple fact is that you were left in the lurch for a very long time and got too used to blaming yourself for getting stuck there. Your inability to believe you could continue living was not entirely your fault. You picked up the glass, but it takes immense pressure and time to get someone to that point."

I considered that.

"What you do *now* is entirely within your control," Dr. French said. He scribbled a fresh prescription onto his pad. "Let yourself be helped. I'm putting you on a graduated dosage. Mild. You'll be off it by Christmas."

He held the slip of paper out to me. I stared at it.

"Will it always feel like so much at once?" I asked.

"Will what?"

"Living."

Dr. French squinted at the middle distance of his coffee table.

"Happiness," he said with the air of speaking as the words came to him, "is not a thing you can point to and understand as an object. It's a unique state of being made from the individual drams of small, achievable joys. It isn't so glamorous as making a cocktail, but we owe it to ourselves to learn how to brew our necessary remedies if we can't find it anywhere else. Everyone needs to be their own medicine. Some of us just need a little help."

He watched me evenly, calmly, a studious and careful gaze. I stared at the delicate shapes of the molding trim at the base of the wall.

I would be alright, wouldn't I? I could learn.

A silence hung between me and Dr. French like a hawk lingering back on its keeper's arm, afraid of the wilderness.

"The majority of life is rarely an ecstasy," Dr. French said gently, "and often confounding. But people aren't good wine meant to be kept in cellars. When the rubber meets the road, we're all cheap stuff, better in the company of others."

Dr. French gestured at me with the prescription as though insisting to pay for something I was trying to give him for free.

I took it.

Before I made for the bus back across town, I shut myself in the phone booth on the corner.

I dug into my purse for the torn-off corner of a *Playbill* for Judy Garland's September premiere Wesley had left on the kitchen counter, on which I'd scrawled a Texas number that Ezra had left with our answering service last night.

"Alpine Construction," Jesse answered, chipper as anything.

"Hello, this is Margaret Shoard, calling for twelve cords of lumber?"

A single, bright rap of a chuckle cracked down the phone line. "Shit, Ezra owes me a hundred bucks. Didn't think you'd actually call."

"How are you?"

"Oh, same as ever. Living the dream. Got to go kick up some rabble down in Terlingua couple weeks ago, can't complain."

"Do you think you'll be stopping by New York any time soon?"

"And why might I do that?" he asked. I could hear the sideways smile in his voice.

"For the theater, of course."

"Of course! The bastion of American arts, paved by only the dirtiest Rockefeller dollars."

"I'd like to meet," I said, staring at my toes, scuffing one idly against the piss-stained edge of the call box. "If you have the time, of course. I take it you'll be busy."

"I've got nothing but time for you, Cherokee Park. What needs doing?"

"Just a chat. I want to make sure we're square."

Jesse made a considering sound. "You know, Ezra said he's putting together *Hamlet* next."

"Is he."

"By Gis and by Saint Charity, alack and fie for shame," Jesse sang to himself in blithe falsetto as Ophelia, "Young men will do 't, if they come to 't, by Cock, they are to blame." Without skipping a beat, Jesse snapped back to his own voice. "You know Minnie's?"

I blinked. "The burlesque bar?"

"I prefer 'girly club,' doesn't sound so full of itself, but technically, yes. The burlesque bar," he said, chewing pointedly on the consonants, "just off Forty-Second."

"I know it." Lisette still had friends there.

"Good! I'm due in town sometime next month. I'll be in touch when I'm in spitting distance," Jesse said, all cheek, and hung up.

I stared at the handset tolling monotony.

I missed the cradle the first time I tried to hang up before hurrying to the curb and flailing for the first cab I saw. I needed to talk to Edie.

◆ ◆ ◆

I TOOK THE stairs two at a time on the last flight up. I knocked briskly on Edie's door, tried the latch, and found it open.

"It's me," I called as I stepped inside, but froze—my greeting rang baldly through the apartment, and it took me several seconds stopped stock-still in her foyer to realize it was because the walls were bare.

"Hello?" I called out, and heard my voice echo again with a strange, museum-like nakedness.

"Margaret." It came from deeper in the apartment, with a keen note of surprise as though I'd caught her off guard. Edie was *never* off guard. Her footsteps rapped stiff against the bare floor where she was supposed to have several rugs arranged in the piano room.

She stopped at the end of the front hall, and I looked at her awash in a bath of daylight shot through with stray motes. I had never seen Edie look anything besides put together. In all the years I had known her, she was the very picture of grace in even her lowest moments—ripped drunk, or spitting mad at a bad review, or simply ego-bruised by someone saying the wrong thing. In every case, she had still been *Edie*, poised and perfect and holier-than-thou without even having to try.

Standing in her strangely bare apartment, for the first time, Edie looked small and afraid and very, very lost.

"What's going on?" I asked, barely making enough air to speak. The door hung partially open behind me.

Edie huffed a tight sigh and drew a hand over her brow. Her hair was tied back with a lopsided scarf, and she was in a pair of Capri pants with a men's golf shirt tucked messily into the waist. "I have to go back to Melbourne for a little while," she said haltingly to the floor.

The air left me as though I'd been kicked in the gut. "What's happened?"

Edie shook her head and came to stand across from me, her hands on her hips. "My mother. She's been off for a while, but it's—worse, now. I knew it was bound to happen, I just wish she wouldn't have taken her bloody *time* and done this before the fall season picked up." She paused and shut her eyes to draw a breath, hold it, and blow it out again. "Well. She never did do anything for anyone's convenience but her own, why start now after ninety-odd years?"

She gave her usual piquant smile, but the sparkle was gone. I stared at her in quiet shock, until Edie's wherewithal caught up to her.

"My God, your *hair.*"

"Edie."

"When did you do this? It looks marvelous."

"Edie."

She stopped plucking at my head and sighed before reaching out to draw her hand down my arm, stopping at my wrist to curl my fingertips up in her palm.

"I was going to go down and tell you both when I had my head on straight again," she said. "But I've had to figure this whole mess so quickly, and I only . . . well. It's a lot. I'm sorry if all the packing has been making a racket."

I hadn't even noticed anything amiss through the ceiling. I'd been so absorbed lately in the process of being truly aware of the days happening around me, that even inconveniences like a few extra bumps and rumbles felt miraculous in their mundanity.

"No," I blurted, scrambling, shaking my head quickly. "No, it's— obviously, you have to go. You have to see her. Right? You're her daughter."

I tried to keep it in, I really did. But no matter how many dirty jokes Ezra made about her being *my* mother, or what kinds of rumors flew around about us, Edie had filled the gap I'd made by leaving home and raised me into the person I was now.

It was as though I'd been plunged into cold water and left to figure out how to kick my way back to the surface. I didn't even realize I'd begun getting emotional until Edie clicked her tongue tenderly at me and kissed my knuckles.

"For better or for worse," she murmured.

I would be shattered to lose her. But if I could weather what happened in Sumner, I could weather anything.

It would be alright. This was change, and to change was to remain. I would live.

Edie held her arms out and bundled me close. I accepted the embrace immediately, squeezing tightly around her middle.

"I have to tell you," she said, her chest buzzing gently at my ear, "and I hope you take this as the compliment it's meant to be, but I don't feel any doubt leaving you here for a little while. I might have before, but right now, Margaret, you're the sharpest I've seen you since we met."

In lieu of saying anything, unable to really speak at all, I nodded. She was right.

"Do you remember that *Midsummer* performance, early days?" she asked, with the hint of a smile in it.

"I fucking hate *Midsummer*," I muttered into her shirt.

Edie laughed. "Oh, I know. Remember how nervous you were?" She stepped back and held both my shoulders to take me in. Edie shook her head again in happy disbelief and pursed her mouth for a moment as it buckled with her own emotion. "You could face the entire world now, darling. *Really* face it, truly. You could. And you will, won't you?"

I hesitated before nodding again. Edie gave me another one of her most earnest smiles, the kind that reached through her whole face, and leaned in to kiss me on the corner of my mouth.

"Jesus." I swiped at both my clammy cheeks and gave a wet, miserable huff. "I'm gonna miss you."

"I'll keep in touch. Cross my heart. And you aren't rid of me for good; the subletter is an old friend. We'll get a drink together before I go, introduce you and all."

She looked at me for a moment before pressing another kiss to my forehead. I shut my eyes and memorized her warmth.

"If you knew the whole truth of what happened out there," I said before she pulled back, so I didn't have to look her in the eye as I admitted it, "I think you'd be really proud of me."

Edie remained with her mouth against my skin for a long, considering silence.

"When I was a girl," she murmured without moving away, "the bush started directly off our porch. I always stayed up later than I should have, and I'd hear the wild dogs scrapping sometimes after dark. There was a real mess of it one night, so I went out to try and catch sight of them—I stood there with a torch in my little hand and watched a female tear out the throat of whatever mangy cur had been trying to mount her."

I swallowed around the thick fist of feeling closing up around my throat, and held tight to Edie's wrists.

"It was the most extraordinary thing I'd ever seen. *You're* extraordinary, Margot. Look at you." She leaned back and appraised me. "Lit right up from the inside out. You'll be just fine."

"Ezra is doing *Hamlet* next," I said, remembering suddenly why I'd come up here in the first place. "I want to go for Ophelia."

Edie smiled and pretended to catch sight of an old friend at the back of my gaze. "*There* she is."

30

Minnie's Burlesque

THREE WEEKS LATER, Wesley and I had dinner at the Jane West. We had started sleeping in the same bed again two nights before.

After we parted ways on the sidewalk, I watched Wesley disappear down Washington Street to make his call time covering for Chap, walloped with a flu after the raucous summer, as emcee at the club on the corner of Eleventh.

Dr. French's regimented weaning had helped even my keel back out, as much as taking it the first few times made me think of Lake Sumner with a stinging, gut-turning avoidance. I stole down the very small pinch of my evening dose from my new compact in the back seat of the taxi taking me north along streets fizzing with traffic.

Going alone to Forty-Second Street would have scared me once—the unknown, the furtive desperation of sex clubs, the profusion of loitering men who stared at women as though any would be brave enough to charge if only the price was right. But now, any fear slid from my mind like oil on water.

By all counts, I didn't fit there. I wasn't dressed to entertain, and I wasn't a man in a suit looking to be catered to. I'd arrived early. I ordered a drink and sat neatly at the far end of the bar, avoiding eye contact and enjoying a martini just dirty enough to count, and watched the dancer onstage perform a number about losing her clothes piece by piece in a wind tunnel.

I could feel people looking at me. I didn't have to look back.

I was unafraid of myself.

I was free.

At nine-twenty, I hailed one of the bartenders and asked to see Jesse. He came around the counter and led me into the back. As I followed him, I caught my reflection in the low red light throwing itself off the glass of several framed, racy show posters. I looked powerful.

The bartender knocked on an unlabeled door, bowed neatly at me, and returned to the club room. *Come in,* Jesse's voice called muffled through the jamb.

He went without a hat, and a silk shirt hung open over his scarecrow shoulders—he sported another massive belt buckle, this one made of hammered silver and inlaid with chips of turquoise around a curved tooth.

"Mrs. Margaret Shoard," he said, mocking a hat tip, holding out his hand. I shut the door behind me and gave him a firm handshake. "Love the haircut."

"Thank you, it was a rash decision."

"My favorite kind." Jesse had several stacks of cash counted out across the heavy desk behind him and two different ledgers splayed open among them. "So, how can I help?"

I hadn't done much thinking about what I would say to him when I got here. Preparing for a conversation with this man was like preparing for a storm that was going to level the whole block anyway. I only knew I didn't want to waste his time.

"You know one of the crew didn't come back with us," I said, averting my eyes to the abstract painting hanging ever so slightly off-center across the room.

Jesse hummed the affirmative. In my periphery, he put his hands on his hips. "I did recall hearing about that."

"He had ties." I took a pause to taste the words, the reality of them: I was telling someone. "To me and Wesley."

"I figured something of the sort," Jesse said, entirely unbothered.

"I want to make sure nobody will ever find out about it."

Jesse was smiling at me when I looked up at him. "Do you know what our plan for that place has been from the get-go?" I shook my head, and his grin sharpened. "Our old friend Vaughn took out a handsome insurance policy on the playhouse. Dry air and the piss-poor electricians he hired, you know how it goes—fires break out all the time in the desert, even with a wet summer." Jesse examined his knuckles, the faded smears of tattooed letters punctuating the ends of each fist. "Whole place is cursed now. Nobody will look at that land for *years*."

"If . . . they find him," I said haltingly, and tried to continue but couldn't corral my thoughts into a single question that made sense.

Jesse gave me a calm smile as he skimmed a mind-boggling number of bills from the top of one of the piles. "Cross my heart, Cherokee Park, nobody will find him. He'd been overstepping all sorts of boundaries, thinking he and Vaughn could get one over on the rest of us. Far as I'm concerned, I'm in *your* debt."

I stared at the cash. "I don't—"

"Come on, don't wound my pride. It's a few cents above the dollar on market price, same as I'd have given anyone to take him off my hands." He gestured with the money. "It's a figure of speech. I'm not trying to put you in a net. Just paying you for your work. One and done, if that's how you want it to go. Buy yourself something nice; take your mab out somewhere fancy, my treat."

I dug into my purse and retrieved the knife, which I had washed and stowed and kept in my lipstick drawer like a talisman.

Jesse lit up. "There she is! Clean as a whistle, too. Hell, you treat your tools nicer than half my guys."

I looked Jesse straight in his bright, laughing eyes. "I don't want debts," I said. "We're square. *Nobody* finds out—that mab of mine is real tore up about it all, and I need to be able to mean it when I tell him he can relax."

Jesse nodded his chin at the knife. "Don't worry. This one doesn't kiss and tell. She's a good girl."

"Are *you*?"

"Yes, ma'am. When it matters."

I accepted the money. He took the pocketknife back.

Jesse spat on his palm and held it out to me.

I spat on mine and clapped it together with his. As we shook, Jesse weighed the pocketknife in his free hand. "You sure you don't want to keep it? Looks nice on you."

"I'm sure."

"Will you have a drink?"

Jesse offered his elbow. I took it.

"It's a shame you're a dangerous man, Jesse," I said breezily as he led us from the office.

He grinned at me. "And why's that?"

"You have a way about you."

Jesse clicked his tongue and held two fingers up to someone across the room. He steered us to a table right at the front of the stage with a small RESERVED plaque beside its tea candle. "Now, now, Mrs. Shoard. I'm flattered, but I really do prefer blonds."

I shot Jesse a smile as he pulled out my chair for the best seat in the house. "So does my husband."

◆ ◆ ◆

AS I SLID my shoes off in the foyer, I saw the bathroom door spilling light into the hall.

Wesley was in the tub. His hair was wet, slicked back from his forehead, and he had a cigarette burning between two fingers. His knees were drawn up to his chest, his skin warmed lobster-pink.

I wanted to have our life back. I wanted to see him smile with his whole face again, the effortless brightness that used to emanate from him and fill a room.

"I'm going to take a bit of a break," Wesley said before I could speak.

I blinked. "What?"

He took a shallow mouthful of smoke. "I'm taking a page out of your book. Hiatus. We have plenty of money left after the last Sumner paycheck, so I'm going to take a few months to—I don't know. Get my nerves back under control. I'm not . . . alright, right now, Jack. Ezra agrees. Once *Two Gentlemen* is done, I'm taking a season off."

I stared at him.

"Is it really that bad?" I asked gently. "For you?"

Wesley's gaze flashed. His lips twitched, holding in what I could tell from the tightness in his jaw was a bitter smirk. He shut himself up with another quick drag. "Yes. It really is That Bad. For me."

I swallowed. "Nobody's ever gonna find out."

Wesley huffed one dry, bitter chuckle. "How—" He stopped himself, his tone barely breaking its glassy surface, and rubbed his thumb briefly against one temple. He shook his head and gestured at the water. "Come here. Get in."

I stripped down and left my clothes in a pile on the floor. I flinched at the heat of the water but soldiered ahead to sink in down to my shoulders, facing him and drawing my legs in to mirror him. Wesley held out the cigarette.

"How can you be so sure," Wesley asked with trained-in evenness, "that we're in the clear?"

"Withhold your judgment."

"What?"

"Promise me you won't say anything until I'm done explaining. Withhold your judgment."

Wesley took a steadying breath. With his elbow on the lip of the tub, he tilted his chin into one hand. "Fine," he said lightly.

I began to draw shapes on the surface of the water with meandering fingertips and told him the truth, the whole of it: Haas's drugs, Jesse's affinity for me, how I got the pocketknife, and the promise I'd received earlier tonight that our hands were clean.

Wesley was very still for a very long time when I finished. He stared at me with a serious draw to his brow and his mouth firmed by deep concentration. The ends of his hair curled lightly in the rising steam.

"It is *extremely* risky for you to be talking to that man," he said, his voice shaking softly. "I know what they're like, they—"

"So do I. My mother was married to one of them."

Wesley shut his eyes. We were silent for a long, humid stretch.

"The hardest part," he finally said, so gently it almost sounded like innocent wonder, "is that it doesn't *stop*. You know? Nobody calls scene, or hold, or gives us a—a fucking five; it's real. It's all real. I need to . . . I don't know. Figure out who I am now."

I held out a hand for the cigarette again. "Are you still my husband?"

He passed it to me and watched as I nursed a shallow draw. "Of course I am," he whispered.

I slid my feet forward under the water, touching our ankles together. He didn't move out of the way.

"I'm angry at myself for going along with it," Wesley said after a long moment. "I'm angry at myself for even . . . *starting* that arrangement in the first place; I'm angry at *him* for hurting you; I'm angry at *you* for getting wrapped up in his—his *shit;* I'm angry at you for moving on; I—I mean, I know I must sound like a broken record, Jack, but I'm angry."

His eyes were heavy and sad and so bright with his own truth that it made me ache.

I passed him the cigarette. "At least you're feeling something. I'd be more concerned if you were numb."

Wesley nodded distantly before finishing off the last puff and leaning down to tap the end out in the ashtray on the floor. "Yeah. It's something."

We were silent for another dense stretch. I made more shapes in the water.

"The Players are doing *Hamlet* next," I said to my wavering reflection. "I'm going to audition."

The body is with the King, but the King is not with the body.

I looked up and found Wesley watching me. "Ezra's hoping you will. Says he's seen a change in you."

"It's the hair," I hazarded at joking.

Without ceremony, Wesley produced a fresh bottle of Wild Turkey from the floor on the other side of the tub. "Congratulations, Jack," he said, quietly emphatic, and managed to smile back before cracking open the top. He took the first pull and passed it to me.

31

1957

I HADN'T DONE Ophelia in years. Her lines were more melodic than I remembered—the poetry enchanted me.

I felt the weight of character as never before: not with the urgent press of assuming her desperate sorrow as my own, but with once-removed sympathy I could put on and take off like a jacket. Rather than *being* Ophelia, I was inviting her in when she served me and ushering her back out again when I was through working. I played the part.

And I played it well. Ezra went so far as to explicitly compliment my mad scene—not only with backhanded kudos, but with a curt nod and a *Good work*, as though I'd really moved him.

Wesley was coming back to himself, slowly. I wrote Edie twice a month in Melbourne, so she could keep abreast of the most essential gossip. Her subletter was a patrician pianist who only ever practiced at very appropriate hours. My new favorite pastime between rehearsals was sitting on our balcony to listen through his open window from below.

Autumn turned over into an icy winter, and after the new year rolled over all frosted about its edges, we arrived at the opening night of *Hamlet*.

I got to the theater an hour early to set my room just the way I liked it. I organized my makeup on the dressing table, checked to see if any of the mirror lights needed replacing, and made sure all my costumes were hung and ready in the proper order on the wire rack at the far end of the room. Whoever had used the space in my absence kept the hair tools in a different drawer, which I changed back immediately.

The rug had been replaced, and the sofa reupholstered. Once the vanity was set to rights, I sat and smoked a slow, meditative cigarette as I stared at where I had bled out.

That version of Margaret was unreachable now. I had put her to bed where she belonged—not exiled but retired into the calm fields of the past at the edge of memory. I knew her, of course, but she could finally rest. After all of it, rest was what she deserved.

Three tidy knocks rapped at the door. I extinguished my cigarette and stood to answer it.

Ezra proffered a single columbine to me. "From Wesley, he sends his best from the house. I made him forgo the whole bouquet until I'm sure you can be trusted with a vase in here again." He peered at the room over my shoulder.

I accepted the flower and kissed him on the cheek. "There's that old confidence in me."

I took my time preparing. Once my face was painted, I stood and did my warm-ups—voice runs, leg stretches, and breathing patterns lying on my back in the middle of the floor.

I stared at the ceiling. I could do this. The dress rehearsal had been rocky. Tonight would be great.

I sat up, stepped into my costume for the first act, and primped at my hair. I looked at myself in the mirror. I looked exactly like her, as well as I could recall from her visits.

In the wings, I sought the dresser on stage left and peered out at the audience through the edge of the curtain as she cinched up the back of my dress. I found Wesley in the front row with the rest of his bouquet across his knees, sitting beside a new man he'd been seeing lately. He was a poet called Victor who fancied himself somewhat of a modern Oscar Wilde—scintillating, challenging, but not technically dangerous. They flirted privately with each other as they perused the *Playbill*, Wesley's elbow brushing Victor's every time he leaned over to point someone out in the cast notes.

The lights in the house went low. The murmur of the audience quieting settled in like a thick wool blanket. I shut my eyes and took a deep, stilling breath.

A gift.

The performance was unparalleled. Being back in front of an audience was like arriving home at dawn after a very long night spent wandering in the dark.

At curtain call, Wesley leapt to his feet and began flinging the bouquet at me one by one—rosemary, pansies, fennel fronds, more columbines, and fistfuls of daisies: every flower from Ophelia's armful in the play. I caught them as best I could, my eyes blurring with happy tears as the flowers pelted me.

"*Bravo, Jack!*" he shouted. Victor joined him, throwing flowers and leading the cheer. "*Bravo!*"

I took another bow. More of the house joined the cheer over their applause, swelling with praise.

I was Ophelia, I was Jack, I was Margot, I was Margaret, I was Margie; I was meant to be nowhere but here—all of me at once, seated firmly at the helm.

◆ ◆ ◆

THE NEXT MORNING, I met Wesley for a late lunch in the park. He brought a paper sack of sandwiches, last night's suit impressively un-rumpled from a stay at Victor's place after we'd wrung ourselves out at the third after-party.

I'd grabbed a newspaper as I crossed Sixth on the way here for the express purpose of flipping directly to the Arts and Culture section—we had four inches of a very nice review, and I shoved it triumphantly into Wesley's hand as he passed me my sandwich.

"'. . . and the return of Margaret Wolf is not to be missed,'" Wesley read aloud, his eyebrows up with pleased surprise. "'Her Ophelia frets and yearns and *dissolves* with all the proper anguish. The arresting chemistry she brews even without her usual foil is well worth the price of entry.' Well, look at *you*."

Wesley swatted my knee fondly with the rolled-up paper and tucked into his own sandwich. We ate in companionable silence as the trees winnowed on a breeze, dappling the light streaming down over our bench.

"Is it strange to you from here?" Wesley asked.

"Is what, a good review?"

"Opening something." Wesley thumbed a fleck of mustard from the corner of his mouth. "Particularly as Ophelia, after . . . all of it."

"What do you mean?"

"She drowns herself," Wesley deadpanned.

"It's different now."

"Is it?"

I let him sit with that for a moment as I neatened my lipstick with the crumpled edge of a paper napkin.

"Is it weird to see me up there without you?" I asked, examining the bread for the next ideal bite.

When he was silent, I turned to look at him. I could tell something was making him itch. Wesley caught me watching and shrugged. "It's alright. Really. It only feels sometimes like I'm still waiting for another shoe to drop," he said gently.

"That will pass."

"You keep saying that."

"I keep meaning it."

I balled up the wax paper and crusts into the paper bag and passed it to Wesley to toss into the trash can on his side of the bench.

He put an arm around me and his gaze skated over the milling strangers, the valiant leaves browned and still clinging to their branches.

"How's Victor?" I asked. I leaned to lay my head sideways against his shoulder.

"Perfectly lovely. He's all the right things at once."

Across the pathway at the edge of the pond, there was a family with a baby carriage and a little girl in a bright pink jacket who couldn't have been older than four. She had floated a plastic boat into the water and was reaching for it, her stubby fingers out wide with the unfounded confidence of a child's unflappable curiosity.

Her foot slipped. She overbalanced, pitching toward the pond, but a man who looked like her father was quick to react and snagged her swiftly by the back of her collar before she could go in. He reached forward to rescue her boat in the same gesture. Wagging the water from it, the man deposited her back on her feet without skipping a beat of conversation with the girl's mother.

The little girl clutched the boat to her chest and stared at the pond, her eyes wide as saucers. For a moment, it looked as though she was going to burst into tears—but instead she broke into a cherub-cheeked, dimpled grin and dissolved into a fit of hysterical giggles at her own fear.

Good kid.

We remained in the park, sitting and ambling and running into a few friends, until the cold grew a few too many legs around us. On the way back home, we stopped into the grocer and split as usual—Wesley to the produce aisles and me to the deli counter—and met back up on the corner of Hudson outside the exit. We walked home with Wesley between me and the road. He juggled the door open for me on the way back up to the apartment.

"Did you see Ezra laying into Richard's new assistant?" Wesley muttered, raising a hand hello to the porter as he let me board the elevator first.

"They'll be all tied up in each other in under a month," I said. Wesley's attempt to swallow his chuckle failed miserably.

The lift stopped on the fifth floor. Wesley stood aside to let me out ahead of him, and then hoisted my bag onto his arm so I could dig into my purse for our key.

Through the west-facing window, a long shaft of light fell into the apartment. In the mirror on the wall across from the door, I watched us shed our coats and hats and shoes, shucked into the privacy of the life we insisted on sharing for the rest of our days.

"Do you want a double?" I asked over my shoulder, on the way to the bar cart.

"Use the last of that old port, would you?" Wesley called as he unpacked the groceries at the counter.

I uncorked the bottle and poured for us both.

Acknowledgments

This was not a story that lacked fuel for the fire. Margot and Wesley remain two of the most entertaining, magnetic characters I've ever had the pleasure of pulling from my own marble, but theirs was a heavy boulder to push for a long time. It feels lighter now. Thank you for reaching the end. Every book is itself a process, and I hope this one has been as fulfilling for you to read as it was for me to write. I thank first and always the unknowable thing that lives in me, which makes this practice possible.

To my agent, Chris Bucci, for not pumping the brakes on this plot the second it crossed his desk—and knowing how the hell to even sell it—and to my editor, Kate Dresser, for once again trusting me with your world-class collaboration: this book wouldn't have been half so bold without your support. If there are two people who would have treated this story with more care than you, I would love to meet them, but I don't think they exist. Your belief in what I am capable of has sustained me from draft to print, and I can never thank you enough.

To the rest of the powerhouse at Putnam, particularly Tarini Sipahimalani, Katie McKee, Jazmin Miller, and Molly Pieper: you are the best at what you do. I am lucky beyond measure to be part of your story. Thank you.

Luke, this is not *The Lord of the Rings*. I love you in dialects we haven't yet learned to speak, and discovering them together is the greatest joy I've ever known. You are my favorite reader.

Thank you to Jess, Kelly, Gabe, Kat, Jen, Erika, Tori, Meghan, and Clayton for the bar names I so wish were real places, and to Dr. Later and friends for Edie's Aussie-isms.

Thank you, variously and heartily, to everyone who has taught me something about myself along the way: to Rose, Katie, and Janna, for always being there; to Sandro, for the photo of the aftermath of *Titus* on the boards; to Will, George, Mike, and the Santa Fe Opera crew of 2015; to Anna and Hannah, from day one of all this book stuff; to Katy and Elena, from day zero; to Laura Harte, for teaching me how to fall in love with Shakespeare; to the Archive, for making sure I never take myself too seriously; and to my parents, Karen and Rolf, who have never shied away from showing up for me—and could not be further from the demographic of this book but clamored all the same to read it. I love you.

Many thanks as well the those who fed my imagination with their art and helped this book become, chief among the many: Celine Loup, Joëlle Jones, Wilsen, Pitou, Torres, Jonny Greenwood, Marika Hackman, Sarah Kinsley, Julie Taymor, Neil Newbon, Andrew Scott, Sir Trevor Nunn, Dame Judi Dench, and Sir Ian McKellen.

Lastly, thank you to Robert Clift and Hillary Demmon, the filmmakers of *Making Montgomery Clift*. It was not only a boon for research purposes into the social strata of actors in the 1950s, but presents a tender portrait of a deeply mythologized man whom I hold in great regard. He is described best by Lorenzo James:

> Being with Monty was like standing in front of a fireplace in the dead of winter, and you get all this wonderful kind of sincerity. It's a pity that everybody— and I would have shared Monty with everybody— did not get some of the medicine that Monty was brewing. He'd give off a glow.

Do watch the film if you can find it, it's very good.

Thank you again for being here. It is a singular feeling, to finish a book. Go give off your glow. I'll find you in the next one :)